Lorene

CLIFF WALKING

A Novel

STEPHEN RUSSELL PAYNE

Cedar Ledge Publishing

ISBN:0-615-49362-9
ISBN-13:978-0-615-49362-6
LCCN:2011930490

Manufactured in the United States of America

For information, permissions and appearances, please visit our website at www.StephenRussellPayne.com or on facebook at Stephen Russell Payne, Vermont Writer.

To Marietta, Christopher and Meghan,
for surrounding me with love and giving me the time to write.
You are my greatest treasures.

ACKNOWLEDGMENTS

It is with deep gratitude that I thank the following people for their help in bringing the story of *Cliff Walking* to life. For your painstaking and honest reviews of the manuscript: Toby Sadkin, Trine Wilson, Paul Ruoff, Nancy Hickey, John B. Payne, Jane McGill Cooke, Melissa "Missy" Van Marter Rexford, Robert H. Hallowell, III, Alden "Jerry" Clark, Jan Morse, Walter Blasberg, and (through *many* revisions,) my wife, Marietta. To Judge Ronald Kilburn, for his wealth of legal expertise, Bob Shiel, Esq, for his help in researching Maine law, and to Vermont State Police Colonel John Sinclair, and the late, Caledonia County Sheriff, Clement Potvin, for teaching me about the hard realities of rural law enforcement. To Mrs. Louise Swainbank, who, in 1967, invited a young Galway Kinnell to speak at our seventh grade English class. It was his generous sharing of and utter devotion to his gift of writing that lit the fire. And to my dear friend and literary confident, Angela Peck, for your wonderful insights and for putting up with me when I became "beyond bereft." With a smile and a stern rebuke, you always pulled me back from the edge.

To my mentors extraordinaire, X. J. Kennedy and Howard Frank Mosher, who have graced my life with their wisdom, friendship, humor, and humanity. To my Surgeon-in-Chief, John H. Davis, MD, for encouraging me to keep writing despite the rigors of surgical training. To Jennifer Finney Boylan and Chris Bohjalian for their help and encouragement over the years. And, finally, to my renowned editor and friend, Lesley Kellas Payne. You have patiently taught me how to always go deeper, enriching my stories beyond my dreams. I simply could not have done this without you.

"The ideals which have lighted my way and time after time have given me the energy to face life have been Kindness, Beauty and Truth."

- Albert Einstein

CHAPTER 1

Francis stepped to the window at the foot of the bed and looked out past the thorny hedge roses to the glistening surface of the sea. As he did every morning, he cupped his hands around the blown glass whaler's lamp on the window ledge and closed his eyes. As his palms absorbed the warmth of the glass, he bent toward the flame and blew it out. The relentless vigil had worn him down.

Downstairs, Francis pulled on his field coat, picked up his easel and canvas, and ducked through the doorway. Outside, sweet salt air filled his lungs. He set the easel up in its usual spot by the pine tree then turned and walked down the stone path toward the ocean. He descended jagged steps carved into the cliff, down to the black rocks at water's edge. He untied the lines holding his wooden skiff to a pair of rusty iron rings that had been drilled into the rocks of this tiny, protected inlet a hundred years before.

As he headed out onto the bay, the waters of the Atlantic lapped gently against the curved wooden bow of his boat. The strenuous, rhythmic pulling of oars kept his mind from racing back to that day she disappeared. He tried not to look down into the water, tried not to search the ledges and lobster traps for some trace of her. In his mind he had seen her many times—crawling, struggling beneath the surface, desperately trying to get home. But it had been over a year. While his heart had agonized over letting go of her, his mind had to acknowledge that Rachael was gone.

When he reached the spot a quarter-mile from shore, Francis let go of the oars. They thumped against the side of the skiff as it turned slowly toward the east. He closed his eyes and felt the warmth of the rising sun on his face.

How Rachael had loved sunrise. She would often slip silently from their bed, descending the staircase to brew fresh ground coffee in the kitchen. Still under the covers, he would wait for her return, her cold feet sliding between his legs. She'd climb on top of him, the comforter over her shoulders, her face radiant in the morning light streaming through their seaward window. His hands cradling her breasts, the rhythm of Rachael's soft cum cries had brought Francis into many a new day.

He sat drifting in the skiff for some time, his gaze resting on the small islands ringing the outer edge of Penobscot Bay. After a year of living alone, the acute mourning had worn off, leaving Francis both unsettled in how he remembered Rachael and unable to find new bearings for his life. For all their compatibility and success, the further he got from her death, the more he had to own that something vital had been missing. As the years had worn on they'd lived a very comfortable life, but rarely had looked into each other's eyes when making love. One of them always left the bed afterward while the other fell asleep. He remembered many a time he'd sat in the bathroom after love making, wanting to go back and lie next to her, to share his creative dreams and fears, particularly the mounting vulnerability he felt: a famous artist who for years had painted nothing of internal value. Bobbing on the gentle waves, Francis was finally facing how much he and Rachael had missed.

When the sun had lifted off the horizon, Francis headed back toward shore. Though the waves were with him, rowing home alone again was always harder. After tying the skiff securely to the rings, he climbed the cliff stairs back to the bungalow. Inside, he glanced at the sagging cot that had made his back ache for a year. Perhaps it was time to sleep upstairs again.

Francis took his wooden box of paints and brushes from his studio then walked to the door and stopped. He frowned. A boy stood on the lawn in front of his easel, someone he had never seen before. Francis watched silently from behind the screen door. No one came onto his property these days.

The boy was barefoot and a bit chubby. His hair was unkempt, and wet sand was splattered on his black baggy pants. Francis was uncomfortable around kids, feeling they didn't mix well with an artist's life. He flinched as the boy reached up to the canvas and traced his fingers along the figure of a naked woman crouched on a rock at the edge of the sea.

"You there, don't touch that," Francis called out, pushing the screen door open with his arm. The boy's hand curved through the air with unusual grace, down the inside of the woman's leg to the sole of her foot. Francis set his box on a red metal chair and stepped toward the intruder.

"She's beautiful," the boy said, moving back from the easel.

Francis knew he was staring at her breasts. He stepped between the boy and the canvas. "This is a private piece. Not for public view."

"Where'd you learn to paint like that?" the boy asked, moving to get a better look.

"I'm a painter. That's what I do." Francis looked into the boy's face. "Who are you? What are you doing up here?"

"Name's Stringer. Just moved to town."

"Didn't you see the no trespassing signs?"

"Nope. None down by the water."

"You came up the cliff steps?"

"Yeah, great rocks down there." Stringer was staring at the painting again.

Francis shook his head. "That's a long, dangerous walk around Wagner's Point. You could've gotten hurt."

"I'm used to the ocean."

There was a light in this boy's eyes, a genuine curiosity. He was still a kid— annoying, disruptive—but authentic. Francis watched his eyes and doubted the boy would try and rob him. "Where're you from?"

"California. Moved here with my mom a few weeks ago."

"Long way to the coast of Maine."

"I guess."

"Why'd you move?"

Stringer looked away from the canvas. "That asshole, Leland. It was out of control."

"Who's Leland?"

"My dad. He's a crazy drunk." Stringer looked back at the painting. "How'd you get the light to do that? Under the girl?"

Francis stepped away from the easel and looked at the canvas. Rachael's body cast a striking shadow across the water-slicked rock. "I studied her, what her shape and spirit did to the light."

Stringer stepped closer to the canvas, tracing a line from her belly to her hip, the delicate movement of his hand in striking contrast to his appearance.

"Did you love her?"

Francis's heart tightened. He wanted to kick this little wise ass off his property. He felt disarmed and violated. But he also felt something good. He relaxed a bit and turned toward the sea. "It's none of your business, but yes, I loved her. Very much."

The bright yellow-red sun was slowly rising and the salt mist was beginning to lift. A trio of seagulls circled gracefully on air currents above the cliff.

"I knew you did," Stringer said.

Francis turned back to the boy.

Stringer looked straight at him. "Thanks for telling me the truth." He turned, started toward the path then momentarily looked back at Francis. "My mom's beautiful too."

Stringer ran down the path toward the cliff, his head quickly disappearing below the hedge roses. After a few moments, Francis got up and walked to the bluff. Below him, springing from rock to rock like a young bear, Stringer made his way past the skiff, back along the treacherous shoreline toward Wagner's Point.

Francis did not paint much that day. He sat on the bluff watching the rocking of the waves—white suds over green over blue. He closed his eyes and watched Stringer's young fingers explore lines in the air. He had to admit that, surprisingly, it felt good to have a visitor, someone new to talk to.

The next morning, after he had come back from the sea, Francis set to work. He painted with more vigor than he had in months. He felt an urge to start a new painting, but instead stayed focused on Rachael kneeling on the rock. And although he was accustomed to the solitude—liked it really— he wanted to see Stringer again.

By eleven o'clock the Indian summer sun was too hot to work. He pulled his easel into the shade of the lone pine tree in his yard and went inside. He prepared a ham and brie sandwich with some of the lettuce and bean sprouts brought each week by his kind neighbor, Kasa Mokanovitch, an elderly woman who lived at the foot of the road.

He took his lunch outside where he found Stringer standing in front of the easel. "You again. I didn't think you'd come back."

"Yes, you did," Stringer said without taking his eyes off the canvas. "You're lying."

Though taken aback, Francis sort of smiled then took a drink of iced tea.

"Her breast—why'd you paint it so many times?"

"What do you mean?" Francis felt his defenses rising.

"You know, her breast—there must be twenty layers of paint on there."

"Observant, aren't you?" Francis walked over to the easel. "You're right, except there's probably a hundred."

Stringer cocked his head at Francis and then, for a few moments, their eyes met. In the shade amongst the aroma of decaying pine needles, Francis felt something open inside of him. Something began to fall away.

"My wife's name was Rachael. She died on her windsurfer out there in the bay a little over a year ago." Francis squinted.

"The wind was blowing like hell. She'd even caught a little air that day. It was beautiful watching her."

Stringer took a step away.

"I turned to get my pencils to draw her, but when I looked back, all I saw was her sail tossed about in the surf. Just like that, she disappeared and was never found. I've searched for her every day since."

"What do you mean, 'searched'?"

Francis felt strangely self-conscious. Stringer waited. Francis gestured toward the water. "Every morning I row out to where I last saw her and search the bottom."

Stringer gave Francis a quizzical look. "You look for her body?"

"I guess."

Stringer watched Francis's eyes. "Sounds like you're searching for something else."

Francis looked away. "Maybe." For the first time since her death he felt a bit embarrassed, seeing more clearly how reclusive and obsessed he'd become.

Stringer shoved his hands deep in the pockets of his pants and turned back to the painting. "So why'd you paint her breast so many times?"

Francis's face drew tight. "She...lost her breast to a surgeon's knife the winter before she died. Cancer. It had spread. She wouldn't do chemo; she'd only use her own herbal remedies.

"Though we didn't speak of it, we both knew she was dying." Francis looked toward the water. "That last week she had regained some energy and was thrilled to be on her windsurfer again. There was a strong offshore breeze. Her arms were weak, but she made it out there three days in a row. Her spirit was back and my god, she seemed so alive. Then she was gone."

"Maybe it was just her time," Stringer said. There was nothing glib in his response, only candor, a caring of sorts.

"Perhaps."

"You missed touching her breast after the surgery?"

Francis recoiled.

Stringer stepped around in front of him. "Tell me the truth. Please."

Francis met Stringer's gaze. "Yes," he said, hesitantly. "I missed her breast. I miss all of her." He turned into the delicate shadows of the pine.

"It'll be okay," Stringer said. "That's what my mom always says." Then he was gone.

The next morning Francis drove south along the coast, spending the day walking along the edge of the ocean. Barefoot, he hiked for hours, aware of his footprints disappearing behind him along the miles of Saco Bay's white sandy beaches. He stood at the edge of the summer carnival at Old Orchard Beach. In their stillness, he saw a certain majesty in the colorful, gravity-defying rides that thrilled summer beachgoers by the thousands. He bought a Philly cheese steak from the one boardwalk vendor still open then sat in the cool sand watching a lone maintenance man repairing a gearbox on the aging red and blue Tilt-a-Whirl. This kid, Stringer, had given Francis a good nudge out of the obsessive grief he'd been hiding in. It had seemed easier to go through familiar motions than to risk moving on with his life. Talking to Stringer seemed to give Francis the bit of courage he'd been lacking.

By nightfall, exhausted and sore, Francis drove home under a September sky filled with stars. He turned at Kasa's withering garden and drove up the hill to the bungalow. There was a definite chill in the air. Soon the first frost would cover the ground.

The following day Francis awoke with a start as light streamed through his seaward window. He had missed sunrise. A cool breeze blowing through the partially open window sent chills across the muscles of his back. He got off the cot and hurried upstairs to the whaler's lamp. It was cold. He turned, looked at the empty bed, then at the picture of Rachael and him on Jacob Bernstein's yacht sailing off St. Lucia. Though Francis hadn't felt like talking much after Rachael's death, he'd appreciated that Jacob had always been a good friend and had called regularly to check on him.

Francis turned back to the window and realized he didn't feel sad this morning. He showered and dressed then walked outside to the bluff where there was no sign of Stringer. He drove to town and parked in front of the county courthouse across from the Congregational Church. Its tall white steeple soared into blue sky, the brilliant lamp in its belfry a beacon of hope for sailors and fishermen for nearly two hundred years. On misty nights, Francis could see its glow from the bungalow and hear the muffled peal of its bell drifting across Wagner's Point.

He walked down Main Street toward the harbor. Several people on the sidewalk spoke to him. "Good morning, Mr. Monroe. We've missed seeing you in town. Can't wait to see some new paintings." The faces looked familiar, but he couldn't remember names. It was strange to be in town without Rachael by his side, but it felt good to get off the cliff.

He stopped in front of a small, well-cared-for storefront. The prominent black sign over the doorway was inscribed in gold leaf letters: Francis Monroe Gallery – Classic Maine Seascapes. There was only one original oil left in the window: waves crashing against the skeleton-like remains of a beached fishing vessel. A small sign hung in the window that read: "Closed until further notice. Sorry for any inconvenience."

He turned away and walked straight to the local art supply inside a small clapboard shanty teetering on a stone parapet overlooking the water. The metal hinges of the sign were covered with sea rust. "Cove Cards– Pens, Paints, Buoys, Fresh Lobster."

Francis walked in and went to the art supplies at the back of the shop. He looked around for a few minutes. "Got any other easels?" he called out to Ginny, who was arranging postcards in a rack beside the cash register.

"Nice to see you too," she grumped. "Where the hell you been?"

Despite her refined Westchester County upbringing, Virginia Wentworth was very much a local. Through running Cove Cards and owning a pair of lobster boats for thirty years, she'd seen and heard it all.

"Haven't been to town much," Francis replied.

"Damn smug artists. Now what're you looking for?"

"An easel, smaller than this one. Got any others?"

Ginny made her way around the racks of Maine souvenirs and magnets toward Francis. "There isn't exactly a lot of call for easels. Seems the artists we've got right here under our noses never buy anything." She tapped the top of the easel. "That's the only one I've got."

"All right, I'll take it."

Ginny turned and headed for the cash register. "Bring it on up with you. Give you five dollars off 'cause the box got wet and I had to throw it out."

Francis folded up the easel, selected a box of watercolor paints and a package of his favorite French pencils, and carried them to the counter.

As Ginny rang up the sale, her demeanor softened. "People miss you, Francis. You've been a big part of this town for a lot of years." She tore off a large piece of brown wrapping paper and laid it on the counter.

"It's been hard for me to go out." He pulled his checkbook from his coat pocket. "Rachael was the people person, my social spark plug."

"She sure made you produce. Nobody likes the gallery being closed. Can't tell you how many tourists come in here asking when you're going to reopen." She grinned at him. "You'd think you were famous or something."

She folded the wrapping paper over the easel and the other items then secured the edges with masking tape. "I see your old buddy Andrew Wyeth's having a show down in Portland in a couple of weeks."

"Francis brightened. "Really?"

"I saw it in the *Sunday Herald*."

"That sounds great. Thank you for telling me. I don't even get the paper anymore."

Ginny shook her head. "You really don't make a very good hermit, Francis."

He leaned over the counter and made out a check. Then he straightened up and glanced across the street. Stringer. His mother. He squinted. Long dark hair fell gracefully over her shoulders as she walked beside him. Francis left his checkbook on the counter and stepped quickly to the door. She had one arm around the boy. He watched her move briskly behind the parked cars; her figure, the way she moved, more striking with each glimpse.

"You going to pay me or keep gawkin'?"

Francis returned to the counter, straining to watch them through the windows, which were cluttered with sale ads and community announcements. He smiled at Ginny. She grinned back at him. He quickly picked up his purchase and walked to the door.

"Hey," Ginny said, as he opened the door. "Good to see you."

"You too," he said and walked outside.

He looked up Main Street in the direction Stringer and his mother had been walking but they were gone.

CHAPTER 2

When Francis got home he set up the new easel on the lawn next to his. He adjusted it so the light was just right and left the watercolor box next to it on a lawn chair. Feeling a bit restless, he walked down the hill to Kasa's house. He found her in the summer kitchen, scrubbing a bushel of large, deep orange carrots, her broad brow beaded with fine sweat. Her eyes brightened when she saw him.

"Francis, you've finally come to visit." She dropped the carrots into the old metal sink. "So good to see you. Sit yourself down." Francis sat in one of the chairs in the small greenhouse off the kitchen. Kasa wiped her hands on her apron and sat down next to him. Despite her hard seventy-eight years—or maybe because of them—she had an indomitable twinkle in her large brown eyes. Big boned and rugged, she was a gentle, caring soul. She and Rachael had gardened together for many years, and this was where they drank coffee and shared their lives. Francis thought about how much Kasa missed Rachael. As he looked at his old friend it hit him how hard his own reclusiveness had been on her.

"So long since you've sat in my house," she said, smiling.

It felt good to be in her powerful presence, in the warmth of her gaze.

"Gets kind of lonely, leaving vegetables in your mailbox all summer. Worried the postman might think I'm crazy. But I haven't wanted to disturb you."

Kasa slid her chair closer, laying her rough-skinned hand on his forearm. "So troubled, my friend, speak to me." She took his hands in hers.

He started to stand, but she held him. He looked into her eyes. "The other day, this boy, from California, came to the bluff. He saw the painting."

"Of Rachael?"

"Yes." The words did not come easily. "Meeting him has sparked something inside of me—something good—but it's also made me feel restless, guilty even." He fell silent.

"My dear Francis—" She gently rubbed his palms. "Sometimes God opens us even if we don't feel ready." She tightened her fingers around his. "Rachael is gone. Don't die alone painting on that bluff. She'd not have wanted that."

"Kasa, I'm feeling strange things."

"Go on—"

"Like Rachael and I missed so much, caught up in too many superficial things. Our life had become so much about business and prestige and not matters of the heart. And not just with her but with my painting as well. I haven't felt inspired for years. I just kept pumping out those damn seascapes wealthy tourists hang in their beach houses."

Kasa watched his face. "You both did the best you could and those paintings have given you a generous living." She paused. "Life isn't simple or easy. Over time our dreams become less pure."

Francis nodded. "I know it's time to move on." He gently withdrew his hands.

After a few moments, Kasa stood, straightened her back, and stepped back into the shadow of the summer kitchen. Standing at the sink, she wet her brush and went back to scrubbing carrots.

Francis walked to the door and turned back. "Kasa…"

She stopped scrubbing and looked up.

"I'm sorry I've been so preoccupied. I know how much you miss her. I've just felt paralyzed."

"You don't have to stay that way," Kasa said. "We all have to learn how to move on from certain things to survive."

"You've been a wonderful friend. I'll do better."

"I'd like that," she said, managing a bit of a smile.

Back home, Francis found the paint box untouched on the chair, but Stringer stood in front of the new easel, his hands moving through the air. Lines, graceful lines curving with inspiration that comes only from within, from knowing the lines before you draw them.

Francis stood at the corner of the house, watching.

"I know you're there," Stringer said.

Francis walked over to him. "Have you ever painted before?"

"Some drawings, is all." He looked uncomfortable.

"Would you like to paint?"

"Can't."

"Why not? You paint in the air."

"That's nothing—jes' bullshit." Stringer jammed his hands deep into his pockets.

"You see the lines. I know you do."

"You got this easel for me?"

"Yes. It's yours."

"Why?"

"What do you mean, why?"

Stringer cocked his head, looking at Francis suspiciously. "Why'd you buy me an easel? You don't even know me. What do you want?"

"I thought you'd like to paint," Francis replied.

Stringer's hands fidgeted in his pockets. "I can't paint."

"Why not?"

"Not s'posed to."

"Says who?"

"That asshole."

"Leland?"

"Yeah." Stringer became more anxious at the sound of his father's name. He rocked back and forth in his sneakers in front of the canvas, intermittently touching the clean white surface with the tips of his fingers.

"What did Asshole do to you?"

13

Stringer rocked harder, back and forth on the coarse grass. "Nothin'."

"Stringer..."

"He yelled at me when I was drawing a picture of my girlfriend. Said art was for sissies." Stringer rubbed his forehead with the back of his hand. "I kept working on it. He kept yelling and came over and knocked my picture on the floor. He ground his boot into it like it was one of his cigarettes."

Stringer's jaw tightened; he stared at the ground. "I got down, tried to pull his boot off the picture, but he kicked me in the stomach. I bit him. On the leg."

Francis frowned.

Stringer raised his head and looked Francis in the eye. "Leland picked me up, threw me into a chair, and broke my arm." Stringer grabbed his right forearm as he spoke. "He said that would keep me from doing pussy work. Mom tried to stop him—she really did—but he hit her so hard in the face she..."

Stringer walked away and sat down at the edge of the cliff. A thick, down east fog was blowing across the bay.

Francis walked to the bluff and sat beside Stringer. "I didn't suffer as much physical abuse as you did, but I have some idea what you've been through." Francis pulled his knees into his arms. "I'm an only child. My mother was a mad woman, in and out of mental institutions, always on one tranquilizer or another. A parade of European nannies took care of me. My father was a tough businessman, totally into money, Wall Street, and sports. When he came home from New York on weekends he'd ask me what I wanted to do and I'd say I wanted to paint. He'd tell me I was wasting my life, that I'd never amount to anything. He wanted me to go to Yale like he had, like his father before him. Play football, get into the stock market, and make new fortunes for the family."

Francis felt the first cool licks of fog on his face. "When I was your age, I wasn't sure why, but I knew I wasn't going to do what I was supposed to. I left home when I was sixteen. I couldn't paint there and the only truth I knew in my life was I *had* to paint." Francis glanced at Stringer. "Kind of like I'm feeling since I met you."

Francis took in a deep breath as misty white fog surrounded them. "We're all learning new things, Stringer. If you want to paint here, you're always welcome."

CHAPTER 3

Kate walked in from work and threw her bag on the couch. Waitressing for ten hours was way too long on her feet. She was fried.

"Stringer," she called out, walking toward his bedroom. He was never home. She stuck her head inside his room, glanced around, and saw nothing that worried her, just papers sticking out from under the sheets. She turned and walked across the small living room and looked into her bedroom. She wondered if she'd ever feel safe enough to come home and not check each room for signs of danger.

She stepped into the cramped bathroom next to her bedroom, unbuttoned her blouse, and took it off. She unhooked her bra and let it fall to the floor. She reached behind the plastic shower curtain and turned the hot water on full. For a few moments she stood watching herself in the metal-rimmed mirror over the sink. Her eyes looked permanently tired, but for a woman of thirty-eight, her breasts were still firm, her belly softened by only a little extra fat. As steam obscured her image, Kate closed her eyes and took in a deep breath. At least they'd made it safely to Maine. The three thousand miles between Leland and them was a comfort.

She stood in the shower until the hot water ran out then dried off and pulled on a thin Indian robe her mother had given her many years before. She walked into the kitchen, slid a Lean Cuisine chicken something into the microwave, poured a glass of pulpy orange juice, and sat down at the table.

Too wired to relax, she got up and walked back to Stringer's room. She sat on the bed and pulled back the covers. There, in the middle of his bed, were several paintings. She picked up the first and slid it onto her lap. She followed the sharp black lines connecting a geometric collage of brilliantly colored shapes stretching to the edges of the paper.

"Wow," she said, sliding the second painting across her knee. A sleek white boat, black rocks, waves, a disintegrating lighthouse, a human figure at ocean's edge. The third painting still lay on the bed. Kate stared. It was a portrait of her—abstract, but beautiful and strangely accurate. She reached down and touched the soft peach shadow beneath her cheek then ran her finger over the light, earthen shading of the scar above her right eyebrow.

"Mom!" The kitchen door slammed.

Kate quickly slid the paintings back under the covers and got up. "Hey, String." She hurried into the kitchen and pulled her dinner from the microwave.

Stringer dropped his pack on the kitchen table and opened the fridge.

"How's your day?" Kate peeled the plastic cover back, the aroma of orange glaze rising off the chicken.

"Good. School sucks, but the skate boarding's good."

"You'll get used to it. Takes a while. You hungry?"

"Already ate."

"Homework?"

"Yeah, I'll do it." He dropped a silver Hershey's kiss on the table beside her. She watched him walk across the frayed living room rug to his room. She stared at the glazed chicken. Stringer returned to the kitchen almost immediately. He sat down across the table from her. "You saw them."

She couldn't lie. "I'm sorry. You left the edges sticking out. How could I resist?"

Stringer looked pissed.

"When did you do them?"

"They're not for public view."

"Good. I'm not the public."

"You know what I mean."

"String, those paintings are great. I had no idea you were drawing again."

"I'm not drawing. I'm painting."

"Whatever. How can you say school sucks when you have such a good art class?"

"Yeah, well." Stringer got up and poured a glass of soda.

"I'm sorry, I won't look at any more unless you show them to me."

"Okay."

Stringer walked back to the door of his room. Kate relaxed and ate a fork full of rice.

"I didn't do them in school," he said, a bit sheepishly. "I don't even have an art class."

Kate looked up, surprised. "You've been painting here?"

"Nope."

"So…?"

"I've been taking lessons—sort of." Stringer jammed his hands into his pockets. "There's this old guy outside of town who lives up on a cliff."

Kate stopped eating, turned and looked squarely at Stringer. "And what? You paint with him? Who is he?"

"Some artist who works on his lawn right over the ocean. He said I could paint up there."

"Is that where you go after school?"

"Yeah, most of the time. He's a good guy. Bought me an easel."

"What are you talking about, bought you an easel?" Kate got up and walked over to him. "Stringer, after all the shit we've been through, how do you know he's not some pervert?"

"He's not a pervert, Mom. He's nice to me."

"No one's nice for no reason."

Stringer walked toward the kitchen. "You should meet him. He's cool."

Kate was tired and exasperated. She ran her fingers through her wet hair. "You can't spend time with someone I don't know."

"So I'll take you up there. He won't mind."

"I don't want to meet some old man who lives on a cliff."

"He's not that old and I thought you liked the paintings."

"I do, but look, I've had a long day and I can't deal with this now." Kate walked to the living room window that faced the cove and sat in the overstuffed chair.

Stringer walked over and sat on the arm of the chair. "I'm happy when I'm up there and he's teaching me a lot about painting: how to look at the light and stuff."

Kate saw genuine enthusiasm in her son's eyes, something she hadn't seen in a long time. She reached up and put her hand against his cheek. "String…"

Stringer's face brightened. "That means you'll meet him?"

"It means we'll see. What's his name?"

"Francis. Monroe. He has a gallery over on Main Street."

"We'll see."

"Okay, Mom." He walked toward his room. "Oh, and his wife Rachael died last year. He's lonely too."

Kate turned in time to catch a glimpse of Stringer's back as he disappeared. She finished her chicken then pulled on a sweatshirt and walked into his room. He was looking at an old surfing magazine he'd brought from California. "All right, String, I'll have to meet this guy if you're going to continue to go there."

"Good. Let's go after school tomorrow. You're working the early shift, right?"

"Yeah." Kate looked at Stringer and shook her head. "You can talk me into anything."

The next morning they both woke up a bit late so they had to hurry to get ready.

"I'll pick you up behind the school as soon as you get out, right?" Kate asked anxiously.

"Yeah. How we getting there?"

"Shelly, a girl at work, is letting me borrow her car."

"Okay, meet you around the side by the gym—not out front. Three o'clock." Stringer picked up his backpack and headed for the door.

"String, what should I wear? Should I bring anything?"

He paused at the door. "Just bring yourself, Mom. That's plenty." He gave her a smirky smile and left.

Kate walked into her bedroom and looked at her sparse selection of clothes. She picked a wrinkled skirt up off the floor and held it up to her waist. "No way." She threw it into the tiny closet and walked back to the kitchen and called Shelly.

"Hi, Shelly, it's Kate. If it's okay, I'll pick the car up after lunch. And..." she hesitated. "I've got another favor to ask. Can you tell me where I can find something decent to wear—cheap?"

"Who *is* this guy?"

"Some old guy my son met. He's teaching Stringer to paint. I've got to meet him and see if he's okay. It sounds weird, but I want to look decent."

"To hell with what it sounds like. What's *he* like?"

"I don't know. String says he's nice."

"Nice? Know anything else about him?"

"His wife died last year. That's all."

"Shit, girl! You talking about Francis Monroe, out past Wagner's Point?"

"Yeah, that's his name."

"Why you Southern California slime lizard, borrowin' my car to go see Francis Monroe!" Shelly laughed on the other end of the phone.

"What are you talking about?"

"Don't you know nothin', girl? Monroe's gorgeous and he's one of Maine's most famous painters. He was inspired by Andrew Wyeth, who lives up the coast. He's kind of a recluse, but a nice guy."

"You're kidding."

"Honey, after forty there's some things a girl don't kid about."

"How do you know him?"

"I don't, really. Everybody knows who he is but nobody's seen much of him since his wife died. She was real sick with cancer then she drowned. Heard it wasn't pretty." Shelly paused. "She was a real looker—dark hair, green eyes, tight ass. I hated seeing her around town 'cause she acted like she was too good for us locals. She traveled all over the place, writing books on arts and antiques or something like that. She built that fancy gallery of his on Main Street and got his paintings into big magazines. Rich people used to come from all over the place to buy his work. He's got a couple of paintings hanging in the museum up in Rockland."

Shelly took a breath and sighed. "I can't believe he invited you to his house. Baby, you're in for a sweet surprise."

Kate ran her fingers through her hair. "Shelly, you're scaring me. I'm just going to check things out for String. He really likes going up there."

"Well, girl, while you're up there checking things out for your son, you just check 'em out for yourself, too. God didn't make too many Francis Monroes, even on a good day. Now go over to Cynthia's, down at the pier, and pick out something nice. Put it on my charge."

"I can't do that."

"Do it. We only get so many chances, girl."

* * *

Bucking as though it was having a seizure, Stringer watched the rusty white Subaru lurch around the side of the gym, coming to an abrupt halt in the middle of the parking lot. The woman inside was waving at him.

"Shit," he said, seeing his mother in the driver's seat. He motioned for her to drive closer to the building. Kate motioned harder for him to come out to the car. He glanced around to see if anyone was watching then ran across the pavement and jumped in.

"I know, I know. I can't drive a stick, but I'm trying."

Stringer sunk down below the dashboard as Kate jerked her way out of the lot. She was already so nervous that he didn't give her a hard time. Five minutes north of town, Kate turned into the long driveway that led to Francis's house. She impatiently ground into low gear to climb the hill. "Calm down, Mom, it'll be okay," Stringer said. He glanced over at her. "Besides, you look good."

"Thanks," Kate said, "I needed that."

Stringer waved to an old woman digging in a garden behind a split rail fence at the corner. She leaned on her spade and smiled at them. Kate tried to smile back but the shifting was getting the better of her.

Halfway up the hill, revving the engine, working the clutch, the car stalled out and died. Kate dropped her head against the steering wheel and let out a stifled scream. She fumbled for a moment then yanked up on the parking brake.

She turned to Stringer. "We're walking the rest of the way."

"But, Mom, we're almost there."

"Good." She opened her door and stepped out. Her new pants felt too tight, making her aware of the extra weight she'd put on since they left California, which, based on how thin she'd become before they left, was probably a good thing.

Stringer shook his head and got out. "You're going to leave the car *here*?"

"The brake's on. It's not moving. This is good."

Kate shut the door then looked at her reflection in the dusty car window.

"C'mon, Mom."

She curled her hair behind her ear and followed Stringer up the hill.

When they reached the back of the bungalow, he turned to her. "Thanks for coming. Now be cool."

"Yes, sir." She followed him around front.

"Hey, Francis," Stringer said, pulling open the screen door.

"Don't just go in," Kate said under her breath.

"It's okay, Mom."

He held the door for her. She stepped inside and stood in a small hallway filled with the sweet aroma of paint, warm cinnamon and spices. As she stood in this stranger's house, Kate felt—strongly, clearly—the presence of another woman. Among the other aromas, a distinctive fragrance lingered. Kate had stepped into her space. Strangely, it felt good. Safe. She glanced around the room. Rachael was everywhere: delicate Italian planting pots on a wooden table by the window, a gold hair barrette on the window sill. Worn boat shoes still waited beneath the coat rack.

In the kitchen at the back of the house, she could see a tall man standing in front of a black cook stove. His back was straight, his shoulders and jaw square. He lifted a tea kettle from the flame and turned toward them. Steam rising from the kettle's curved spout caught the afternoon sunlight streaming through a window.

"Stringer, Kate, please come in. I'm just making some tea." His voice was warm and perhaps a bit shy; a little uncomfortable, Kate guessed, with the ritual of afternoon visitors. He poured hot water into a teapot that sat in the middle of a hand-painted metal tray, surrounded by china cups, a creamer, and sugar bowl.

Backlit by sunlight, Kate watched Francis walk from the kitchen into the hallway.

"Shall we go outside?" he said, motioning toward the door. His sandy hair was thinning, his eyes bright, alive.

"Sure," Stringer said.

Kate followed Stringer out onto the lawn. Francis came last, the screen door slamming behind him. Kate started at the sharp sound.

Out in the sunlight and salt air, Kate took in a deep breath and turned toward the man standing beside her son. And although she had not yet met him, interestingly he did not feel like a stranger.

"So nice to meet you, Kate," Francis said, extending his hand. She watched him delicately lift her hand into the air between them as if it was someone else's—Cinderella's, Dorothy's, Meg Ryan's—not hers. "I'm glad you came," he said, gently shaking her hand. You have quite a son, who's a talented artist."

Kate felt momentarily disconnected from the world around her. Francis was not at all what she'd expected and was so totally different from other men she'd known. Aware of Stringer staring at her, she brought herself into focus. "Nice to meet you too, Mr. Monroe. Stringer talks about you all the time."

Stringer frowned. "No I don't."

Francis smiled. "Please, sit down." He motioned to several colorful metal lawn chairs. "And please call me Francis." He poured each of them a cup of tea and handed one to Kate. "I'm glad you came. I've asked Stringer to invite you out several times since we met. I've felt a little awkward with him here without having met you."

Kate gave Stringer a sideways glance. "Well, I work in town and don't have a car yet, so I don't get around much."

"I should have offered to come into town to meet you, but I rarely leave this place, at least since my wife died last year."

"Stringer mentioned her. I'm sorry."

"Thank you."

Stringer seemed to enjoy watching the two of them talk. After a short silence, Kate put her tea cup and saucer down on the grass. A chilly breeze curled over the cliff raising goose bumps on her arms.

"You look cold," Francis said, getting up from his chair. "I'll get you a wrap."

"Oh, that's okay." Kate wasn't used to this.

Francis returned quickly with his brown field coat. "I'm sorry, this is all I have handy." He bent forward and slid it around her shoulders. The sun-bleached hair of his forearm brushed her cheek.

"Thanks."

Kate felt the collar's soft lining against her skin. Francis's scent surrounded her. She slid her arms inside the sleeves.

"So now that you guys have met, can I keep painting up here?"

Kate looked at Francis, who smiled back at her. She heard Shelly's voice in her head: "We only get so many chances, girl." Kate needed to be a responsible mother first. She pulled the coat tightly around her. "How often does Stringer come up here?"

"About every other day. Didn't you know?" Francis frowned at Stringer, who stared off at the ocean.

"I wasn't sure," she replied. "You think he has talent?"

"Yes, I do. Considerable."

"So do I. He's a gifted kid," Kate said. "If he'd only had a chance earlier—"

"You mean if Asshole'd left me alone," Stringer interjected.

"Stringer!" Kate snapped. "Don't talk like that in front of Mr. Monroe."

Francis changed position in his chair.

"It's true," Stringer said, crossing his arms.

Kate frowned. "I did the best I could." There was a long silence.

"Sounds like Leland screwed up everybody's life," Francis said.

Kate's eyes opened wide. She stared at Francis. "You know about Leland?" She turned toward Stringer.

He awkwardly set his teacup on the ground, stood, and started pacing. "I told him—a little."

Kate's lips pursed; her body tightened. Heat rose in her cheeks.

"I didn't mean to upset you," Francis said, leaning forward.

Kate stood, holding the coat tightly around her. She turned to the sea. Embarrassed, humiliated by having been tortured for so long, she wanted to run, but something deep inside held her. She was aware of Francis watching her.

"I'm sorry, Mom. I like talking to Francis."

Kate turned back, looked at Stringer then at Francis. The cries of seagulls carried over the sounds of waves crashing against the rocks below. "I don't really know what to say." Pain, rage, terror from her past, attraction to this handsome, compassionate man, fleeting moments of safety and peace all collided inside her.

"Why don't you sit down and finish your tea?" Francis said quietly.

At the sound of his gentle voice, tears formed in her eyes. She squinted and looked back at the fog bank creeping across the bay.

Francis stood and stepped behind her. "You must have been terribly frightened to come all the way from California."

Kate spoke without looking at him. "Trust me, I was way beyond *frightened*."

"I know it's none of my business, but I find it extraordinary that you made it all this way. May I ask how you got here?"

"In a smelly train," Stringer interjected.

Kate looked directly at Francis. "You must promise not to tell anyone about this."

"Of course. Not a soul."

Kate settled into her chair again. "An old friend of my father's, an engineer on the Canadian Pacific, took us as far from Venice Beach as we could get by rail. We weren't official passengers and even had to ride in a freight car for one leg of the trip, but we made a clean break."

As she spoke, Kate was amazed at the relief she felt sharing the story that had terrified her for so long.

"Leland hates cold weather and traveling, so northern New England seemed like a good place to go. Even if he located us, I don't think he'd ever come way out here." She paused and looked at her son. "It's been the hardest on String. He had to just up and leave in the middle of the night. He couldn't tell his friends anything.

Settling down in a totally new town is hard, but the relief of not having to look over your shoulder every second is worth it. Besides, String has the ocean here too. A lot rockier than the beaches we're used to, but it's still the ocean. He's a real strong swimmer and a good surfer too."

"I didn't even bring a surfboard with me," Stringer said, "but there's not much for waves anyway."

"Wait till the fall storms come," Francis said.

Stringer perked up a bit. "Yeah?"

"The surf becomes very powerful heading into winter. You'll see."

The three of them sat back in their chairs. Kate watched Stringer handle his cup of tea, something completely new for him. He looked good. And Francis's kind mannerisms and his considerate voice moved her. Sitting between them she could feel something being reset inside of her. She didn't know exactly what, but she felt it as surely as the salt air against her face. For the first time in ages, she actually felt okay. Not someday, but right now, in this moment.

Fog suddenly blanketed the yard. Shivering, Stringer came over to his mom. She opened one side of the field coat and wrapped it around him.

"We have to go," Kate said. "I'm not good driving in fog and the car's parked halfway up your hill."

"Would you like me to give you a ride home?"

"No. We'll be fine if we get going."

Appearing a bit awkward, Kate shook hands with Francis. "Thank you for letting String come here and for teaching him to paint."

Francis smiled. "You're most welcome and please come back anytime."

Kate slid the coat from her shoulders and wrapped it tightly around Stringer. "Can I return this in a few days?"

"Yes, of course." Francis reached in his pocket, pulled out a small package, and handed it to Stringer. "These are for you."

Stringer took the package, opened it, and pulled out a thin black pencil. His eyes lit up. "These are cool. Thanks."

"You're welcome. They're my favorite French drawing pencils. They have a wonderful lead."

Embarrassed, Kate put her arm around Stringer and they walked toward the road.

"Kate—" Francis called out.

She turned back to him.

"Thank you for coming."

Kate and Stringer rode home in silence. Meeting Francis had had an unexpected, powerful effect on her.

"He's pretty cool, huh?" Stringer asked as they arrived back in town.

"Yes, he is," Kate said, turning at the courthouse and heading down Main. She slowed as they passed the Monroe Gallery. "I'll drop you off then take the car back to Shelly's."

"I'll go with you and we can walk home."

"You sure?"

"Yeah."

Kate smiled at Stringer, pulled a surprisingly smooth U-turn in the middle of the street, and drove the half mile to her friend's house. "Wait outside, I'll be right back." She ran up the stairs and knocked on the door.

Shelly called for her to come in. At the sight of Kate, she turned in her old recliner, set down her beer can, and muted the TV.

Kate walked in and dropped the keys in Shelly's hand. "Thank you so much, this was a huge help. I gotta go, String's waiting outside."

"Hey, girl. Let me see your face."

Kate hesitated then looked her in the eye.

Shelly broke into a smile. "Oh, Kate..." She got up from her chair. "Are you okay?"

Kate smiled. "I'm a little overwhelmed. He seems like a really nice guy."

"I told you." She nudged Kate. "Not bad looking, huh?"

"Not at all." Kate stepped back. "Sorry, but I gotta go."

Shelly nodded. "See you tomorrow at work?"

"Yeah." Kate walked to the door. "I'm not good at this, Shelly. I didn't have any real friends in California. The only time anybody helped me was when they wanted something." She paused. "Thanks again."

"You're welcome. I hope something works out for you."

"Stringer's got a good place to paint. He's really into it and Francis is kind to him. That's enough."

"I s'pose so," Shelly said. She waved to Kate as she left.

Walking home, Kate looked up through a row of tall maples at stars set into a cobalt blue sky. They walked beneath the glow from the belfry of the Congregational Church, past the courthouse with the lighted "Sheriff's Department" sign hanging on the side, down the abandoned sidewalk to their apartment.

"Any homework?" Kate asked as they walked into the kitchen.

Stringer took off the field coat and dropped it on the kitchen table. Kate sat down next to the coat.

"A little math. I'll do it then hit the sack."

"Okay."

"Hey, Mom…"

"Yeah?"

"I've never seen you like that before."

Kate looked up. "Like what?"

"Like you were with Francis. You were cool; even let him get near you. You didn't bolt."

Kate remembered Francis sliding his coat around her shoulders.

"Maybe you guys can be friends." Stringer raised his eyebrows and smiled. He took his mathematics book from his backpack. "We're square about me going up there now, right?"

"Right."

Stringer nodded. "Maybe this won't be such a bad place after all. Good night."

"Night, String."

Kate sat at the table for a long time, kneading the worn sleeve of Francis's coat. Around ten, she got up, walked into Stringer's room, and pulled the covers over him. He had fallen asleep with one of the new drawing pencils in his hand, a sketch pad beside him.

Kate slid the pad out from under his arm and held it to the light coming through his window. A graceful bird with broad wings lifted above the earth on a current of air. Tiny people on the ground waved. Kate traced the edges of the wings with her finger then set the pad on the foot of his bed.

"I love you, String," she said, gently pushing the hair back from his eyes. Then, in the dim light, she slid her fingers over the lump by his temple, the wound where skin and skull had healed. "Please forgive me," she whispered then leaned down and kissed his head.

CHAPTER 4

Though fall was definitely in the air, Francis felt the change of seasons more intensely within than in the fading of the grass and brilliance of the leaves. There was a new clarity to the coming of morning, a sense of freedom he hadn't felt for many years. The quiet desperation that had all but smothered him was, mercifully, lifting.

The next morning Francis continued his sunrise routine, but instead of searching for Rachael, he laid back against the bow of the skiff and thought of little beside Kate and Stringer. He was drawn to their authenticity and also had to admit he felt a powerful physical attraction to her. He replayed in his mind the simple task of sliding his coat over her shoulders while breathing in the entrancing smell of her hair.

Stringer didn't come to visit for a couple of days, which wasn't unusual, but Francis found himself missing him. He kept looking out the window and down the path for him. He hoped he hadn't said something that had offended Stringer or Kate, but he didn't think so. He felt they too were adjusting to these strong changes of heart. Francis figured he could not be feeling the connection so strongly if they weren't feeling it too.

On the third evening after they had visited, Francis ended up pacing about the house, walking out to the bluff and back several times. He very much wanted to call them, to see how they were doing, to hear their voices. He held off as long as he could but finally, around ten o'clock, he couldn't stand it any longer. He pulled on a jacket and headed into town.

✳ ✳ ✳

Kate had spent the last few days working overtime at The Claw while Stringer spent a lot of time at a friend's house working on a social studies project about California street musicians. When Kate tucked him into bed that night, he seemed distant and dejected.

"You okay?" she asked, sitting on the edge of his bed.

"I haven't had time to go to Francis's for a few days. Have you talked to him?"

"No," Kate said, reaching to push his hair out of his eyes.

Stringer turned away. "Why not? You said you liked him."

"I *did* like him, but I've been busy and I felt uncomfortable, especially after talking about Leland. And I was a little embarrassed. I mean, who are we to this famous guy?"

Stringer frowned. "He's not like that."

"You're probably right. It's just me. I have to admit…"

"What?"

"Well, I felt safe at his house; it made me feel better about this town and I've worried less about Leland the last couple of days."

Stringer nodded. "Me too." He sat up on his elbows, looked Kate in the eye. "And remember, Mom, before we got on that train I promised I wouldn't let Leland hurt you again."

Kate smiled. "I know you did."

"And I meant it."

Stringer lay back again and Kate pulled the covers up around him. "It's late and you've got to finish that social studies project tomorrow. Get some sleep."

Stringer relaxed under the covers. "Good night."

Kate said good night then stood in Stringer's doorway watching him fall sleep. She pulled his door shut, crossed the small living room, and sat in the overstuffed chair. It was chilly by the window and she found herself suddenly feeling very alone and a bit frightened. She looked out at the harbor, which was quiet except for two men who were unloading a lobster boat beneath a street light on the dock. Though it was so different than Venice Beach, this *was* a beautiful place to have landed, made all the more interesting by this Monroe fellow. She realized that each day away from Leland felt like she was incrementally shedding a constricting snake's skin. She was being freed from a horrible bondage.

Kate realized she was biting her nails. She sat back and had the unusual thought that she wouldn't want Francis to see her chewed nails. She pictured him beside Stringer at the easel he'd bought for him, then she walked to the kitchen and pulled Francis's coat around her. She sat back by the window, amazed at how her life had changed for the better in such a short time. And though she'd probably be looking over her shoulder for a long time to come, she did feel a modicum of peace.

The white moonlight reflected off the mast of the few sailboats left in the harbor. Unlike the never-ending street life of Venice, Winter's Cove had gone to bed for the night. She did miss the muscle-shirted men at the gym on the beach and the in-line skaters, joggers, strollers, and power walkers constantly parading up and down the promenade. The problem was she could never truly relax and enjoy that California life. Between the drinking and drugs before she got sober and Leland's craziness to the end, there'd been little or no peace. But now in this new place, with these new people, she was aware of how sick and tired she was of being sick and tired. She was glad that Stringer reflected this change in her when he mentioned she'd acted differently around Francis. She could feel Francis's anguish that, in ways, had some similarities with her own. She was grateful to be sober and relatively sane on the coast of Maine with her son and, yes, with Francis Monroe nearby.

Kate pulled her knees up under his coat and began drifting off to sleep. Suddenly she started at the sound of a car door shutting outside the window. Her eyes opened wide as her heart raced. She couldn't clearly see the car so she got up, quickly checked on Stringer then snuck into the kitchen where she had a view of her steps. She thought of calling the police and checked to see if the set of carving knives were in their wooden block by the sink. They were—all four of them. Kate felt her pulse pounding in her ears. Could Leland have found them already?

Someone climbed the steps and knocked—softly—on the door. Kate approached from the side, out of sight. A man's figure obscured the light from the street. She stood by the refrigerator, frozen, feeling as if she was going to vomit. Another knock then the storm door closed quietly and the man disappeared.

Taking rapid, shallow breaths, Kate pulled out a knife then slid over and peered out the corner of the window. She saw Francis walking toward his Jeep, which was parked at the curb. He paused, looked up at her apartment then pulled his collar up around his neck and climbed in.

Kate relaxed though her heart kept pounding for a different reason. She opened the door and hurried down the steps just as Francis started to pull away. Timidly she stepped into the light. He stopped, putting the Jeep in park so suddenly its gears ground.

They met in the middle of the street.

"I hope I didn't startle you. I know it's late but I wanted to…" He hesitated then continued. "I've really missed you and Stringer the last few days." He appeared a bit awkward, as if he didn't quite know how to handle himself. "Would you like to take a walk down to the old harbor?"

She looked up at Stringer's window. "Stringer's asleep. I don't dare leave."

"You can easily see your apartment from the wharf."

She looked down toward the wharf just a short distance away. "Okay," she said, "I'll be right back."

Back inside, Kate made sure Stringer was sound asleep then checked the latches on the windows to be sure they were all secure. She wrote a quick note and left it on the kitchen table then locked the front door and rejoined Francis.

They walked side by side the short distance to the harbor. As they stepped onto the wide plank wharf used by local fishermen and sailors, Kate stopped and looked around. The moon, nearly full, hung above the steeple of the Congregational Church, its brilliant white light reflecting off the water.

"Beautiful, isn't it?" Francis said. "A little town built where the sea wore an opening in the rocky shore." He took a few steps down the wharf. "I haven't been down here in a long time. I've missed it."

"It is beautiful and very different than LA's miles of sand beaches." Kate's voice was raspy in the night air. He watched her, the turning of her head, the movement of her perfectly shaped lips as she spoke.

"I wonder whose boat that is," she said, motioning to a sleek wooden sloop tied at a private dock off the main wharf. *Maiden* was lettered in gold across its upward curving stern. In the moonlight, the boat appeared to be smiling.

"She belongs to Delbert Ready," Francis said as they walked toward the sloop. "He had it built twenty years ago by Ralph Stanley up in Southwest Harbor. One of the best boat builders in Maine. Delbert leaves her in the harbor late every year. He likes to take the last sail of the year, a tradition he brought with him from Long Island when he retired."

Kate stepped out onto the dock's burgundy-colored carpet and ran her hand along the sloop's smooth teak rail. Francis watched her fingers trace the letters "R. W. Stanley Builder" carved into the wood.

"Why does he sail so late? It's already pretty cold."

"Delbert was a prominent magazine editor in New York who traveled with an upper-class crew off Long Island. Every fall he and his buddies had a competition to see who would be the last to sail their boat for the season. He introduced the same custom when he moved up here and for a few years a number of locals competed with him. We had some real frosty outings back then; even sailed on Christmas Eve once. But years ago everyone except Delbert lost interest. One of these days he'll take the *Maiden* for her last sail of the season—around Wagner's Point, across the bay in front of my house and back to the harbor here. Then they'll haul her out of the water and into storage until spring."

"It's a beautiful boat," Kate said, turning back to Francis.

"Let me show you something." Francis motioned for her to follow him down the main wharf and onto a narrow floating dock that stretched out into the harbor. It ended at a set of stairs leading to a wooden shack built on creosoted pilings twenty feet above the water. The sign on the railing read "Private."

"A special place," Francis said to Kate at the bottom of the stairs.

"Can we go up there?"

"Yes." Francis climbed the steep stairs, looking back to check Kate's footing. "Careful at the top here. A couple of boards have come loose."

He pushed open the door and held it for Kate. She stepped up into the shack as Francis held his hand out to guide her. She held on tightly as they walked across the creaky wooden floor. Through the cracks moonlight reflected off of the water below.

They stepped through another door onto a small deck. Three elderly Adirondack rocking chairs sat facing the water. Francis motioned for Kate to sit in the one that afforded a view of her apartment as well as the cove. As they sat down the door slammed behind them. Kate started and glanced around.

Francis reached over and touched her hand. "It's okay. No one's here."

He put his feet up on the railing and they sat listening to the lap of waves against the pilings beneath them. Occasionally the mournful cry of a seagull rose above the sound of the surf.

"What is this place?"

"The old harbormaster's house. Been here in one form or another for well over a hundred years. Some folks got together and rebuilt it many years ago, but it's fallen into disrepair again. The town built a fancy new harbor office over on the hill there a few years back so no one comes here anymore except nostalgic folks like me and a few local kids. A lot of people think this place is haunted, which is just fine with me. Our ignorant sheriff and others have tried to tear it down, but a group of us preservationists have been able to save it so far."

"It's pretty creaky up here, but peaceful. And it's a great view of the town." Kate paused. "Why did they name it Winter's Cove?"

Francis smiled. "In a few months the harbor will freeze over. It's amazing how beautiful it is with layers of sea ice on everything. Sometimes the waves form crystals that look like huge diamonds. On a moonlit night like tonight, the whole town shimmers like someone scattered tinsel everywhere. At Christmas most people decorate their houses with thousands of tiny white lights and luminaries line the street. It's very beautiful."

"What do people do here all winter?"

"They don't swim much."

Kate frowned at him.

"Well, they skate and ski. The lobstermen work on their boats all winter and everyone tries to stay warm and get ready for Festival."

"Festival?"

"It's our New Year's celebration. Pretty near the whole town comes out." Francis pointed. "The firemen run hoses from the hydrants and flood Cliff Street over there, making the street a gigantic slide that goes out onto the ice-covered harbor. On New Year's Eve we have a parade with school bands, magicians, fire eaters, fire trucks, and at least a dozen decorated floats. People dress up like they're at a winter Mardi Gras.

"After the parade, anyone who wants to picks up a torch from the lamplighter at the top of Cliff Street and jumps onto the ice slide. They go like a bunch of screaming banshees down the shoot out onto the harbor. Often, there are several generations of one family, even grandparents, holding hands sliding together. It's really cool."

"So to speak—" Kate interjected.

Francis smiled. "Then there's a huge bonfire on the ice in the middle of the cove. At midnight, everyone throws their torches onto the woodpile and it ignites. I love watching the light of the flames on people's faces. Kids eating marshmallows, drinking hot cocoa and cider. And a lot of very cold champagne flows pretty freely. And I hate to admit it, but even that horse's ass, Sheriff McNeal, lightens up a little. Fire crackers and sparklers go off all over the place, and toward the end of the night, the mayor sets off a barrage of fireworks that explode over the village." Francis smiled. "People come from all over. Every bed and breakfast for miles around is full."

"Doesn't the fire melt the ice? Isn't it dangerous?"

"After an hour or so, the bonfire melts through and gradually sinks into the ocean. By the time the fire goes out, most folks head home. The firemen clean up the debris in the spring."

Kate and Francis sat silently for a few minutes.

"Why do you come here, Francis?" Kate asked, looking over at him.

Francis put his hands up to his face and blew warm air through his fingers. "This place comforts me, makes me feel safe."

"From what? You don't seem afraid."

Francis chuckled. "I don't, huh? I'm not half as tough as you."

Kate searched his face.

"I think it's the rhythm of the waves lapping against the pylons and the boats, the townspeople asleep on the hillside. I don't feel so lonely here."

"Do you feel lonely a lot?"

"Sometimes." He turned to her. "I don't feel lonely tonight."

They sat in silence again. A large wave splashed against one of the pilings beneath them. Kate pulled the collar of the field coat more tightly around her neck then leaned forward and looked over at the windows of her apartment. Everything appeared quiet.

"Will you tell me more about you?" Kate asked.

Francis felt her nervousness and knew he needed to go first. "All right. In the late sixties I was burned out, living in New York doing awful commercial work—what they called art—to market condo developments, golf courses, that kind of thing."

Francis pulled his feet off the railing. "Rachael wrote books on European and American antiques. She was also a fine illustrator. We met working on a project together and fell in love. She was good for me, got me organized. A year later we were married and moved into a house her family owned in the Hamptons." Francis watched a seagull dive below them and skim over the surface of the water. "She came from lots of money so she set me up in a studio near the pool."

Kate looked quizzical, as if such a thing was hard for her to imagine.

"The bungalow I live in now originally belonged to my grandmother who lived there for fifty years. My neighbor, Kasa, was her best friend. Grandma left it to me, and for several years Rachael and I spent part of each summer here. It's a wonderful place to paint, so fifteen years ago we decided to move up here permanently."

Kate listened attentively, her eyes bright in the moonlight. "What happened to your parents?"

Francis looked away. "They died in a car accident when I was twenty, but I had left home and come up here to live with my grandmother when I was sixteen. I'm an only child. My house was a bad place to grow up."

"How come?"

Francis thought for a few moments then continued. "My father was a tough businessman who never approved of my wanting to be an artist. He was emotionally and, at times, physically abusive." Francis took in a deep breath, letting the warmed air slowly escape. "I had a life-changing experience that summer I stayed with my grandmother. She took me to an art show where I met a famous local artist, Andrew Wyeth, who still spends his summers near here in Port Clyde. Meeting him was a huge inspiration, and following that, I had an enormous creative rush and did some pretty interesting, impressionistic paintings. That is, when

I wasn't doing the commercial work that paid the bills. A lot of my creative pieces were pretty wild, but I felt great painting them.

"After Rachael and I came to Maine, she encouraged me to do seascapes and I developed a successful style. It wasn't very imaginative, but tourists liked them and we made a lot of money. I got so busy keeping up with the growing demand I didn't have time or energy for anything else. Until she died a year ago, seascapes were all I painted for many years."

Francis shook his head. "Stringer is helping me realize how sick to death of them I really am. And how far away from Wyeth's inspiration I had gotten." Francis's eyes brightened. "Speaking of which, the Museum of Art in Portland is having a new Wyeth show soon. It'll be great to see some new paintings and have a chance to spend time with older works he keeps in his private collection."

"Isn't he the guy that painted that crippled woman crawling across a field?" Kate asked.

"Yes," Francis replied, seeming pleased she knew of Wyeth. "That's his most famous painting – Christina's World."

"My mother had a poster of it in her van. I always liked it. There's a desperation in that scene that I can relate to."

"Yes, exactly."

"That's amazing you met him." Kate smiled. "You really must be famous."

"Well, I haven't seen him in years. It's been a long time since I've painted anything that would be of interest to him."

"You never know," Kate said encouragingly.

"Maybe you'd like to go with me to the show."

Kate looked surprised. "Thanks, but I'm not the art museum type."

"Oh, I think you'd enjoy it, Portland's a wonderful city."

"We'll see."

After a few moments, Francis sat forward. "You've probably heard plenty enough about me."

Kate shook her head and leaned forward. "No, please tell me more."

"Aren't I doing all the talking?"

"Yes," Kate said, smiling again. "I'm really enjoying myself."

Francis sat back in his chair. "Well, Rachael traveled a fair amount and I painted. She bought a storefront on Main Street and turned it into a gallery—for tourists mainly. I tried my wilder stuff, but it was seascapes that sold. Somehow over the years, I became sort of famous."

Francis smiled. "Barbara Bush bought a painting for their house in Kennebunkport. She wrote me a nice thank you note that Rachael had framed for the gallery. But I tired of doing the same kind of thing over and over and I don't know if my heart was ever truly in it." Francis looked down at the water. "The day Rachael died was the last time I painted the sea. She was dying of breast cancer when she drowned windsurfing in the bay."

Francis fell silent. The night air was cool and moist. Kate unfolded her arms and slid a hand over his sleeve. He rested his other hand on hers, feeling solace in her touch.

"The cancer was awful. After the surgery, neither of us dealt with her pain or disfigurement very well and she wouldn't allow any other treatments. I pushed her to go down to the Leahy Clinic in Boston or Sloan Kettering in New York, but she refused. I felt helpless, completely deflated. I'm sorry to say I haven't done much with my life since."

"You've helped Stringer," Kate said, looking into Francis's eyes.

"I'm glad," he said. "Stringer's been good for me." He paused then continued. "Rachael didn't want children and I guess I've never had much use for them either—mostly out of ignorance—until I met Stringer."

"He trusts you, which is amazing for him. You're really good with him and with me too."

Francis squeezed her hand.

"You know how long it's been since I sat and had a real conversation with a man?"

"I'd guess a long time."

"Yeah, like forever."

Another seagull swooped past the deck railing and landed on top of an abandoned piling.

"You don't have to tell me anything, Kate. After these months of being alone, I'm grateful just to sit here with you."

"You're an interesting man, Francis." Kate stood and ran her hands through her hair. She tested the strength of the railing. Cold air blew under her coat, chilling her back. She sat down again and crossed her arms. She could see her apartment clearly in the moonlight. "For the first time in many years I feel like telling someone about my life, but it's hard. Besides, if you really knew my past, you'd probably run like hell."

"I doubt that."

Kate looked out at the chocolate-blue ocean. "I grew up on the plains of North Dakota and Montana. Mom was part Lakota Sioux, part Cheyenne. She traveled from reservation to reservation in an old woody station wagon, teaching school kids traditional music and art. Lakota songs were her gift, most of them sung to honor Wakan Tanka, Great Spirit of the Sioux Nation.

"When I was a little girl, if Mom was feeling good, she'd sometimes take me with her. She was a very intelligent woman, but often strange and moody, especially when she was at home where she was on edge most of the time. Out on the road teaching she was different." Kate smiled. "It was beautiful watching her sing with the children.

"Other times, when she was drinking heavy, she'd just disappear, sometimes for weeks at a time. She drove my father crazy worrying about her. He was a good guy, an engineer for the Canadian Pacific Railroad, working the east-west routes—freight, passengers, whatever was running. Sometimes he'd take me away for days, riding on his knee up in the engine. When he was busy I'd stand in the window and stretch my arm out as far as I could to catch the wind. I missed a lot of school and I loved it.

"The rest of the time I'd get passed around among friends until Mom finally showed up or Dad returned from a run. I spent a lot of time alone, listening to scratchy tapes of Mom singing Lakota songs mixed in with Bob Dylan, Janice Joplin, and Kris Kristofferson." Kate shook her head. "Mom and Bobby McGee. Somehow I think the music saved me."

Francis smiled. "That was great music. I used to listen to those guys while I painted. They brought me relief from my family."

"Same here," Kate said. She felt the ocean breeze blow through her hair, chilling the back of her neck. "Mom and Dad were a fiery pair, but they loved each other till the day he died. Heart attack on the Sunday Night Hauler out of Vancouver. It was the summer I turned fourteen. Mom went crazy and drank night and day. I couldn't stand it so I started drinking with her. First it was beer, but by sixteen I'd drink anything I could get my hands on. After a while she sent me to her sister's in Los Angeles. I'd never seen a city like that before. It was good getting away from Mom. She'd lost it—she couldn't even sing anymore.

"My aunt was pretty crazy too, and she didn't really want me around so I mostly hung out on the street and down by the beach. I was drinking heavy and doing drugs. I got pretty far out there for a while. I don't remember a lot except the next spring Mom hung herself from an old ancestral tree by the Little Bighorn River back in Montana, near where her great-grandfather, Red Cloud, had died. I didn't even know about it until a few months later when my aunt got around to telling me. I'd moved out of her place by then and was living around Muscle Beach in Venice. That's where I met Leland."

Though Kate's story made Francis a bit uncomfortable, her forthrightness was inspiring. He marveled at how this woman and her son had so quickly changed his life.

Kate took in a long breath, adjusting herself on the wooden railing. She felt a bit nervous sharing all this but also felt compelled to get it out. "I went downhill fast. Drugs, booze, anything I could get my hands on. I lived on the street and started stealing money, jewelry, hand bags, whatever it took to get a fix. I got arrested a few times, but some of the cops I knew from the beach helped me out. I never did any real time.

"Leland worked as a bouncer at the Baja, a shitty little bar just off the beach. He wasn't bad looking back then. He looked after me, kept me from getting killed a few times." Kate paused and looked up at the moon. "God, I was such a moron."

"Sounds like your life was pretty desperate."

"It was. For a while I thought I was living the California dream, but it turned into a long nightmare."

Francis nodded.

"Leland let me stay at his place. He drank, but he wasn't into it as heavy as I was. We fought all the time. Then I got pregnant, but I didn't even know it till I was three months. When I told Leland he was furious. He didn't want a kid around, thought it would interfere with his drug deals. He got ugly a few times, but the real beatings didn't start then. Just the yelling and screaming and pushing me around."

Kate stood, put a foot up on the railing and leaned on her thigh. She stared out to sea and found herself humming a calm Lakota melody. "Everyday Leland made sure I knew what a good-for-nothing piece of shit I was. He told me I'd be dead if it wasn't for him. Ironically, he was probably right." Kate watched a seagull lift off the piling and fly into the darkness. She checked the apartment and saw nothing to alarm her.

"I tried to stop drinking while I was pregnant with String, but I couldn't, at least not for more than a few days. I'd shake and sweat something awful. My skin felt like it was going to crawl off of me. Leland always got me something to get by, to keep me hanging on. By the time I was due, I was really messed up on coke and cheap vodka. I hated him, but I was terrified he'd leave me if I had a kid around. I didn't think I could make it alone. I didn't know how I'd get my next fix without him."

Kate suddenly felt very uncomfortable. A sense of dread crept in, making her feel nauseous. She'd said way too much. She folded her arms tightly across her chest. "Can we go back now?"

Francis watched her for a few moments. "Of course," he said quietly. "I do appreciate you sharing this with me."

Kate stared nervously at her apartment. "I gotta go."

He gave her plenty of space on the deck and made sure the door didn't slam behind them. Kate followed him across the creaky floor to the steps and down to the dock. They walked in silence to the end of the wharf.

In front of her apartment, Kate stopped in the middle of the street, turned, and looked straight into Francis's eyes. "I'm sorry, Francis," she said, peeling off his coat. "I can't do this." Without looking at him, she pushed it into his arms, turned, and ran to her steps.

Inside, Kate pushed the door shut, slid down the kitchen wall, and sat in a heap on the floor. When she heard the Jeep drive away she began to cry.

CHAPTER 5

The next morning Francis rose before sunrise, blew out the candle in the lamp upstairs, and walked to the skiff. Out on the bay, he let go of the oars and drifted on the nearly placid surface of the sea. He leaned back and looked at the bungalow on the cliff, the spot where he sat the day Rachael died, the place he had painted her image for a year. He thought of Kate, her dark hair on the collar of his coat, moonlight on her face. As beautiful as she was, he could see where Leland's fists had fallen. She didn't have to tell him everything. He knew her pain in a way he had not known Rachael's. Rachael had denied hers, as if her wounds didn't exist. So neither did his. Kate was different, authentic rather than cultured, with a striking rawness an essential part of her beauty. Her lack of pretense, her rough edges, and the ability he sensed in her to survive, even grow, under the harshest circumstances intrigued and pulled on him.

Kate and Stringer were unquestionably opening his heart. He hadn't meant for them to, but he couldn't stop it. Couldn't explain it either. He just knew it from the place his need to paint came from, a place he had avoided for years. He realized how extraordinarily self-absorbed he'd been and how Rachael had enabled him to live a comfortably controlled life of privilege. But he also realized that he had deprived their marriage of levels of emotional intimacy that could have come from sharing his deeper dreams. Dreams way below the surface of his famous but predictable seascapes. Dreams that Kate and Stringer were helping bring to the light of day.

Francis took up the oars and rowed swiftly back to shore. Inside his studio, he stared at the dusty virgin canvases standing on edge beside his drawing board. He then lifted the painting of Rachael from his easel, pulling hard to separate it from the thick layers of dried paint at the base. He carefully placed the painting in the corner then picked up his easel, supplies, and a new canvas and walked out into the yard. Instead of placing the easel in its usual place by the pine, he walked to the cliff and set it up there. The sweet, salty air was refreshing. He felt good.

Francis stood before the empty canvas for a long time then closed his eyes and reached out, felt the arc of lines as Stringer had. He opened a tube of dark blue paint. Then burnt sienna, sunflower yellow, crimson, and seashell white. He squeezed generous dollops onto his worn pallet, then, brush in hand, leaned toward the canvas. Thin lines from the edge of the brush formed the corners of city high rises, their windows reflecting orange sunlight. Broad blue-brown strokes for rooftops and tiny lines for TV antennas, clotheslines and balconies brimming with Mexican pots, red geraniums and purple and white petunias. Delicate green vines stretched over old brick facades and off-kilter fire escapes.

Exhilarated, moved by the energy of brush strokes, Francis painted through the morning. A semi-abstract cityscape: a warm, steamy deli with red and white awnings shadowing the sidewalk; a bag lady and a bag man, unshaven, sprawled on park benches; a child's chubby arms stretched skyward chasing a flock of pigeons across sparse grass.

By one o'clock, Francis was tired. He sat down and stretched his legs on the lawn. His mind raced. He was full of energy he hadn't felt in years. It was exhilarating but also a bit uncomfortable. He walked to the cliff and looked down at the black rock where Rachael had crouched so many mornings. He closed his eyes tightly as if finally, mercifully, squeezing out the sight. A lick of sea breeze blew against his face. He simply couldn't do it anymore.

Francis felt overcome by an urge to run to Kate and share his new freedom with her. But he also knew that she, like him, had been stuck in her life for many years and that it would take time in a safe space to heal and adjust. For the next couple of days he did not light the whaler's lamp nor did he go out searching in the skiff. He did, however, continue to paint with new fervor. Stringer did not visit though he and Kate were never far from Francis's mind. He was worried she'd been scared off at the harbormaster's shack but had an inkling she was drawn to him as he was to her.

The third day he awoke feeling filled with Kate: her scent, her eyes and smile, her intriguing mixture of raw sensuality and vulnerability. He couldn't resist seeing her any longer so he left his paints in the rack, climbed into the Jeep, and drove down the driveway past Kasa's onto the main road.

Suddenly he pulled to an abrupt stop then backed into Kasa's yard. As the dust settled, he heard the familiar creak of her kitchen door. He looked up and saw steam streaming out into the cool air.

Wearing a red-stained apron, Kasa walked around the edge of the garden and approached Francis's window. "You look like a crazy man."

He smelled the bittersweet aroma of stewing tomatoes then felt her strong hand on his arm. "I feel like one."

"My dear Francis," Kasa said, shaking her head. "Come out of there and let me have a look at you."

He stepped out and leaned against the side of the Jeep.

"What's goin' on?"

Francis worked the dirt with his shoe. "Knowing how close you and Rachael were, would you be disappointed if I started to care for another woman?"

"Have you found someone?"

"Yes."

Kasa put her hand to her chin and studied Francis's face for a few moments. "Well for heaven's sake, tell me about her."

Francis fidgeted. "I don't think this is the right time."

Kasa looked into his eyes. "Yes, it is."

"All right," he said uneasily. "Her name is Kate, that boy's mother, and she's not like Rachael. Kate's had a very hard life and certainly doesn't come from money. I don't mean to compare them, I just…" He shook his head. "I feel like a schoolboy talking like this."

Kasa reached up and put her hand on his chest. He smelled tomato juice on her fingers. "Francis, if she touches your heart, embrace her. Something wonderful will happen to you."

Emotion welled inside of him. "It already has." He felt tears form in his eyes.

"I'm so glad you've come alive again," Kasa said. "You've always been a good man, Francis. You've just been stuck in your sorrow."

They hugged each other.

"Thank you," he said.

Kasa smiled and walked back to her kitchen.

Francis climbed into the Jeep and drove to town. At Kate's apartment, he climbed the stairs and rapped on the storm door. No answer. He rapped again, hard enough that the aluminum door frame rattled. Again nothing. He peered inside. No lights on. No one around that he could see.

He walked back to the Jeep feeling like he just *had* to see her. Maybe she was waitressing. He walked toward the harbor. He hadn't been in The Claw for years because Rachael wouldn't go in a place like that; too townie for her. He looked over at the harbormaster's shack where they'd sat and talked a few nights before. Three seagulls sat on the roof's cap, which was covered with white gull poop.

Francis hesitated when he reached The Claw then slowly stepped onto the porch and looked in the window. There she was: blue denim jeans with a white polo shirt open at the neck. Her dark hair was pulled back in a braid and apron strings fell smoothly over her buttocks.

Francis opened the door and stepped inside. The smell of fresh perked coffee and The Claw's famous buttered apple crumb cake permeated the air. Kate glanced his way, then hurried between tables and disappeared into the kitchen.

Jake Armstrong, The Claw's owner, greeted Francis. "Mr. Monroe, good to see you." Considerably overweight, Jake spent most of his life sitting behind The Claw's antique brass cash register, watching over his money and gossiping with the locals. "How ya been?"

"Fine, thank you," Francis replied, staring at the swinging door to the kitchen.

"Here for lunch?"

"Actually I need to speak with someone for a moment."

Kate reappeared through the swinging door, steak and eggs in one hand, a large slice of crumb cake in the other. She placed the plates in front of two white-haired men then curled a loose strand of hair behind her ear, picked up a tub of dirty dishes, and carried it to the bussing station.

Jake saw an old couple come through the door behind Francis. "Let the paying customers through," he said, motioning Francis to the side.

Francis started to walk toward Kate then stopped. She was hard at work. This wasn't right. Struck by her sense of dignity, he quickly left. He walked down the sidewalk, around back of the restaurant onto the rocks at water's edge. He sat watching the incoming tide.

After a short while, the air became chillier as a storm was building offshore. Francis stood up when he heard a door at the back of the restaurant swing open. Wiping her hands on her apron, Kate stepped to the railing of the metal fire escape and looked down at him. "So what is it?" She crossed her arms tightly against her chest.

Francis looked up at her. "I shouldn't have bothered you here."

"Men—you've got the guts to barge into the middle of the restaurant where I work, get me out here on a damn fire escape, but you can't tell me what you've got to say."

This was certainly a much feistier Kate than he'd seen before.

"I didn't get you out here. I was watching the harbor."

"Like hell. You knew I'd see you out here."

Francis walked over and climbed the metal stairs to where Kate stood. Her face was red and goose bumps covered her forearms. Layers of thick black paint peeled from the metal railing behind her. "I wanted to tell you…" It was hard for him to get it out. "Since I met you, something's happening to me…"

Kate squinted at him. He sensed that she was softening.

She turned away and held onto the railing. She spoke without looking at him. "I'm scared, but I feel it too."

Francis gently touched her shoulders. Slowly she turned to him and looked into his eyes. She slipped her arms around his waist.

Suddenly the metal fire door flew open and slammed against the railing. Jake took up the whole doorway. "Do ya think I pay you to stand out here kissy facin' with the locals? Get back in here." Jake slid an unlit cigar from one side of his mouth to the other. Then he glanced at Francis. "You can see she's one of my new girls. Ain't got her trained yet."

Francis glared at Jake. "You can't talk to her like that."

Jake's large jowls tightened. "She works in my restaurant— I'll talk to her any way I damn well please."

Kate put her hands on Francis's chest and pushed him away from Jake. "He's right. I'm on duty. Go, Francis."

"Californians," Jake said, shaking his head. He lumbered back into the restaurant, the red door slamming behind him.

Francis looked at Kate. "You can't let him treat you like that."

"He's an old fool and I need the money. I've got two mouths to feed." She briefly put her hands on his chest again. "You're a kind man, Francis Monroe, but you don't have a clue about people like me. Just go home and paint."

Francis started to speak, but Kate stepped away, opened the door, and walked back inside. He stood leaning against the cold railing for a few moments then climbed down the stairs.

He didn't remember driving home, after which he sat out on the bluff for a long time. He watched long strands of shiny green seaweed and pieces of driftwood churned up by the storm that was fast approaching the coast. Below him, the skiff bobbed back and forth on its mooring. He pulled his field coat around him and closed his eyes. He felt the strong, onshore winds against his face.

After a while a sailboat appeared, trying to make its way around Wagner's Point. It looked like the boat was having a hard time. Francis got up and retrieved his binoculars from the bungalow. Back at the bluff, he brought the boat into focus and realized it was the *Maiden*.

Delbert was in trouble. His mainsail was partially up, flapping hard in the wind. The bow pointed straight toward the huge rocks that jutted into the sea from the point. Francis squinted just as the *Maiden* smashed into a jagged outcropping, throwing Delbert about the cockpit.

Francis ran to the house and called the nearby Coast Guard station, the same number he had called the day Rachael drowned. Then he dialed 911 and told the local dispatcher Delbert was in serious trouble. He grabbed his foul weather gear, a life preserver, and his nylon rescue rope and ran to the Jeep.

With his emergency flashers on and large raindrops splattering hard against his windshield, Francis raced past Kasa's house, down the half-mile road to the point. He parked by the walking trail and ran across a field to the edge of the cliff. The fierce wind raked cold rain across his face. Below, Delbert clung to the mast, hard surf battering the *Maiden* against the rocks.

As Francis started descending the slippery ledges he saw someone standing on an outcropping near the boat, trying to help Delbert.

Francis secured his balance. "Hey!" he yelled. "Be careful on those—"

As the person turned toward him, Francis's throat closed around his words. Stringer. He'd been on his way to the bungalow to paint.

CHAPTER 6

"Stringer, get back!"

Stringer waved Francis off. A thunderous wave crashed over the boat and onto the ledge where Stringer stood. The main sail tore loose and flapped violently over Delbert's head. Stringer edged down the face of the rock outcropping, moving closer to the boat. A pair of powerful waves slammed into the hull, jamming it into a crevasse between the rocks. Stringer waved his arms and yelled at Delbert, encouraging him to jump. A ways off shore, a white Coast Guard boat made its way through the surging waves toward the point.

Francis cupped his hands to his mouth. "Stringer, wait! I've got some gear. Wait!"

Stringer ignored him. Several more waves pounded the *Maiden*. The boat lurched onto its side, the sleek wooden hull splintering against the rocks. Delbert clung frantically to the rigging as the mast broke away from the boat and crashed onto the rocks next to Stringer, who looked as though he was readying to dive.

Life preserver in hand, rescue rope over his shoulder, Francis crawled across the slick rocks, getting as close to Stringer as he could. "For God's sake, don't jump!" he yelled at the top of his lungs.

Another wave ripped over the damaged, tangled sloop. Delbert lost his grip and plunged into the dark, foamy water below Stringer.

Francis knew Stringer was going in after Delbert so he had to do something. He crouched down and tied the rescue line to the life preserver. "Stringer! Grab this!"

Stringer glanced back. Francis threw the preserver as hard as he could. It landed close enough that Stringer could grab it. He slid his arms into the life jacket and fastened one buckle. Francis sat down and dug the heels of his sneakers into a crevice in the rock. He ran the rope around his waist and held tight with both hands.

Stringer stepped closer to the edge of the outcropping, searching for Delbert. Seconds later Delbert surfaced about ten feet in front of the *Maiden*, apparently unconscious, his face bobbing in and out of the water. For a few moments, the waves subsided.

"Don't do it, Stringer. Wait for the Coast Guard!"

Ignoring him, Stringer crouched and jumped out into the water. He surfaced quickly and swam straight at Delbert, who was only feet away from smashing his head into the rocks.

Francis stiffened with fear. The Coast Guard boat was within a hundred yards of the *Maiden*, an officer in a blaze orange suit yelling over a loudspeaker. "Get back from there!"

"Two men overboard!" Francis yelled back, but of course they couldn't hear him. His fingers were white from holding the rope.

Stringer swam in front of Delbert, whose forehead and cheeks were red with blood. Stringer struggled to hold him away from the rocks and, with remarkable agility, maneuvered his arm around Delbert's chest from behind. Fighting to keep Delbert's head above water, Stringer kicked furiously, pulling hard through the surf with his free arm.

Francis shimmied across the rocks to line up with Stringer. "Swim, String, swim!" Francis yelled as he continued to pull hard on the rope.

A wave clobbered Stringer and Delbert from behind, pushing them under the surface. Pulled forward by the force on the rope,

Francis lost his foothold and was yanked, chest-first to the edge of the rock. Regaining his balance, he wrapped the rope around his right hand, grabbed a crack in the rock with the other, and held on. He felt the rope stretch taut. He couldn't see either Delbert or Stringer.

"Stringer!" Francis shouted. He pulled until his palms bled. The rope felt as if it was caught on the rocks. He edged down the ledge to a small bit of gravelly shoreline. Waist deep in water, Francis squinted against the storm, frantically looking for Stringer. The awful crunch of the *Maiden* against the rocks sickened him.

"Stringer!" he yelled. "Stringer!"

Francis pulled himself along the rocks toward where he had last seen them. During a moment of calm he saw an arm break the surface. He pushed deeper into the frigid water. An incoming wave smashed him in the face, knocking him off his feet. He struggled up again, pushing through the surf, clinging to the edges of the rocks. "Stringer! Over here!"

Finally Stringer's head emerged from behind a boulder a few yards away. Francis lunged forward and grabbed his outstretched hand. Waves crashed over them. Their heads surfaced again. Pawing, grabbing hand holds in the rocks, Francis pulled Stringer toward shallow water. All the while Stringer kept Delbert locked in tow behind him.

Exhausted, they finally crawled onto the stony shore. Stringer slumped against a rock. Francis dragged Delbert out of the water, holding him upright against his chest. Remarkably, he was still breathing.

Francis looked over at Stringer. His face was bloody, the life preserver half torn off of him.

"You okay?"

Stringer nodded weakly. His right arm dangled oddly.

"Your arm—is it broken?"

"Yeah," he said between heaving breaths.

Francis heard sirens above the cliff, and shortly several fire-men descended the rocks. A Coast Guard Zodiac landed on a stretch of gravel nearby.

Rescuers surrounded Delbert and immobilized his spine. They placed an oxygen mask over his face then started an IV. They loaded him into a litter basket, tucked a blanket around him then rescue ropes lowered from the cliff above pulled him to safety.

Firemen attended to Stringer. They put an air splint on his arm and a stiff collar around his neck. One took off his rescue coat and wrapped it around him. In another litter basket, they raised Stringer from the rocks. Finally they guided Francis to a safety rope and helped him climb to the top where an ambulance was leaving the scene, rushing Delbert to the hospital.

"May I ride with him?" Francis asked, seeing Stringer being loaded into the back of another ambulance. An older fireman with a gray beard nodded. "Sure, Mr. Monroe. Slide in there on the bench."

His whole body aching, Francis climbed in and an attend-ant shut the doors. Stringer's skin had a sallow, blue hue. He was shivering uncontrollably so an EMT covered him with a couple of blankets. Francis reached over and put his hand on Stringer's good arm, the one that had clung to Delbert. "Hang in there, Stringer, you did a hell of a job."

Stringer tried to smile but was in too much pain so he grim-aced instead. Francis held his hand on the way to the hospital.

The emergency room was hectic. Some folks had heard about Delbert's accident on their scanners while others had followed the ambulances from the scene. The Coast Guard and the fire and sheriff's departments were there, as well as a local TV news crew.

As soon as they arrived, Stringer and Francis were taken into separate triage bays. For the most part, Francis was cold and tired. Only his right hand needed treatment. A nurse bandaged his cuts, gave him some dry scrubs to wear, and released him.

Francis immediately hurried into the trauma room, took hold of Stringer's good hand, and asked a nurse about his condition.

"He's stable and receiving IV hydration," she said. "We're waiting for x-rays to be taken. After that his lacerations will need suturing and his arm needs to be set."

"I'm going to call your mom."

Stringer looked up at him, concern in his eyes. "Do you have to?"

"Of course I do. You okay for a few minutes?"

"Yeah."

"You were amazing out there," Francis said, gently squeezing Stringer's fingers. "I'll be right back." He walked into the hallway, found a phone, and called Kate.

"Stringer's okay," he said when she answered, "but there's been an accident."

"Oh my God. Is he all right?"

"Yes. Nothing critical, but he's broken his arm."

"How? What happened?"

"He was out on the point, on the way to my house, and he saw a man thrown off his sailboat when it crashed into the rocks. He would have drowned if Stringer hadn't saved him. It was Delbert Ready."

"Oh my God—" Kate's voice cracked. "Where are you?"

"At the emergency room. I'll stay here with Stringer and send someone over to get you. Hang on a minute." Francis looked around the waiting room, put the phone down, and walked over to a deputy sheriff he knew who was standing by the door.

A few moments later he came back to the phone. "Kate, a friend of mine's coming to get you."

"Right now?"

"Yes. His name's Charlie Lord. A deputy sheriff."

"Francis…" He could hear her crying.

"Kate. String's going to be okay. I promise you. I'm going in with him now. I'll see you in a few minutes."

"Tell him I'm on the way."

"I will."

Francis watched Charlie's cruiser pull out of the parking lot, its blue lights flashing through the rain. He had known Charlie for years, ever since he taught Charlie's autistic son, Nathan, to paint as a young child. Charlie had been a loyal friend ever since. Especially at this moment, Francis appreciated that.

He walked over to the x-ray department and asked a receptionist where Stringer had been taken. She pointed to a small exam room. Inside, partially obscured by a curtain, Francis saw Stringer's bare feet against the white sheet.

Two x-ray techs were working on him. One of them, a young brunette, spoke in a calm voice. "We're going to pull traction on your arm to get a better view. We'll be as gentle as we can, but it's going to hurt some." The other tech, a tall, lanky guy, steadied Stringer's shoulder as she pulled. Stringer yelled.

Francis stayed outside the room while they took the x-rays. When Stringer yelled out in pain, Francis grimaced and shook his head, knowing that Stringer would not have been out on the point if he hadn't been coming to paint.

Suddenly the curtain was pulled back and Kate rushed to Stringer's side. "String—" She looked him over. "What happened to you?"

"It's just my arm. Got crunched against the rocks."

"But your face—it's a mess."

"You should've seen this awesome sailboat—these huge waves just smashed it into the rocks. This old man was stuck on the boat and the surf was kickin' the shit out of him."

"Oh, my God," Kate said. "It was the *Maiden.*"

Francis nodded.

"It happened right in front of me, Mom, on the way to Francis's." Stringer turned to Francis. "Man, thanks for that life preserver and the rope. I wouldn't have kept afloat without it." Stringer's eyes were filled with excitement. "Those waves were screamin'. Did you see the one that tore off the mast?"

Francis nodded his head. "They were something, all right. I told you the surf comes up strong in the fall."

"That guy was hurt bad. His face was in the water."

"You saved his life, String," Francis said. "It was a crazy thing to do, but you were amazing."

Kate sat on the edge of the gurney. "You really did this?"

Stringer nodded.

Someone knocked on the open door. A handsome, middle-aged man stepped into the room. "I'm Dr. Conklin," he said, nodding first at Francis then at Kate. "Our hero here has a fractured radius." The doctor pointed to his own forearm then held an x-ray up to a light box on the wall and pointed to the break.

"Is it serious?" Kate asked.

"No. It's pretty well aligned. We can treat it with a cast and get another x-ray in a couple weeks."

"That doesn't sound too bad," Kate said, looking at Stringer.

"Easy for you to say."

"I'll be back in a few minutes to put the cast on. We'll finish up then a local TV news team would like to interview you. You should be real proud of yourself, young man." He stepped out of the room.

"That's great," Francis said, smiling. "Stringer deserves recognition."

Kate suddenly turned and glared at Francis. "Are you *crazy?*" She leaned closer to him. "Stringer is *not* going to be on TV! All we need is for Leland to see him on the news saving some guy in Maine."

"But you're safe now. Leland can't touch you up here."

Kate turned and faced Francis squarely. "You don't know shit about Leland. He's a goddamn monster. He'd come and get us."

"Well, we won't let anything happen to you or Stringer."

Kate shook her head. "Sure, Francis, Stringer damn near drowned saving one of your locals while you watched, and *you're* going to protect us from the meanest sonovabitch in Southern California? Bullshit."

Kate was so angry her neck veins bulged. "Do you know what it took to get from California to Maine, to escape that bastard without leaving a trail?"

"Mom, leave it alone." Stringer's excitement was gone. He sounded defeated.

Kate paused and looked at her son's face. "I'm sorry, String. You know what he's like."

"Yeah, he's a bastard. But let's not talk about him anymore. Today's okay. I did something good."

Kate settled down. "I know you did." She leaned over and kissed him on the head. "I'm sorry."

"And another thing: when I smashed my arm on that rock, Francis swam out in that crazy surf and dragged me and that other dude to shore. I never could've made it alone. We would've drowned."

Kate slowly looked back at Francis. She seemed surprised, perhaps a little embarrassed.

Just then a nurse walked into the room followed by a young blond woman in a blue business suit and a cameraman with battery packs attached to a black hip belt.

"Dr. Conklin's been called to a cardiac. It'll be a few minutes before he can put your cast on. In the meantime the TV people can come in."

Francis stepped between the newswoman and Stringer. "The boy's mom would rather there be no interviews. He's very tired and in a lot of pain with his broken arm and all."

The newswoman tried to get around Francis, but he held his arm up and stopped her. "It's been a traumatic afternoon. Let him rest."

The nurse looked at Kate, whose steely face answered her question. The nurse told the news crew they'd have to come back the next day. Disappointed and annoyed, the reporter turned and pushed her cameraman toward the door. "We'll be back first thing in the morning," she said over her shoulder.

"Oh no you won't," Kate said, half under her breath.

The nurse walked to the sink and prepared the plaster. Dr. Conklin returned and formed the padded cast around Stringer's arm. He placed him in a sling and showed him how to cradle the cast against his body.

"I'm sorry you broke your arm, but you did a great job out there today. It took a lot of guts. Delbert, the guy you saved, is an institution around here." Dr. Conklin looked at Francis. "We're airlifting him to the medical center in Portland, but thanks to both of you, I think he's going to make it. Anyway, if you feel ready to go home later, you can be discharged. Just let the nurse know." The doctor said good-bye and left the room.

Kate looked at Stringer for a few moments then turned to Francis. "Thank you for getting rid of them. And I'm sorry I got nasty. We aren't used to being with someone we can trust. I'm used to doing it alone."

"Maybe you don't have to anymore."

Kate looked at him out of the corner of her eye. "Maybe."

Stringer was clearly exhausted. The nurse gave him a pain shot so he could get some sleep. Kate and Francis left the room and walked outside onto the lawn. The rain had stopped and the wind had calmed considerably. It was getting dark and the air was turning cold. Kate had on only a light shirt.

"There's a little cafeteria inside. Let's get a cup of coffee."

"Okay."

Back inside they each got a hot coffee and a bagel then sat down at an empty table. A TV flickered from up on the wall in the corner.

"Thank God String's going to be all right." Kate said, taking a sip of coffee. "I'd be lost without him."

"I know." Francis held his cup in both hands. "I had no idea he'd come out today, especially with that storm blowing in."

"He missed you; he just can't stay away." *And neither can I*, she thought to herself.

"Despite the danger, I have to tell you he was incredible out there. I've never seen a kid with so much courage."

Kate shook her head. "Or craziness."

"Probably both," Francis said.

The Portland station's six o'clock news was coming on the TV.

"Shit, Francis, look!" Kate said, rising off her chair. She ran over to the TV and turned up the volume. Someone had captured Delbert's rescue on a home video and there were fairly good close-ups of Stringer. The reporter identified him as a twelve-year-old boy, a strong swimmer from the West Coast.

"Those bastards," Kate said, pounding her fist on a table so hard the salt and pepper shakers danced. "We've got to get him out of here!"

"Kate, he's in a hospital. This is just a local news program. There's no way Leland could see this."

Kate turned to him and took hold of his shirt with both hands. "Please call them. Tell them not to put this story on the national news. They know you. You're a big deal here. We're nothing to these folks, a couple of strangers from California. Please, Francis."

"Okay, but I think we're overreacting."

"We're *not* overreacting. Trust me." She searched his eyes. "Promise you'll trust me on this."

"I promise. I'll call right now."

Francis walked over to a pay phone, looked up the number for the Portland TV station, and dialed. After an intense exchange, he hung up, stared at the phone for a few moments then walked back to Kate. He did not sit down. "The wire services have already picked it up. There's no way to stop it. It may even make the evening news; one of those upbeat human interest stories."

"Damn," Kate said, backing against the wall. She put her head in her hands.

"Delbert was a well-known magazine editor from New York. He knows people all over the world. It's a big deal your son saved his life."

"I can't fucking believe this!" Kate said, leaning against a vending machine full of plastic-wrapped food. "We're screwed.

We can't stay here." She slammed the front of the machine with the palm of her hand. "We finally get to a safe place thousands of miles away and Stringer has to save some famous guy in a shipwreck." She threw her hands up. "We can't get a break."

Francis walked over to her. "If you don't feel safe going to your apartment, why don't you both come and stay at my place. I'll call Charlie and ask him to keep an eye out for anyone who even vaguely resembles Leland."

Francis took Kate into his arms as tears ran down her cheeks. He sounded confident, but he too was worried. He'd never dealt with a guy like Leland Johnson. Still, as surely as he'd had to search for Rachael, he was resolute that he would help Kate and Stringer in whatever way he could.

Francis felt an unmistakable power in holding Kate. Something spiritual coursed through her that had awakened his ability to feel, to care deeply, to get out of himself enough to help someone else.

"Come on. If Stringer feels strong enough, we'll take him to the bungalow tonight. You can stay for a few days until this blows over."

Kate lifted her head and wiped her eyes with her sleeve. Francis gently curled long strands of hair behind her ear and, in that moment, was indelibly struck by her unpretentious humanness and beauty. "Kate, I know you feel scared and lost, but in letting me help you, you're also helping me find who I am again."

Kate looked at him as if she understood.

He helped her to her feet and they walked back to Stringer's room. Though he was sleepy, Stringer said he wanted to go home. Francis borrowed several pillows from the hospital, propped them up in the back seat of the Jeep, and loaded Stringer in.

They stopped at Kate's apartment to pick up a few things then drove out of town. Stringer said he was glad they were going to Francis's. At the bungalow, Francis and Kate helped Stringer out of the back seat. He hobbled toward the door then stopped and looked at the horizon, where sharp white cracks of lightning illuminated low-lying clouds, dancing between them as if the sky was short circuiting.

"Cool," Stringer said, supporting his casted arm on his hip.

"It's late in the year for heat lightning," Francis said. "There must be another storm coming."

As they walked inside, Francis caught the screen door with his hand so it wouldn't slam. Kate and Stringer stood in the small hallway, not sure where to go.

"You and Stringer will be most comfortable upstairs in the big bed, if that's okay. Unfortunately, I have only one bathroom. Downstairs."

"That's fine," Kate said.

Francis led them up the narrow staircase. Kate helped Stringer, brushing against pictures hanging on the wall. Her arm caught a photograph of Rachael, nearly knocking it off its hook. She stopped, carefully straightened it, and continued up to the bedroom.

"There're towels, blankets, and more pillows in the bureau there," Francis said, pointing to an ornate piece Rachael had bought in Paris years ago. In the dim light, he watched Kate as she pulled back the quilted comforter, supporting Stringer's arm as he got into bed. She carefully snugged the comforter up over his shoulders then looked around the room. "This is great," she said. "Real cozy."

Kate stepped to the window and curved her hands around the glass lamp. "I've never seen a lantern like this. Where did you get it?"

"It's a whaling lamp. My grandmother left it to me when I inherited the bungalow. It's very old, from Gloucester, Massachusetts." Francis stepped closer to Kate. "In the nineteenth century when the great whaling ships went out to sea for months, even years at a time, families placed these lanterns in seaward windows and lit them each night to guide the men safely home. 'Beacons of hope,' Grandma used to call them."

Kate reached inside the blown glass and ran her finger over the thick, melted wax layering the bottom. "Do you light it often?"

"Until recently, every night."

She looked into Francis's eyes, lightly touched his chest then stepped to the bed.

Francis walked to the top of the stairs. "If you need anything, just give a yell."

"Thanks. I will."

"Goodnight, String."

Stringer waved the fingers sticking out of his cast.

Francis descended the stairs, smelling Kate's lingering scent in the hallway. He heard the familiar creak of the bed springs as she lay down next to her son. Francis listened as she sang softly to Stringer in the twilight. He assumed it was a Lakota lullaby. Soon the upstairs light went out and all was quiet.

Francis walked into the kitchen and pushed open a window above the sink. A new moon slid behind gathering clouds. He leaned on the sink with both hands, cool night air circulating through his hair.

After a while, he filled the kettle and lit the stove. Blue gas flames burst forth under the iron kettle. He took down a tin, pulled out two tea bags, and placed them in stoneware cups. He lifted the kettle from the stove just before it whistled, filled the cups, and put a stick of cinnamon and a half-teaspoon of clover honey in each cup.

He took his tea, sat down in the studio, and dialed the sheriff's department. He thanked Charlie for picking up Kate then, speaking in a low voice, told him the little he knew about Leland Johnson. He asked him to keep an eye out for him, to find out whatever he could. Charlie said he'd run Leland through their computer and call him back in a day or two. Francis asked if Delbert's rescue had made it onto Dan Rather. Charlie said he was disappointed that it hadn't, that it would have been good publicity with Festival coming up in a few months. Francis was relieved.

After he hung up, Francis pulled the painting of Rachael into his lap. He ran his finger over the thick layers of paint forming the breast she had lost. He had not admitted to Rachael that her mastectomy scar had disturbed him; that it was hard for him to look at, to touch. That he too felt her violation. He'd known his feelings were of less importance, but now he wished he'd shared more of his pain with her. It might have made it easier for Rachael to do the same with him. He placed the canvas back against the wall and walked outside.

The wind blew against his face as he walked to the bluff. Waves crashed hard against the rocks below. He sat down, dangled his feet over the cliff, and closed his eyes. Francis heard voices in the wind, ancient songs rising from the surging sea. He listened carefully and heard Rachael and Kate and Stringer, their cries mingling in the night.

A short while later, he heard footsteps behind him on the path.

"Thank you for the tea." Kate crossed her legs and sat beside him.

"You're welcome."

"And for letting us stay with you. It's beautiful here. And I do feel pretty safe." Kate watched the moon move behind clouds in the southeastern sky. "I hate it, but I've lived in fear for a long time. Leland's a wicked man. Relentless. Told me many times if I ever tried to get away he'd hunt me down. I seriously think he might kill me." Kate pulled a blanket more tightly around her shoulders.

There was something powerfully sensual in her honesty.

"Sounds terrible," Francis said.

"It was. I tried to fight him, but the system doesn't work. Cops would come and he'd lay off beating me for a while, but he'd keep pounding me mentally. That was the worst of it and it's the hardest to escape. It's like he got inside my head and twisted my brain."

Kate pulled her knees up tight to her chest. "'Till I met you, I hated men. I couldn't imagine wanting to be close to one again." She looked at Francis. "But it feels good, the way you treat Stringer and me."

Francis reached up and gently held his hand to her cheek.

Kate took one side of her blanket and wrapped it around Francis's shoulders.

They sat holding hands for some time. Then Kate turned to Francis. "I'm really beat. I'm going to go back inside. Are you okay?"

"I'm fine."

They gently let go of each other's hands. Kate stood, took the blanket off her back, and slid it around him. Then she kissed him on the cheek. "Good night, Francis."

He wanted to take her in his arms and kiss her but hesitated. "Good night, Kate."

Kate walked to the bungalow. Francis sat huddled on the cliff, watching silver-capped waves dance across the bay. He felt full of her. Even in the cool air his face felt flushed. He reached up and touched the spot on his cheek where Kate had kissed him. Under the crescent moon, a lone seagull screamed from the direction of Wagner's Point.

CHAPTER 7

Off and on during the night, Francis was awakened by movements in the bedroom above him. He tossed and turned on the cot until just before daybreak when he got up, made a cup of coffee, and took his easel onto the lawn. Outside, the morning had a wonderful clarity about it. The last of the storm clouds had blown through, and bright sunlight streamed across the bay. He looked down at the skiff bobbing gently at its mooring then turned and noticed that Stringer was waving to him from the upstairs window. Kate appeared next to Stringer, dark tousled hair about her face and shoulders.

"Good morning," Francis called up to them. "Did you sleep well?"

"Yeah, 'cept for Mom's snoring."

Kate dropped a towel on his head. "We slept fine. You offering coffee?" She sounded relaxed.

"Yes. I'll be right in."

Kate stepped to the open window. She was wearing one of his T-shirts. "No. You paint. I'll take a shower and fix breakfast. Do you have eggs I can make?"

"Yes, there's some in the fridge."

"Scrambled or over easy?"

Francis smiled up at her. "Over easy, please."

"Great. Breakfast in half an hour." She and Stringer disappeared into the bedroom. Just seeing them up in the window made him feel joyful.

Francis adjusted his easel to the light and began to paint: barefooted New Yorkers tossing a Frisbee on spring grass in Central Park; women in tank tops and Bermuda shorts. Skyscrapers rose above the pastel green of budding treetops. A chocolate lab arched in the air, stretching toward a yellow Frisbee. At the edge of the park, a small flock of pigeons lifted from the grass.

Kate fixed eggs over easy for Francis, scrambled with melted provolone and bits of broccoli for her and Stringer. They ate outside, and despite it being late September, the sun was warm, the air pleasant. Kate gave a sigh of relief when Francis told her the rescue hadn't made the network news.

When Stringer finished eating, he turned to his mother. His face was scratched and swollen. "Can I paint today? Not go to school." He glanced at Francis for support.

Kate looked at them both. "Okay. One day," she said.

Francis nodded. "I'd say he's earned a day off."

Kate stood and gathered the dishes together.

"I'll help you with those," Francis said.

"No. You and String spend some time painting or doing whatever you guys do up here. I'll clean up then I think I'll take a walk."

"A nice hiking trail starts across the road from my neighbor at the foot of the hill. Her name is Kasa."

"Sounds good."

Kate walked inside, washed the dishes then stepped into the hallway. She saw Francis's field coat hanging on the back of the door. She took it off the hook and slid her arms inside. It felt and smelled wonderfully familiar.

Outside, Francis was settling Stringer into a lawn chair in front of his easel, carefully tucking pillows under his casted arm.

"See you later," Kate said as she left.

"Have a good walk," Francis said.

"Watch out for the rocks," Stringer called out, a bit sarcastically.

"I will." Kate put her hands deep in the coat's pockets. "Nice coat."

Francis smiled.

Walking down the hill, Kate grinned as she passed the spot where she and Stringer had stalled out in the Subaru. At the bottom of the hill, she stopped next to Kasa's garden. Deep orange pumpkins sat on withering vines. By the fence lay half-rotten zucchinis, cucumbers, tomatoes, and a few squash on a bed of laid-over corn stalks. A wooden wheelbarrow in the middle of the garden overflowed with old newspapers and straw. Kate walked over and rested her hands on top of the weathered picket fence separating the garden from the road. She closed her eyes, enjoying a potpourri of scallions, chives, mint, and basil mingling in the crisp fall air.

"Do you like to garden?"

Kate was startled by the voice. An older, large-boned woman stood in the doorway at the back of the house. She wore a heavy denim apron, her frizzy white hair done up in a bun. Kate stood back from the fence and slid her hands into her pockets. "I've haven't gardened since I was a girl."

Kasa stepped into the sunlight. "Isn't the color of the pumpkins wonderful?"

"They're great," Kate replied. Feeling intimidated by the woman's large presence, she stayed outside the fence.

The woman walked across the garden toward her, wiping her hands on her apron. She reached over the fence and shook Kate's hand. "I'm Kasa. You must be Kate, Francis's friend."

Surprised but pleased that Kasa knew her name, Kate shook her hand. "Yes. I was just going for a walk."

Kasa pointed across the road. "Trail starts over there between the cedars and the bayberries. It'll take you to the point. Would you like a cup of coffee first?"

Kate hesitated. She would, but it didn't feel quite right. "Thank you, but I really need some exercise. Maybe some other time."

"Have a good hike then."

Kate walked across the road to the where the trail began. She looked back at Kasa, who was bent over, pulling up the stubborn stalk of a large pumpkin vine. Suddenly the vine snapped and Kasa fell backwards into the dirt.

Kate hurried back across the road. "Are you all right?"

"I probably could use a strong hand to get up," Kasa said, steadying herself on her elbows.

Kate came around the end of the fence into the garden, set her feet in front of Kasa, and gave her both hands. Kasa took hold, let out a groan, and righted herself. Kate was surprised by how much Kasa weighed and by the strength of her arms.

"Thank you." Kasa said, small clumps of earth falling from her dress. Then she returned to pulling up the remaining vines.

"I could help you with those," Kate said.

"That would be wonderful."

Kate pushed up the sleeves of the field coat and grabbed hold of a plant. The tiny spines of the vine were sharp, but Kasa was handling them without gloves so Kate figured she could. She tugged hard with both hands and the stalk slowly came loose. She threw the plant on the pile Kasa had made in the middle of the garden, bent forward, and pulled up another one.

Soon she shed the field coat and hung it on a fence post. Kate and Kasa worked until all the pumpkin, squash, and zucchini plants had been uprooted. Before they were done, Kate too had fallen in the dirt, making them both chuckle.

"Now we must have a cup of coffee together," Kasa said, looking with satisfaction at the pile of uprooted vines.

"Okay." Kate followed Kasa through a deeply gouged wooden door into a sunny, glassed-in room.

"Sink's over there," Kasa said, pointing. "I'll put the kettle on."

Kate washed her hands in the sink. She loved the smells of Kasa's summer kitchen, particularly the scent of mint coming from a planter in the window. Kate sat down at a small table bathed in sunlight.

Shortly Kasa came back with two cups of hot coffee and a saucer holding two warm biscuits. "Do you like cream and sugar?"

"Yes, please."

Kasa poured a generous portion of cream into Kate's mug, slid the sugar bowl toward her, and sat down in the other chair. She looked tired.

They both took a sip. Steam rose from their mugs into the sunlight in delicate curls. "Have you known Francis long?" Kate asked.

"Since I came here from Yugoslavia after the war. His grandmother, Gracie, lived in the bungalow then. She was kind to me and we became friends. Francis was just a boy when he first came from New York to visit. He used to paint on the lawn even then. Handsome boy, seemed like every girl in The Cove came round to play with him."

Kate sipped her coffee, already feeling more comfortable.

"After Gracie died, Francis and Rachael moved in. Rachael and I gardened together for many years before she died last year. Breast cancer. She fought like hell, but it took over her body. Her spirit was strong till the end. Francis always stood by her, as much as she'd let him."

Kate set her mug on the table. "Didn't she drown in the bay?"

Kasa nodded. "Yes. She knew it was her last day. There was just too much pain. She said every single bone ached; even her teeth hurt. We sat here at this table early that morning and she told me she was going for one last sail. I never thought she'd find the strength, but she was determined." Kasa's gaze drifted out across her garden. "She said good-bye to me and gave me a long hug. Rachael rarely hugged. I knew I'd never see her again."

A gentle breeze passed over the table from the partially open door. Kate felt a chill run up her back.

"You have known a lot of pain too," Kasa said.

"How do you know?"

"Your face carries your past. You are a beautiful young woman and your beauty hides much, but I see it."

Kate blushed. Kasa reached over and lightly touched a welt of scar tissue over Kate's eye from when Leland shoved her into a stove. Then Kasa raised the blue cotton sleeve of her work dress, revealing several old scars. She lifted her sleeve a bit higher and a vague number tattooed in black ink appeared.

Kate froze. After a few moments, she bent forward and gently touched it. "My God, Kasa, what happened to you?"

Kasa's large eyes turned to Kate. "I grew up in Yugoslavia. When I was sixteen, my parents sent me to Jewish friends in Austria to work for them. When war broke out, their family was captured by the Germans. I'm not Jewish, but I am strong. I spent three years in a Nazi work camp."

Kate sat motionless.

"After we were freed by the Allies, I made it to England, then America. I was one of the lucky ones."

Tears filled Kate's eyes.

"I'm sorry," Kasa said, sliding her chair toward Kate. "I didn't mean to upset you."

"It's okay," Kate said quietly. "I'm sorry for what you've been through, but it's a relief to talk with someone who really knows what pain is."

"Me too," Kasa said. She cleared her throat and sat upright in her chair. "You go for your walk now. Fresh air is good."

Kate stood. She put her hand on Kasa's arm. "Thank you."

Kate hiked along the trail through browning scrub then along a salt marsh where a lone egret stood at the edge of the water. The trail led to a rock ledge that ran parallel with the shore. She stopped, tied her sneakers more tightly, and then climbed up the rocks.

Halfway up, she stopped. Carved into dark stone were a half-dozen hearts encircling initials. Some were so worn away by the salt air you could hardly make out the letters. She ran her fingers over one carving: "J. L. + B. W. Forever." Kate wondered who the lovers might have been. Teenagers who'd just lost their virginity? A sailor and a shore girl who'd met on a hot Saturday night? Some old couple, married for years, helping steady each other's arthritic hands? She could only imagine those kinds of feelings.

Kate continued across a grassy area that led to Wagner's Point. As the ocean came into view, she slowed her pace. There it was, jammed between huge rocks just off the point. Kate shuddered as she stared at the battered remains of the *Maiden*. After a few moments, she gingerly climbed down to an outcropping just above the wreck. She was shocked by how little was left of the smooth mahogany bow she had touched that night in the harbor. It was hard to believe Stringer had rescued someone from that wreck and survived. And it was clear he couldn't have done it without Francis's help. Kate looked north toward the bungalow. She thought of Francis and how much she appreciated how he was helping Stringer recover the part of his soul battered and beaten down by Leland.

Kate sat on the rock, elbows on her knees, watching the waves push against the remains of the boat still held together by strong hardwood ribs. Farther out, two lobster boats were headed into the cove. Though the breeze was chilly, the sun was warm on her face. She sat for a long time, gently rocking back and forth. She had been moved, and a bit unnerved, by Kasa, but somehow comforted too. She knew about being battered, so Kate hadn't needed to explain it. And it was wonderful to be away from Leland, to feel even a little safe. She was mindful, though, they had been in Maine but a short time and she still worried about him finding them. But for the first time in many years, she at least had some realistic hope.

Kate closed her eyes, imagined Francis painting on the bluff with Stringer, the blond hairs of Francis's forearms illuminated in the sunlight. He was like no one she'd ever known. He made her feel important, even beautiful. He was a man worthy enough to spend time with her son. She smiled and wondered if she would ever kiss him.

After a while, Kate couldn't sit any longer. She climbed back up over the ledges, crossed the field, and headed toward the bungalow. Half an hour later she passed Kasa's and turned up the dirt road. Her heart pounded. Sweat formed at the base of her neck. She stripped off the field coat and carried it over her shoulder.

At the bungalow, Kate paused in the shadow of the eaves and watched Francis and Stringer, who were still painting on the lawn. As though dancing without touching, their arms moved in smooth arcs across the canvases. She watched the muscles of Francis's forearms and the arch of his back.

"Hey, Mom," Stringer yelled without turning his head.

Kate stepped into the sunlight. "You guys still at it?"

Francis turned to her. A handsome face—tanned and weathered just enough. Like that of a Nebraska wheat farmer she'd once met traveling with her mother.

"Look at this," Francis said, gesturing to Stringer's canvas. Stringer finished a series of strokes then put down his brush.

Kate looked at the painting. "String, this is amazing."

He was painting the wreck of the *Maiden*. Kate felt as if she was right there, sitting on sea-glazed rocks in fierce winds, waves pounding the sleek ship to pieces.

"You like it?"

"It's great."

"And with one arm in a cast," Francis said. "Your son has unusually keen insight." He smiled approvingly. "He's becoming an artist."

Kate felt Francis standing behind her. An unfamiliar longing burned deep inside her. She put her arms around Stringer and hugged him. "I'm really happy you're painting." Then she turned and took Francis's hand. "Thank you for all you've done."

"The pleasure is mine."

"Okay if I get a bite to eat? That was quite a walk."

"Of course. Did you make it to the point?" Francis asked, catching her eye and motioning toward the bungalow.

She felt his gaze glide slowly over her body. "Yes." She followed Francis to the house.

"You must have been moving right along to make it back this soon."

Kate's stomach felt like a cage of butterflies. "Yeah, I was." Francis held the door and she passed under his arm, her shoulder brushing against his chest. He let the door close softly. She walked into the kitchen, leaned against the stove, and turned to him.

He searched her face. "You are so beautiful."

Kate looked at the floor. He reached up and gently lifted her chin. Kate glanced at the front door. Francis leaned toward her, drawing her lips to his. Kissing him, Kate let out a sigh of pleasure. She cradled his cheek in her palm, raising her thigh against his groin.

With some difficulty, Francis pulled away. He took Kate's hand and led her up the staircase to the bedroom. He looked out the window and confirmed that Stringer was still busy painting. He turned and kissed Kate softly along her neck. She unbuttoned his shirt and undid his belt. He slid her sweatshirt over her head, peeling it off her arms. Beneath her white cotton bra, her breasts were magnificent and firm, rising toward him with each breath.

Bare-chested, his khakis loose around his waist, Francis could not take his gaze off her. He hadn't realized how much he had longed to touch a woman's tender places again. So much sadness, loss, and despair. He closed his eyes. Rachael's scar flashed in his mind. He heard Kate unclasp her bra, then felt it fall at his feet. She took his hand in hers and gently raised it to her breast. Francis felt the curving fullness then her nipple between his fingers. His penis was hard.

Slowly he opened his eyes. Kneeling, Kate slid his pants down his legs, kissing the insides of his thighs. Holding each other, they settled onto the bed. Francis pulled off her jeans, slid his fingers inside her panties, and felt the soft hair of her mons.

Naked, they lay intertwined, hands searching each other's warm bodies. Francis lifted her breasts to his mouth. His tongue played with her hard nipples. Kate massaged his penis with her hand.

Kate gradually rolled onto her back, her thighs opening to him. Francis felt her bare skin against his, looked into her eyes, and kissed her, drawing her tongue deep into his mouth. She pulled him closer and he slowly, smoothly entered her. He tried to hold back, but knew he was ready to climax.

Then, suddenly, tears appeared in Kate's eyes. She looked away and pushed against his chest with her hands. Feeling an orgasm cresting, Francis withdrew as Kate rolled away from him onto her side, crying. Climaxing powerfully, Francis fell against the comforter, ejaculating into the bed clothes.

As soon as he quieted, Kate rolled back toward him, resting her hand over his back as it rose and fell with his breathing. "I'm sorry, Francis. I thought I was ready, but I guess I'm not."

Francis didn't move.

Kate leaned over and kissed him. Francis rolled up on his side and looked at her. He felt awkward, embarrassed.

Kate glanced down and saw what had happened. "I'm so sorry," she said, breaking into an unexpected smile.

He grinned. Kate started to giggle. Francis's awkwardness melted away and he too cracked up. They lay there on the bed, holding each other, laughing.

Francis raised himself on one elbow, delicately lifting sweaty hair from her eyes. He kissed her tenderly on the lips. "You're worth waiting for."

Kate slid off the bed and pulled a sheet around her. She stepped over and looked out the window to check on Stringer.

Just then the phone rang. Francis sat up and answered it. "Yes?" He caught Kate's gaze as she turned and looked at him questioningly.

"Mr. Monroe, Charlie Lord."

"Charlie, could I call you back in a bit?"

"I've got bad news for you."

"About Leland Johnson?"

"No. About this Kate lady, Leland's wife. I'd be careful of her."

Francis held the phone more tightly to his ear. He felt Kate's hands on his back.

"She's got quite a rap sheet."

"Charlie, I'll have to call you back," Francis said, rather sternly.

"It'd be better if you came down to the station."

Francis felt his chest tighten. "Okay," he said, "I'll be down shortly."

CHAPTER 8

Francis rang off. Kate pulled a sweatshirt over her head, glanced out the window at Stringer then spoke to Francis. "What's going on?"

"I've got to go down to the sheriff's office," he said, quickly dressing.

Kate stepped in front of him. "Has Leland found us?"

"No, nothing like that."

"Then what?"

Francis picked up a shirt. "Charlie's a good guy, but he gets in a huff sometimes."

Kate stared at Francis. "Is it about me?"

Francis nodded. "Well, partially."

"What about me?"

Francis looked out the window. Stringer was walking toward the bungalow. "I was worried Leland might try to find you so I asked Charlie to run him through their computer. He said they didn't find much on Leland but something came up about you."

Kate's cheeks turned red. She looked at the floor. "Why's Charlie after me?"

"I don't think he's *after* you. Folks are a little provincial around here. And that damn sheriff rides him hard." Francis tried to look reassuring. "Some locals get nervous when there's even a hint of outside trouble. I'm just going to go down and talk to him."

Kate looked chilly. Francis opened the drawer of the Parisian dresser, took out a warm pair of sweatpants and handed them to her. She sat down and pulled them over her long legs.

Francis felt his stomach churning. "I'll be back soon." He walked toward the stairs.

Kate touched his leg as he passed. "Please don't let them hurt us."

Francis stopped. For the first time since they'd met, Kate looked broken, as if she'd barely survived Leland. As if everything had been as bad as she'd said it was.

He crouched beside her, put his hand on her forearm. "I won't. I promise."

He leaned forward and kissed her forehead. Then he walked downstairs, grabbed the field coat off its hook, and opened the front door, where he was met by Stringer.

"Let me help you," Francis said, taking Stringer's pallet and paint box, which he was balancing on his cast. "I'm going into town and I'll pick up pizza on the way home. What do you and your mom like?"

"Pepperoni and pineapple with extra cheese. We hate anchovies. Where *is* Mom?"

"Upstairs. She could probably use a hug. I'll see you in a while."

"Hey, Francis—"

"Yeah?"

"Mom loves ice cream with pizza. Cherry Garcia's her favorite."

"Got it."

Unsettled by a mixture of curiosity, concern, and fear, Francis drove silently into town. He wanted to be protective of Kate and Stringer and, if he could, spare Kate harsh judgment from townsfolk. *A little provincial* was, after all, a bit of an understatement, especially with Sheriff McNeal on the prowl. On the other hand, and even more unsettling, Francis had to acknowledge how little he really knew about this woman who had quickly become a central part of his life.

In town, Francis parked next to the courthouse. Charlie's cruiser was in the lot, but not the sheriff's, which was good. Larry McNeal was a hot-headed, closed-minded bigot from a tough paper mill family. Francis—and lots of other folks—had little use for the man. Some would even admit to being scared of him, knowing the near absolute power county sheriffs can wield. McNeal did keep the county safe, but beyond that it was a good thing Charlie was his chief deputy. As best he could, Charlie kept the running of the county more humanized than McNeal would have on his own.

Built in the middle of the nineteenth century as the county jail, the imposing building still had a few functional jail cells, their windows reinforced with heavy iron bars bolted through thick brick walls. Every fall, Sheriff McNeal gave the junior high school class a tour of the place. He took his time highlighting the cells' best features, including the warped metal bunks with inch-thin mattresses held to the wall by pairs of chains. The exposed porcelain toilet was situated under the tiny, dingy window on the outside wall. McNeal was sure the apparently low drug use in Winter's Cove stemmed directly from his scaring the shit out of kids by taking them through the county's "Hell Hotel."

Francis shook his head and walked inside.

"Hey, Mr. Monroe. Thanks for coming in." Charlie was working on reports at his desk. "Can I get you a cup of coffee?"

"No, thank you." Francis walked over and shook Charlie's hand.

Charlie motioned to the heavy wooden chair next to his desk. "Have a seat."

Francis pulled the chair a few inches away from Charlie's desk and sat down.

"So what's this you've found?"

Charlie opened a folder and took out a computer printout. "I looked into this Leland Johnson like you asked. The only things I found on him were a misdemeanor drug possession and a domestic abuse order from a few years ago. Strange though, the abuse complaint was withdrawn by the complainant—his wife—a week after it was ordered. And one DLS he got fined for."

"DLS?"

"Sorry. Driving with license suspended. Figuring I'd check everybody out, I ran Kate Johnson through the computer too." Charlie picked up another printout and slid it across the desk to Francis. "She's good lookin', but this lady's trouble." Charlie leaned toward Francis. "Look here," he said, pointing to a line he'd highlighted in yellow. "Shoplifting, trafficking narcotics, possession of controlled substance with intent to sell."

"But those were back in the early nineties."

"Some are felonies, Francis. Serious offenses."

Charlie's finger slid down a few more lines. "Supplying alcohol to a minor."

Francis frowned. "There must be more to it. She's not like that now."

Charlie pointed at the paper again. "It's right there, Mr. Monroe. Rap sheets don't lie."

"Well, maybe in the past she—"

Charlie became a bit agitated. "Can't you see she's trouble? And now she's living in Winter's Cove. God knows what she's up to."

Francis's back stiffened. "Look, Charlie, I know she's been through tough times in the past. She's told me herself, but this Leland guy's a bastard who held her against her will, physically and emotionally abusing her. She tried for years to get away from him and couldn't—until she and Stringer finally found their way here."

Charlie stood and squinted the same way Sheriff McNeal did. Francis had never seen Charlie look like that before. "*If* this Leland guy beat her up, maybe she, well, mighta had it coming."

Francis gritted his teeth, rose from his chair, and stared Charlie hard in the eye. "Because I've known and liked you for a long time, I'm going to pretend you didn't say that." Francis leaned closer. "No one has the right to beat up someone else, Charlie. No matter what."

Charlie was taken aback. His countenance softened a bit. "Look, Mr. Monroe, what you do in your personal life is none of my business, but folks are talkin' about you having her and the boy stayin' out to your place. You're right, we've been friends a long time and I still appreciate what you did for my boy, but I gotta tell you, this Kate lady's bad for you and for this town. We don't need this. Last summer's tourist season was down and now Festival's coming and we need it to be a good one." Charlie looked away. "Besides, sheriff's up for reelection in the spring and he's already told me to do something about her."

"Really?" Francis replied, anger rising inside of him. "Like what?"

Charlie shifted his weight from one foot to another. "Look, Kate's still this guy's wife. They're legally married. He reported her and their son missing a month ago. She'll be wanted for interstate kidnapping next and you'll be an accessory. They've crossed state lines. That's a federal offense."

Francis sat back in the chair and looked at the gold sheriff's department star on the wall behind Charlie. "You remember when you first brought Nathan to see me, when Dr. Perrin couldn't do anymore with him and thought he might respond to watching me paint?"

Charlie looked embarrassed. "Of course I remember."

"After Nathan started painting that summer, you told me nobody had gotten through to Nathan like I did. You said I had a sixth sense about him."

Charlie nodded. "You turned his life around and saved our marriage too. We were about crazy with Nate. Until the day she died, my wife was thankful to you."

Francis slid his chair close to Charlie's. "Well, I'm telling you I've got the same sense about Kate. She is a good, courageous woman. She deserves everything positive this town has to offer, including a chance for a new life. A safe life. Whether you like what you see or not, you have an obligation to protect her like everyone else who lives here, and I'm going to make sure you do."

Charlie slid back in his chair.

"Besides, Charlie," Francis said, remembering Charlie's tumultuous affair with the town clerk a few years back, "none of us is perfect."

"No, sir, I guess not."

Francis stood and walked to the door.

"Be careful, Mr. Monroe."

Francis let the door close with a bang behind him. Disturbed and confused, he drove home with the window rolled down, the sharp night air refreshing against his face. Halfway to the bungalow, he remembered the pizza, made a U-turn in the middle of the road, and drove to Dan's. While the pizza was in the oven, Francis walked across the street to the town grocery. He smiled when he found a pint of Cherry Garcia in the ice cream freezer.

On his way home, Francis saw a cove taxi drive by him heading into town. Francis made the turn at Kasa's and climbed the hill to the bungalow. He put the ice cream on top of the pizza and, balancing, pushed the door open with his back and walked inside.

"I'm back," he called out, walking into the kitchen. "Anyone hungry?"

Silence.

Who was he kidding? He knew they were gone, down the road in that damn taxi. The house was terribly quiet. He climbed the staircase and peered into the bedroom. The bed was made, the windows closed. The whaler's lamp was cold.

Francis sat on the edge of the bed, pulled back the covers, and ran his hands between the sheets. He could smell Kate's entrancing scent. He laid back and closed his eyes; saw her lying next to him, naked, laughing.

He got up and unlatched a window. Moist salt air rushed in. The moon rode high over the cliff, casting shadows beneath the pine tree on the lawn. He closed the window and picked up a book of matches from the windowsill. "The Claw" was printed on the front. He realized how much he liked having Kate and Stringer in his house. He lit the lamp—this time for them—then walked downstairs. In the bathroom, he ran cold water onto a hand towel and held it to his face. Then, sliding the wet cloth around the back of his neck, he caught his reflection in the mirror. Somehow he looked younger since he'd met Kate. He was not at all sure where it was going, but his life was undeniably changing, and for the better, it seemed.

In the kitchen, he dropped three spoons into the bag with the ice cream, picked up the pizza box, and drove straight to Kate's apartment. The light was on, so with pizza and ice cream in hand, he walked up the steps and rapped on the door. No response. He looked inside and saw Stringer's backpack on the kitchen table, a can of Coke by the sink. He rapped again. Still nothing. He backed out of the doorway, turned, and looked up and down the street. It was quiet. The only person in sight was a woman walking her dog on the opposite sidewalk. In the distance, moonlight reflected off the tin roof of the harbormaster's house. Worried about them but not sure where to look, he figured the best thing he could do was go home in case they returned or called.

Francis drove uptown and saw Charlie's cruiser idling next to the courthouse. He remembered what Charlie had said about Kate, and though he probably meant well, it made Francis angry. She had scars and pain enough from her past without some deputy sheriff giving her a hard time. Besides, he knew how much people could change. Though he had questions, he trusted his own instincts about Kate. He was letting her into his heart, and he didn't do that sort of thing lightly.

Out on the highway, Francis rolled down his window, letting in the night air. Driving along a stretch of road beside a salt marsh, he noticed a bright set of headlights coming up behind him at high speed. He reached up and adjusted his rear view mirror.

Suddenly a large pickup with a rack of glaring roof lights was right on his tail, the roar of its engine unnerving.

"What the—" Francis squinted and pulled to the right.

The truck swerved toward the Jeep, forcing Francis to the shoulder. The truck's windows were rolled down and a wild eyed, black-haired man with a scraggly beard was at the wheel. He swerved the pickup into the side of the Jeep, laughing like a crazy man as their fenders crunched together.

His heart pounding, Francis held tight to the wheel and jammed on the brakes. The man floored the truck and raced off. Francis caught a glimpse of the Maine license plate: BLKHRT.

"Goddamn redneck!" Francis yelled. He rolled his window down and looked at the side of the Jeep, but it was too dark to see the damage. With his headlights shining through mist rising off the marsh, Francis sat long enough to catch his breath, and then drove on.

A quarter mile down the road, Francis saw the lights again, coming at him around a corner on his side of the road.

"Shit," he said to himself, pulling toward the shoulder.

The guy was coming straight at him. Francis considered crossing into the other lane but didn't dare. With nowhere to go, he pulled the wheel as hard as he could to the right and the Jeep dug into the shoulder. Francis shielded himself with his arm and yelled. The pickup roared along his door, tearing off his rear view mirror and pushing him off the road.

The Jeep tore into the swamp, rolled over, and plowed into a mound of marsh grass, driver's side down. Francis flew forward, cracking the windshield with his head. Freezing water rushed in his open window. As the hood submerged into the weeds, the Jeep's hot manifold let out a sickening hissing sound.

CHAPTER 9

Cold swamp water rose over the seat. Dazed and in pain, Francis pushed back from the steering wheel and managed to undo his seat belt. He felt blood dripping from pieces of glass imbedded in his forehead and cheek. With the wet sleeve of his coat, he wiped his eyes enough to see then tried to open his door, but it was jammed into the mud. Something sparked under the dashboard, sending up a whiff of smoke. The Jeep settled more deeply into the marsh as cold, muddy water sloshed through the window. Francis strained to pull his legs out from under the partially collapsed dashboard.

Realizing the danger he was in, Francis pushed himself up so he could roll down the passenger window. He braced his feet against the steering column and pushed hard enough to climb out the window onto the roof. Resting for a moment, he dipped his hand into the water and rinsed the glass and blood from his face. A stabbing pain shot through his left shoulder.

A few moments later, lights appeared on the horizon. Heart racing, Francis slid off the Jeep and crouched down in the swamp. Suddenly flashing blue lights shone over the embankment and a vehicle pulled up near where Francis had gone off the road. He waited in the water until he saw a man in uniform get out, then he pulled himself back up onto the passenger's side of the Jeep.

"You okay?" the officer yelled.

"Yes. Got run off the road," Francis yelled back.

The officer hurried down the bank, his flashlight flickering in Francis's direction. "Anyone else hurt?"

"No. I'm alone. Is that you, Charlie?"

"Yeah." Charlie stood at the edge of the marsh. "Shit, I didn't know that was you, Mr. Monroe. We gotta get you out of there. Can you walk?"

"I think so. It's cold, but it's not that deep." Francis slid off the Jeep into the water. Soaking wet and shivering, he slogged his way through the muddy sea grass.

Charlie walked in up to his knees to give Francis a hand climbing up the bank to the road. His body cold and sore, he leaned against the warm hood of the cruiser.

"What the hell happened?" Charlie asked.

"Some maniac in a pickup crashed into my Jeep and drove me off the road."

"Probably a logger," Charlie said. "Lotta them in town drinking this weekend. Did you catch a plate number?"

"Yes. BLKHRT."

"Blackheart. Shit. Mitch Trager. That asshole lives up north, clear cuts for the paper companies." Charlie stared at Francis. "Come on, it's cold out here. Let's get you into the cruiser and warm you up."

Charlie helped Francis into the front seat. "I'll take you to the hospital."

"I'm all right. Just take me home."

"Shouldn't Doc Conklin take a look at those cuts?"

Francis felt his cheek as he looked in the rear view mirror. "They aren't that bad. I'd appreciate it if you'd just take me home."

"Okay."

Francis fastened his seat belt and lay back against the headrest. Charlie turned around in the middle of the road and headed for Francis's place. "Don't worry, we'll track down old Blackheart. We've had trouble with him before. Comes to town and gets drunker 'n hell. He's always starting fights. First time he run someone off the road though." Charlie accelerated. "We'll get the bastard."

At the bungalow, Charlie walked Francis to the front of the house.

"Thank you, Charlie."

Charlie held the screen door open. "By the way, I'm sorry if I offended you at the office this afternoon. Sheriff Larry likes to keep everything under control, doesn't want anyone—especially from away—stirring things up. I was trying to protect you. I didn't know you were so sweet on this Kate lady."

"Thanks. The whole Kate thing kind of snuck up on me too."

Charlie nodded. "Call me if you need anything," he said as he walked toward his cruiser.

"Good night, Charlie." Francis walked inside and locked the door. He peeled off his wet clothes, turned on the shower as hot as he could stand it, and stepped in. Mud, dried blood, and pieces of marsh grass flowed off his body into the drain.

As the hot water ran out, Francis stepped out of the shower and wrapped himself in a large, soft towel that held Kate's scent. He climbed the stairs to the bedroom and closed a seaward window blown open by the wind. He relit the lamp with the matches from The Claw and lay down on the bed. For the first time since Rachael died, he went to sleep upstairs.

Francis slept until noon. When he got up, he thought about going out in the skiff, but he was too tired and sore. He made a cup of tea, walked onto the front lawn, and sat in a metal chair. He thought about the jerk who'd run him off the road. It had scared the hell out of him. In all his years in Maine, nothing like that had ever happened before.

The sun's warmth felt good on his face and aching shoulder. He missed Kate and Stringer and wondered if they were all right. He remembered he'd wanted to more formally ask her to go to the Wyeth exhibit in Portland and then out to dinner at Walter's, his favorite restaurant.

Francis walked back inside and phoned the sheriff's department to check on his Jeep. Charlie told him they'd had it towed to Moses' Garage in town and that they had a loaner Francis could use.

"Any luck with this Blackheart guy?" Francis asked.

"Well, strange thing. An hour or so before you got run off the road the Portland PD arrested Mitch for fighting outside a bar near the airport. Looks like somebody stole his truck. We're working on it, but he couldn't have been driving it."

Francis thanked Charlie and rang off. Concerned, he sat and thought for a couple minutes, then called Moses', which said they would drop off the loaner car for him. Then he phoned Kate and was relieved when she answered, though she sounded a bit distant.

"I'm sorry you left last night."

"I had to get out of there." There was a pause. "What did Charlie tell you?"

"Nothing you hadn't mentioned. Mostly minor drug stuff." Silence.

"Listen, Kate, I'd really like it if you came with me to the Wyeth exhibit tomorrow night in Portland. It's a rare chance to see some of his best private pieces that he's never sold."

"I don't know, Francis. Things seem a little out of control around here."

"Please come. We could have dinner afterwards at a great restaurant down in the Old Port."

Francis waited.

"I can't leave String alone, and Shelly's out of town. I don't know anyone else I'd trust."

Francis thought for a minute. "I bet he could stay with Kasa."

"She wouldn't mind?"

"I think she'd love the company. Does Stringer play chess?"

"Yeah. He used to play a lot."

"She *loves* to play chess. She's one of the best players I know. I'll give her a call."

"All right, if you're sure he'd be safe with her."

"She's tougher than nails."

"Okay."

"I'll call you back shortly."

His spirits lifted, Francis decided to walk down to Kasa's. She said she would be delighted to have Stringer spend an evening with her. Francis returned to the bungalow and called Kate, and though she was still a bit hesitant, she agreed to go.

"Great. Pick you up at six."

After Francis rang off, a bright blue Chevy Malibu, followed by Moses' wrecker, drove into the yard. Pete, a mechanic with a stubble of a beard and a cigarette hanging from his mouth, jumped out of the Malibu and tossed Francis the keys. "Have fun," Pete said as he climbed into the wrecker. He and his buddy drove off.

Francis studied the Malibu. It was old and gaudy, but clean and in good shape. On the fender was a Holley 4-Barrel Carburetor sticker. He shook his head, walked inside, and checked the flyer for the Wyeth exhibit. It was open until nine. Perfect. He'd take Kate to dinner afterwards. Then he stood in the hallway for a few minutes wondering who had run him off the road. The whole thing had unnerved him and he had to suppress a sense of dread creeping into his thoughts.

He phoned Walter's and made a reservation for nine-fifteen at his favorite table overlooking the cobblestone streets of the Old Port. His shoulder was aching, so he grabbed a bag of ice and walked upstairs to lie down. But after a few minutes he got up, opened the closet, and looked over the rack of his dress shirts, none of which he had worn since Rachael's memorial service. Each one had memories.

He took his favorite long-sleeved white silk off the hanger. Rachael loved for him to wear it when they went out on summer nights. Francis felt the smooth fabric, remembered the last time he had worn it—a luncheon with her publishing friends on a yacht off Falmouth Foreside. Despite her obvious weight loss and the sallow color in her cheeks, she was still beautiful that day just a few weeks before she died.

A wave of sadness came over him. He laid the shirt on the bed, walked over to a photograph of Rachael, and took it down from the wall. He held it in his hands. For reasons he wasn't entirely sure of, it was finally time to say good-bye. He kissed the photograph, laid it on the bureau, and then took down two others. He carefully wrapped them in linen, placed them on the overhead shelf in the closet, and closed the door. He picked up his shirt from the bed and walked downstairs.

The next evening Francis was so excited about going out with Kate that he arrived at her apartment a bit early.

"What happened to your face?" Kate asked as Francis walked into her kitchen. She wore a blue cotton dress that moved softly over her hips.

Stringer looked up from his homework at the kitchen table. "Man, you look bad."

"Thanks," Francis replied, frowning at Stringer. "Some crazy logger ran me off the road driving home last night. My shoulder's banged up, but I look worse than I feel."

"I hope so," Kate said. She gently touched his forehead. "That looks sore. Did you put something on it?"

"Not yet."

"Hang on a minute." Kate walked to the bathroom and returned with some cream. "This will help. Here, sit down."

Francis sat in a chair, rolling his eyes at Stringer. Kate crouched beside him and applied a thin layer of cream to his cheek and forehead. Francis watched her eyes as she tended to him, the cool cream quickly relieving the stinging.

After Kate finished, Francis turned to her. "We should get going. I want you to have enough time to enjoy the exhibit. And I'm sure Kasa has the chess board set up and ready to go."

"I'm sure String will be glad to play with someone who really knows what they're doing."

Stringer grinned. "You mean as opposed to you, Mom?"

On the way to Kasa's, both Kate and Stringer seemed a little nervous, but they all relaxed after Kasa welcomed them into her fragrant house warmed by her woodstove. In the middle of her kitchen table sat an elegant inlaid chess board. After saying hi to

Kasa, Stringer immediately sat down and examined the beautifully detailed pewter pieces. "These are awesome," he said.

"They're very old; hand poured in England over two hundred years ago. The set was left to me by a family I worked for during the war." Kasa turned to Kate and Francis. "Now you two run along and let us get down to some serious chess."

Kate gave Stringer a kiss on the head to which he slightly recoiled. She handed him a piece of paper. "Here are the numbers where we'll be. Call me if you need *anything.*"

Kasa appeared to pull her large frame up to her full height. "Don't worry; we'll take care of each other."

"I know you will, it's just..." Kate paused.

"I don't need protecting," Stringer said, shedding his coat.

"I know you'll be fine," Kate said. She stepped over to Francis, who slid his arm around her waist.

"Cute couple, aren't they?" Kasa said to Stringer, smiling.

"They're all right," he said a bit sarcastically.

As they walked to the door, Stringer looked over at them. "Have fun. Be cool down there in the 'Big City'."

On the way to Portland, Francis told Kate about Andrew Wyeth's career. To Francis's mind, Wyeth was one of America's most gifted and fiercely independent artists. "The summer I turned sixteen, my father and I were at serious odds and Mother was back in a mental hospital. Thankfully my father sent me to spend a month with my grandmother in the bungalow. For my birthday, she took me to a Wyeth exhibition in Rockland after his landmark painting, 'Christina's World,' came out." Francis paused. "It was so powerful, feeling the depth of his passion as he discussed his works. He just penetrated the canvas with his unvarnished emotions—anger, frustration, and joy—all infusing the work. I was blown away. I knew then what a true living artist was."

As they exited the interstate heading into Portland, Kate turned to Francis. "Did you try to keep in touch with Wyeth?"

Francis shook his head. "No."

"Why not?"

Francis turned at an old sea captain's house and headed uptown. "I barely met him. Anyway, I was just a kid, barely able to draw, and I hear he's very reclusive, values his privacy."

Kate thought for a few moments. "But you said he's your mentor, and you're one of Maine's best painters. It seems you two would naturally connect." She looked over at him. "Has he ever been to your gallery?"

The art museum was a block ahead of them. Francis pulled into a parking space and turned to Kate. "Andrew Wyeth is way out of my league. He isn't interested in tourist trade seascapes, no matter how good they are. When I was younger I produced work he might have appreciated, but not in the last twenty years. I'd be ashamed. Besides," he said, "he'd never remember me."

Kate frowned, obviously confused by his answer.

"Let's go in. You'll see what I'm talking about."

They walked to the museum entrance where Kate stopped in front of the large glass doors.

Francis waited. "Are you okay?"

"I'm nervous."

"We'll wait then." They sat on a granite bench under a portico next to the entrance. The cool night air felt good. Across the street was an open air café filled with people enjoying drinks and dinner. Lively conversation rose from beneath the red and white umbrellas standing over the tables. A hint of fresh seafood was carried uptown by a light breeze from the many fishing boats tied up down in the harbor.

Kate watched a woman in a pale yellow dress cross the sidewalk toward them. She carried a plain canvas bag and her light blue sneakers were noticeably worn. She kept her eyes down as she passed Francis and Kate, opened the glass doors, and walked into the museum.

Kate looked through the glass into the lobby. An imposing portrait of the artist hung over the entrance. Beneath it, the woman in the yellow dress purchased her ticket and walked into the exhibit.

Kate stood. "Let's go in."

Francis took her hand and they walked inside.

A striking lady dressed in a navy jacket with a gold lapel pin greeted them. Kate felt herself withdraw.

"Mrs. Vidich, nice to see you." Francis turned to Kate. "This is Kate Johnson, a friend of mine."

Mrs. Vidich extended her hand across the counter to Francis, then to Kate. "How nice to meet you. We always love having Mr. Monroe visit us. Andrew Wyeth's probably the only Maine painter more famous than he is." She smiled at Kate. "You two go right in."

"Thank you, but I'll pay the admission," Francis said.

"There's no need—"

"Please."

Francis paid for their tickets, then handed Kate a glossy brochure. Inside, Kate stepped over against the wall near the entrance to the exhibit. A couple dozen people in suits and evening dresses milled about sipping tall glasses of wine. She leaned toward Francis. "I shouldn't be here."

"Why not?"

"I feel like a tramp. I don't belong here with you."

Francis walked slowly around Kate, his hand on his chin, observing her. "Really? It appears to me you are the singularly most beautiful woman in sight, maybe in the whole city. You are honest, unpretentious, and incredibly sensual. I don't see *any* reason you shouldn't be here. In fact, standing against that cold granite wall in that lovely blue dress, *you* are a work of art. The museum has never looked better."

Kate blushed and looked at the floor. "You're crazy."

"It's a prerequisite for being an artist. Besides, one of the things I most admire about Mr. Wyeth is that he paints authentic people just like you."

Kate gave Francis a puzzled look. "What do you mean?"

"You'll see." Francis offered her his arm.

The moment they stepped into the presence of the paintings, Kate felt different. As she started to look at Wyeth's work, something shifted inside of her. After a few minutes, she walked over and stood in front of a painting from Wyeth's personal collection entitled "Barracoon." A placard explained that Barracoon was a name for slaves' quarters back in Thomas Jefferson's time. The painting captivated her. A naked black woman lay on her side on rumpled sheets, her back to Kate, the palms of her hands and soles of her feet catching indirect sunlight from a window. Her head was pressed into a pillow, her posture and weight, her worn feet and hands bearing witness to her dignity, the depth of her courage and surrender. Kate studied the back of the woman's long body, particularly the intense red of her palms.

After a while Kate moved on to a painting of a blond-haired girl who stood naked, arms crossed, behind a cracked open door. A shard of light illuminated her young breasts, full hips and golden pubic hair. Kate bent forward, read the card on the wall then studied the canvas. In her father's rough-planked chicken coop, fifteen-year-old Siri looked toward the stream of sunlight angling in from outside. She exuded a natural confidence heightened by Wyeth's sparse style. Kate was drawn to the canvas, struck by the lack of arrogance or pride in the girl. She reached to touch Siri's warm skin, her fingers stopping short of the canvas. A fresh young woman authentically revealed—naturally beautiful, imperfect, and strong.

Kate left Siri, slowly passing other nudes: Helga lying beneath an open window, partially exposed beneath a sheet. A robust young man from Maine named Eric, standing naked in a clearing, his blond hair blown back in the wind. She walked slowly through the gallery, stopping in front of an unusual seascape entitled "Pentecost." The card described the scene as being along the edge of a wharf on the rocky coast of Allen Island where fishing nets, suspended like spider-webbed sails, dried in the wind. Spirits seemed to dance among the flowing nets.

The placard explained that Wyeth painted the scene after a young girl was swept out to sea in a fierce storm, her body later found off Pemaquid Point. Wyeth was thinking about the girl floating under the water when he envisioned the wind-blown nets as embodying her soul.

Kate sat there, thinking of the artist somehow pulling this delicate, airy painting from the depth and darkness of the ocean. She thought of Rachael and of Francis searching for her in his skiff; of Delbert Ready in the *Maiden*, riding the deceptive surface of the sea. She saw Stringer in the surging waves, struggling to recover a part of his soul lost years before at the hands of Leland.

She stepped closer to the painting, her fingers hovering over the silvery nets, tracing the edge of the water where it flowed into jagged crevices along the rocky shore. Staring at the painting, Kate felt something break free inside her. She imagined the black woman, her imperfect skin, her exhaustion and her strength; Siri, full of life's promise, naked in the sunlight of her father's chicken coop.

An unfamiliar freedom rose within Kate. She stepped back from the canvas and turned to look for Francis. The museum, except for the gallery she was standing in, had been darkened. She'd become so engrossed with the paintings she'd lost track of time. She hurried toward the entrance where she found Francis waiting on a bench near "Barracoon."

"There's no hurry," he said quietly.

Kate stopped. "You scared me," she said, catching her breath. Their voices echoed in the empty hall. "I'm sorry. I was in the far room there."

"It's all right. The curator's a friend of mine. He said we could stay until he's ready to leave."

Kate sat beside Francis beneath a wall of paintings illuminated by low spotlights.

"There's this incredible painting in there with fish nets blowing in the wind."

"Ah yes, "Pentecost." Remarkably powerful, isn't it? It's another painting from Wyeth's private collection that he lent for the exhibit."

Kate gripped Francis's arm. "This place is amazing. It's like the paintings give off a spiritual energy."

Francis smiled. "I know. They have the soul and vision my commercial seascapes lack."

Kate stood and walked around in front of the bench. "Francis, I want to tell you something." Her eyes were intense. "I tried to tell you this once, that first night you took me to the harbormaster's shack, but I couldn't."

"I remember—about when Stringer was born."

"Yes." Kate paced back and forth then sat down again. "This is so strange; I don't feel as ashamed as I always have."

Francis listened quietly.

"For years people told me to get away from Leland, to do whatever it took, but I couldn't leave. He was not only my drug connection; he was the only one who knew about what happened after Stringer was born."

Kate got up, walked around back of Francis, and looked at "Barracoon" again. "Francis, I did a horrible thing." Her voice caught. She cleared her throat.

"My pregnancy was a nightmare. I was drinking heavy, doing any drugs that Leland would give me. He was dealing all the time, hanging out with some real creeps. He'd had a shitty childhood and ended up hating kids, and once I really started to show, he'd come back to our dingy little apartment and fly into a rage. Sometimes I couldn't get out fast enough and he'd beat me up: punch me in the head, kick me in the stomach. He tried to get me to bleed, to abort. I was pretty out of it a lot of the time, just too sick to fight back. It was a nightmare, but somehow Stringer and I made it through the pregnancy.

"After I delivered, I began shaking uncontrollably. I knew I had to have a fix. So I took off from the hospital that same night. I walked home with the baby under my coat. I was so dizzy by the time I got to Muscle Beach, I collapsed on a bench. I was wicked thin and so weak I could barely walk. One of Leland's henchmen saw me and told me I'd better get rid of the kid or Leland would cut off my drugs, maybe even kill me. This guy didn't joke around. I believed him."

Kate ran her fingers through her hair then stared at the floor for a few moments.

"The baby started crying, wailing so loud people were staring at me. I tried to nurse, but I didn't have any milk. My heart was racing and I was sweating that awful greasy addict's sweat. I stuck my finger in his mouth so he'd suckle, but he just screamed louder. I thought my head was going to split in two. Finally I stuffed the baby back inside my coat, got up, and walked down an alleyway just off the beach."

Suddenly Kate felt nauseous. She struggled to take a deep breath, then looked at Francis and started to cry. "He wouldn't stop screaming."

Though he was taken aback by her story, Francis felt the power of her pain. He slid his hand onto her forearm. "It's okay," he said softly. "You need to get this out."

Kate wiped her eyes. "There was a dumpster in back of this bar. I walked over and..." Kate crumpled against Francis, sobbing.

She felt his arm slide around her shoulders. She knew she had to continue though she had to force the words out. "I lifted the lid of that stinking dumpster and pulled the baby out of my coat. He just kept screaming, so I closed my eyes and dropped him in." Kate's hands shook as she spoke. "He whimpered for a few more seconds and then there was nothing."

Kate turned slowly to Francis. "I was terrified. I thought I'd killed my baby." Tears streamed down her cheeks. "I dragged a wooden box over to the dumpster and climbed inside where I found Stringer's head bloodied, but he was still breathing, still whimpering."

Kate wiped tears from her face. "I was so happy he was alive. Somehow I got him out of the dumpster and we made it to an ER. He had a bad cut on his forehead and his skull was cracked." Kate paused, shaking her head. "That's how he got the scar over his eye. Those people took great care of him. They saved his life."

Kate fell silent. After a minute or so her breathing quieted and she wiped her eyes with Francis's sleeve. "I've been terrified String would show signs of brain damage either from the drugs or from the injury, but thank God so far he seems okay. Leland said he'd get me arrested and tell Stringer what I did if I ever left him. I didn't care about the cops, but I'd die if Stringer found out. It was worth putting up with Leland's abuse."

Francis straightened on the bench and shook his head. "Man, you've been through some kind of hell, my friend."

Kate appeared relieved. "You don't think I'm a monster?"

"I think you were living with a monster and trying to survive." Francis gently lifted matted hair from her cheek. "How'd you finally get away from him?"

"For a few years I just existed. I tried to get clean but couldn't. Finally, with the help of a very cool social worker from that same hospital, I got sober four years ago. She took me to an AA meeting on the beach and the people there saved my life. Staying sober that first year was really hard. And as I got stronger, Leland lightened up on me but started beating on Stringer and acting strangely with him." Kate's jaw tightened. "That pushed me over the edge.

"Last winter things got worse. Leland took Stringer off with his crazy friends on a couple of drunken escapades including a package store robbery. That's when I decided we had to get out of there, no matter what. It took a while, but I found us a ride across Canada on a freight train. A guy named Big Frank, an old railroad engineer who worked with my father, got us out of LA without anyone knowing. He knew what we'd been going through. His old man had beaten the hell out of him too. He connected us without tickets, without a trace, all the way through to Sherbrook and then down to Portland. We got a ride north and ended up here in Winter's Cove by chance. This was as far away from Leland as I could get us."

Francis listened as Kate's words echoed in the empty gallery. He looked into her eyes. "You have survived more than most could ever imagine. I have great respect for you and Stringer."

They sat quietly for a few minutes before a man in a black dress coat appeared at the entrance to the exhibit. "Francis, I'm sorry, but I have to leave now."

Francis looked at his watch and was surprised at how late it had gotten. "Yes, of course. Thank you for letting us stay." He motioned to Kate. "John, this is Kate Johnson."

"Pleased to meet you, ma'am," John said.

Kate nodded sheepishly. They followed John to the museum entrance where he opened one of the glass doors and held it. Kate managed a smile and then followed Francis out into the refreshing night air. On the sidewalk, she took hold of Francis's arm and leaned her head on his shoulder. "Thank you for bringing me here. Wyeth's paintings are very powerful."

"I think he would be pleased by what happened for you tonight."

"And thanks for being a kind listener. I can't believe I actually told you all that."

"Thank *you*. I'm deeply moved by what you shared with me."

"After keeping it inside all these years, it feels good to finally get it out."

Francis smiled.

The streets of Portland were quiet. A light sea mist had blown in from the harbor.

"Shall we walk?" Francis asked.

"Yes, that would be good."

They strolled arm-in-arm down through the financial district to the cobblestone streets of the Old Port, arriving at Walter's Restaurant at twenty after ten.

"Guess we're a little late for dinner," Francis said as he looked through the steamed-up windows. "I've never missed a reservation before," he said, looking at Kate. "Until now, I never had anything important enough come up." He smiled and took her hand in his. "Let's keep walking."

Heading down toward the water, the lights burned brightly at Beal's Homemade Ice Cream on lower Fore Street. Kate stopped and turned to Francis. "Seems you promised me an ice cream."

Francis nodded. "So I did."

They walked down several scalloped granite steps into the ice cream shop. Kate ordered a vanilla grape nut, Francis a cherry-chocolate swirl. They sat at a white wicker table, sharing their cones with each other.

"You're a remarkable woman," Francis said. "I've never known anyone like you."

They stopped eating and gazed at each other, smiling.

Kate licked ice cream off her lips. "Let's go home."

Francis agreed. Back in the Malibu, Kate sat close to Francis as they drove out of the misty city heading north to Winter's Cove. When they arrived at Kasa's, the house was quiet. As they stepped into her summer kitchen, Francis slid his arm around Kate's waist and turned her toward him. They shared a long, deep kiss in the moonlight. Kate sighed as Francis ran his hand over her smooth bottom, then she gently disengaged. "You're crazy," she said.

"I'm falling in love," he replied and kissed her again.

Then they both heard someone moving inside.

"We're out here like a pair of teenagers," Kate said under her breath.

Francis smiled.

"I've got to go in and get String."

Kasa met them at the door, said she and Stringer had a wonderful time playing chess and telling each other stories. She looked at Stringer who was asleep on the couch by the fire. "He's a fine boy."

Kate stepped over and gently kissed his forehead, awakening him enough to walk out to the car. They thanked Kasa and left for town.

Stringer slept in the back seat while Kate held Francis's hand in the front. Despite her reservations, she'd had a great evening, different from anything she'd ever done before.

"That was really cool, seeing his paintings with you."

"Yes," Francis said. "It brought up a lot of things for me too."

She squeezed his hand. "You know, you're also a great artist. You can paint anything you want to."

Francis nodded. "I hope you're right."

At Kate's apartment, Stringer was still half asleep as Francis helped him out of the car. Kate opened the door and Stringer walked in and headed straight to bed.

Francis kissed Kate at the door. "Do you want me to come in?"

"Not tonight, lover boy." Kate smiled, devilishly lifting her thigh against his. "You'll just have to suffer."

Francis frowned. "They say that's what artists are supposed to do."

Kate closed the door and watched Francis drive off. Then she walked into Stringer's room and sat on his bed. As she tucked him in Kate noticed that his window was open.

"Do you want your window open that much?"

Stringer rolled over. "I didn't open it."

Kate stared at the window. Pressure rose in her chest.

"String, what is that smell?"

Her fingers dug into the bedclothes.

"What smell?"

Fear gripped Kate like a hand around her throat. She slowly rose, glancing around the room.

Stringer awakened and sat up on one elbow. "Mom, what's the matter?"

"You stay *right* here," she said, inching toward the door. She peered into the living room. Seeing no one, she bolted for the phone on the counter in the kitchen. Halfway there, a wild-looking man with a scraggly beard shot out of her bedroom, grabbed her around the waist, and tackled her into a chair.

Kate let out a terrified scream as Leland pulled her head back by her hair.

"Thought you'd gotten rid of me, didn't you?" he growled, his sour breath reeking of beer and chewing tobacco.

Kate struggled to free herself, but Leland had her pinned in the chair. "Get away from me, you bastard!" she yelled.

Leland drove his knee into her side and slapped her across the face.

Just then Stringer opened his door, squinting against the kitchen light. "What's going on?" Coming fully awake, he recoiled at the sight of his father. Kate screamed at him to run and get help.

"Good to see you too, boy," Leland snarled.

"Leave her alone!" Stringer yelled. He charged out of his doorway and jumped onto Leland's back. Leland let go of Kate, grabbed Stringer, and threw him against the wall so hard his cast dented the plaster.

Leland lurched back to Kate and tore open her shirt. "Where's your new boyfriend, Katie? You been fucking him right here in front of String?"

Stringer tried to get up, but Leland pushed him against the wall, spitting a greasy wad of tobacco at him.

Kate bolted out of the chair and got Leland in a headlock from behind. She tightened her arm around his throat so hard he gagged. Stringer pulled himself up and slugged Leland in the groin with his cast. Kate loosened her chokehold and Leland staggered back against the wall. A few seconds later a psychotic look flashed from Leland's eyes. He pushed off the wall and charged at Kate.

"Get out!" Kate yelled at Stringer.

As Leland kicked her back into the chair, Stringer hit Leland in his lower back as hard as he could, crying out in pain from his fractured wrist.

"Come on, darlin'," Leland said, catching his breath. "Time you gave me a good fuckin'." He shoved Kate through her bedroom door onto the bed. Trembling as Leland dropped onto her, Kate cried out as she struggled to get up. Leland slapped her back down on the bed.

Stringer held his broken arm in close to his side and headed into the bedroom. "You bastard!" he cried out as Leland ripped open his mother's jeans.

Leland glanced at Stringer. "Think you're going to whup me, boy?" An insane grin broke over Leland's face.

Kate came up off the bed and hit Leland in the head as hard as she could. Momentarily dazed, he swung around and punched her in the chest, knocking her over backwards to the floor. She lay there moaning in pain.

"Leave her alone!" Stringer screamed from the doorway. Tears streamed down his cheeks.

Drunk and dazed, Leland looked at Stringer in disgust. "You worthless piece of shit," he said. "She should have finished you off when she had the chance."

Hearing this, Kate rose from the floor, grabbed a metal lamp from the bedside stand, and smashed it into the side of Leland's head. Stunned, he slumped to the floor under the window. Suddenly the room was silent.

CHAPTER 10

Despite the great evening he'd had with Kate, Francis's sleep was tumultuous; vivid, disturbing dreams almost awakening him before they'd vanish. About five in the morning, he rose and sat on the edge of the bed. Myriad feelings passed through him. Kate's story was a bit shocking, but he was inspired by her and Stringer's remarkable ability to survive. And he found Kate *so* sensual, as if every imperfection revealed from her past magnified her present beauty. It had been hard not to seduce her the night before right there in Kasa's summer kitchen.

Francis walked downstairs and made a cup of coffee. Standing in front of the warm stove, he could still smell Kate's scent on his chest from holding her the night before. A shower could wait.

The wind had blown hard during the night so he walked down the cliff steps to check on the skiff, which he should have pulled from the water weeks ago. One of its lines had loosened and was caught in a tangle of seaweed, which had allowed the gunnels to wear against the rocks. Holding the skiff steady with his foot, he starting pulling knotted strands of kelp from the line.

"Francis!" he heard someone call out. He looked up and saw Stringer at the top of the cliff stairs. Even from a distance he looked distraught.

"I'll be right up," Francis yelled back. He let go of the lines and hurried up the stairs where he found Stringer in a torn sweatshirt, trembling, his face black and blue. "What happened?"

Stringer's face contorted when he tried to speak.

"My God, did he find you?"

Stringer nodded. Tears streaked down his cheeks.

Filled with anger and fear, Francis wrapped his arms around Stringer and held him.

"He was hiding in our apartment last night. He beat the shit out of us."

"Is your mother all right?"

"Yeah, but he's crazy, says he'll kill us if we don't go back to California."

Francis held Stringer at arm's length. "No way. We're going to stop him."

"You don't know him."

"Come inside," Francis said. He hurried Stringer into the bungalow and wrapped him in a thick trapper blanket. "Where's Kate now?"

"In the apartment. He finally passed out drunk, but she doesn't dare leave. It's just like it was before. Even worse."

"Damn—" Francis said. "I had no idea he was there last night." He thought for a few moments then said, "I'm going to get the sheriff and go over there."

Stringer looked at him incredulously. "They won't do anything; not here, not in California."

"They *have* to help. They can't just allow him to come in here and beat you up."

"Bullshit, Francis!" Stringer pulled away from him. "The sheriffs came over last night—including one of your buddies— and he just talked his way out of it. Mom and I were standing there beat up the whole time and they didn't do anything."

Francis looked at the bruises about Stringer's head and neck. "Okay then I'm going to call the State Police." He picked up the phone and called the barracks outside of town. He spoke with the sergeant on duty who explained that the State Police stayed out of domestic situations unless local law enforcement asked them for assistance. They knew nothing of Kate and Stringer's situation and didn't see the need to get involved.

Not able to get anywhere, Francis hung up and turned to Stringer.

"If you're not going to help, I'm going back," Stringer said, throwing off the blanket. He headed toward the door.

Francis cut him off. "You can't go back there. It's too dangerous. I'm going to give the sheriff's office one more try."

Stringer glared at him.

Francis picked up the phone again just as it rang. It was Kate. "Are you all right? I can barely hear you." He pressed the receiver to his ear. "Kate? Kate, are you there? Shit!" he said and hung up.

"What did she say?" Stringer demanded.

"The line went dead."

"We gotta get over there!" Stringer yelled.

Francis grabbed his coat. "I'm going. You're staying here."

"The hell I am."

Francis took Stringer by both shoulders. "I can't let you go back there. Your arm's broken and he's already beat you up. You're safe here."

"She's my mother."

"I know. That's why putting yourself in more danger won't help her." Francis let go of him and hurried to the door. "Lock the door behind me and I'll call you as soon as I can."

Stringer stomped his feet. "This is bullshit, Francis!"

Francis kept running, climbed into the Malibu, and tore down the hill. In town, he pulled into the courthouse lot, got out, and burst through the sheriff's department's door. Charlie was sitting at his desk and did not look surprised to see Francis.

"Why haven't you arrested that bastard?" Francis demanded as he crossed the room.

"Don't see where I can."

"Why the hell not? Can't you see how crazy he is? He's abusing Kate and Stringer just like I told you."

"That's not what my deputy and I saw. Leland was a little drunk and he ain't much to look at, but there wasn't any fighting goin' on. We saw Kate and the boy through the door. They looked a little shook up is all."

Francis leaned over Charlie's desk. "Really? Stringer came out to my house and looked pretty beat up to me." Francis stared Charlie in the eye. "Don't you see he's got them so damn terrified they don't dare say anything? He's threatened to kill them!"

Charlie's lips pursed. He too leaned forward across the desk. "Listen to me, Francis. The sheriff isn't happy 'bout all this. Town's starting to get ready for Festival. You know how many folks come and spend their money in the cove over the holidays? Last thing we need is anymore of these goings on. Tourists want to see the quaint coast of Maine, not some goddamn Jerry Springer show."

Francis set his jaw, staring straight at Charlie. "I don't give a damn about the tourists or the festival. I want you to take care of Kate and Stringer."

Charlie leaned in so close Francis could smell black coffee on his breath. He saw a frightening mixture of anger and fear in his eyes. "Frankly, Francis, the sheriff don't give a sweet shit what you think. He's the boss. In fact, he gave me a message to deliver to you, personally." Charlie's frown deepened. "You go near Leland's wife again and he'll throw *your* ass in jail. The sheriff gets re-elected this coming March and he's not going to let you or that California bitch screw things up for him."

Francis felt the spirit drain out of him. This made no sense.

Charlie didn't move. "Are we clear on everything, Mr. Monroe?"

Francis glared back at him. "You go to hell, Charlie Lord."

They stared at each other for a few moments, and then both straightened up. Francis turned and walked out of the office, knowing he was the only one who could help Kate. He got in and drove down the street, pulling to the curb across from her apartment. As he ran across the street to Kate's steps, he was surprised to see her frightened face in the door window. Quickly she opened the door enough to slip out onto the porch. Holding onto the doorknob, she glanced back through the window then turned to Francis. "He's in the bathroom," she said between shallow breaths. Her cheeks were bruised and swollen, the corner of her mouth cut. Her hair was matted against her scalp with dried blood.

Francis took her arm. "Kate, you've got to get out of there. Come with me. Now."

"He's crazier than ever." Her chin began to quiver. "He's taking us back to LA. He might kill us if we don't go."

Francis saw the terror in her eyes and heard it in her voice. Her hand shook so badly the doorknob rattled. His heart pounded. "Kate, you haven't come this far to go back—"

Suddenly a fist smashed through the door window. Shards of glass flew around them. A war whoop filled the air. Francis ducked, keeping hold of Kate's arm.

Leland's bloodied hand grabbed Kate by the throat and pulled her against the door, which swung open into the kitchen. He reached around the door with his other arm, grabbed her by the hair, and threw her on the floor. "Fucking bitch."

Francis pushed through the doorway and grabbed hold of Leland's arm. Leland punched him in the face with the other fist, sending him reeling back onto the porch. He glanced toward the street looking for help. Instead he saw Stringer screech to a halt on a bicycle. "Stringer! Go get help!"

Inside, Leland stood over Kate, holding her by the hair. The apartment reeked of stale beer. Francis heard Stringer run up on the porch behind him. "It's over, Leland, let go of her," Francis said in a loud, steady voice. "The State Police will be here any minute."

Leland's bloodshot eyes opened startlingly wide. He bared his teeth. "We'll see about that!" He let go of Kate and grabbed Francis by the coat. Francis ducked a punch. Kate crawled over to the sink. Francis tried to wrestle Leland's hand off his coat, aware of Stringer behind him.

Leland kneed Francis in the groin, buckling him. He slammed him into the refrigerator, sending magnets and pictures to the floor. Francis regained his balance, grabbed Leland's right arm, and pushed him backwards into the kitchen table. He lost his balance and fell onto the sink. Kate scurried into the living room on her hands and knees.

"Leland," Francis said sharply, trying to reason with him. "Quit before something worse happens."

Leland righted himself.

"You can get help," Francis implored him. "We'll help you—"

Ignoring Francis, Leland pulled a heavy, serrated knife from the wooden rack on the counter. "Fuck you, asshole!"

Leland rushed at Francis, swinging at him with the knife. Francis deflected Leland's arm, the knife piercing the metal skin of the refrigerator door.

Kate screamed, crawled over, and hid behind the overstuffed chair by the window.

"Watch out, Francis!" Stringer yelled.

Francis lunged toward Leland as he pulled the knife from the metal. He grabbed Leland's arm, but Leland wrenched himself loose, swung around, and drove the knife into Francis's thigh.

Francis cried out, clutching his bleeding leg. Leland struck again, slicing through Francis's coat into his ribs. Suddenly Francis couldn't breathe. Pain seared through his chest.

Stringer edged his way into the kitchen. "Get out, Francis! He'll kill you!"

"Shut up!" Leland yelled. "You wouldn't be such a miserable little fuck if your momma had taken care of you like she was supposed to."

"You leave Mom alone!"

Leland laughed. "Yeah, ask her about that dumpster in Venice."

Kate moaned.

"You bastard!" Stringer yelled. Holding his cast up like a battering ram, he charged into Leland. Francis had regained his breath, and he now pinned Leland against the wall and slammed his hand into the cabinet, trying to dislodge the knife. Leland held on to it with a deathly grip.

Stringer slugged Leland hard in the groin with his cast. Leland bent forward then let out another war whoop. He tore his arm from Francis's grip, turned, and kicked Stringer across the room.

Kate shrieked.

Francis tried to get hold of Leland's arm again, but he was too fast, ripping through the air with the knife, driving it into Francis's shoulder. Francis yelled in pain. Blood streamed down the sleeve of his shirt.

Leland slammed the butt of the knife into the side of Francis's face, sending him to the floor inside the living room near Kate. He was vaguely aware of Stringer running into his bedroom.

Leland dropped on top of Francis. "Who needs help now, lover boy?" Leland wiped bloody snot from his face with his arm as he pushed a knee into Francis's stomach.

"Can't...breathe."

"Shut up!" Leland backhanded Francis then spat on the floor next to his head. "I've always wanted to kill one of you smart fuckers. Cut your goddamn tongue out." He cackled with delight.

Francis could barely get any air in.

Stringer came out of his bedroom, moving to within a few feet of Leland. "Get off him," he shouted.

"Fuck off," Leland snapped back. He drove his knee harder into Francis's gut as he raised the knife in the air.

"Don't make me do this," Stringer said. "Drop the knife."

"What are *you* going to do about it?" Leland said without looking up.

Stringer raised his good arm, pointing a small pistol at Leland's head. "Drop it."

Leland glanced at Stringer. "You little bastard, that's my gun!"

"I said drop it!"

"Gonna shoot me with my own gun?"

Francis watched in horror, unable to move.

Stringer's face contorted. A sick smile broke over Leland's face. "Watch your friend die!" he said, aiming the knife at Francis's throat.

Stringer squinted, leveled the barrel, and yelled, "Nooo!" He closed his eyes and squeezed the trigger.

At the sound of the blast, Leland winced. His shirt jerked where the bullet entered his left chest. Still holding the knife over Francis, Leland's right arm trembled as though he was having a seizure. He turned toward Stringer. "You little fucker—"

Another shot blasted out of the steel barrel, tearing flesh off Leland's left shoulder.

"Drop it!" Stringer yelled again.

Bleeding, his lungs rattling, Leland came down at Francis with the knife.

Three more deafening shots rang through the apartment. Bullets thumped into Leland's body, which jerked and twisted. Hemorrhaging from chest wounds, vomiting blood, he slumped to the floor. His eyes still wide open, he shuddered, coughed, and expelled his last wheezing breath.

CHAPTER 11

Warm blood dripped from Leland's abdomen, soaking through the leg of Francis's jeans. He heard Kate whimpering behind the overstuffed chair, a ricocheted bullet hole in the window behind her. A thin stream of sea breeze entered the room through the glass, curling the white curtain against the arm of the chair.

Francis had a hard time getting a full breath. His arm and leg burned with pain. He pulled his legs out from under Leland and pushed himself back against the wall. He took in several partial breaths. The intense ringing in his ears from the gunshots made it difficult to concentrate.

Stringer sat on the edge of a kitchen chair, his mouth ajar, staring at his dead father. The pistol lay on the floor.

Kate's hand appeared from under the curtain and slid over the arm of the chair. She pulled herself up to a standing position, her face drawn as though she'd aged a lifetime in a few moments. Her arms trembled as she steadied herself against the wall and stepped past Leland into the kitchen. She knelt next to Stringer.

Stringer was shaking. He turned his head to her, his eyes brimming with tears. Kate wrapped her arms around her son, his head falling against her breast. He cried in her arms then retched onto the floor. Kate gently wiped vomit from his mouth and chin then rocked him in her arms.

Through the broken window, Francis heard sirens approaching. Tires screeched to a halt out front. Heavy footsteps sounded on the pavement then there were men at the kitchen door. Broken glass crunched under their feet.

Someone was on a megaphone in the street. "This is the police! The building's surrounded! Step out where we can see you with your hands in the air."

Francis looked at Stringer cradled in Kate's arms, then glanced back at Leland's contorted body. The guy on the bullhorn yelled again. It all seemed surreal.

Francis pushed himself off the floor and limped over to Kate and Stringer.

Another siren. The bullhorn blared again. Francis surrounded their trembling bodies with his injured arms. Then, struggling for breath, holding his hands over his head as best he could, he stepped into the doorway.

"Come out slowly!" an officer barked over a megaphone. "Keep your hands where we can see them."

Francis pushed the screen door back with one knee, his other leg threatening to buckle under him. Officers stood on both sides of the small porch, weapons trained on him. Main Street was filled with police cruisers and ambulances, blue and red lights splashing off the buildings. Townspeople watched, half-hidden behind parked cars and in darkened doorways.

"All right. Walk down the steps and lie face down on the sidewalk."

Francis looked at the deputy sheriff next to him, staring past the steel barrel of his revolver. It was Serge Martin's youngest son who'd always wanted to be a cop. "It's okay," Francis said quietly. "The shooting's over. Leland's dead."

Charlie stood next to Sheriff McNeal, who grabbed a bullhorn from one of his deputies. "Shut up and get down on the sidewalk!"

Wincing at the sound of the sheriff's voice, Serge's son was polite and professional. "Please, Mr. Monroe."

Francis faced Sheriff McNeal and walked down the steps. Keeping his hands in view, he lay down on his stomach, his face against the gritty cement. Ralph, one of the deputies, stepped over to cuff him. He grabbed hold of his injured arm and pulled it behind his back. Francis cried out.

Ralph relaxed his grip. "Mr. Monroe's injured, Sheriff." He crouched down and turned Francis over onto his back. "Leg's cut too."

Francis slid his hand up over the wound to his chest. "He stabbed me in the ribs. Hard to breathe," he whispered.

Ralph motioned across the street to an ambulance crew. "Got an injured man here."

Charlie stared at Francis, a look of horror on his face. McNeal dropped his megaphone onto the hood of his cruiser, walked over, and stood next to Francis's head. "What the hell's going on here, Monroe?"

Francis lifted his face from the cement. "Leland Johnson went crazy. Beat up Kate and Stringer. Stabbed me with a butcher knife." Francis caught a couple of breaths. "He was on top of me, going to kill me when..." He paused again. The pain in his chest was nearly unbearable.

The sheriff slid a wad of chew from one cheek to the other. He was nervous, impatient. "When *what?*"

"When Stringer shot him and saved my life."

"Sheriff!" Deputy Martin yelled from the doorway of the apartment. "There's a dead guy in here, and a lady and a kid."

McNeal turned. "They dead?"

"No, but wicked shook up."

McNeal glanced at Charlie. "Get Monroe to the hospital. We'll get a statement later. I gotta see what the hell's going on in there."

Sheriff McNeal, followed by two deputies, climbed the stairs, pulled open the screen door, and walked inside. Through the open door, Francis heard the sheriff barking orders. "You two, put your hands on your heads. Cuff 'em so they won't try anything."

"Sheriff, the kid's got a cast on his arm. I can't cuff him."

"Then just put him in a cruiser," McNeal snapped.

Francis heard the sheriff's voice moving through the apartment into the living room. "Well, isn't this a fine goddamn mess. Get this place cleaned up before the news people get here."

"But it's a crime scene, sir," a deputy said.

"I know it's a crime scene, for Christ's sake." Francis heard the sheriff stomp around, grumbling to himself. "Never had anything like this before. It's a goddamn disaster."

A deputy led Kate, then Stringer out of the apartment onto the porch. Stringer stopped and looked back inside the apartment. "Sheriff, I shot him."

Sheriff McNeal stepped into the doorway and spat a wad of spent tobacco on the porch floor. "Is that so?"

"Yes, sir."

"You sure it wasn't your mother's boyfriend there?"

"Leland was killing Francis and I shot him."

The sheriff twisted his face, staring at Stringer as if he was waiting for the kid to come unwound. Stringer didn't budge.

"Well, you take a ride up to the office with my deputy. We'll get to the bottom of this."

Deputies led Stringer and Kate down the stairs to the cruisers. Francis struggled to stand, but the paramedics and Deputy Martin prevented him from getting up. He could only watch as the deputies opened the back door of the cruiser and hurried Stringer and Kate inside. Then it pulled away and sped up Main Street.

An EMT with rubber-gloved hands assisted Francis onto a stretcher. "We need to take you to the hospital. You're bleeding and your breathing's getting worse."

Francis was loaded into the back of an ambulance. They put an oxygen mask on his face, started an IV in his good arm, and then covered him with a blanket.

Just before they closed the door, Sheriff McNeal stuck his head in the doorway. "Some fucking mess you've made, Monroe."

Francis ignored him.

"Did the kid really do the shooting?"

"Yes."

"Self-defense?"

"He saved my life. Probably saved all of us."

McNeal worked a wad of tobacco with his tongue. "Lotta bullet holes in that corpse."

Francis looked away. It was hard to talk through the oxygen mask.

McNeal spit a wad of brown chew onto the pavement then shook his head and wiped his mouth with the back of his hand. "Got a real rat's nest here. Somebody's gonna have to pay."

CHAPTER 12

Francis heard the siren wail then felt the ambulance move. The next thing he knew there was a very bright light over him and a man in blue scrubs was rubbing something cold on his left chest. An oxygen mask was uncomfortably tight on his face. He could not get a full breath.

"You have a pneumothorax, Mr. Monroe—air that's leaked around your lung. I have to insert a tube into your chest to let it out. You're going to feel a little prick."

A needle pierced his skin. In a few seconds the area became numb. "Okay, there's going to be some hard pushing then your breathing will get better."

Francis focused, recognizing Dr. Conklin. A nurse took Francis's hand and held it firmly. He felt tremendous pressure against his chest, then a sharp, painful pop as Dr. Conklin carefully slid a large clear tube between his ribs. Francis's breath caught. He tried to roll away.

"Please hold still. I'm almost done."

It felt like a blowtorch was burning through his chest. The nurse squeezed Francis's hand harder. He heard a rush of air, and his breathing started to ease.

"I'm going to put a stitch in and we'll be done."

Dr. Conklin tied the suture then removed his gloves. "We'll keep this tube hooked to suction overnight; then, if your x-ray looks good, we'll remove it. Luckily your lung didn't suffer major damage, but you'll have to take it easy for a while. My assistant will repair your shoulder and leg wounds." Dr. Conklin gestured to Francis's thigh. "You've bled into the muscle so you won't be able to walk much for a couple of days." He paused. "Do you have any questions I can answer at this point?"

"No," Francis said quietly.

"I hope you feel better," Dr. Conklin said then left the room.

"How's your breathing now?" the nurse asked.

"This tube hurts, but my breathing's better." Francis looked up at her. "Are Kate and Stringer okay?"

The nurse glanced toward the door then back at Francis. "I'm not supposed to say." She lowered her voice. "But I think they're all right."

"Are they here?"

She checked the door again. "They were checked out then taken away by Sheriff McNeal. That's all I know." She pulled a warm blanket over him. "Now try to relax and let the pain medicine work. Dr. Conklin's assistant will be in to sew you up in a few minutes."

"But I need to—"

"You need to rest," she said, placing her warm hand on his forearm. "You can't do anything for anyone else until you get better."

Francis's head fell back against the plastic pillowcase.

Sam, the physician's assistant, spent over an hour suturing the lacerations in Francis's thigh and shoulder. The procedure was painful, but the narcotics took the edge off. Afterwards Francis was admitted and for the rest of night was aware of little besides nurses taking his vital signs, checking his bandages, and giving him medicine.

Francis awoke as red sunlight tinged the thin blinds covering the window. His whole body felt stiff as cement. His chest burned, his head throbbed, and he needed to urinate. He sat up as best he could and with his good arm wrestled the urinal under the sheet and relieved himself. He set the half-full container on the bedside stand and fell back exhausted.

Someone cleared her throat. In the dim light, Francis turned and saw Kasa sitting in the corner.

"Kasa—"

She pushed herself up on the arms of the chair and stepped to the bed. "Francis, what a sight you are." She shook her head. "Thank God you're alive."

"Have you seen Kate and Stringer?"

"Yes."

"Are they all right? What have they done with them?"

"I drove Kate home from the jail last night after they locked up Stringer. She's at the bungalow."

His eyes were heavy, and it was hard for him to focus for very long. Kasa's voice seemed to come from far away.

"Francis, I must speak with you. Can you stay awake?"

Francis forced his eyes open again. "Yes."

"The town's in an uproar. People are scared. On the news last night the state's attorney said she'll be bringing very serious charges." Kasa shook her head. "I don't like this; I fear for Stringer and Kate."

"He would have killed us, Kasa." Francis frowned. The chest tube hurt more when he tried to talk. "They have to see that."

"The sheriff doesn't think it was self-defense. Says it was murder."

"That bastard —"

"He's a mean, stupid man," Kasa said, leaning closer. "Now listen, Francis, I also heard from Ginny that the town council's meeting tonight to discuss what's happened and they conveniently didn't invite me."

"That doesn't sound good."

"I know. I don't trust them, but don't worry, I'll be there."

Francis straightened a bit. "I need to call Jacob in New York."

"Isn't he your art lawyer?"

"Yes, but he was a brilliant criminal lawyer for years." Francis took a couple of slow breaths. "I know he can help us, at least point us in the right direction."

Kasa adjusted her weight from one leg to the other. "Do you have his number?"

"At home in the black leather book by the hall phone."

"I will get it right now and call you."

Francis managed a smile. "You're a wonderful friend."

After Kasa left, the room was quiet save for the steady hum of the IV machine on the pole next to him. The clock read five after six. He wanted to call Kate but, in case she was sleeping, decided to wait. He adjusted his position so the chest tube didn't pull so hard on his ribs and closed his eyes.

The next thing Francis knew, a soft hand slid over his forearm and warm fingers intertwined with his. He felt a kiss on his cheek and smiled when he smelled Kate's herbal hair conditioner. He opened his eyes, and though she looked tired and drawn, he was so relieved to see her.

Without letting go of his hand, Kate pulled a chair next to the bed and sat down. "How are you doing?" she asked, gently pushing hair off his forehead. "You look awful."

Francis slid his good hand over hers. "Are *you* all right? I feel terrible about what happened. My God, you and Stringer could have been killed." Francis took several short breaths. "I made him stay at the house. I didn't dream he'd ride my bike to town. I—"

Kate put her finger to his lips. "You did the best you could. It was impossible."

The phone rang. Francis motioned for Kate to answer it.

"Yes, Kasa, just a second." Kate picked up a pen from the bedside stand. "Go ahead." She wrote down two numbers on the back of a hospital menu, listened for a few moments, and then said good-bye.

Francis stretched to see the menu. "You have Jacob's number?"

"Home and office. This is your lawyer friend?"

"Yes. Would you dial his home number?"

Kate dialed and handed the phone to Francis.

"Jacob—" Francis raised himself in the bed a bit. Kate slid a pillow behind him. "Yes, it's Francis. I'm sorry to call so early but I need your help."

Francis explained the situation and then listened for quite a while. At one point he could no longer hold the phone so Kate held it for him.

"Thank you so much, my friend. Stringer and Kate are extraordinary people."

After Francis said good-bye, he wet his lips with a spoonful of ice chips. "Jacob has an old friend, Buster Hurd, who lives north of here. They went to Harvard Law together. Jacob says he's the best criminal defense attorney he's ever known." Francis took a couple of breaths. "He's not sure if Hurd is fully retired or not, but said he'll call him and see if he'll represent Stringer."

"How old is he?"

"Must be in his early seventies."

Kate frowned. "He sounds too old."

Francis rested for a moment. "I don't think so. I recognize Hurd's name. He's a legend up north. Years ago he defended a Canadian logger, Felix Giroux, accused of the gruesome murder of a Presque Isle girl. Her partially dismembered body was found under a skidder at a remote logging site where Felix was working."

Francis paused, spooning a few more ice chips onto his tongue. He felt a bit better as he recounted Hurd's history. "I remember people were out for blood, wanted somebody hanged. Against incredible odds, Hurd proved Giroux's innocence, figuring out that the son of a local mill owner killed the girl after he'd gotten her pregnant." Francis looked at Kate. "Jacob says Buster was the smartest guy in their class, and I trust Jacob."

Kate nodded. "Okay. So when will we hear from him?"

"Soon."

The phone rang. Kate answered it. "This is Kate Johnson." She listened then her face lit up. "Yes. That's great." Kate listened intently. "Of course. I'll be right there." She clutched the phone and looked at Francis. "They're letting Stringer out while the state's attorney decides what to do. He has to stay at your house and we can't leave town."

"That's good news," Francis said. He pushed the button on the rail, raising the head of the bed. "I've got to get out of here." Moving caused a stabbing pain in his side.

Kate shook her head. "You've got to let yourself heal. Besides, you're connected to all these gadgets. You can't just up and leave." She looked deep into Francis's eyes then kissed him on the lips. "I need you to get better." Kate stood. "I'll bring Stringer by. It'll be good for the two of you to see each other. And maybe we won't need a lawyer after all."

Francis pushed out a smile. He wished that were true.

After Kate left, Francis slept for a couple of hours. He awoke when the door to his room slowly opened and Stringer stepped inside. Kate stood in the doorway behind him.

Francis looked up. "Stringer," he said, smiling. He motioned for him to come closer. Stringer's shoulders were slumped, his countenance dull. He stepped to the bedside and stood there quietly. Francis expected Stringer would be traumatized but was shocked at how terrible he looked.

"Sit down, my friend."

Stringer lowered himself into a chair. His mouth was partially open, the way it had been after he'd fired the shots and dropped the pistol to the living room floor. Francis pushed hard against the bed with his good arm and sat up. Gritting his teeth, he swung his good leg onto the floor. Despite the chest tube pulling at his ribs, he leaned forward and took Stringer into his arms. Stringer slowly slid his hands around Francis's neck.

"I'm so glad you're okay," Francis whispered in his ear. He held onto Stringer until the pain was too great then let go and fell back against the bed.

Kate stepped behind Stringer and rested her hands on his shoulders.

Francis struggled to think of something comforting to say.

Without looking up, Stringer spoke. "I thought we could stop him this time. I thought he might listen to reason." He paused and shook his head. "I didn't want to shoot."

Francis held his hand to Stringer's cheek. His chin was quivering. "I know you didn't. You had no choice."

Stringer stood. Francis took his hand and looked him in the eye. "You saved all our lives. Don't ever forget that."

"I hope you feel better," Stringer said flatly then walked out of the room.

Kate crouched at the side of the bed and she and Francis held each other. He felt her warm tears against his cheek.

"Whatever it takes," he whispered. "Whatever it takes."

CHAPTER 13

Horace Bagley, Winter Cove's mayor, looked at the clock over the door to his office. It was eleven o'clock. "Where the hell's Larry?"

Serge Martin, chairman of the town council, glanced at the clock. "He'll be right along. Don't be gettin' nervous, Horace."

"Don't get nervous?" Horace sat his coffee cup down hard on his desk and stared at Serge. "Last night some kid from California fills his father full of lead in front of his mother and the most famous artist in the state of Maine, who she just happens to be banging, and you're telling me not to get nervous?" With his neck veins bulging, Horace began coughing and wheezing. He finally settled down, pulled a cigarette from his shirt pocket, and sat back in his chair.

"Have a little couth, Horace. Don't smoke those in here," Ginny Wentworth said, frowning.

"Oh, let him smoke," Serge said. "It'll calm him down."

Horace lit the cigarette and took a furious drag. "Ah, I'll open the window to keep you from bitchin'." Horace got up, unlatched the heavy oak-framed window, and pushed it open. A cold breeze crossed the room.

Just then, a large figure in a Stetson appeared at the frosted glass door to the office. The door swung open and Sheriff Mc-Neal walked in, followed by Charlie Lord and Gwen Chadbourne, the state's attorney. Gwen was born in Blue Hills, Maine, eldest daughter of a Republican state senator. Skinny and severe, she'd earned her law degree at Boston University, cum laude, and then came home to practice. Having never liked the bleeding heart defense side of the courtroom, she became a prosecutor. She was smart and tough, a touch sleazy when need be, and every bit as conservative as her daddy was.

"Sit down, Larry, we've been waiting for you," Horace said, motioning to several chairs at the side of his desk. "Nice to see you too, Ms. Chadbourne."

Gwen nodded, folded her skirt underneath her, and sat down. She set several files on the desk. Serge got up, checked the hallway, and shut the door while Larry took off his dusty Stetson, set it on the desk, and sat down.

"Horace, you can call me Gwen. Especially at this hour."

Horace nodded then turned to Larry. "So what have you got for us?"

Sheriff McNeal reached into his pocket and pulled out a small tin of tobacco. "A goddamn mess, that's what." He gathered up a good-sized wad of chew and pushed it into his left cheek. He looked like a lopsided chipmunk.

"Could you be more specific, Sheriff?" Ginny asked, trying to hold back her sarcasm.

"This Leland Johnson guy came out from California last week looking for his wife, who he found shackin' up with Monroe. Somehow they ended up in the apartment together and that crazy kid, Stringer, shot his father at point blank range." McNeal shook his head. "What kind of name is *Stringer*, anyway? Even used his father's gun, which he stole from him before they left California. I just figure the kid wanted to knock off his old man. Liked Monroe better. Ginny said they've been painting together and Monroe bought him an easel a while back. Can you imagine that?"

Horace turned to Ginny.

Ginny nodded. "A month or so ago, Francis came into the shop and bought an easel and a beginner's paint box for the kid. I think he was doing it just to be nice, but when he was checking out he saw Stringer and this Kate lady walking up the sidewalk and I thought he'd go right through the window after her." Ginny paused and shook her head. "First time I'd seen Francis since Rachael's service and there he was chasing after some young thing."

"Nobody said she wasn't a looker," Charlie chimed in. Gwen frowned over her glasses.

Ginny thought for a moment. "On the other hand, we can't ignore the fact that this kid saved Delbert Ready's life. That ought to count for something."

Sheriff McNeal pushed his chew along his gum to the other cheek. "That's got nothing to do with the killing. No question it was murder. Kate and the kid lured him out here from LA to kill him. Pure and simple. They thought way up here nobody would know the difference." He paused, looked at Horace, then at Gwen. "We can't have people coming out here from the goddamn West Coast to murder someone. Got to set an example so nobody else tries it. And we've got to get this trial over with. Festival's coming. After the lousy weather last summer, folks are hurting; they're advertising like hell, planning on a big crowd for New Year's. We sure need the money. Hell, the council's talking about canceling my new cruiser for next summer if the coffers don't fill up. It's up to the state's attorney here, but I'd hang the little bastard."

Everyone turned to Gwen.

"The sheriff's mentioned what we're up against, though I want to be clear about something from the start. The fact that Festival's only a couple of months away can't have any bearing on due process. This boy—or young man really—deserves a fair trial with enough time for all sides to prepare. Now, with that said, I'll just say this was a heinous crime. Worst I've seen since I came back to Maine. And I understand concerns over the publicity this trial will undoubtedly bring. I pledge to do everything I can to bring it to a prompt end. Hopefully before Christmas. Although who knows, maybe this'll attract more people to come see what's going on."

Serge set his coffee cup on the desk. "You may be right, but this isn't exactly the type of publicity we need. This sort of thing can attract all kinds of crazies. I say we get this over with as fast as we can." He grinned at Horace. "And I think we can count on Judge Thornton to move things right along."

Horace nodded in agreement then leaned toward Gwen. "So what you going to charge him with?"

Just then there was a firm knock on the door.

"Who the hell is that?" Horace snapped, looking at the door. "Well, go ahead and open it."

Charlie reached over, turned the large brass knob, and the door swung open. Standing square in the doorway, her frame blocking much of the light from the hallway, was Kasa.

"Shit," Serge said under his breath. Ginny looked at the floor. Gwen straightened her dress again and adjusted her glasses. Horace jammed his cigarette into the ashtray.

Kasa took one step into the room. "Having a council meeting without me, are you?" She shut the door behind her so hard the glass rattled.

"This isn't an official meeting," Horace said.

Kasa looked around the desk. "Well, I'm the only council person that wasn't present, so now it's official." She marched over to the last chair in the corner, pulled it between Gwen and Horace, and sat down. Apprehensive, Horace and Larry looked at each other. Serge shrugged his shoulders.

Kasa folded her arms across her chest. "Well, get on with your meeting."

Horace coughed, cleared his throat, and reflexively pulled another cigarette from his shirt pocket.

"Don't smoke," Kasa said sternly. Horace slipped the Camel back in his pocket.

Gwen glanced at the faces around the room then turned to Kasa. "I'm Gwen Chadbourne, the state's attorney."

Serge interjected, "This is Kasa Mokanovitch, a member of the council."

Gwen extended her hand and Kasa shook it firmly. "We're discussing how best to handle the Johnson murder," Gwen said.

"Who said it was murder?"

"I said it was a murder," the sheriff snapped. "What would you call it?"

"Don't know," Kasa answered. "Haven't heard the facts yet."

Gwen glared at Larry then turned back to Kasa. "Mrs. Mokanovitch, I believe I speak for everyone—"

Kasa interrupted her. "You don't speak for me, young lady."

Chadbourne continued. "Under the law, we have the elements needed to bring a murder charge: motive, the murder weapon with Stringer's fingerprints on it, and two eyewitnesses. I don't see any need for a grand jury. I just need to decide if we'll move to try him as an adult."

Kasa's eyes widened. "He's just a boy, for God's sake! You can't treat him like a hardened criminal."

Gwen looked straight at Kasa. "He murdered his father."

"In cold blood," McNeal added emphatically.

Kasa didn't flinch. "Sounds like self-defense to me. Plus he saved Francis and his mother from being killed by that evil man."

McNeal scowled at Kasa. "You can't blame the guy for coming out here to get his wife back."

Kasa's eyes lit up and her back straightened. "He abused them—badly—for years."

"How do you know that?" Ginny asked.

"I have sat and talked with Kate."

The sheriff shook his head. "That doesn't mean anything."

Kasa turned and glared into his eyes. Suddenly she reached over and pinned his wrist to the table with her hand so hard his fingers blanched. Gwen recoiled.

"I know the face of someone who's been abused—beaten and tortured. Kate is one of them."

The room was silent. Kasa didn't need to roll up her sleeve to reveal the coarse black ink tattooed into her skin. She gradually released her grip on McNeal's arm.

Gwen nervously straightened her papers and slid them back into an expandable manila folder. "Mrs. Mokanovitch, maybe there was an element of self-defense, but that in no way justifies shooting someone five times—emptying the gun—at point blank range. I haven't seen anything as gruesome as this since I interned in South Boston."

Kasa stood and looked down at Gwen. "So you've made up your mind then?"

"Yes," Gwen said, pushing her chair back. She stood. "Murder one."

Kasa stepped to the door and opened it. "May God have mercy on your souls," she said from the doorway as she walked out.

Gwen remained standing. "For the record, I don't like this anymore than anyone else, but I have a responsibility here and I will carry it out to the letter of the law." She picked up her files and walked toward the door.

Ginny spoke up. "You know, Gwen, if you try him as an adult, the press'll go after us like a pack of hungry wolves."

Gwen turned. "Then so be it. As my father used to say in the Senate: do what's right and damn the detractors. Goodnight."

When the door had closed behind Gwen, Horace, Sheriff McNeal, Charlie Lord, and Ginny sat motionless, staring at each other, their collective faces wrought with uncertainty and fear.

CHAPTER 14

Francis was awakened early the next morning for another x-ray. A short while later Dr. Conklin walked into the room followed by a nurse. "Your lung remains re-expanded so we can take the chest tube out."

Francis adjusted himself in the bed. "Good."

Dr. Conklin shed his white coat and opened a sterile instrument pack. He cut the stitch securing the tube and pulled it out. "That looks good, now we'll get your IV out and take your oxygen off. If you do well getting up with physical therapy, you can go home this afternoon, but you'll have to take it easy for a while." He paused for a few moments. "Do you have any questions, Mr. Monroe?"

"No. Thank you for taking care of me. I guess I was in pretty bad shape when I got here."

"Yes, but luckily nothing critical." Dr. Conklin slid his hands into his pockets. "It was a terrible thing that happened." There was both sadness and fear in the doctor's countenance. "And it's sure got Sheriff McNeal in an uproar and that's not good."

Holding his chest dressing as he sat up, Francis was surprised at what he was hearing. "Why are people so worried about Larry McNeal?"

"'Cause he's the sheriff," Dr. Conklin replied rather sternly. "He runs the county."

They exchanged glances then the doctor stepped to the door. He started to open it then turned back to Francis. "This is my wife's hometown, Mr. Monroe. It's where her elderly parents live and where we want our children to grow up. This is the only ER job around these parts and I've got a ton of debt to pay off so I have to work for the county. They own this hospital."

Francis said nothing.

"I hate to see someone like you beaten up, but I would think you'd realize this Kate lady is nothing but trouble—for you and everyone else."

Before Francis could speak, Dr. Conklin walked out of the room, the door closing behind him. Francis lay there seething. He couldn't believe a doctor would talk like that, that he could be that full of fear. It made him detest McNeal even more.

Late that afternoon Francis was discharged, and Kate and Stringer took him back to the bungalow where he settled onto the couch by the woodstove. Kate brought him a cup of tea then covered his shoulders with the trapper blanket and sat beside him. Stringer seemed very edgy, unable to focus on anything, so he decided to go out for a walk.

"Don't go far and stay away from the cliffs," Kate called to him as he headed out the door.

After Stringer left, Kate spoke to Francis. "We got a call from Buster Hurd this morning."

Francis perked up.

"He sounds interested in Stringer's case. He hopes he can drive down here tomorrow afternoon."

"Great," Francis replied. He tried to get more comfortable on the couch.

"Kasa also stopped by and said she'd call you about some council meeting."

Francis didn't say anything.

Kate leaned forward. "What's the matter?"

"Kasa told me at the hospital the council is meeting with the state's attorney to decide what to do."

"I thought it was a good sign they let String come home." Kate frowned. "Do you think they'll charge him with anything?"

Francis thought for a moment as he adjusted his leg on the ottoman. "I wish I knew. I just know I don't trust the sheriff. He's a cold, self-serving man. I've never met the state's attorney, but I've heard she can be tough just to make a point."

Kate shook her head. "Leland would have killed you—probably all of us. It was self-defense."

"I know," Francis said, feeling exhausted. "I think I'll take a pain pill and rest a bit."

Kate helped him get comfortable on the cot in his studio, which was close to the bathroom.

After Francis fell asleep, Stringer returned and he and Kate had a bowl of soup and fresh bread left earlier by Kasa. A while later, after Kate went to bed, Stringer went in to check on Francis. He helped him roll from one side to the other, adjusted his pillows then sat on the floor next to him. In the dim moonlight, Francis reached over and cupped Stringer's cheek. "You know, you're a very special kid."

Stringer looked at the floor.

"What happened to you the other day was horrendous," Francis said. "Are you hanging in there?"

Stringer looked at Francis. "What do you think they'll do to me?"

"Honestly?"

"Yeah."

Francis raised himself on his good elbow. "I think they'll probably charge you with something. I doubt they'll just let it go."

"I heard men talking at the jail. They called me a violent little bastard." Stringer frowned. "They don't like outsiders here."

Francis shook his head. "I'll tell you something, Stringer. You have as much right to live in this town as anyone else. And another thing: I've lived in Maine a long time and I know the people pretty well. Most folks aren't like the sheriff; they've got bigger hearts. Whatever happens, I believe they'll do the right thing. It's hard because right now you're at the mercy of the system, but we're going to fight like hell if we have to."

Francis lay back against the pillows. Stringer stood and tucked in Francis's blanket. "Why do you care so much about us?"

Francis smiled. "Well, for one thing, since the day I met you, you and your mom have helped save my life—in more ways than one."

"But if we'd never come here you wouldn't be all messed up. Your life would be quiet like it was before."

"Exactly," Francis said. "I wouldn't have you as my friend and I wouldn't be in love with your mom."

"I guess that beats the quiet life, huh?"

Francis smiled. "Yes, it sure does."

Stringer nodded. "So if you need anything, just yell," he said.

"I will. Good night."

Stringer left the studio and walked upstairs to bed.

A few hours later Francis awoke with a start. Someone was outside calling his name. He pushed himself up in bed and swung his legs over the side of the cot. He strained to unlatch and open the window. Kasa stood on the lawn in her long wool coat.

"Francis, I must talk to you—now."

He leaned through the open window, whispered as loudly as he could, "Come in." He stood, forced his stiff legs into a pair of sweatpants, and stepped into the hallway. The clock said one-thirty. His heart beat uncomfortably hard as he unlocked and opened the front door.

Kasa walked in quickly, her eyes wide, as if she'd been frightened. "Francis—" she said, out of breath.

"What is it, Kasa? What's going on?"

"You must take the boy from here. They'll come for him—soon—and they'll hang him. I heard it in their voices. I've seen this before."

"Why? What's happened?"

"The sheriff and his cronies—they want Stringer to pay, to make an example of him."

Francis frowned. "How do you know this?"

"The council meeting."

"Who was there?"

"Sheriff McNeal, Charlie Lord, Ginny, and the other three council members. Plus the mayor and that state's attorney woman, Chadbourne. She's no good. Her heart is stone." Kasa's chin trembled as she spoke. "I told you they tried to keep me out."

"Did Chadbourne decide what to do?"

Kasa paced the hallway, her hand holding her chin.

"Kasa?"

She stopped and turned squarely toward Francis. "First degree murder. She wants the judge to let her try him as an adult."

Francis staggered backwards against the door jamb. "You can't be serious."

Kasa stared at him. "The sheriff convinced Chadbourne that Stringer killed his father in cold blood, that he and Kate planned it all along and thought they'd get away with it way up here."

Francis shook his head. "This is madness. Leland Johnson came here after *them*."

"I tell you, they're crazy like a lynch mob. You must get out of here and take Kate and Stringer with you."

"We can't run, Kasa. For God's sake, I can barely walk." "We have to let our attorney handle this. Buster is coming down from Blue Hills tomorrow." Francis looked Kasa in the eye. "It would be madness to run from the law."

Kasa shook her head. "Francis, you don't understand. These men, they don't care about justice, only their own power." She leaned toward him. "If you can't go, Kate must take Stringer away from here tonight. To Canada."

"To Canada?" It was Kate's voice. Francis and Kasa turned. She was crouched on the stairs.

Kasa walked over to her, gesturing with her hands. "Dear girl, they want to take your baby. You can't let them. You must go."

Terror took over Kate's face. She descended the staircase and stood in front of Kasa. "You know something. They're coming after him, aren't they?"

Kasa nodded.

"There's not going to be any justice, is there?"

Kasa shook her head. "In the war, we didn't heed the warnings that came from other towns where the Germans had already killed people, where they had sent them to camps in trains. We didn't believe what they said the Nazis were doing." Her eyes welled with tears. "They came and took the children I cared for. I tried to fight, but they beat us with their guns, tore Elise and Hans from my arms. I couldn't stop them."

Kate embraced Kasa. "I'll leave with him tonight."

Francis closed and locked the front door then looked at Kate. "You can't just run away."

Kate stared back at him. "Why not? That's how we got here, isn't it?"

Kasa continued to stare at Kate. "You *must* go."

"Kasa," Francis said, stepping in front of her. "This is not World War II. There are no Nazis coming."

Kasa turned to Francis. "You do not know this kind of fear, of being pursued, your family in danger. Let her go."

"But—"

Her face hardened. "You don't know what it is to *have* to run, Francis."

Kate nodded grimly. "Even dead, Leland's still after us. Only now it's through the police. Kasa is right. There'll be no justice. The police have never helped us, never believed us. Not in California. Not here. You tried, Francis."

He shook his head. "Buster is coming tomorrow. The truth will—"

Kate's face tightened. "The *truth* is that bastard beat us for years, nearly killed us, and now they want my son for murder for saving our lives, saving *your* life. You call that justice?" Palpable strength galvanized Kate. She was setting her next course in their struggle for survival. "I will take Stringer. Tonight."

"Running will make things worse," Francis argued. "You can't hide in Canada. They'll find you, bring you back, and charge you with more crimes." He searched her face and his countenance softened. "Besides, how will *I* find you?"

She looked Francis in the eye. "If you come with us, you won't have to find us."

Francis looked at the floor.

Kate crossed her arms. "What's it going to be, Francis?" Her voice wasn't threatening, just dead serious.

Francis turned, hobbled to a chair beside the phone stand, and sat down. He thought for a few moments then looked at them. "I'll help you as much as I can: give you money, names of some friends up north. I'll stay here and work with the attorneys." Francis winced with pain, as much emotional as physical. "But I can't go with you. I can't do something I think will make matters worse than they already are."

Francis and Kate looked at each other then she turned to Kasa. "I'll go wake Stringer."

"I'll get my car. There's a full tank of gas and a map of Maine in the glove box."

"Thank you, Kasa."

"You will be okay. Francis and I will make a list of people you can call for help. When you get to Caribou, the border is easy to get across."

Within minutes, Kasa drove up in her old Ford Escort and parked close to the front door.

Kate put some snacks together then brought Stringer downstairs. He had a blanket around his shoulders and was still half asleep. Kate paused at the front door. "Can I borrow your field coat? For luck?"

Francis nodded. "Of course." Walking to the phone stand, he took a sizable wad of bills from the desk drawer, along with a page of phone numbers. He stepped into the studio, pulled a large book from the shelf over his drawing table then limped across the lawn to the Escort. Kate was in the driver's seat.

"This is for you," Francis said, handing Kate the money and names. Then he handed her a book.

Kate hesitated then turned on the small dome light. She stared at the cover for a few moments then ran her fingers across the title: *Andrew Wyeth — an Autobiography*. She held the book to her chest with both hands.

After a few moments, Kate nodded. Then she turned off the dome light and slid the book in between the two seats. Francis stood back from the car.

Kate shifted into gear and the Escort lurched forward, its dim rear lights disappearing down the driveway into the mist.

CHAPTER 15

Feeling more torn than he could ever remember, Francis limped toward the cliff. The moon was obscured by clouds gathering from the west, and as he walked past the pine tree, an eerie wind whistled through its upper branches. In the darkness, it was hard to tell exactly where the edge of the cliff was. Listening for the crash of waves below, he inched his way to his usual place then slowly lowered himself to the ground. After a few minutes he began humming a poor rendition of one of Kate's Lakota songs.

Francis thought of Kate and Stringer heading north as fugitives on the run, panicked at the sight of every police cruiser along the way. For a moment, Francis felt a fleeting touch of relief that they were gone. He could have a sane life again and the town would get back to normal. But then he cringed, revolted by his own cowardly thoughts. He closed his eyes and once again saw Stringer tracing lines on a canvas. He felt Kate lying next to him, her fingers running through the hair of his forearms.

Francis turned toward the bungalow and noticed that the candle in the whaler's lamp had burned out. He walked back inside, up the staircase to the bedroom. At the window, he slid both hands under the lamp and lifted it from the windowsill. Its feet made little snapping sounds as it came loose from the paint. Carefully he carried the lamp downstairs and set it on the windowsill in the studio. He lowered a new candle inside the glass and lit it. As the wick flickered to life, he turned his easel toward it and gathered together several tubes of paint. Dark and light colors: black, burnt sienna, ghost white and sunflower yellow. He squeezed a dollop of each color onto the dry wooden pallet, then without looking pulled a brush from a cubby hole above his drawing table.

He turned to the canvas and bore down through the aching of his heart, pushing disparate feelings out through his brush. He spent the night painting a turbulent, moonlit ocean; tiny tufts of white pigment riding the backs of black and blue waves. In fact, it was the first time he'd ever painted the nocturnal life of the ocean, had put to canvas the dark, mysterious currents of the coast of Maine, currents that seemed so familiar to him these days.

This was not a painting Rachael would have liked or shown at the gallery. But that didn't matter. Feeling a sense of satisfaction and relief, he stripped off his clothes and lay down on his cot. He fell into a fitful sleep, dreaming of Kate and Stringer driving northward through the night. He saw strange, frightening shadows racing by them in the underbrush, the dark hulks of moose standing in the middle of the road staring them down.

As he tossed and turned on his narrow cot, he saw Kate leaning over a pool table under a lighted Budweiser sign, a townie's hand on her jeans. He tried to visualize Stringer, but his image wasn't clear.

Francis began to rouse at the sound of car doors slamming outside the bar. They were coming to take Kate away—finally—for the dumpster, for adultery and murder, for ruining a nice town in Maine. Huge policemen leaned down, their faces filling the windows of the bar. Terrified, Kate crouched behind the pool table, frantically trying to protect Stringer.

Francis awoke so suddenly he snapped his neck as he sat up. Voices on the lawn—someone banging on the front door. He squinted at the clock beside the drawing table. It was six o'clock. He turned and looked out the window. "Shit—" he said under his breath.

Sheriff McNeal was at the door, papers clutched in his hand. Getting out of a second cruiser in the driveway were Charlie and Ralph.

Francis pulled on his sweatpants and stepped into the hall.

"Sheriff McNeal here, Monroe. Open up, we've got an arrest warrant."

Francis opened the door. Sunlight nearly blinded him. He held up his hand to shield his eyes.

McNeal handed him a bunch of folded papers. "Got an arrest warrant for Stringer Albert Johnson for the murder of Leland Johnson. You gotta let us in."

Francis took the papers and stepped back from the door. The sheriff and his deputies walked into the hallway. Charlie kept his eyes down.

Francis unfolded the papers and scanned down the first page. "First degree murder?"

"That's what it says. All signed by Judge Thornton. Now where is he?"

"He's not here."

"You know we're going to search the place." The sheriff motioned to his deputies.

After a minute or so, Ralph called down from the top of the stairs. "Bed's cold, Sheriff. They must've left during the night."

"Look everywhere. And down by the water. That crazy kid likes to climb on the rocks."

Ralph headed for the cliff. Charlie searched the yard. Francis stood in the hallway barefoot. McNeal stayed by the door, working tobacco back and forth from one cheek to the other.

Ralph came back inside. "No sign of him, Sheriff."

McNeal stepped to the door, spat a wad of wet chew on the grass then stepped back over to Francis. "Where are they?"

"I don't know."

McNeal stepped closer, so close Francis could hear him sucking tobacco juice between his teeth. "Tell me where they went, Monroe."

"I said I don't know."

"You know, for a smart fella, you sure are stupid about some things. I could arrest you for harboring a fugitive, aidin' and abet-tin' a murderer, and obstruction of justice. Hell, you're pretty damn near an accomplice." The sheriff took in a somewhat labored breath. "If you weren't such a famous fellow, your ass would be in a sling too."

Francis looked straight at McNeal. "Get out of my house."

"You'd better tell me where they headed."

Francis stared at McNeal without speaking.

Finally the sheriff wiped his mouth with the back of his hand and took a step back. "We'll put out an APB. Every cop in New England'll be looking for them. They're probably headed to Canada. That's how they got here in the first place. Don't worry, we'll get the border zipped up good and tight."

The sheriff cocked his head to the side. "Come on, boys." He looked back at Francis. "State's Attorney Chadbourne's gonna charge the little bastard as an adult. He's on the run, probably armed and dangerous." McNeal leaned toward Francis. "Hope we can bring him in alive."

McNeal walked outside, letting the screen door slam behind him. He and his deputies climbed into their cruisers and sped off down the hill.

Once Francis had steadied himself, he called Kasa, who came up to the bungalow. They spent the day comforting each other, anxiously waiting for word from Kate. None came. They called friends whose numbers they had given her but no one had heard from her.

Kasa and Francis talked about all that had happened since the day Stringer appeared in Francis's yard. He told her that meeting Kate and Stringer had changed his life, opened his heart and reawakened his deep love of painting. He talked about moments of feeling the way he did that afternoon in the presence of Andrew Wyeth, about the unspoken power certain people have.

Kasa mostly listened, often checking the driveway.

The day after Kate left, Buster Hurd arrived in town and drove out to the bungalow. He was a large, well-dressed man in his seventies. He had a full head of white-gray hair, and his broad shoulders filled his wool sport coat. His face was tanned and weathered, and he appeared to be a thoughtful man. His eyes, rimmed with gold glasses, were bright and alive.

Francis and Buster sat in the parlor sipping Jameson's Irish whiskey and talking about what had happened. At first Buster appeared frustrated, annoyed that Stringer and his mother had fled, but as he listened to their story, he became increasingly empathetic and wanted to help. He told Francis that their running was a potentially grave choice and that it was likely the authorities would be rougher on Stringer and maybe they'd also charge Kate with a crime.

As they talked, Francis studied Buster's countenance. He saw a sadness behind his bright eyes. "May I ask you something personal?"

Buster nodded.

"Why are you interested in this case? You're a famous lawyer who's retired and I assume it's not for the money."

Buster took a long swig of whiskey and set the glass down. He clasped his hands together over his protuberant abdomen and looked at the stove. "I suppose you have a right to know." He cleared his throat. "In part, it's because I would do anything I could for a friend of Jacob's. And I do sorely miss being in the courtroom. But there's another reason."

There was a long pause.

"It goes back many years. One Sunday morning a few months after I won the Felix Giroux case, my son, Travis, rode off on his bike to deliver newspapers on his route along a winding coastal road outside of town. He didn't show up for church, so we called the police and went out looking for him. We didn't find a trace so we thought he might have been kidnapped. Maybe revenge for my getting Felix off, which led to a local mill boy getting convicted."

Buster took another swallow of Jameson's and wiped his mouth with the back of his hand. "Just before sunset the police chief called and said they had a drunk driver sobering up in the jail who thought he'd hit something that morning out on the shore road. We raced back to the area and began searching again."

Buster cleared his throat again. "I found my son's damaged bike at the top of a ravine about thirty feet from the side of the road. My best friend and I climbed down into the ravine with flashlights. We found Travis's body at the bottom. He was dead."

Buster paused for what seemed like a long time. "From the bloody scrapes we found on the walls of the ravine, it looked like he'd struggled terribly trying to save himself, to get help." Buster looked at his hands. "The skin was worn off most of his fingertips." He shook his head. "Seeing your flesh and blood like that...I felt like I'd been gutted."

Buster sat back and looked at Francis. "A substantial part of me died that day,

Mr. Monroe. I didn't have a chance to save my own son. All these years it's haunted me, knowing he had been alive, struggling to survive for God knows how long." Buster shook his head.

"I'm terribly sorry. I had no idea."

"The bastard that killed Travis was a drunkard like Leland Johnson. He'd killed an old woman in a crosswalk six years before—drunk, of course. He'd been out of jail less than a year when he killed Travis."

Francis leaned forward in his chair. "I can barely imagine how you've suffered."

Buster raised his gaze to Francis. "From what you've told me and what I know of you, I suspect you have a pretty good idea." Buster paused. "I read about your wife, that she died windsurfing last year. I'm sorry."

"Thank you," Francis said. "So where do we go from here?"

"I'm going to stay in town and start working on things. This Chadbourne lady's tough. I knew her old man. A conservative bastard, he served in the State Senate for many years. We've got to be ready for her. She wants to make a name for herself and start climbing the political ladder."

"You're assuming Stringer and Kate will be back?"

Buster raised his eyebrows. "Oh, they'll be back—one way or another. Let's hope that crazy sheriff of yours doesn't do anything really stupid when he finds them."

The next day, Francis rose just before sun up. The candle in the whaler's lamp burned low on a mound of melted wax. He leaned over and blew it out. Though he'd tossed and turned, worrying about Kate and Stringer most of the night, for the first time since the stabbing, his body felt like his own again. His leg was sore but more limber, the burning sensation almost gone. He looked out the window. Only a couple of dissolving cirrus clouds lingered over the horizon. For a few moments Francis closed his eyes and, in his own meager way, prayed they would be all right.

He lit the gas heater in the studio, walked to the bathroom, and splashed cold water on his face. Then he pulled on an old parka, picked up his easel, and set it up out on the lawn next to the pine tree. Trying to distract himself, he worked on a new painting, a pair of rapscallion deckhands duking it out on a nineteenth-century New England wharf. After a couple hours he saw an out of breath Kasa struggling up the drive.

Francis walked toward her. "What's happened?" he asked.

"Kate phoned."

"Thank God! Are they all right?"

"I don't know. She sounded scared—said she couldn't run anymore. Wants us to come get her."

"Where is she?"

Kasa grabbed Francis's arm. "First of all, she made me promise I'd tell you that she's wanting to drink."

"Where *is* she? We have to go at once."

"What did she mean about the drink?"

Francis looked Kasa in the eye. "Kate had a bad time with alcohol and drugs. They nearly killed her before she got sober a few years ago. I'll explain more later, just tell me where she is."

"She called from Bucksport, three or four hours from here."

"That's as far as they got?"

Kasa frowned. "Yes, and I don't think she's doing well."

"I know. I've been half out of my mind worrying about her. Let's just go. Do you have an address?"

"They're staying in a shelter in the basement of Trinity Church, somewhere downtown. She said some friends had been helping her but she couldn't stay there much longer."

"Is Stringer all right?"

"I don't know, but I can't believe he's too well off." Kasa's shoulders drooped. "I was a fool to tell her to run, but I was terrified for her." Tears formed in the corner of her eyes.

Francis put his hand on her shoulder. "You did what you felt was best. This has affected all of us in unexpected ways. Now I need your help to bring them home. I don't think I can do it without you. Is there a phone number where we can call her and tell her we're coming?"

"No. She called from a phone booth—at a gas station, I think. It was noisy. Besides, she knows we'll come."

They headed northeast on Route One. Traffic was heavy with seemingly endless tractor trailers and logging trucks rolling north and south. It took almost two hours to cover the first sixty miles.

"I need gas," Francis said as they approached Thomaston.

"And a cup of coffee," Kasa said.

Francis pulled into a Texaco station, stuck the nozzle in the tank, and leaned back against the car. Feeling anxious and tired, he stared at the roadway. Kasa got out and stood beside him, stretching her back.

"This is the worst fall traffic I've ever seen. Damn tourists. It's going to take us forever to get to Bucksport. Do you think Kate will hold on?"

Kasa thought for a few moments. "Yes, I think she will. She loves you, Francis. And she adores Stringer."

Francis checked the dial on the gas pump. "I hope she loves herself enough."

"I think she does."

Fresh coffee cups in hand, they headed north again. By supper time, they were still driving. Francis's palms felt sweaty against the imitation leather of the Malibu's steering wheel. He missed the familiar comfort of the Jeep. Kasa rode quietly, saying only, "We'll make it," when Francis became irritable. By the time they hit the outer edge of Bucksport, it was close to sunset, heavy clouds having blown in from the west.

They drove into town and stopped at a coffee shop where Francis asked how to get to Trinity Church. The girl behind the counter wasn't sure, but gave him the best directions she could. "If you can't find it, go down Main Street to the police station. They'll tell you how to get there."

Yeah, right, Francis thought to himself. He followed the girl's directions carefully, but when they rounded the corner of Pine and Katahdin streets, the church wasn't there. Frustrated, he jammed the car into park, took off his seat belt, and got out, banging on the roof with his hand. "Damn it!"

Kasa leaned across the seat. "Francis Monroe, get back in this car."

Francis grumbled then climbed back in.

"We *will* find her. Go down this street and take a left. Maybe we haven't gone far enough."

Francis put the car in drive, rounded the corner, and there at the end of the street was a white church with a short steeple, paint peeling around its small stained glass windows.

They parked in front of a hand-lettered sign that read "Trinity Church — Our Lady of the Blessed Sea." They got out and stood at the curb. Some kids were playing basketball on a playground across the street.

Francis looked at Kasa. "Do you know where they are?"

"She said there's a set of stairs in the back that goes down to a basement door. It was noisy on the phone, but I think she said to ring the doorbell and wait for someone to answer."

"Let's go."

"Francis," Kasa said, touching his arm. "Kate may be in bad shape. Go slowly."

He nodded. "I will."

They walked around the side of the church to the back where they found a set of cement stairs leading to a wooden door. As Francis walked down the steps, he felt crumbling cement underfoot. Kasa stayed close behind him.

Francis approached the door. A dank smell filled the stairway, like that of an old well. He glanced over his shoulder at Kasa.

Before he could knock, the latch unlocked and the door opened a crack, revealing the thin face of an old woman. She was hunched over, but did not appear frail. "Are you Francis?"

"Yes."

"What is your friend's name?"

"Kasa."

The woman closed the door, undid a security chain then opened the door wide enough for them to enter. Warm, musty air rushed past them. In the low lighting Francis saw tables piled with rummage clothing and tag sale items. On one wall were the cut out tracings of children's feet over which hung a hand-lettered poster: "Footsteps of the Lord." To the left was a small kitchen. On the counter sat two large steel coffee pots. Their tops were inverted and black electric cords were draped over the side like escaping snakes.

"Enter here," the woman said, motioning to a small room in the corner of the basement. She held back strings of wooden beads with her arthritic hand. Francis motioned for Kasa to go first, but she nudged him toward the parted beads then followed him into a sort of meditation room.

"Please, sit down."

Francis and Kasa sat on a wooden bench in front of a small, hand-crafted altar. Half-burned candles stood in polished brass candlesticks. A picture of a young Jesus was centered above a wooden cross on the wall over the altar.

The woman sat on a metal chair next to them and folded her hands together. Her eyes were kind, her countenance calm. "I am Madeleine. We have your friend here. Miss Kate. She came to us two days ago. One of the sisters found her crying in an alley downtown. Sister had seen her sitting in the back of a meeting— a recovery meeting—and she seemed very upset. On her way back here, Sister found her next to a trash container."

"What do you mean a recovery meeting?" Kasa asked.

The woman looked at Francis. He turned to Kasa. "I think she means an AA meeting. Alcoholics Anonymous. Remember what I told you in the car."

"A boy was with her. He was frightened by how distraught his mother was."

"Is he here?" Francis asked.

"Fearing for their safety, Sister brought Miss Kate and the boy here. They have slept in a makeshift room in the back. We have it for people in crisis, mostly women and children in danger. It was not until today she told us who she was and that she couldn't run anymore. The boy is outside playing ball with the two sons of a woman who helps us. He has a cast on his arm, but he badly needed some fresh air."

"May we see her?" Francis asked.

"Can you help her?" Madeleine replied. "We fear she is running from the law. We want to help her, but we cannot endanger the sisters or our church."

"I understand," Francis said. "We'll take them home with us tonight."

Madeleine looked into Francis's face. "Will you promise to take care of them? They are precious children of God."

"Yes," he said. "I love them very much."

Sister Madeleine placed her hands around his. "I will take you to her."

Madeleine stood, stepped through the wooden beads, and walked to the other end of the basement. Francis and Kasa followed.

Before entering the small "room" constructed of moveable Sunday school partitions, Madeleine stopped and made the sign of the cross. She turned to Francis. "I think she is sleeping."

Francis looked in and saw Kate lying in a fetal position on a thin mattress on the floor. A blanket covered her hips, and though she was sleeping, she clutched something tightly in her hand.

Francis took a step closer and saw between her fingers a page torn from the Andrew Wyeth book he had given her. It was a picture of the painting "Barracoon."

Madeleine whispered to Francis, "She was clutching that print when Sister found her in the alley. She holds it like I hold a crucifix."

Francis crouched beside Kate's mattress. He reached toward her head, hesitated then lowered his arm. "My dear Kate."

Moments later he felt her fingers slide into his palm. "Francis—"

He slid his arms under Kate's shoulders and lifted her into an embrace. "I love you," he whispered.

Her chin on Francis's shoulder, Kate began to cry. Then she saw Kasa. "You came," Kate said, reaching for her. Kasa took her hand.

"What happened to you?" Francis asked.

"I had an accident. Got a flat and hit a tree a few miles from here. The car wasn't drivable." Kate looked at Kasa. "I'm sorry." She looked down. "I ran. Stringer and I spent a day on foot until he said he couldn't go any further. The poor kid was dead on his feet."

Kate pushed herself up and sat back against the wall. "We were wet and cold and hungry. I took Stringer into a pub in Bucksport to get something to eat and suddenly I really wanted a beer. I craved it—more than I have in years. Stringer was playing pinball. I sat down at the bar and he flipped out. He ran out of the pub yelling. I ran after him but couldn't find him. I searched all night, thought I'd lose my mind." Kate caught her breath and looked at the Wyeth print in her hands.

"The next day I went back to the bar and ordered a beer. I sat there staring at it for quite a while." Kate shook her head and looked at Francis. "God, Francis, I had it right at my lips then I threw it across the bar. I spilled it all over the place. I wanted to lick the beer off my fingers *so* badly. I screamed at the bartender that I was an alcoholic, to give me a wet cloth to wipe off the beer." Kate held her head in her hands and cried. Francis put his arm around her shoulder.

"The bartender got me cleaned up then took me around the corner to a church where there was an AA meeting. I was going crazy without Stringer. I don't remember the meeting, just that I got there without drinking." Kate shook her head. "But I was *so* close to relapsing.

"Some people offered to help me. I blew them off and went looking for Stringer. I was so exhausted I must have finally collapsed in an alley. A woman found me and brought me here. The next day they found Stringer. He was petrified I'd been drinking, but I hadn't." Kate turned to Madeleine. "Right, Sister?"

"Sober as a judge, my dear." Madeleine smiled then stepped out between the partitions.

Francis rubbed Kate's hands. "I'm so glad you're safe and sober. I was worried sick. I never should have let you leave."

"I had to try, but I guess my running days are over. I'm just too tired."

Francis held Kate's hands tighter. "You know there's a warrant out for Stringer?"

Kate looked at the floor. "I knew there would be."

"Does he know?" Francis asked.

"I'm not sure. He's been too scared and angry to talk much." Kate looked at Francis. "Does String know you're here?"

"Not yet."

"What should we do, Francis?"

"I'm going to call Buster Hurd, Jacob's friend. He's down in Winter's Cove. I told him about the situation when he arrived yesterday. He'll know the best way to proceed."

Francis winced. His leg was sore from crouching so long. He gently slid his hand over Kate's forearm. "You know we've got to bring Stringer in. There's no other way."

Tears came to Kate's eyes.

"Things are pretty riled up and I don't want some trigger-happy deputy doing something crazy. I hate to say it, but at this point he's probably safer in jail." Francis stood. "I'll be back soon. Kasa will stay with you."

Kasa sat against the wall next to Kate.

Francis walked back through the basement and up the stairs. Across the street he was relieved to see Stringer and two other kids shooting at a netless hoop. Tufts of grass pushed through the many cracks in the pavement. Francis watched them for a couple of minutes, knowing this might be the last freedom Stringer would see for a long time.

Stringer saw Francis and immediately stopped playing.

"String," Francis said, stepping over to him. He extended his arms.

Stringer was chewing a wad of gum. He kept his arms to himself. "So we going to get this over with?"

Francis took a step back and caught his breath. There was no bullshit with this kid. "Yes. Buster Hurd, our attorney, said we should go to the sheriff's office north of town, for you to turn yourself in. There are cops all over the place looking for you."

Stringer spat on the pavement. He looked like he'd aged several years in just a few days.

"I'll get your mother."

"Yeah. I'll wait here."

Back in the church basement, Francis found Kate and Kasa kneeling beside Madeleine at the altar in the small sanctuary room. Francis walked quietly through the partitions, crouching beside Kate's mattress. Her only possession was the crumpled print of "Barracoon." Francis picked it up from the bed clothes and flattened it against his thigh. He ran his finger over the red of the woman's palms and the soles of her feet. Then he stood, folded the print, and placed it into his pocket. He walked to the door of the meditation room and waited for the women to finish their prayers. Their soft murmurings comforted him.

After a few moments, the women got up and Madeleine walked Kate to the door. Francis put his arm around her. "Thank you," he said to Madeleine.

Madeleine laid her palms on their backs. "The Lord God be with you."

Kate hugged Madeleine and said good-bye. Then Kasa, Francis, and Kate walked up the stairs.

At the car, Kate walked up to Stringer and hugged him, running her hand over his head. After a few moments, he took a step back. "Let's go, Mom."

The four of them climbed into the Malibu. Kate edged across to the middle of the front seat. Stringer got in on the passenger's side and sat with his casted arm out the window. Kasa climbed into the back seat and folded her hands in her lap.

Francis held the wheel with both hands and took a deep breath. "Here we go." As they drove through town he glanced down each side street checking for police. Buster had said it was very important for Stringer to turn himself in voluntarily if at all possible.

They turned onto Route One heading north. "It should only take ten or fifteen minutes to get to the sheriff's station." He reached into his pants pocket, pulled out the Wyeth print, and placed it in Kate's hands. She held it tightly.

A couple of minutes up the road, a State Police cruiser came up behind them. Francis's gaze darted back and forth from the road to the rear view mirror. His shoulders tightened, a thin film of sweat forming on his forehead. After it had followed them a short distance, the cruiser pulled around them and disappeared. Francis relaxed a bit.

"Stringer, we've gotten you an excellent lawyer. His name is Mr. Hurd; he's from up in Blue Hills. We met yesterday and he's already started working on your case."

Stringer didn't say anything. He just hung his head out the window, letting the wind blow around him.

"It's going to be okay," Francis said, mostly to himself. He sped up to fifty-five as they crested a hill.

From out of a side road came the state trooper, blue strobe lights flashing, siren wailing. Stringer pulled his head into the car. Kasa sat bolt upright as Kate wrapped her arms around her son.

Up ahead, three police cruisers formed a road block. Officers were crouched behind cruisers, holding their shotguns at the ready. Another cruiser came in from the left and quickly edged in close to Francis's door. Kate screamed. For a moment, Francis thought of flooring it, blasting through the road block and making a run for the border.

"Goddamn it," Francis said, hitting the wheel. As the distance to the road block disappeared, Francis eased off the accelerator and slid his foot onto the brake. As he slowed, the cruisers flanking him backed off a bit.

Francis brought the Malibu to a stop a few feet from a sheriff's cruiser. "Those bastards," he said, jamming the car into park.

An officer spoke over a PA system. "Put your hands on your heads. Keep them where we can see them." All four of them stared straight ahead and obeyed.

Heavily armed officers approached the car from both sides and opened the doors.

"Step out with your hands over your heads and lie down on the pavement."

Francis slid off the seat, looking the officer closest to him in the eye. "We were taking him in to surrender."

"Sure," the officer responded sarcastically. "Heading north to surrender." He motioned to the pavement with his gun. "Face down."

"We were going to the sheriff's office up the road."

"I said, face down—now."

Francis glanced across the seat. One cop had taken Stringer out of the car and another had Kate's arm and was pulling her from the seat.

"Get your hands off her!" Stringer yelled.

"Shut up, kid! You're under arrest. Get down on the ground."

Stringer ignored him, wrested free, and grabbed the gun belt of the cop pulling on Kate.

"Hey!" yelled another officer. He grabbed Stringer by the neck and tore him off the other officer. Kate screamed. Stringer elbowed the cop in the ribs then kicked him in the knee.

Francis lifted his head from the pavement. "Stringer, don't fight them!"

An officer with sergeant stripes pulled a long black flashlight from its holster and strode around the back of the car. As Stringer struggled, he cracked him across his good wrist. Stringer yelled in pain, but still turned and tried to scratch the officer's face. The sergeant clobbered Stringer across the lower back with the flashlight. Kate screamed again as she tried to crawl to Stringer.

No one seemed to notice that Kasa had stepped out of the back seat and was standing beside the car. Suddenly she let out a bellowing yell, bringing her hand down on the roof of the car so hard she dented the metal. "Stop!"

Everyone froze.

"He is but a boy!" Kasa said, her eyes wild, her jaw set. She stepped over in front of the sergeant, took a deep breath, and looked him in the eye. "Treat him like a human being. Do you hear me?"

The sergeant and his officers appeared stunned. Without saying a word, Stringer glanced at Kasa, got to his feet, and put his hands together. Handcuffed, he was led to a cruiser and placed in the back seat.

Not wanting to make things worse, Kate restrained herself, holding onto Francis's arm as a state trooper read Stringer his rights. Stringer appeared to ignore him, gazing through the cruiser window at his mother, a look of deep desperation on his face.

CHAPTER 16

As the police cruiser holding Stringer sped south, Kate, Francis, and Kasa stood silently in the gravel at the side of the road. On the orders of Sheriff McNeal, Stringer was being taken back to Winter's Cove to be formally charged.

Francis mustered enough strength to get everyone into the Malibu then pulled a u-turn and followed after the cruiser. He passed a couple of cars, trying to keep up, but couldn't. He slowed down and the three of them watched the blue lights disappear into heavy traffic in the distance.

Kate and Kasa were quiet as Francis called Buster on his cell phone and told him what had happened. After he hung up, Kate turned to him, her eyes red and swollen. "What did he say?"

"He'll be waiting for Stringer at the sheriff's office." Francis glanced at Kate. "He's relieved Stringer's coming in alive."

"Yeah," Kate said. "And beat up." She stared out the side window. "But he'll be all right. He's tough. Leland beat him a lot worse than this."

Francis glanced in the rear view mirror. Kasa looked drained. "You okay?" he asked.

Kasa nodded, leaned forward, and touched both his and Kate's shoulders with her large hands. "Don't worry about me. I'm tough too."

It was late that night when they arrived back in Winter's Cove. They left Kasa off at her house then drove into town and parked at the courthouse. They hurried up the granite steps of the sheriff's office where they saw Charlie sitting inside. He appeared uncomfortable as he opened the door and let them in. Kate said she wanted to see Stringer.

"We had Dr. Conklin take a look at him. He's got a couple bruises but nothing major."

"I want to see my son," Kate said, staring Charlie straight in the face.

Francis couldn't look at Charlie, who turned and led Kate down a narrow brick corridor to Stringer's cell. Francis followed behind them.

"Mr. Monroe—"

Francis stopped and looked into a small room off the corridor. Buster sat behind a wooden table, working by the yellow light of a desk lamp.

"Come in and sit down so I can bring you up to speed."

Francis glanced down the corridor as Kate disappeared around a corner. "I'll be back in a few minutes," Francis said to Buster then hurried down the hall after Kate. He heard a clang then the opening of a cell door.

When he rounded the corner, Francis saw Stringer sitting on the edge of a metal cot suspended by chains from the brick wall. Kate was on her knees in front of him, holding him in her arms.

Charlie opened the cell door a little wider and let Francis pass. "I'll be down the hall if you need me." He closed the door and threw the steel lock.

Francis stepped over and crouched beside Kate. "Hey, String," he said, placing one hand on her shoulder and one on Stringer's arm. They were both crying.

After a while, Kate sat back and looked Stringer over. "Did those bastards break anything?"

"No," Stringer said quietly.

Francis cleared his throat. "Kate, I don't mean to rush you, but Mr. Hurd wants to go over some things before he leaves. He's just down the hall. Will you speak with him for a few minutes?"

"It's okay, Mom," Stringer said.

"All right," Kate said. She leaned over and kissed Stringer on the head. "I'll be right back."

Kate called to Charlie who let them out. They walked down the hall to the interrogation room. Inside, Buster held a Styrofoam coffee cup in one hand, a ballpoint pen in the other. He looked over his bifocals as they stepped into the room. He stood and warmly offered his hand to Kate. "I'm Buster Hurd, Mrs. Johnson. It's a privilege to meet you."

Kate shook hands.

"There's not a lot of room in here, but please sit down." Buster motioned to two folding metal chairs next to the table.

"Can I get you some coffee?" he asked as Kate and Francis sat down.

Kate shook her head.

"Actually, I could use a cup," Francis said, adjusting his sore leg under the table.

"I'll get it," Charlie said from the doorway. "Cream or sugar?"

Francis looked at Charlie for the first time since they'd arrived. "A little of both, please."

Charlie nodded and walked away.

Buster sat down, adjusted his belly against the edge of the table, and took off his glasses. "I can barely imagine what you must be feeling, Mrs. Johnson. I know you're exhausted, but it's still important we go over a few things."

Buster put his glasses back on and picked up a yellow legal pad. "Nathaniel Thornton will be presiding over your son's case. He's been a judge around here a long time. He's conservative, but generally fair, and he likes to keep things moving in his courtroom. He's a native who loves to snowshoe and fly fish. Supposed to retire in the spring. This will probably be his last major trial, and I bet he'll get his fill on this one."

Buster set the legal pad on the table and took his glasses off again. "Judge Thornton's going to arraign Stringer tomorrow morning in the courthouse next door. From the little I could dig up today, it's not clear what this Chadbourne lady—the state's attorney—is going to charge him with. She's sharp, but at the moment the prosecution's a bit disorganized. Before she came back home, she worked in South Boston where she saw a lot of violent crime. But having it happen in a small Maine village is very different. And I don't think Thornton's ever had a case of a juvenile shooting his father before. I'm not sure he's clear on exactly how he's going to proceed either.

"Normally the judge appoints a guardian ad litem, a responsible member of the community experienced in juvenile legal matters to advise and guide the defendant. And seeing he's only twelve, I could probably demand Stringer be released tonight, but—"

Kate perked up. "Then get him out."

Buster shook his head. "Instead of pushing the issue at this hour, it's better if Stringer spends the night in jail."

Kate frowned. "Why?"

"It'll make him more sympathetic to the town and the prospective jury. The State will look rather heartless." Buster put his hands together and leaned forward. "You see, the theater aspect of the trial begins now. With every move we make, every word we speak, we have to think about how it will affect things, how it will play in the minds of the jury. And there're always two juries: the community at large and the twelve members who eventually sit in the box."

Kate crossed her arms. "This isn't a damn game."

Buster slid his glasses back on and looked at her compassionately. "Unfortunately, in part it is, Mrs. Johnson. A deadly serious game and we've got to play it better than the prosecution." Buster looked over his glasses. "Let me assure you, my solitary goal is to win Stringer's complete freedom, to hear 'not guilty' spoken by the foreman of the jury."

Buster watched Kate for a few moments. "Look, Mrs. Johnson, we're all too tired to get into it all tonight. Please just trust me on this." He made a notation on his pad then looked at Kate again. "Tomorrow at the arraignment Stringer will plead not guilty. The judge will decide what to do with him while we prepare for trial. He may appoint a guardian or—and this would be unusual—he may let you serve in that capacity."

Kate's face tightened. "I'm his mother. He doesn't need a guardian."

Buster looked at Kate, a mixture of compassion and concern on his face. "Kate—may I call you Kate?"

Kate nodded.

"This is a complex system. Under the tremendous emotional pressures of a trial, you'll have to consider if you can be objective, steady enough to advise Stringer on a host of difficult and sensitive issues: your family, Stringer and your past, your life in California, and, of course, Leland's killing. It's very tough to do when you're related to the defendant, especially when you're his mother. And it's evident how deeply you care for him."

Kate looked uncomfortable and angry. Francis felt her body tighten. He looked at Buster. "Perhaps she can think it over tonight and we can talk more about it in the morning."

Buster sat back, his sport coat sliding to the sides of his belly. "Fair enough."

Kate looked at Buster. "Will Stringer be safe in here?"

Buster nodded. "He'll be all right. The sheriff's a jerk, but his chief deputy out there—Charlie—seems okay. Besides, they're scared of the publicity this trial will undoubtedly bring. I don't think they'll let anything bad happen."

Kate set her jaw. "They'd better not."

Francis stood and pulled Kate's chair out for her.

Buster pushed himself up from the table. "And I should mention a couple of other things," he said, motioning for Francis to close the door. "I don't think it's a good idea to let this thing drag on. What has happened will change Stringer and you forever, but if pretrial legal maneuvering goes on too long, it'll wear Stringer down something awful. It might destroy him, even if he's eventually found innocent."

There was a seasoned calm in Buster's voice that felt reassuring to Francis.

"The State will expect us to make motions to cause delays. Of course we need enough time to properly prepare, but it'll unnerve them if we move for a speedy trial, especially with the holidays coming." Buster looked at Kate. "The last thing is will you authorize me to bring in a child psychologist to meet with Stringer and do an evaluation? There's a very good one at Maine Medical down in Portland. Jack Hardy. He's an old acquaintance of mine and knows his way around the legal system."

Kate nodded. "All right, but I don't want him making Stringer crazy with a bunch of psychobabble."

Buster's countenance remained calm. "I think he'll be able to help us." He slipped his glasses into his pocket then touched Kate's shoulder. "I promise you two things. I'll make them take good care of Stringer and I'll put everything I have into defending your son as if he were my own. If what I'm doing seems confusing, even contrary at times, please trust me to do what's best for Stringer in the long run. We'll talk again tomorrow and on a regular basis after that."

Kate studied his face for a few moments then slowly nodded. "Thank you, Mr. Hurd."

"Please, call me Buster. Everyone does."

Kate nodded. Francis shook Buster's hand and thanked him. He opened the door and they walked into the corridor. Francis followed Kate back to the cell then waited in the corridor as Charlie let her in to say good night.

Kate tucked a wool army blanket around Stringer's shoulders then leaned over and kissed him. She reached into the pocket of her jeans and pulled out the folded print of "Barracoon" and secured it to the steel hook in the brick wall holding the chains to the bed frame.

Francis turned and walked toward the sheriff's office. Charlie was back at his desk, a full cup of coffee sitting on the corner. He stood, glanced at the cup then at Francis. "I didn't want to disturb you."

Francis walked to the desk and picked up the coffee cup. "Thanks."

Charlie looked as though he wanted to say something but then just nodded his head.

"Will you tell Kate I'm waiting in the car?"

"Yeah."

Francis walked outside and leaned against the Malibu. Ten minutes later Kate came out, his field coat pulled tightly around her, her eyes filled with tears.

CHAPTER 17

After a restless night, Francis was awakened at sunrise by Kate taking a shower. After quick cups of coffee they left to visit Stringer and meet Buster before the arraignment. In town, as they rounded the corner onto Main Street, they saw a couple of TV news vans set up in the sheriff department's parking lot, as well as several reporters standing on the courthouse steps.

As soon as they parked, Charlie came out of the sheriff's office and hurried over to the Malibu. He told Kate and Francis to follow him. Inside, Charlie led them into the small interrogation room where they had met with Buster. Charlie seemed nervous as he closed the door and stood against it. "Things are pretty tense around here." He paused and looked at Kate. "I just checked on Stringer. He's okay. Even got a little sleep."

Charlie adjusted the gun belt on his hip. "Sheriff likes things quiet. Those TV people outside have got his blood pressure up. And this morning we got word there may be protesters coming in from Boston. Some children's rights outfit."

"That's great," Kate said. "People *should* be protesting."

Charlie checked his watch. "Anyway, if you make it quick, you can say hi to Stringer before we take him over to the court-house."

"Can't Francis go in?"

Charlie shook his head. "Just immediate family and you're supposed to visit for only ten minutes. Sheriff's clampin' down on the rules."

Kate shook her head.

"I'm sorry, Mrs. Johnson. I've got no choice. One other thing I wanted to warn you about is the sheriff's making us move your son in and out of the courtroom in leg irons. Considers him high risk." Charlie looked at the floor. "We'll do our best." He stepped to the door. "Arraignment's in fifteen minutes. You'd better hurry."

After Charlie left, Francis placed his hands lightly on Kate's shoulders. "I'll wait for you here."

She took a deep breath and walked out.

Francis walked through the sheriff's office over to the windows that looked out on the parking lot. A small gathering of people stood on the sidewalk behind yellow plastic tape strung between barricades.

For a few moments Francis thought of Rachael before she died, remembered the awful feeling of not being able to help her. He squinted against the sunlight. With Kate it was different. It wasn't easy, but they were finding ways to let each other in, to help each other. Despite the pain and tumult and the unfamiliarity of all that was happening, Francis felt profoundly grateful to have Kate and Stringer in his life.

He walked back to the doorway of the interrogation room and waited until Kate returned.

"Mr. Monroe." Francis turned and saw a deputy he didn't recognize. "There's a phone call for you in the office."

Francis walked to the phone. It was Buster.

"I'm outside the courtroom waiting to meet with you. We have only a few minutes." Buster sounded tense.

"I'm sorry, we've been tied up in here. Kate's with Stringer."

"Francis." Buster lowered his voice. "It may get rough in there today. Judge Thornton's feeling a lot of pressure. The state's attorney isn't letting out any slack. They've got a strong old boy's network around here so we'll have to play it by ear."

Francis watched Charlie lead three deputies down the corridor toward Stringer's cell. "All right," he said into the phone. "We'll see you in the courtroom."

When Francis hung up he saw Kate standing at the door to the interrogation room, her hands covering her face. Francis walked over and held her. He heard the sound of chains as the deputies prepared to move Stringer.

After a few moments, Kate straightened and dried her eyes with her hand. "I've got to get over there. I don't want Stringer alone in that courtroom."

Francis nodded. "I know. Neither do I." Charlie led them to the courthouse through a rather stately vestibule, beneath an etched glass chandelier, to a large paneled door. Kate and Francis stepped inside a high-ceilinged room with rows of long wooden benches curving from one side to the other. Sunlight filtered through a round window over the bench. The lemony scent of wood polish lingered in the air.

Stringer was nowhere in sight. Buster sat at the defense table. A thin woman with perfect posture in a dark blue suit stood at the prosecution table studying papers in a manila folder.

Kate and Francis followed Charlie down the center aisle. He motioned for them to sit up front close to Buster. Scattered about on the benches were several dozen people, including what looked like a few reporters. As Francis sat down, a figure in the back corner caught his eye. He turned and saw Kasa sitting alone, her hands clutched in her lap. Francis nodded to her.

Standing beside a small desk in the front near the jury box was a man in his sixties dressed in a worn tweed sport coat. A small plaque on the front of his desk read "Lester Rollins, Court Officer." After a few minutes, Officer Rollins stepped around his desk to a dark wooden door at the front corner of the room. He walked with a considerable limp, as though one leg were shorter than the other. With his hand on the door knob, he turned to the courtroom. "All rise," he said, his voice clear and commanding. "Court is now in session. The Honorable Nathaniel Thornton presiding."

Lester opened the door and a tall, thin man in a black robe stepped into the light coming from the round window. His hair was a mixture of black and gray, his shoulders square. His forehead was set in a frown, his ears a bit too large for his narrow face.

Judge Thornton strode to the center of the bench and sat down. He looked first at the prosecutor then at Buster. "Are you ready to proceed?"

Gwen Chadbourne snapped to attention, flicking a hair off her face. "Yes, Your Honor."

Buster looked over his glasses at the judge and nodded then everyone sat down.

For a few moments there was silence in the courtroom, save for the slightly off-balance whirring of the large-bladed fan hanging from the middle of the ceiling. The brass pole supporting the fan swayed back and forth an inch or two every few seconds accompanied by a slight but annoying squeak.

Judge Thornton nodded to Lester who pushed a button on the side of his desk. A buzzer sounded and a metal door at the rear of the courtroom swung open. A deputy sheriff entered. Francis heard the clanging of chains before he saw Stringer.

Kate pulled her hands to her chest and leaned into Francis.

With a deputy in front and back, Stringer walked awkwardly toward the front of the room. The restrictive leg irons made him walk as if he'd had polio or suffered from some congenital anomaly. He wore a blaze orange jumpsuit too big for him, the collar partially obscuring his face. Though he didn't turn his head, Stringer glanced at Kate and Francis as he stepped in beside Buster.

"Be seated," the judge said. "Regarding the death of Leland Johnson of Los Angeles, California, killed in the town of Winter's Cove, Maine, on Sept. 19, 1998, Stringer Albert Johnson is accused of murder in the first degree. The State is charging the defendant as an adult under Maine state statute."

A murmur spread through the courtroom.

Judge Thornton looked at the attorneys. "Is everyone clear on the charges?" Both Chadbourne and Buster nodded.

Francis had a hard time getting a full breath. Kate stared at the back of her son's head. The chain around Stringer's waist was visible between the wooden spindles of the chair.

The judge turned to the defense table and folded his hands. "Let the record reflect that the court offered, in fact encouraged, the appointment of a guardian ad litem for the defendant. Defense counsel, however, requested that his mother be allowed to function as his guardian. With some reservation, I am granting this request, as long as it appears his mother, Kate Johnson, is able to adequately serve the needs of her son."

Judge Thornton paused and looked across the front of the courtroom. No one said anything. "Will the defendant please rise."

Buster pushed his chair back and stood. He helped Stringer to his feet then looked at the judge.

"Mr. Hurd, how does the defendant plea?"

"Your Honor, the defendant pleads not guilty."

Thornton nodded and looked at the clerk. "Please enter a plea of not guilty. You may all be seated." He put on his glasses then studied something on his desk. "Regarding imposition of bail…"

Gwen Chadbourne stood. "Your Honor, the defendant is accused of a violent capital crime. The State believes he is a danger to society and poses an unusually high risk for flight from this jurisdiction as evidenced by already having tried to flee to Canada. Additionally, he has no long-term ties to this community or to the state of Maine. Because we have no juvenile detention center, the State requests the defendant be held in the county jail without bail under SRS supervision." Chadbourne paused a moment. "Thank you, Your Honor." She smoothed her skirt and sat down.

The judge thought for a moment then looked at Buster. "Mr. Hurd."

Buster pushed back from the table and stood. He looked over his bifocals at Chadbourne then at the judge. "Your Honor, the killing of Leland Johnson was an act of self-defense and the defense of others in imminent danger from a man with a long history of violent abuse. Stringer has no criminal record whatsoever and we do not feel he is a danger to anyone. In addition, this is where he and his mother have chosen to live—a place they thought safe, where in fact they have a strong connection with a prominent member of the community, Mr. Francis Monroe. We request the boy be released in the custody of his mother and County Social Services and that he remain within the confines of Mr. Monroe's home until trial. Thank you, Your Honor."

Francis was aware of how shallow his breathing was. Kate seemed only to watch Stringer.

Before the judge could turn back to the prosecutor, Chadbourne was out of her seat. "Your Honor," she said, unable to contain her annoyance, "what the defense is asking for is absurd. *Both* the defendant's mother *and* Mr. Monroe were involved in the murder of Leland Johnson. How can they possibly think the court would allow—"

"Your Honor," Buster broke in sharply. "I see no evidence from the court that either Mrs. Johnson or Mr. Monroe stand accused in this matter or that they have been charged with any crime."

Chadbourne stepped hard on her shoe, grinding it into the wooden floor. "Your Honor!"

"That's enough," Judge Thornton said firmly. "Counsel, approach."

Bristling, Chadbourne stepped to the front of the bench and stood a good three feet away from Buster. The judge leaned forward and spoke in a stern voice. Francis strained to hear what he was saying, but couldn't. The courtroom was silent save for the whirr and intermittent squeak of the ceiling fan.

The judge motioned for the attorneys to step back, reached down, and pulled a heavy book from under his desk. Everyone waited as he opened it and silently read a passage. Chadbourne and Buster remained standing.

Judge Thornton took his glasses off and set them on the open book. He looked at the defense table. "The court must consider the least restrictive conditions that will assure the defendant will appear at trial. Additionally, the public must be protected from the potential actions of the defendant. In the case of a minor, the defendant must be protected in terms of his constitutional rights and from any possibility of physical harm. Taking all of this into consideration, especially the extenuating circumstances of this case and the intense reaction of the community, I order the defendant remanded to the county jail in joint custody of the sheriff's department and the department of social services with generous visitation rights by the defendant's mother."

Buster raised his hand. "Your Honor, I must—"

Judge Thornton rapped his gavel on the bench. "Court's adjourned." As the judge left the bench, Lester got up from his chair and straightened his leg. He quickly limped to the door and opened it for the judge.

Three deputies surrounded Stringer. Buster took his hand and spoke to him. After a few moments the deputies pulled Stringer away and hurried him up the outer aisle. Kate raced over, trying to catch him, but she was too late. The heavy metal door slammed shut, the lock activating with a loud click.

Francis stepped into the center aisle and walked straight to the bench. He looked at the book the judge had read from, its edges coated with worn gold leaf. Francis squinted at the passage marked by the judge. It was from the Gospel according to John: "You shall know the truth and the truth shall set you free."

CHAPTER 18

Kate and Francis rode home in silence. Back at the bungalow Kate took off for a walk. When she returned to the house, Francis smelled the scent of cedar on her clothes and knew she had walked the path to Wagner's Point. Exhausted, she pulled off his wet field coat, dropped it on the hall floor, and went upstairs. Francis picked up the coat and hung it on its hook to dry. He stood in the hallway and listened. It sounded like Kate was crying into a pillow. As he climbed the stairs he fought off feelings of despair, trying to rally himself to support Kate but feeling as if he weighed a thousand pounds.

Kate was half-wrapped in blankets, her head covered with the comforter. Francis sat on the edge of the bed and gently placed his hand on her lower back. She flinched. He began slowly massaging her, sliding his hand over the smooth skin of her back and shoulders. At first the muscles along her spine were knotted tight but they gradually began to relax.

After a while, Francis lifted the comforter away from her face. Her long black hair, moist with tears, was matted against her face. He slid his fingers beneath the strands and lifted them from her cheek.

Kate curled into a fetal-like position.

Francis noticed Rachael's silver-handled hair brush on the Parisian dresser next to the bed. He lifted the brush from its tray. Intertwined with the fine bristles were strands of Rachael's hair. He turned back to Kate and studied the soft curve of her cheekbone and lips, the subtle cowlick at the side of her forehead where her hair curved upward like a star burst.

Francis gently ran the bristles through her hair, brushing it back against the white pillow. After a while, Kate's breathing quieted and she fell asleep. He must have also fallen asleep for the next thing he knew, Kate was sitting cross-legged on the bed next to him, her hand on his arm. He lifted his head, squinting against the hazy light. Through the bedroom windows he saw it was drizzling outside and a light fog surrounded the bungalow.

"What are we going to do?" Kate asked.

Francis slid the comforter off his legs and sat up. He had been in a deep sleep. "What do you mean?"

"How are we going to get Stringer another lawyer? A *good* one."

Francis was puzzled. "He has the best attorney around."

Kate crossed her arms against her chest and leaned back against the headboard. "He let them charge String as an adult. That's not being a good lawyer."

"It was the prosecutor's decision."

"She's a bitch, but Buster didn't fight worth a damn to get Stringer out of jail."

Francis stood and stepped to the window. "I know you're scared," he said, looking out at the mist. He turned back to Kate. "But I think we need to trust Buster. My gut says he knows what he's doing."

Kate pulled her knees tight to her chest. Her eyes welled with tears. "I feel so out of control. I want to stay sober. I want to save my son and I want to trust Mr. Hurd, but he seems like an old man who wants another moment of glory, like he had with that French logger he got off." Kate wiped tears from her cheek with her sleeve and looked at Francis. "I don't really think he's committed to Stringer like he would be to his own son."

Francis looked Kate in the eye. "Do you know about Buster's son?"

Kate shook her head. "I wasn't sure he had one." She lowered her head. "Help me, Francis. I don't know what to do."

"Kate, Buster lost his own son as a teenager and I believe saving Stringer is very near and dear to his heart."

Kate looked surprised.

"I think it would help if you spent some time with Buster and got to know each other a little. I think you'd understand why he's doing this."

Kate looked up. "Would he do that? Take time for me?"

"I'm sure he would."

Kate looked a bit hopeful. "You'll come with me?"

Francis squinted. "It would be better if you did this alone."

"Why?"

"Kate, we are truly in this together, but I think there are some things each of us has to do alone. Like your needing to leave for Canada and my needing to stay. Right now, I think it's best if you see what Buster is about for yourself, without my influence." Francis paused for a few moments. "I'd be happy to call him if you'd like."

Kate stared out the window. "No. I can call him myself."

Francis stepped into the doorway. "All right. The keys to the car are on the phone stand."

Francis walked downstairs into the kitchen and leaned against the cook stove, his palms flat on the cold black iron. He closed his eyes.

After a few minutes he heard Kate descend the staircase and phone the hotel where Buster was staying. She made arrangements to meet him in the hotel coffee shop.

Francis turned from the stove. "I'll be waiting when you get back."

She looked at him, searched his face then turned and walked outside. Through the kitchen window he watched the lights of the Malibu disappear into the fog.

Francis pulled on a sweatshirt and walked down to Kasa's. He found her putting up red-slatted snow fencing along her garden at the side of the road.

Kasa straightened when she saw him.

Francis leaned against the fence. "May I ask you something, Kasa?"

"Of course." She pulled off her gloves, set them on the edge of the wheelbarrow then sat on a roll of snow fence. "Sit down."

Francis sat next to her. "Kate's on her way to the hotel to talk with our attorney, Buster Hurd. She wanted me to go with her, but I said she should go alone."

Francis felt an uncomfortable chill spread over his back. "Kasa, I never felt like I was there for Rachael the way I wanted to be. I desperately want to be here for Kate, but I think it's best she talks with Buster alone. But I also don't want her to feel I'm abandoning her."

Kasa reached down beside her leg, grasped a strand of fence wire between her fingers and twisted the sharp ends away from where they had broken her thinning skin. Light fog drifted silently past them.

"The night the Germans came to our town I had just turned sixteen. I was terrified. At the train station, SS soldiers herded us into boxcars that smelled of animals. There were smears of excrement on the floor and walls. They jammed us in so close we had to ride all night standing up pressed against each other. In the morning we arrived at a cold, miserable work camp exhausted and hungry.

"Winter soon settled in. In the coming months, many women and children died. Most of us who survived learned we had no one to depend upon but ourselves." She paused. "Francis, you have not abandoned this woman you love. You're giving her a precious gift of learning how to save herself. And I suspect she is giving you the same gift in return."

Francis nodded. "You're right, but it's hard to hold back when you love someone."

"I know. It's a delicate balance, but it's the right thing to do. It's also a matter of respect. Just as when Rachael wouldn't take chemotherapy. I held back then too."

Francis looked at her, surprised. "But you helped her make those herbal remedies. You were with her every day."

"And at night I prayed she would let the doctors treat her. All I could do was help her in ways she would allow. Many nights I cried for Rachael, feeling unable to adequately help, knowing she was dying."

Francis leaned forward and slid his hand over Kasa's. "I never realized."

"Things are usually not quite as they appear. You know this. I have seen your paintings." Kasa straightened her back. "Well, my friend, back to work. Snow will soon fly." Kasa put her hands on her knees and pushed herself up off the roll of fence.

Francis stood. "Thank you." He walked around the edge of the garden to the road then turned back to her. "Before she died, my grandmother told me you were the wisest woman she had ever known. She was right."

Kasa looked uncomfortable. "Kate's running to Canada wasn't such a good idea."

"She would've gone anyway. She needed to at least try."

Kasa nodded, picked her gloves up from the wheelbarrow, and went back to work. Francis said good-bye and headed to the bungalow where he set up his easel by the front door and began to paint. Black lines against a gray sky; buildings lining Main Street leading to the water; a trio of seagulls circling over the harbormaster's shack. He leaned in close, painting tight lines from the edges of the canvas toward the center. After a flurry of work, he stood and observed his work. Then he sat down again and picked up a fine, pointed brush. He drew Stringer's head and shoulders in front of a prison window, surrounded by the bricks, mortar, and steel of Sheriff McNeal's jail. Francis felt the crushing pressure on Stringer.

A short while later, Francis heard the Malibu pull up outside. He stepped to the window and wiped a layer of moisture from the glass. For a minute or so Kate sat hunched over the steering wheel, staring at the sea. Then she got out, pulled her collar around her chin, and walked toward the cliff. Francis was concerned as he watched her fade into the fog.

He hurried outside where the wind howled around the corner of the bungalow, whistling through the thin upper branches of the pine. The air was damp and cold and made the muscles of his injured leg ache. Light rain froze against his face. He lowered his head and walked down the path toward the cliff.

Instinctively he stopped a few feet from the edge. Hearing Kate's voice coming from the rocks below, he descended the cliff steps, stopping half way down on a cold stone. He cupped his hands behind his ears and listened to her song mingled with the voices of the wind.

There was a sharp change in the air; a colder, biting wind snaked along the cliff from the north. Francis watched Kate turn toward him on the stairs below, ice crystals suspended in her hair. Fine snow flurries swirled about her. Her face seemed different, her eyes calmer. She was extraordinarily beautiful.

Kate stepped closer. Francis glanced down at waves crashing against the rocks then gave her his hand. "Be careful. It's very slippery."

Kate hugged the black cliff wall; she spoke softly, deliberately. "I need to tell you something." She looked deep into his eyes. "It's hard for me to talk about but…" She paused. "I'm falling in love with you. I think it started the day we met. You were so kind."

Kate looked down at the rising sea. "I swore if I ever escaped Leland, I'd never be with a man again." She looked at Francis, a subtle smile cracking the corner of her mouth. "Then *you* came along."

Francis felt a tremendous rush of warmth inside. He reached out and wiped snowflakes from Kate's cheek. She was shivering.

"You're wonderful," he said, smiling. "Perhaps we could move up to where it's a bit safer? And warmer?"

Kate nodded. "Sure."

Francis took Kate's hand and led her back to the bungalow. Inside, they pulled off wet boots, socks, and jackets. Francis led her to the small parlor next to his studio, wiping away cobwebs strung in the doorway. He motioned for Kate to sit on the love seat in front of a woodstove. He lifted a patchwork quilt from the arm of a chair and wrapped it around her shoulders. He carefully tucked the ends in around her bare feet. She curled up beneath the quilt as Francis knelt in front of the stove and opened the creaky iron door.

"First fire of the season," he said, reaching into the dusty wood box. He crisscrossed sticks of dry kindling over tightly crumpled newspaper and, without looking, pulled a long match from a tin on the wall and dragged it across the side of the stove. Pieces of driftwood and fine-split maple snapped to life, enveloped by bright yellow flames.

Francis sat on the floor beside Kate. "You and Buster must've had quite a talk."

"We did."

Francis leaned on the edge of the love seat next to her. "Did he tell you about his son?"

"Yes."

They watched flames lick their way up onto the larger pieces of wood. The first warmth of the fire spread across the room.

Kate pulled the quilt around her shoulders. "Can you imagine finding your son like that?" She lowered her head onto her knees and stared into the firebox. "Buster said he saw where Travis tried to claw his way out of the ravine. His fingertips were—" She fell silent for a few moments then continued.

"Buster told me he feels like Stringer is in *his* ravine, that he needs all of our help if he's to get out." Kate's jaw began to quiver. She wiped her eyes with the edge of the comforter. "He thanked me for letting him help my son. Hopes it might end the torture he's suffered for the last thirty years." Kate put her hand on Francis's shoulder.

Francis closed the door of the stove then sat watching flames lick the inside of the glass. "Human beings," he said after a while, "we want to be better than everybody else, yet deep inside, we have a need to be kind, to help take care of each other." Francis shook his head. "Ironically, it was Rachael who taught me this. She hated goody-two-shoes and gratuitous people who did nice things for others. They drove her crazy. She liked her life and the people in it to have a hardened edge. But she suffered for not letting people in, by not letting herself be very kind much of the time. It's taken me a long time to admit I didn't like that about her."

Francis looked at Kate. "You're different. You've had to be tough to survive, but you're vulnerable at the same time."

"You've helped me discover some things about myself. And talking to Buster made me feel lucky that at least my son's still alive. Though I know Buster's really worried about Stringer."

Francis sat back a bit. "Did he tell you anything new?"

"That psychologist, Dr. Hardy, came up from Portland last night. He asked Stringer a lot of questions about his and Leland's past. Stringer closed down and wouldn't talk to the guy much." Kate paused. "I want him to leave Stringer alone, but Buster says Stringer has got to open up, especially about things the psychologist thinks may have happened with Leland."

Francis looked at Kate. "What kind of things?"

"I'm not sure, exactly." Kate frowned and looked away. "I didn't like what he was insinuating."

"What did he say?"

Kate's lips became terse, her forehead tightening into a frown. "He thinks Leland may have abused Stringer. Sexually. Said he's seen it before."

Francis felt his stomach tighten. Though the house had warmed, he felt an unsettling chill move up his spine.

CHAPTER 19

Buster called early the next morning and said Stringer was so angry and closed down he wouldn't talk with him. He also made it clear that whatever nerve Dr. Hardy had touched, Stringer's talking about it would help reveal the extent of Leland's pathology and that would most likely be key to Stringer's defense. Kate and Francis left for the jail as soon as they could. Once there, Francis followed Kate down the dark hallway to Stringer's cell where they found him sitting backwards on a wooden chair, his face against the iron bars over the window.

Ralph, one of the deputies, walked past Kate and rapped a key on the bars, startling Stringer. "Got a visitor, kid."

Stringer glanced over his shoulder, his forehead indented from the pressure of the bars. He turned back to the window.

Ralph opened the steel lock and swung the door open. Kate hesitated. Francis took her hands in his and squeezed them. "You can do this," he whispered.

Kate stepped inside the cell.

Ralph turned to Francis. "Are you going in?"

Francis looked at Kate who nodded. Ralph closed the creaky door behind them, locked it, and walked away. Kate stood looking at her son, trying to hide the fact that she was trembling. Stringer didn't move.

Francis took a step forward and slid his hand over Kate's shoulder. She reached up and put her hand over his. She took a deep breath and moved to the window. "String…"

Stringer's shoulders tightened.

Kate reached out and gingerly touched him.

He flinched. "Go away."

Kate left her hand on his shoulder.

Stringer shrugged, trying to shake off her hand. "Leave me alone."

"I love you, String." Kate's voice was serious but loving. "I need to talk to you."

Stringer wheeled around, stumbling off the chair onto the floor. His face was swollen but the rest of his body appeared thinner. He looked at Kate. "Talk about what? How they're going to execute me?"

Kate flinched but held steady. "We need to talk about what happened with you and Leland."

"Leave me alone!" Stringer crouched in a heap against the wall and covered his head with his hands. Kate knelt and put her arms around him. Stringer pushed her off. She reached out again. He glared at her, pushing her so hard she fell back against the metal bed.

"Stringer—" Francis said, stepping over to Kate.

She held up her hand. "Please go home."

"You could get hurt," Francis said.

Kate glared at him. "Leave me alone with my son."

Francis stepped back as Ralph appeared from the shadows. He unlocked the door and Francis walked down the hallway to the sheriff's office. He heard Stringer yelling at Kate again. He made himself keep walking, past Ralph who was sitting at the desk under the gold shield on the wall. "Would you call me when she's ready to come home?" Francis said as he passed.

Ralph nodded. "Sure, Mr. Monroe."

"Thank you." Outside, Francis climbed into the Malibu and sat with his head and his hands on the steering wheel. He started to cry. After a few minutes he wiped his eyes, started the engine, and drove to Moses' Garage. He walked into the small office, which was cluttered with boxes of engine gaskets, spark plugs, and black rubber fan belts hanging on the wall. Used carburetors and other oil-stained gizmos held down piles of parts catalogs and old work orders stacked all over the place. Air from an oscillating fan wired to an overhead water pipe rhythmically blew back the soiled pages of the catalogs.

Pete Moses was at the counter wrestling with a windshield wiper replacement. He looked up at Francis. "Hi, Mr. Monroe."

"Hi, Pete. Could you tell me when my Jeep will be fixed?"

Pete smiled. "Isn't that Malibu a hot rig? Got a 393 four-barrel under the hood. Didn't think you'd ever want the old Wagoneer back."

"Actually I'm kind of fond of the Jeep."

Pete set the wiper blade on the counter and pushed open a grease-laden door leading to the service bays. "Sealy, when's Mr. Monroe's Jeep going to be done?"

A young man's head popped out from under the hood of a rusty Ford Bronco. "Just waitin' on them steering parts. Ought to be in next week. First set we got wasn't the right ones." The man's head disappeared back under the hood.

Pete let the door swing shut. "You heard the man. Another week."

"All right. Please call me as soon as it's ready."

"Will do."

Francis started to walk out.

"Real bucket a shit them California folks got themselves into, huh?"

Francis stopped at the door.

Pete spat a wad of chew into a dented steel wastebasket at the side of the counter. "Paper said they's gonna start drawin' a jury here pretty quick. Sure hope he gets a fair trial, being from away and all."

Francis let go of the doorknob and stepped back to the counter. He placed both hands on the deeply worn wood and leaned toward Pete. "He'd *better* get a fair trial, Pete."

Looking surprised, Pete backed up a half-step. "Yes sir, Mr. Monroe."

Francis left without saying another word. When he got home, he milled around the bungalow then walked to the cliff. He kicked pieces of flaking shale into the surf below then went back inside. He hadn't felt this much anger and frustration for a very long time. He felt kind of like he had when his father had chastised him on weekends for wanting to paint: incompetent, insignificant, unable to get his bearings.

Francis sat on a stool in front of his easel. He painted hard, forcing thick, dark layers of paint onto the canvas. He painted till well after dark when his arm was so sore he had to stop. It was after ten when the phone rang. He rushed to answer it.

"Mr. Monroe? Ralph Simonds."

"Yes, Ralph."

"I had to ask Mrs. Johnson to leave a couple hours ago. Sheriff's orders. She didn't want me to call you like I said I would, but on my rounds just now I saw she's been sitting outside against the front of the building. It's pretty cold out tonight and she doesn't have a very heavy coat on. I tried to give her one, but she said she was okay and was going to stay till visiting hours tomorrow morning. She had a pretty rough time with the kid. Probably wouldn't be too good if the sheriff found her out there."

Francis gripped the phone. "I don't care about the sheriff, but she'll freeze out there. I'll be right down."

"Good."

"Ralph...Thanks."

"It's okay."

Francis hung up then stood in the hallway thinking. He picked up the phone book, found a number, and dialed.

"I'd like a large cheese—half-mushroom, half-pepperoni. Can you make it soon? Thanks."

Francis hung up and opened the hall closet. Hanging there was one of Rachael's favorite coats: English wool lined with soft, cream-colored sheepskin. He ran his hands up inside the coat and lifted it to his face. He breathed deeply, smelling the faint, lingering scent of French perfume. He took the coat off its hanger and folded it over his arm. Then he walked into the parlor, gathered up the quilt he had wrapped around Kate that morning, and left for town.

He drove straight to the jail and parked in one of the visitor spots. Jacket and blanket in hand, he found Kate sitting against the granite foundation in the shadow of some shrubbery. He walked over and knelt down in front of her. She was shivering.

She lifted her head from her knees and looked at Francis. He slid the sheepskin coat around her back then wrapped the quilt around her legs. "I'll be back in a few minutes."

Kate looked a bit puzzled as Francis took off. He drove to the pizza shop, picked up his order, and drove back to the jail. He sat back down beside Kate and put the pizza box on his lap. "Mushroom or pepperoni?" he asked, opening the box. He saw Kate's eyes brighten as she caught a whiff of the fresh dough. "Mushroom."

He placed a steaming slice onto a paper plate and slid it onto her lap. He pulled a napkin out of his pocket and handed it to her as she devoured the first slice and motioned for another. They sat on the cold cement and ate half the pie before either spoke again.

Francis licked the spicy sauce from his lips. "So how's it going?"

Kate swallowed the last of her piece and wiped her mouth. "Just great," she said, managing a grin.

"Good," Francis said. He smiled then started to chuckle. "Things are going great for me lately too."

They looked at each other. Exhausted and scared, they started to laugh.

Francis put his arm around her and they leaned back against the granite foundation. "So did Stringer say *anything?*"

"Except for swearing at me, no."

"Are you really going to stay here until he talks?"

"What else can I do? It isn't easy, but I've always found a way to reach him, especially when he gets this defensive."

Francis pulled the quilt over them and they rested against each other. The next thing they knew, a pair of headlights flashed across the parking lot illuminating them. Francis put his hand up to shield their eyes from the light. The car pulled to a halt in front of them. The driver's door opened, its gold badge reflecting light from a street lamp.

A large figure climbed out. "What the hell's going on here?"

Sheriff McNeal lumbered toward them. Francis sat upright. Kate threw off the quilt and came up off the ground. "I'm waiting to see my son as soon as your damn jail opens up."

McNeal stopped a few feet from Kate, switching his wad of tobacco from one cheek to another. "You can't be hangin' around outside like this. This is county property."

"The hell I can't. This is *public* property."

McNeal took another step toward Kate. Francis quickly stood.

"You listen here, little missy, this is *my* jail and I make the rules. Now you get outta here or I'll—"

"Or you'll *what?*" Kate got right in McNeal's face. "You'll call one of your deputies to come throw me off? Do your dirty work for you?"

The veins running up McNeal's neck engorged. His face darkened. "Don't you mouth off to me, you little bitch. I'm the sheriff around here and—"

Kate moved closer to McNeal, within inches of his big face. "You're a fat, evil shit sheriff, and you're trying to get my son hanged."

McNeal's eyes dilated. He opened his mouth but didn't speak. Francis was stunned.

Kate pointed her finger at McNeal's face and gritted her teeth, almost hissing at him. "I brought that boy into the world and nothing, not you, not your goddamn hick county—*nothing*—is going to keep me from helping him. You got it, Sheriff?"

For a few seconds there was silence; then McNeal took a step back onto the pavement. He spat a slimy wad of tobacco into the shrubbery, turned, and walked back to his cruiser. He sped out of the parking lot, tires squealing as he tore up Main Street.

Francis watched the street, half thinking McNeal would return. But there was only the crisp silence of an early winter night.

Francis turned to Kate. Her face had softened and she was shaking. He wrapped his arms around her and kissed her on the forehead. "That was amazing. Nobody talks to McNeal like that."

Kate put her hands on his chest. "Could you tell I was scared shitless?"

He shook his head. "Absolutely not."

"Good," she said. Then they sat back down and she nestled her head under his chin. "Hopefully that will keep him out of our hair for tonight."

Francis smiled. "Oh, I think it will."

Leaning against the granite foundation of the old brick edifice, they held each other, watching moonlit clouds pass over the sleeping town.

Shortly after the Congregational Church bell rang at two a.m., the front door of the sheriff's office swung open. Ralph rushed out onto the steps. "Mrs. Johnson—something's wrong with Stringer!"

Kate tore out of Francis's arms, running to the front of the building and up the stairs.

CHAPTER 20

"What's the matter?" Kate demanded as Francis reached the top of the stairs behind her.

Ralph's eyes were wide. "He's throwing up. Blood. In the corner of the cell."

"Shit," Kate said, rushing past Ralph. "Ulcers."

Ralph and Francis followed her down the hallway.

"Open this thing," Kate said, grabbing the bars with both hands.

Ralph pushed a large metal key into the lock and turned it. Kate ran to Stringer, who was slumped against the wall in the corner. A small stream of red-tinged fluid had found its way to the drain in the center of the cement floor.

"Oh, baby," Kate said, gently pulling his head onto her lap. Stringer looked awful. He tried to lift his head but vomited on Kate's leg. She didn't flinch, just carefully wiped the vomit from his face with the sleeve of the sheepskin coat. "Get me a towel," she said in a steady voice.

Ralph disappeared down the hallway and quickly returned with a handful of towels. "Is he all right? Should I call an ambulance?"

Kate put her hand up. Francis turned to Ralph. "Hold on. She knows what she's doing."

Kate sat back against the brick wall, stroking Stringer's head. She slid her arms out of the coat and laid the soft lining around him. After comforting him for a minute, she spoke to Francis. "He's had bleeding ulcers before. He needs

199

medicine: Pepsid twenty milligrams twice a day and a week's worth of Carafate. Twenty-eight pills. And don't give him any caffeine."

Ralph took a step into the cell. "Mrs. Johnson, you can't just prescribe medicine for your son."

Kate looked up at Ralph, motioning with her finger for him to come close. Ralph leaned toward her.

"I know what my son needs and he needs it now. If you don't want to see him bleed to death on *your* shift, you'd better get what I asked. And I don't really give a shit how you get it."

Ralph straightened and stepped backwards. "I'll see what I can do."

Francis glared at Ralph, who locked the cell door and disappeared. Francis crouched beside Kate and touched Stringer's head.

Stringer opened his eyes for a moment, looked at Francis then let his head relax back onto his mother's lap.

Francis leaned toward Kate and whispered. "Are you sure he shouldn't go to the hospital?"

"I can take care of him as long as he doesn't get worse."

A few minutes later, Ralph came back down the hallway. "Doc's coming over from the hospital."

Francis nodded. The three of them sat huddled together in the corner of the cell and waited. The cement floor was cold and clammy. Above Kate and Stringer, Wyeth's "Barracoon" hung from the metal hook.

A short time later Francis heard Charlie speak to someone out in the sheriff's office. Soon Ralph came down the hall with Dr. Conklin and let him into the cell. Francis backed away.

"Let's get him over onto the bed," Dr. Conklin said, stepping over the red vomitous on the floor.

Kate helped Stringer onto the cot where he lay on his side, listless. Dr. Conklin leaned over, examined the bruise on Stringer's forehead, listened to his lungs, and palpated the four quadrants of his abdomen. Stringer winced when he touched his stomach.

Dr. Conklin turned to Kate. "He's had stomach ulcers before?"

"Twice."

"He's obviously under a tremendous amount of stress." Dr. Conklin put his hand to his chin and looked down at Stringer and Kate. Then he turned to Ralph and Charlie. "He's certainly sick—acute gastritis, at the least. I think we should send him over to—"

"Doctor—" Kate interrupted. "I've been through this with him before. If he gets the right medicine and I can stay and take care of him, I think he'll be all right."

Francis frowned. Kate didn't take her eyes off Dr. Conklin, who thought for a few moments.

"I'm not totally comfortable with this, but seeing as the ER is just a mile away and Mrs. Johnson has experience with this—" He paused. "I'll give Stringer the medicine for his stomach and a sedative so he can get some rest." He turned to Charlie and Ralph. "He's totally exhausted and clearly hasn't been eating right." Anger rose in his voice. "He looks like hell. You should have called me before this."

"He looked fine a few hours ago," Ralph said nervously. "Just angry."

Dr. Conklin ignored him, opened his bag, and pulled out a bottle of pills and two syringes. "Get some more blankets and pillows in here. And a rollaway for his mom who will stay with him through the night."

Charlie straightened. "We can't do that, Doc. He's a *prisoner*—in here for murder."

Kate slid onto the cot, curved her hand around Stringer's head.

Dr. Conklin stared at Stringer's bruised forehead then at Charlie. "You know what, Charlie? This has all gone too far. The boy's sick. His mother stays for the night. That's it."

Charlie stepped into the cell. "Doc, I'm going to have to run this by—"

Dr. Conklin glared at Charlie. "The sheriff?" He took a step toward Charlie and looked him straight in the eye. "Who's in charge here, Charlie?"

"Well, at the moment I am."

"Then make a decision. You'd think no one could blow their nose around here without the sheriff's okay." He shook his head. "Including me sometimes," he said under his breath.

Dr. Conklin turned to Kate. "Please undo his jumpsuit." Kate slid the orange garment down past Stringer's hip. Francis looked at Stringer's prominent hip bone. He was no longer the chubby, agile bear in baggy pants he'd watched scramble over the rocks of Wagner's Point.

Stringer didn't move as Dr. Conklin injected medicine into his thigh. Then he gave Stringer a couple of pills and put his instruments back in his bag. "He should rest for a few hours now," he said to Kate. "If he vomits again or starts any bright red bleeding, call me immediately and we'll get him to the ER. I'm on call all night."

"Thank you," Kate said, watching Stringer.

"You're welcome."

Dr. Conklin walked past Ralph and Charlie without saying another word. Ralph locked the cell door and he and Charlie left.

Francis watched as Kate stroked Stringer's hair, gently running her hand over the scar tissue on his head. Francis followed the curves of Kate's body. It didn't seem possible, but she grew increasingly beautiful the more time they spent together.

In the dim light, beneath the black woman's figure, Kate rubbed Stringer's back.

After a while, Francis spoke. "Do you want me to stay?"

"No. We'll be okay. Go home and get some sleep."

"All right." Francis held his hand against her cheek then leaned over and kissed Stringer's head. "I love you both."

Stringer's hand slid from under the blankets and touched Francis's arm. He took Stringer's hand and gently squeezed it.

"Thank you, Francis," Kate said, quietly. "For everything."

Francis shook his head. "Thank you for letting me into your lives. Much better days are going to come."

Francis stepped to the door and rattled the lock. Charlie let him out then followed after him. "Mr. Monroe," he said as Francis headed for the front door.

Francis paused.

Charlie shifted from one foot to another. "You remember when you first came to our house to help Nathan? He hadn't spoken to anyone in months."

"Yes."

"The day he started to come around was the day you brought an easel for him. You set it up in the corner of his room with some finger paints and just left them there. He stayed up half the night playing with it. Sandy and I hadn't seen him that happy in years."

Charlie fell silent. Francis waited.

"Well I thought it might help this Stringer kid if he could paint. He's just shriveling up in there."

Francis watched Charlie's face, saw the pain in his eyes. After a few moments, Francis nodded. "That's a good idea, Charlie."

Francis extended his hand. Charlie, surprised by the gesture, shook it. "Thank you, Mr. Monroe." Charlie looked Francis in the eye for the first time in a while. "This has been awful tough for all of us."

CHAPTER 21

Francis drove home slowly. Thick clouds gathered from the west, darkening the early winter sky. The Portland radio station was forecasting snow flurries overnight. He slowed as he passed Kasa's. All was quiet.

Francis walked into the bungalow and lit a fire in the woodstove. In the kitchen, he found a fresh loaf of homemade oatmeal bread, Kasa's specialty. He picked it up, enjoying the warm texture of the loaf between his hands. Then he walked into the studio and lit the candle in the whaler's lamp. He pulled out a virgin canvas, picked up a brush and a tube of black paint.

He painted furiously—a portrait of the Empire State Building from a bird's eye perspective. He selected a fine round brush and painted in the tall, curved-top fence that kept people from jumping off the observation deck 102 floors above the street. Behind the fence he painted the figure of a boy, his hands—painted in bright red—clutching the iron bars. He placed thin white lines and tiny square dots of yellow on the street far below. For several hours Francis worked the canvas; squinting, cocking his head to one side or another, frequently holding his breath as he leaned in and painted fine details. In the wee hours of morning, he finally set aside his brushes, laid down on the cot, and fell asleep.

At seven Francis was startled by the phone ringing in the hallway. He sat up and heard Buster's voice on the answering machine. He rushed into the hall and snatched the receiver off its cradle. "Hello? Buster?"

"Yes. I was calling to tell you the judge has given us a tight schedule for the pre-trial proceedings. I need to meet with you, Kate, and Stringer this afternoon at the jail. We must go over things and get our witness list together."

"Did you know Stringer is sick? Bleeding ulcers."

"No. Is he getting proper medical attention?"

"Yes. A doctor came from the hospital last night and gave him medicine. After some argument, they let Kate stay with him last night."

"Really?"

"Yes. Kate wanted to stay and take care of him at the jail instead of going to the hospital. I think she's crazy."

Francis heard Buster chuckle. "No, she's not. I know she cares deeply, but in part I think she's learning to play the game."

"What game?"

"The *PR* game."

"Well, the deputies weren't very happy about it, but the doctor ordered it."

"That's a good sign, though it's probably because the sheriff's gone up north on a moose hunt. Anyway, we'll meet at one-thirty at the jail. Think about anyone that might be able to help him out: character witnesses, that sort of thing."

After they rang off, Francis walked outside where fine flurries danced in the air. He stretched his arms over his head and took in a long breath. The soreness in his chest was much better. For a few moments he felt invigorated, even hopeful.

He walked back inside, collected Stringer's painting materials, including the easel, and put them in the trunk of the Malibu. He phoned the sheriff's office and spoke with Charlie, who said it would be okay to bring the art supplies. He said they'd put a rollaway cot in the cell for Kate and that they'd both slept most of the night.

Francis walked into the kitchen, cut two generous slices of Kasa's bread, and made a ham sandwich for Kate then drove to town through an intensifying snow fall. At the jail, he took out the painting supplies and the lunch bag and walked up the steps to the sheriff's department's door. It was locked. He set the easel down and knocked on the heavy glass.

Charlie came and opened the door. "Come in," he said. "It looks like Christmas out there."

Francis stepped inside, the sleeves of his dark denim coat darkening with melting snowflakes.

Charlie glanced at the art supplies. "Stringer will be glad to see you." He picked up a paddle-like device. "Sorry, I've got to check these things for weapons."

Charlie quickly ran the metal detector up over the easel and other art supplies.

"Okay. Go ahead."

Francis took his things and walked down the hallway. He stopped when he saw Kate curled around Stringer on the metal cot.

Kate lifted her head and looked at Francis. Without disturbing Stringer, she slid from under the coat and stepped silently across the floor. She reached between the bars and took Francis's hands. "I'm so glad to see you."

Charlie unlocked the door. Francis stepped inside and set the easel down.

Kate wrapped her arms around Francis's neck and hugged him. He took her into his arms and held her tightly. "How are you two?"

"Better," Kate whispered. "A nurse came and gave him another shot this morning. He's still sleeping." She looked at the things Francis had brought. "These are great. Maybe painting will help get his mind off this place."

"Charlie suggested it."

Kate looked surprised.

"He's trying to help," Francis added. He leaned the easel against the wall. "How's his stomach?"

"He hasn't thrown up since the doctor gave him the medicine."

"Good."

"Did Buster call you about meeting this afternoon?" Kate asked.

"Yes. He said he'll meet us here at one-thirty."

"Do you mind if I come out to the house to shower beforehand?" Kate raised her gaze to his as she spoke. Morning sunlight coming through the small square window caught her smooth cheek.

"Of course not."

Kate saw the paper bag. "What's this?"

"Something for you."

She opened the bag, pulled out the sandwich, and unwrapped it, revealing Kasa's homemade bread. Kate smiled and kissed him on the lips. "Thank you."

For a few moments they looked out the window together. Fine snow was falling through the bare branches of the maples lining Main Street.

"I haven't seen snow in a long time, since I was a girl in Montana. It's beautiful."

"Yes," Francis replied. He turned away from the window. "Do you want to come home with me now, while Stringer rests?"

Kate looked at Stringer, who was sound asleep. "Yes, if I can be back here by noon. I don't want to leave him alone for long." Kate tucked the sheepskin coat around him and kissed his forehead.

Back at the bungalow, Kate took a long, hot shower. Upstairs, Francis found a bottle of Parisian oil Rachael used to smooth her skin after showering. He descended the staircase and placed the bottle on the edge of the white pedestal sink in the bathroom. Waves of steam rolled out into the hall. It smelled of Kate. He stood in the doorway watching Kate's thin figure move behind the frosted glass. Then he quietly closed the door.

Francis tidied up the kitchen then pulled fresh clothes from the dryer in the laundry room and folded them into several piles. He pulled off his sweatpants and dropped them in the wicker hamper on top of which he noticed a pair of Kate's underwear protruding from a pile of towels. He held the soft cotton up to his face.

The bathroom door opened. Francis stood motionless in the sunlit laundry room as he listened to Kate's footsteps moving toward the kitchen. A towel held around her waist, she stepped into the light and stood in the ante way, bare breasted, Rachael's aromatic oil evaporating from her skin. She looked at Francis, her face filled with shyness and passion.

For a few moments they gazed at each other.

Kate walked toward him, letting the thick white towel slide off her hips onto the floor. Francis's eyes feasted on the beauty of her body—her slender legs, her slightly upturned nipples, the fine, dark hair of her mons.

Kate slid into Francis's arms and kissed him. He ran his hands down her back and over her buttocks. Kate slid her tongue in and out of his mouth, her breasts rising against his chest. He swung his arm across the top of the dryer, sending piles of clean linens to the floor. He knelt and licked Kate's nipples, drawing a breast into his mouth. They sunk to the floor on top of the warm laundry. Kate slid off his pants then lay on her back and pulled Francis toward her. Francis looked at her navel, her abdomen, the dark skin surrounding her nipples.

Kate fondled his penis then gently slid it inside of her. Francis penetrated deeply for a few moments then Kate rolled on top, keeping him inside of her. With her hands on his chest, she rocked her pelvis over his. As their breathing intensified, she threw her head back and cried out. Francis held her smooth bottom tight in his hands, watching her breasts move above him.

Kate panted as she reached orgasm. Francis felt her powerful contractions then felt her warm fluid on his thigh. Again she climaxed, her fine sweat mixing with Rachael's Parisian oil. Francis came to orgasm so powerfully he had to calm Kate's rhythm. Her breathing quieted and her pelvis relaxed against his. She leaned forward, her breasts falling against his cheeks.

They lay there surrounded by soft, warm linen. After a while, Kate sat back against the dryer and curled her hair behind her ear. "Wow," she said. "I so needed that."

Francis smiled. "You're wonderful. And sexy as hell."

Kate looked embarrassed then turned more serious. "That was wonderful, but I feel guilty with Stringer sitting in jail."

"I know. I feel it too." Francis pulled a terry towel from the pile and slid it around her shoulders. "Maybe this is part of how we get through this. Together." Francis leaned forward and kissed her forehead. "I have so wanted to make love to you."

Kate looked into his eyes. "Are you really going to stay with me through this? No matter what happens?"

Francis nodded. "No matter what. Kate, I need you at least as much as you need me."

Kate's eyes filled with tears.

CHAPTER 22

Kate and Francis held hands on the way to the jail. The sun's warmth had melted the dusting of snow; the sky over the ocean was azure and cloudless.

When they arrived, Ralph ran the metal detector over them and showed them to a small conference room next to the sheriff's office. Buster was fixing himself a cup of coffee. Stringer sat at the end of a marred oak table; his hands were free, his ankles shackled. His expression brightened when Kate and Francis walked in.

Kate rushed over and wrapped her arms around Stringer. "You look much better."

"I feel better. The medicine helped. And I was glad you were here."

Kate smiled and ran her hands over his. "It's going to be okay, String. I know it."

Francis touched Stringer's shoulder. "Hi there."

He shook Francis's hand. "Is Mom doing okay?"

Francis nodded. "Yes."

"Good morning," Buster said, walking over to the table. He sat in a captain's chair across from Stringer. "We have a lot of work to do, so let's get started."

Francis and Kate sat on either side of Stringer. Ralph stepped into the doorway. "I'm going to shut this door. If you need anything, I'll be at the desk."

Buster nodded. "Thank you, deputy." He turned back to the table. "First of all, I need to tell you a few things." He took off his bifocals and set them on the table.

"This is my last trial. I'm old and tired and diabetes is getting the best of me. I didn't want another trial, but the truth is I *need* to try this case."

Stringer turned to Kate then Francis. "Did you know about his son, Travis?"

Kate and Francis nodded.

Buster turned to Stringer. "Stringer, you've got a vicious drunk trying to kill you. Not by running you off the road, but by slow torture, even though he's dead. You, however, have a chance for a good life. A damn good chance."

Francis nodded. Buster had everyone's attention.

"Now, there're a couple of things you need to know about a murder trial. To paraphrase our political colleagues, 'It's the jury, stupid.' That's why drawing the jury is so important. There're a lot of good people around here and we've got to get some sympathetic ears into that jury box. And that's for me to worry about.

"As far as the stuff you read about how juries behave— whether it's a good sign if they look at you or not—forget all that. Every one of them is a private citizen who would rather be out fishing, drinking coffee at Dunkin Donuts, watching TV, anything but sitting in those seats judging another person. Look at the people of the jury as regular human beings just as you are. Look at them with compassion. It'll help you get through this."

Buster paused, took two swigs of coffee, and set his mug back down. "Though I'm gradually running outta gas, I'm good at what I do—done it for nearly fifty years. Still, I don't have all the answers, certainly not all the *right* answers. In part, my job is to figure out how to win Stringer's freedom as we go along, to stay on top of the complex ebb and flow in the courtroom."

Something slammed in the sheriff's office next door. Francis glanced up, felt his pulse quicken. He hoped that asshole McNeal wasn't back from his hunting trip.

"Trials develop tides of their own," Buster continued. "Sometimes things roll along smoothly and look pretty good. The next minute, the next witness can cause a rip tide that'll knock you over. Whatever happens, you must keep your feet on the floor, your heads on your shoulders. Juries look favorably on competent defendants and reasonable support people."

Buster turned to Kate. "This may be particularly hard for you, Kate. During every good and bad moment of this trial, Stringer is your son, your flesh and blood. There's no distance for you. I know it's hard, but if you feel like you're going to lose it, like you want to shoot the judge or the prosecutor—or me—excuse yourself. Leave the courtroom quietly. Go outside and take a walk, throw up, pound on a wall—whatever—just do it away from the eyes and ears of the judge, jury, and the media."

Kate nodded.

Buster took another swig of coffee. "Lastly, I've listed Jacob as co-counsel on this case. He's the smartest attorney I've ever known. This trial is going to hinge on treacherous issues and I may need him. He said he'll be here in a few hours if I call."

Kate raised a finger. "What do you mean by treacherous issues?"

Buster twirled his glasses on a yellow legal pad. "I guess I'm old-fashioned, but I still believe that in a case of this magnitude, the truth, if it's on your side, will lead you to victory. The truth, however, is like a honed hunting arrow—razor sharp blades pointing in different directions. The faster it flies, the deeper it penetrates. It can drain a life-threatening infection or it can turn in the slightest wind, slice through a vital organ, and bring death."

Buster pushed back his suit coat. His cheeks tightened. "A murder trial should be a relentless process of revealing the truth, and the truth is usually stubborn and tough to get at, often festering beneath the surface of what actually goes on in the courtroom. You pick at it from different angles. It smells and disgusts and hurts like hell before relief finally comes." Buster squinted, staring at the three of them. "Relief only comes if the truth is on your side. And I believe in this case it's on ours."

Buster put his bifocals back on and peered over the rims. "Treat the truth with great respect. In the final measure, it's the only worthy weapon we have, and the prosecution is well armed."

He cleared his throat and picked up a file folder. "I think our strategy should be the just and necessary defense of Stringer's life and the life of a family member in imminent danger." Buster looked at Francis. "You don't qualify under the family defense statute, but we'll claim he was also preventing your attempted murder."

Buster looked at Kate and Stringer. "In the face of a lifetime of abuse from Leland, we can build a strong defense. Stringer and I had a good talk this morning. He told me about things Leland made him do with guns when he was little."

Stringer blushed and looked down.

"I know this is tough, Stringer, but it's your life we're defending here. We've got to explore everything, use anything that can help."

Kate looked at Buster. "Leland forced String to shoot a pistol when he was five years old. He made him shoot rats and stray cats in the drainage ditches around LA. Most of the time Leland was drunk and crazy."

Stringer blushed again. Buster leaned toward Kate, his abdomen indented by the table edge. "Making a child that age fire a gun is a dangerous, reckless thing. But it's not shooting rats that I'm concerned about. It's the sexual things that are deplorable, the most damaging. They'll make the greatest impression; make the jury sit up and take notice. They'll supply the power we need to turn the tide in our direction."

Kate turned to Stringer. "*What* sexual things?"

Stringer looked away.

"*String?*"

"I'm sorry, I assumed you knew." Buster paused for a few moments. "Stringer knows how badly I feel about all this, but I think he also understands that at this juncture we have to deal with it head on." Buster looked at Stringer. "Would you like me to tell her, son?"

Stringer nodded.

Buster took hold of the edge of the table with both hands. "Stringer said his father never had sex with him, but he embarrassed the hell out of him; terrified him, really."

Kate slid her hand onto Stringer's forearm. "What did he do to you?"

Stringer nervously moved his legs, rattling the chains on the floor. He glanced at Buster. "You tell her."

"The most disturbing incident was when Leland made Stringer stand on a picnic bench in a park and take his pants off in front of other drunken men. He yelled at Stringer that he couldn't be his real son because he wasn't endowed well enough."

Buster shook his head. "He pulled on Stringer's penis to demonstrate to the men how short it was and it made him bleed. Stringer was in pain for a long time."

Francis recoiled at what he was hearing.

Buster continued. "I'm not sure that's the whole story, but that's as much as Stringer has told me."

Tears filled Kate's eyes. "My God." She put her trembling hands to Stringer's face and pulled him toward her. "How old were you?"

"Third grade," Stringer said hesitantly.

Kate held him and they both cried. Otherwise the room was silent.

After a few minutes, Kate turned to Buster. "That was the summer that bastard suddenly took Stringer to the mountains for a couple of weeks. I was too sick to stop him. When Stringer came back he had blood in his urine and it burned every time he peed. I took him to some shitty doctor Leland knew, who said he couldn't figured out what caused it."

Kate shook her head and looked at Stringer. "I'm so sorry. I had no idea." Kate's face tightened. "If that bastard was still alive, I'd kill him myself."

Francis leaned forward on the table. "Isn't that enough to show the jury what a monster Leland was? That Stringer had no choice but to shoot him?"

Buster thought for a few moments. "Judge Thornton's a fundamentalist, a fly fisherman who ties his own flies. He's exacting and tough. He'll probably instruct the jury that we all have choices to make; that Stringer had other, less deadly choices that day. That perhaps he *chose* to shoot and kill his father."

Francis felt rage rise inside of him. He looked at Buster. "That lunatic would have killed all of us. For God's sake, his knees were in my chest. He was trying to *kill* me with a butcher knife."

"It's not enough, Francis," Buster said. "The sexual abuse, making a child shoot a gun, are part of what will affect the tide of the case. But we need to carefully, methodically lead the jury through Leland's long-standing abuse of Kate and Stringer to the moment Stringer pulled that trigger. We must show that, in Stringer's frame of mind, shooting Leland was the only reasonable choice he had. It was the only way he could see to survive."

Buster paused and looked over his glasses at Stringer. "The hardest part will be convincing the jury you had to shoot five times."

Stringer crossed his arms and glared at Buster. "I told you, he wouldn't stop. He was an animal, crazier than ever."

Buster closed one file and opened another. "Any questions at this point?"

Francis shook his head. No one said anything.

"All right then, first thing we need to do is get a witness list together, folks who could testify on Stringer's behalf." Buster pulled the cap off a silver pen and looked at Kate. "Are there people in California who knew Stringer well, who might have seen some of Leland's abusive behavior?"

Kate thought for a few moments.

"A grandparent? Aunt? Neighbor?"

"My parents are dead. Leland was abandoned as a kid and grew up on the streets. He never knew his parents. I left my family when I was a teenager and never went back. I'll have to think."

Stringer's eyes opened wider and he looked at Kate. "How about Mrs. Shedrick?"

Francis felt relief at Stringer's sudden willingness to participate.

"Mrs. *Shedrick?*"

"That crazy old lady who lived in the green trailer by the canal where Leland took me shooting."

Kate crossed one leg over the other. "I vaguely remember that you told me about her."

"She used to watch us. One time when Leland knocked me down 'cause I couldn't hit anything, she screamed at him from the door of her trailer. Told him to leave me alone. He yelled back so loud it hurt my ears then he fired a shot through the side of her trailer. She jumped back inside and slammed the door."

"Did she call the police?"

"No way. Nobody called the police on Leland. After that he took me to a camp up in the mountains with crazy friends of his. They drank around the clock."

Buster leaned forward. "Can you tell us more about what happened that summer?"

Stringer turned away. "No."

"Do you know if this Mrs. Shedrick is still alive?" Buster asked.

"I think I saw her a couple of summers ago out by the canal, but I'm not sure."

"Could she testify?" Kate asked.

"If she's reasonably intelligent and believable, she could. We'd probably have to hire a PI to find her. If it looks good we'll fly her out here and get a deposition and see how she'd hold up on the stand. She'd have to be strong; Chadbourne will quickly unravel a weak witness."

Buster made a couple of notes then rested his hands on his stomach. "Kate, this sort of thing can cost a lot of money, and I don't know how much you have to spend. I don't mean on my fees; I'm not worried about that. I'm talking about expenses, like flying in witnesses."

Francis put his hand on Kate's arm and leaned toward Buster. "I'll take care of whatever expenses there are. If bringing this Shedrick lady out here will help, we'll certainly do it."

Kate put her hand over Francis's. "Thank you. I don't know any other way we could do it."

"Any other thoughts?"

"How about Delbert Ready?" Francis asked.

Buster nodded. "Yes. That's a good idea. In fact, he's already come forward. Hard to find a better witness than a man who had his life saved by your client at his own peril."

Kate and Stringer seemed to relax a bit.

Buster turned to Stringer. "Stringer, I know you haven't lived here long, but do you have any close relationships with kids or teachers at school? Anyone who might help you out?"

Stringer thought for a few moments. "No. I don't make friends very easy. Kids around here aren't into the same things I am." He gestured toward Francis. "He's my only friend. I spend more time at his place than anywhere."

Buster leaned back in his chair. "I suppose in many ways Francis knows you better than anyone in town and could really speak up for you."

"I certainly could."

Buster looked at Francis. "The problem is you were being stabbed by Leland at the time Stringer shot him. And as Sheriff McNeal has so eloquently and repeatedly pointed out, you were involved with Kate—who was still married to Leland—in the weeks before the murder."

Feeling blood rush to his face, Francis stood up and stepped to the small window that looked out on dumpsters in the back.

Stringer's face tightened. "You leave Francis alone. He loves Mom. He's never hurt her like Leland did. He's never made her scream." Stringer caught his breath. "He makes her happy."

Francis turned back to the table. "It's okay, Stringer."

Buster pushed his chair back a bit further and leaned forward. "Let me think about this one. Francis, you'll probably be testifying as a material witness in any case."

"How about Kasa?" Francis asked. "She and Kate know each other and Kasa and Stringer have spent time together. She knows how talented he is. She also knows first-hand what abuse and terror are all about."

"What's her standing in the community? Is she well thought of?"

"Yes. Keeps to herself much of the time, but she's honest and well respected. People seek her opinion and she's been re-elected to the town council many times."

"Sounds good." Buster turned to Kate. "Do you think she knows enough about you and Stringer to be able to testify?"

"I think so. She understands."

"Good. We may be able to use her." Buster turned to Stringer. "Now, while we work on finding Mrs. Shedrick, you have an important job to do. I need you to think very carefully about what happened that day. Every moment, every emotion leading up to firing that gun. I need to know what you were thinking, how your stomach felt, how your heart was beating. Everything. Write it down in exact detail."

Stringer stayed silent.

Buster waited. "Agreed?"

Stringer nodded.

Kate frowned. "Why does he have to do that?"

"It's a vital part of how we're going to discover the truth and find our way through this. The truth's in Stringer, not in us." Buster put on his glasses. "And we don't have much time. Jury drawing begins week after next. We asked for a speedy trial and that's what we're going to get."

Buster gathered his files together, slid them into his leather briefcase, and stood. "I'll get to work on finding this Mrs. Shedrick. If you think of anyone else, let me know right away." He lifted his briefcase and stepped to the door. "It takes a lot of faith to get through a trial like this, and I don't necessarily mean the trial in the courtroom."

After Buster left, Ralph appeared in the doorway. "I'll give you folks a few minutes then Stringer has to go back to his cell."

"Thank you," Francis said.

After Ralph closed the door, Francis looked at Stringer. "I know this is terribly difficult for you, but my gut says Buster knows what he's doing, that he's on the right track."

Stringer seemed to ignore what Francis was saying but then his expression suddenly perked up. "Hey, I want to show you guys something I painted last night."

He hobbled to the door, dragging the chain between his legs. He banged on the door and Ralph reappeared.

"I want to show them the painting."

Ralph glanced down the hallway. "All right, but make it quick."

"Come on," Stringer said. He led them down the hallway, passing the sheriff's inner office where Francis noticed a cleaning lady mopping the floor.

Back in Stringer's cell, Ralph took the leg irons off and locked the door.

Stringer pulled out the canvas he had been working on and stood back.

Steaming out of a mountainous forest, a long black passenger train crossed the canvas toward the viewer, its bright yellow headlight piercing the winter twilight. Painted in the windows were tiny profiles of passengers. Hundreds of white specs splattered over the canvas created a dramatic but delicate snowfall. Inside the lead engine were silhouettes of two people riding into the night.

Kate stood motionless, staring at the painting. Francis stepped closer, examining the detailed brush strokes. He ran his fingers through his hair. "Stringer, this is incredible."

Stringer smiled. "You really like it?"

"Like it? It's great. You're developing a unique vision, your own feel for subjects and the canvas." Francis gestured. "This falling snow is wonderful. How did you do it?"

Stringer stepped closer to the easel. "I used that small Russian brush you gave me. Ran it back and forth across a piece of screen I found in the floor drain."

Francis nodded. "That's it," he said. "That's how you find ways to express yourself." He looked Stringer in the eye. "And I have a strong feeling that if you follow Mr. Hurd's advice and do what he asks, he will lead you out of this hell. I don't know exactly how, I just feel it." Francis motioned to the canvas. "In the same way you felt the snow coming down around that train." Their gazes met. "There are instincts we must trust."

Francis embraced Stringer then looked at Kate. "I'll wait outside in the car. See you tomorrow, String."

"Tomorrow," Stringer said.

Ralph opened the cell door and Francis left.

Ten minutes later Kate walked out of the jail and climbed into the Malibu. She put her hand over Francis's on the seat. "I feel a little better—a bit hopeful. The deputies are being nice to String and that helps."

Francis drove out of the lot onto Main Street.

Kate looked out the window. "I'm frightened of what Mr. Hurd wants Stringer to do."

Francis turned at the head of Main and headed north toward the bungalow. "What he wants him to write down?"

"Yeah."

"Why?"

"I'm worried about what Stringer will say. He speaks his mind."

"That's what Buster wants."

Kate curled up on the seat and looked out the window. "I'm worried Stringer knows things I don't."

They rode the rest of the way home in silence. Back at the bungalow, Kate went for a long walk while Francis spent the afternoon painting. She didn't return until almost dark. Francis walked outside to greet her. Her face was flushed, her neck sweaty. "Did you have a good walk?"

"Yeah," she said, loosening her coat. "The worry, the negative energy is awful, but the power of nature out here is awesome. I love to watch the waves crashing on the rocks. All we had in LA were soft sand beaches. The ocean seems much more alive here. And the salt air is so thick; it all takes me out of my head."

Francis nodded. "This place is amazingly beautiful."

Kate looked like she was cooling off fast. "I'm going to go inside."

"Okay. I'll be in shortly."

After Kate walked into the bungalow, Francis stood on the lawn looking at the light dusting of snow caught in the coarse grass. The moon edged its way over the eastern horizon and Jupiter glowed brightly in the southern sky. He took in a deep, cleansing breath.

As Francis walked to the door, he saw the tiny flash of a match in the studio window. He watched as Kate reached down into the whaler's lamp and lit the candle. Then she carried the lamp upstairs to the bedroom.

Back inside, Francis washed his face with a steaming towel then walked upstairs. Kate sat under the covers against a mound of pillows, her arms around her knees. Francis took off his clothes, pulled on a clean T-shirt, and climbed into bed. He lay on his side next to her, his head supported by one hand.

Kate stared at the candle. "Do you believe in God, Francis?" she asked quietly.

Surprised by her question, Francis sat up and leaned back against the headboard. He hesitated.

Kate looked him in the eye. "I think I do." Then she slid down into bed, pulled the comforter up over her shoulders, and fell asleep.

CHAPTER 23

As Saturday morning dawned, wispy clouds drifted out to sea over Wagner's Point. Cool air filled the bedroom from a window Francis had cracked open during the night.

Francis turned in bed and found a pile of covers next to him. Kate was gone. He pulled on a pair of jeans and hurried downstairs where he was met with the warmth of a fire in the woodstove and the aroma of fresh ground coffee.

Kate sat on the floor in the studio looking through a collection of watercolors piled on her lap.

"I hope you don't mind me looking at these," she said as Francis stepped into the doorway.

"Not at all. Most of them are just sketches."

Kate pulled a particular piece from the pile. "This is my favorite."

Francis bent forward. "Really?"

"Yes."

"Do you know what it's of?"

"You watching Andrew Wyeth that day you met him. Where your grandmother took you for your birthday."

Francis smiled. "You're right."

"When did you paint it?"

Francis lifted the sketch from Kate's hands and studied it. "The day after I met Stringer. The way he watched me reminded me of myself with Mr. Wyeth."

Kate looked at Francis. "That day changed your life, didn't it?"

Francis nodded. "Yes, both that day and the day I met Stringer."

Kate smiled. "You've certainly changed his life for the better."

"The two of you have done the same for me."

"We've sure livened up this little town." Kate grinned, leaned forward, and kissed Francis. "I think I'm falling in love with you, Francis Monroe."

Francis broke into a broad smile.

Kate collected the sketches into a neat pile and slid them back in their slot beside the paint rack. "I want to go to the jail early today. If Mr. Hurd finds Mrs. Shedrick and she can tell them the things Leland did to Stringer, I think he's got a real chance."

Francis nodded. "I'm going to take a quick shower then I'll be ready to go." He paused. "Do you want to take a shower with me?"

Kate took hold of Francis's T-shirt and pulled him close. "We'd never get to the jail."

Francis gave her a deep, lingering kiss. "If your son wasn't in jail I'd make love to you all day."

Kate smiled. "I'd like that—both parts."

On the way into town they waved to Kasa, who was splitting wood at the edge of her garden.

"She's something else," Kate said.

Francis nodded. "A remarkable woman."

The sun was unusually warm for the end of November. Francis looked away as they passed the place on the road where Leland had driven him into the swamp. As they drove by Cove Pizza, Francis saw "Happy Thanksgiving" spelled out in large letters on the sign out front. "I'd forgotten that it's Thanksgiving tomorrow."

"Feels kind of weird, doesn't it?" Kate asked.

"Yes. And I forgot to tell you Kasa invited us for turkey at her house." Francis looked over at Kate. "Despite all that's happened we have a lot to be thankful for."

Kate nodded. "Maybe Charlie will let us bring a turkey dinner into the jail."

"I bet he will."

Francis pulled into the lot in front of the jail and stared at the shiny white cruiser in the sheriff's parking spot. "Look who's back."

"Great," Kate said sarcastically.

Francis put his hand on her arm. "Things are getting better. Let's keep our cool."

Kate undid her seat belt. "I'll try."

They climbed out of the car and walked toward the front steps. Suddenly Kate rushed ahead. A bright orange notice was duct taped to the door.

Kate slapped the paper with the back of her hand. "What is this shit?"

Francis scanned the notice: "County Jail visiting hours: 30 minutes – Sundays 1pm. Juveniles in custody: 30 minutes twice daily: 11am and 4 pm. Family only. No exceptions per order of the sheriff."

Francis shook his head. "He *is* truly an asshole."

Kate turned to Francis. "Can he do this?"

"Unfortunately the county sheriff has tremendous power, but we can talk to Buster and see if he can do anything."

"What time is it?" Kate asked.

Francis slid the sleeve of his coat back. "Quarter of ten."

Kate stood on the granite steps in front of the door. "This is bullshit. I want to see my son." She tried to open the door, but it was locked. She banged on the glass with her fist. "Hey!"

"Don't get crazy. You know what Buster said."

Kate ignored him and banged on the door again.

Suddenly she stood back. Charlie appeared inside the door.

"Charlie, let us in," Kate said through the glass.

"I can't." He pointed at the sign.

Kate pulled on the door handle. "Please, Charlie."

Charlie glanced inside then turned back to Kate, opened the bolt, and pushed the door open a few inches. Kate grabbed hold of the edge of the door.

Charlie spoke through the opening. "Sheriff's back—things have changed. And he's pissed off we've been letting you come and go as you please. Went crazy when he found out you stayed overnight."

"But the doctor—"

"Sheriff doesn't care. It's his jail."

"Bastard," Kate said, stomping her foot. She crossed her arms.

Francis leaned closer to the door. "Can't you let Kate in for a few minutes? What harm would it do?"

Charlie shook his head, slid outside, and leaned against the door. "Listen, the boys and I've been trying to treat you and Stringer good. Doin' what we can. We want your kid to get a fair trial." Charlie glanced over his shoulder. "You gotta understand the sheriff's in charge around here. Got the law behind him. He can make all of our lives miserable."

Kate's shoulders slumped.

Charlie opened the door enough to slide back inside then turned to Kate. "Mrs. Johnson, you can come back and visit for half an hour at eleven o'clock. Mr. Monroe, you're not family, but if there's a way I can slip you in at night once in a while, I'll do it. But if you piss the sheriff off, you won't have that." Charlie looked straight at Francis. "So don't mess it up. The kid likes to see you."

Francis felt anger and frustration boil inside of him. He reached out, held the edge of the door open, and looked Charlie in the eye. "I don't trust that son of a bitch McNeal, so if Stringer isn't okay, if he needs anything, you call me." Francis leaned in closer. "Do you understand, Charlie?"

Charlie nodded then locked the door and walked back to his desk.

Francis took Kate's hand. "Come with me." He led her down the steps into the parking lot.

"Where are we going?"

"Some place we can think straight."

They hurried down Main Street to the harbor and across the main wharf. When they got to the stairs leading to the harbormaster's house they stopped and leaned against each other.

"Come on," Francis said after a quick rest. They climbed the steep stairs up into the shack then crossed the creaky floor together. Francis held the rickety door as Kate climbed out onto the deck. One of the Adirondack chairs had collapsed since they were last there.

Kate slumped into the good chair, letting her head fall back against the wooden slats. Francis leaned against the weathered railing and looked out at the dark sea beyond the harbor.

After catching her breath, Kate stood and ran her hand over Francis's back then cuddled against him.

Francis lifted his head and looked at the hillside village. "Spent much of my life in this town. I've loved living here." Francis cleared his throat then shook his head. "But what I've seen this fall—the way they've treated you and Stringer—I don't know anymore. I think of myself as a compassionate man, but with the likes of Larry McNeal and Gwen Chadbourne running things, I'm losing faith."

For a few minutes Kate held him as she hummed a Lakota spiritual. A lone seagull swooped past them, alighting on a decaying wooden piling beyond the shack.

"You know, Francis, the people of this town may come through for us yet. I've watched them, including Charlie and Ralph, and they can't stand McNeal. They know what an asshole he is. And Kasa sees through everyone's bullshit. Including mine."

Kate turned and faced Francis. "Look, I can hardly take a breath without worrying they'll send my baby away for life, or worse. But there's also good in these people—something honest, down to earth."

Kate searched Francis's face. "Look at you. You've taken Stringer and me into your heart. Two desperadoes from California. You love us and you've made us a part of you. And you, Francis, are a very important part of this town."

Kate paused and looked at the ocean. "I listened to what Mr. Hurd said and I know everything rests in the hands of the jury, so I'm going to pray for them and for the prosecution."

Francis lifted his head. "For the *prosecution*?"

"Yes. It's an Indian tradition. Before you go into battle, you must honor your enemy's life by praying for him. My mother said it puts everyone on even ground; it takes much of the fear away."

Francis slid his hand over Kate's. "You're something else," he said, their fingers entwining. "I never met anyone like you." They watched the seagull as it lifted off the piling and flew across the harbor.

"You know what hurt the most when Rachael was dying?"

Kate waited.

"She wouldn't let me help her; she had to do it all herself. I felt emotionally tortured and very alone, unable to help this woman I loved. Maybe worse, I wasn't able to share my sorrow with her." Francis looked into Kate's eyes. "You have given me such a gift by letting me help you and Stringer. By letting me be honest and vulnerable in what is now our shared journey." Francis kissed her on the forehead. "Thank you."

Kate smiled and laid her head in the nape of his neck.

After a while they left the wooden shack and, holding hands, walked back to the Malibu, which was parked in front of the jail. Francis yelled up to Stringer's window but when no one appeared, he turned to Kate. "It's almost eleven o'clock. I can't visit Stringer so I'm going to go get you a car. It'll give you more freedom to come and go."

"That would be great." Kate looked at the Malibu. "Maybe your Jeep's ready and I could keep the Malibu."

"Are you kidding? I thought you hated it."

"I did at first, but it's grown on me. It actually reminds me of a lot of cars in California."

"Sounds good," Francis said, smiling. He climbed into the Malibu and backed out of the parking space. Before he drove off he looked back at Kate who was sitting alone on the granite steps, her face turned up to the sun.

CHAPTER 24

In the days before the drawing of the jury Francis spent most of his time painting—in the studio, in the hallway, in front of the upstairs window overlooking the sea. The Jeep still wasn't finished, so he gave Kate the Malibu and rented an old Bronco with a CB radio bolted to the dash and a loop of rawhide strung with a dried starfish hanging from the rear view mirror.

In town, Francis sensed the pressure surrounding the impending trial. Many people seemed fearful of these strangers who had so disrupted their town. Over the protests of children's rights organizations, including a group from Boston, Judge Thornton held Stringer without bail. He said his decision was based on risk to the public, likelihood of flight, and the unusual violence of the crime. Francis wondered if it was also because Thornton feared for Stringer's safety if he let him out.

Despite a request from Charlie, Sheriff McNeal would not let Francis see Stringer. Francis was able to sneak art supplies in with Kate, and most of the deputies let Stringer paint in his cell at night. Francis talked on the phone with him when they allowed it, and Buster called Francis every day with an update. Despite the hard work of a private eye in California, hopes were dimming that Mrs. Shedrick would be found. Her last known address was now a highway construction site.

Around noon most days, Francis walked down the hill to Kasa's and had a cup of coffee with her. She kept closely in touch with goings on in town through contacts like Ginny Wentworth. Though wanting to be optimistic, Francis knew

Kasa had growing concerns about the way Stringer's case was being handled. McNeal and other hard-core locals wanted to make an example of him. They wanted to ensure that such a thing never happened again in Winter's Cove. And after the rainy summer season they'd had, they badly needed tourists and their money to come for Festival, and for that they needed this nightmare to be over.

The jury drawing was to begin promptly at nine a.m. on Monday, the first of December. Francis let the Malibu warm up in the driveway before he and Kate left for town. It was a bitter cold morning with a northeast wind spitting off the whitecaps in the harbor.

"How're you doing?" Francis asked as he turned onto Main Street.

"Scared as hell."

"You were at the jail late last night."

"Yes, and I stopped at an AA meeting on the way home."

"That's good. The one at the Congregational Church?"

"Yeah. There's a couple of crusty old lobstermen at that meeting that crack me up. It felt good to laugh."

"Did McNeal give you any trouble at the jail?"

"No. I just saw him for a minute and I think he'd been drinking. He was pretty mellow."

"Well, don't trust him," Francis said, turning into the courthouse parking lot.

"Don't worry."

Kate got out of the car and looked around. "I thought there'd be protesters today."

"They're probably waiting for the trial. Besides," Francis said, "it's too cold."

Standing beside the large wooden doors was a deputy named Mitchell. Broad-shouldered with a scruffy beard, he stood with both hands on his unpolished black gun belt. He said nothing as Kate and Francis approached, the morning sun reflecting a rainbow of oily colors in his sunglasses.

In the courtroom, Kate sat next to Francis directly behind Stringer and Buster. Lester announced Judge Thornton and everyone rose. Thornton sat behind the large mahogany bench in a high-backed leather chair. He studied a packet of papers for a few moments then leveled his gaze at the defendant's table.

"We are here today to draw a jury for the murder trial of Stringer Albert Johnson, formerly of Venice Beach, California, accused of killing his father, Leland Johnson, on the eighth day of September 1999 at Winter's Cove, Maine."

Francis felt Kate stiffen beside him. He slid his arm over the back of her seat.

The judge looked at Buster then at Gwen Chadbourne. "Pursuant to pretrial motions, I have before me the agreed upon stipulations. Are there any issues you would like to raise before we begin?"

Chadbourne partially stood. "None, Your Honor."

"No, Your Honor," Buster said from his chair.

Judge Thornton turned to Lester. "You may bring in the potential jurors."

He nodded, limped over, and opened a tall wooden door behind him. A large ceiling fan began slowly turning over the jury box. A row of men and women filed into the courtroom. Appearing uncomfortable, most of them looked to Lester for direction. He seated them in the first three rows of seats behind the prosecutor's table.

Francis looked at the potential jurors' faces as they took their seats. He saw two people he knew: Frank Millhouse, a retired cabinet maker and part-time lobsterman, and Mildred Spears, a school teacher from nearby Cushing, who had once helped Rachael trial a new children's book in her classroom.

On the end of the last row was an elderly gentleman. Short of stature with a round face and a plaid tie, the man wore a forest green sport coat that was too small for him. He sat quietly, hands folded in his lap. His eyes were beady but seemed particularly alive. He didn't speak to anyone.

Judge Thornton read from a paper then turned to Lester and asked him to swear in Mrs. Charles.

Lester stepped beside a heavyset woman in her fifties and motioned for her to stand. She stood, raised her right hand, and he swore her in.

The judge motioned to Chadbourne. "You may begin."

Chadbourne stood and straightened her navy blue skirt. She stayed a good six feet away from the woman. "Are you familiar in any way with the case this trial is about?"

With some difficulty, Mrs. Charles crossed one large leg over the other. "Just know somebody died downtown."

"Have you ever had any contact with the defendant, the deceased, or their families or friends?"

"I seen a picture of the kid's mother in the paper." Mrs. Charles pointed to Kate. "One time she served me coffee at The Claw."

"So you know Mrs. Johnson?"

"Nope."

"You said she served you at The Claw."

"Did."

"Then don't you know her?"

"The lady served me coffee is all."

"Did you ever discuss this case with her?"

"Never discussed nothin' with her. Don't talk to strangers."

Buster jotted a note on his pad.

Chadbourne finished questioning the lady and sat down.

Buster adjusted his glasses. "Mrs. Charles, do you think you could judge this young man based on the facts presented at trial? Judge him fairly, without bias, like you would want to be judged?"

Mrs. Charles looked at Stringer, at Kate, then back at Buster. "Think so."

"Thank you, Mrs. Charles." Buster sat down.

Chadbourne fired a glance in his direction then stood. "Your Honor, I ask that this woman be excused."

Judge Thornton turned to Buster, who stood. "Mrs. Charles is perfectly acceptable, Your Honor."

The judge frowned. "Counsel will approach." The two attorneys walked to the bench and stood a few feet apart. Thornton leaned forward and spoke with Chadbourne. Buster waited patiently. After a brief interchange among the three of them, the judge motioned for them to move back and they returned to their seats.

The judge turned to Mrs. Charles. "Your answers are acceptable to the court. You will be seated on the jury."

"Do I have to?" Mrs. Charles asked.

A slight grin appeared at the corner of Buster's mouth.

Judge Thornton looked over his glasses. "Yes, ma'am, you do."

Mrs. Charles slumped into her seat.

Judge Thornton turned to the pool of potential jurors and, on behalf of both attorneys, asked them a few questions directly, including if anyone personally knew Kate, Francis, Stringer, or anyone else directly involved in the case. The judge dismissed the two people Francis knew, as well as five others. One was a middle-aged man who admitted falling in love with Kate when she served him at The Claw. Four others said they were biased about the case: one for, three against Stringer. Then the judge ordered a brief recess and quickly disappeared into his chambers.

Buster spoke to Stringer then got up and motioned for Kate and Francis to follow him out the back of the courtroom and across the vestibule into the "defense room."

"Please sit down," Buster said, closing the door behind them. "Judge Thornton is urinating. Prostate trouble. We have just a few minutes."

Francis pulled out a chair for Kate and they both sat down.

Buster remained standing. "I need both of you to go home. You can't stay. It's disrupting the flow."

"We haven't said a word," Francis said, a bit indignantly. "I thought the jury drawing was open to the public."

"It is, but you're not exactly the public." Buster looked out through the yellowing Venetian blinds. "I shouldn't have let you come in the first place."

"What's the problem?" Kate asked.

Buster turned back to the table. "There are some good people in that jury pool out there, but you're intimidating them. They're tense to begin with. Having you two sitting there watching them is too much. It's hurting us."

Buster took off his glasses and held them tightly in his hand. "You need to understand, this is a tough call, holding the trial here. The prosecution was expecting us to ask for a change of venue, to have the trial moved to another part of the state. My gut says Stringer will do better here. Problem is everybody knows something about this case. That's why Chadbourne agreed to let Mrs. Charles serve. She's probably as objective as we're going to get."

"I don't want to leave Stringer alone in there."

Buster stared at Kate. "I know it's hard, but it's best for him if you leave. It's the tide I talked about before. Everything depends on the jury—who they are, how they feel. It's already started its flow. You need to trust me on this."

Kate thought for a few moments. "Okay," she said. "We'll do whatever you say."

"Thank you." Buster's countenance softened. "And remember, Stringer is not alone."

Suddenly there was a loud knock on the door, which swung open. McNeal leaned into the room. "Judge is ready. Let's go."

"I'll call you as soon as we're done," Buster said, ignoring the sheriff.

"Tell String I love him," Kate said.

McNeal stood partially obstructing the door so that Kate had to brush against him as she left. He sort of grinned at her. Francis frowned and blew by him. As the jury drawing proceeded, they reluctantly headed home.

Late that afternoon someone knocked on the door of the bungalow. Francis set his paintbrush down on his pallet. Kasa walked into the hallway and gave him a hug. Cold air emanated from her dark wool coat. Her large eyes searched his face. "Have you heard anything?" she asked.

"Not yet.

"Is Kate all right?"

Francis motioned behind him and spoke softly. "She's resting by the fire."

"No, I'm not." Kate said, stepping through the parlor doorway, an afghan around her shoulders. She walked over to Kasa and into her arms. Kasa held her as if she were her own daughter.

"It's good to see you," Kate said. "Waiting is awful."

"I know," Kasa replied. "And there is lots of it."

"Would you like a cup of tea?" Francis asked.

"I would," Kasa replied.

"Kate?"

"Okay."

Kasa and Kate sat on the sofa. Kate opened the woodstove, stoked the coals, and added two pieces of split maple to the fire. Francis made three cups of tea and served them on a silver tray.

Kasa took a sip then set her cup on the saucer in her lap. "Francis, you've been painting. I can smell it."

"Yes. A lot."

Kasa glanced at Kate. "This woman has been good for you."

Francis nodded. "I know."

Kate's expression brightened. "Francis has been painting like crazy. Don't you think he should have a show of his new works? At the gallery, like he used to?"

Francis shook his head. "Kate, I told you, no one buys this sort of thing. They only care about my seascapes."

"How do you know? You told me you haven't painted like this in twenty years."

"Anyway, we've got enough going on."

Kate turned to Kasa. "You've got to see these paintings." Kate looked at Francis. "Is it all right?"

Francis shrugged. "If she wants to."

"Come on," Kate said, taking Kasa's hand and leading the way into the studio.

Francis put his feet up on the ottoman and closed his eyes. He listened to the two women as they looked through his works. After a short while, Kasa stepped into the parlor doorway, her face alive with excitement. "Francis, these are wonderful. I had no idea. So different than your paintings of the coast. Kate is right. You need to have a show. People must see these."

"Thank you, but we'll have to see how things turn out with Stringer."

Kate walked around Kasa and sat next to Francis. "Francis, you must do a show *regardless* of what happens with Stringer." She slid her hand onto his forearm. "He told me you taught him that for artists, the art is essential, that it must not be pushed aside for anything. At its core it is how you survive."

Francis straightened in the chair.

"Didn't you teach him that?" she asked.

Francis looked a bit sheepish. "Yes, I did."

Kate looked to Kasa. "In January then, we'll have a show at the gallery." She looked back at Francis. "A brand new opening for you, different than anything you've done before."

"Yes," Kasa said. "We'll have refreshments, invite whomever you want. Have some of your old artist friends come. Something to look forward to."

Francis watched the excitement on their faces. "I'm not very good with these things, but if you want to put it together, that would be nice."

Kate smiled at Kasa then gave Francis a hug. "It'll be great. You'll see."

Kasa looked at Francis. "When you've a minute, there's a painting in the studio I'd like you to tell me about."

"Sure," Francis said.

The phone rang. Kate jumped up and answered it. "Yes, we're all here. Come right over." She stood holding the receiver for a few moments then turned to Francis. "Buster's on his way. They've picked the jury."

"They're finished?"

"Yeah."

Francis put his hand on her shoulder. "Are you okay?"

"I'm scared. Now my son has his jury. I feel like the trial's over but we just don't know what happens." Kate turned away. "I'm going for a walk to get some fresh air."

Francis took his field coat off its hook and held it while Kate slid her arms into the sleeves.

Kasa stepped closer. "Be careful. It's almost dark; easy to lose your footing."

Kate nodded and walked outside. Francis watched her walk into the darkening mist engulfing the bluff.

Kasa stood in the hallway. "There's an awful lot of pressure on that girl, but she is strong. She'll be all right."

"I know. I swear I'm getting much of my strength from her."

Kasa nodded. "I feel it. Strength you never knew with Rachael."

Francis wanted to protest, but instead looked into Kasa's large brown eyes. "You know me well."

She took Francis's hand in hers and turned it over. She touched his palm, drawing her finger along his lifeline. "Kate is a gift given to you by God. He wants you to rejoice in her, to live your life more fully than you have in the past."

Francis watched Kasa's face. "I don't know how I would've made it without you."

"You would have," Kasa replied, putting on her coat. "I'm going home now. I need to rest. You and Kate talk to the lawyer. Let me know how you make out."

Francis stood in the doorway after she left. The salt air was heavy, changing between freezing rain and snow. He watched as Kasa rounded the corner of the bungalow and disappeared. Shivering, Francis folded his arms against his chest, walked back inside and up to the bedroom window. He worried about Kate walking along the cliffs but remembered what Kasa had said about Kate's needing to learn to take care of herself.

He cleaned the whaler's lamp glass with the tail of his shirt, lit the candle and watched the edge of the cliff as the flame flickered to life.

CHAPTER 25

Car lights flashed across the front yard. Francis hurried downstairs as Buster appeared in the doorway. His necktie was loosened to one side and his shirt was hanging out around his suspenders.

"May I come in?" he asked, his forehead beaded with sweat.

"Of course," Francis said, opening the door as wide as he could.

Buster stepped into the hallway and dropped his leather briefcase to the floor.

"You look exhausted. Can I get you something to drink?"

"I could use a drink," he said, catching his breath. "That Irish whiskey would taste good."

Francis motioned toward the parlor. "Go on in and make yourself comfortable. I'll be right back."

"Thank you." Buster walked into the parlor and pretty much collapsed onto the couch.

Francis brought the Jameson and a couple of glasses from the kitchen. Buster's heavy eyebrows lifted at the sight of the whiskey.

Francis unscrewed the top and filled a glass half full with the amber liquid.

Buster squinted at the glass. "To the top, please."

Francis finished filling the glass then handed it to Buster, who sipped the top portion of the whiskey, swished it around in his mouth then downed half the glass. "Ahhhh," he said, relaxing against the pillows. "A devil of a day."

"Before we start," Francis said, "I need to get Kate. She's out taking a walk."

"In this weather?"

"She was so nervous about the jury drawing she had to get some air before you came." He walked outside. "Kate!" he called out.

No response.

He hurried down the stone path, but in the fog and darkness it was hard to see the separations of cliff, air, and sea. He edged to the top of the cliff stairs and listened. Above the pounding of the waves he heard Kate singing—a harsher song than those he'd heard before.

Holding tight to the rock outcroppings, Francis carefully descended the steps. He waited until Kate finished singing then stepped onto the large flat rocks at the water's edge. "Is that one of your war songs?"

Kate lifted her head. Francis could barely see the whites of her eyes. "Yes. It was taught to my mother by my great-grandfather. It is hard to pray for your enemies. But it must be done; otherwise we are alone in battle."

Kate stepped past Francis and climbed the cliff stairs. He pulled his collar tighter around his neck and followed after her.

Back inside the bungalow, Kate sat on the floor in front of Buster. "So what happened at court?" she asked in a hard voice.

"It was good you both left. Chadbourne would have driven you crazy." Buster's face was flushed. White hair showed through where the top two buttons of his shirt were open. "In spite of her, things went well. With the press of the holidays coming, Judge Thornton just let us keep going till we were done. The court officer brought in pizza for dinner. All in all, the jury pool was good. Thornton was fair and by the book. Neither Chadbourne nor I used all our perogatories—people we're allowed to dismiss without cause. Never seen a felony jury picked quite like that, but I feel pretty good about it." Buster paused, drained the last of the whiskey from his glass. "I think I know who they'll select as foreman."

"Who?" Kate asked.

"Mr. Cleary. Nice old gent. Retired history professor from Colby. Thoughtful. Reserved. Must be pretty near eighty, but the engine's still running well."

"Which one was he?" Francis asked.

"Little man in a green sport coat too small for him. He speaks well and sounds fairly conservative. Chadbourne liked him, but he'll end up helping us."

"How do you know?" Kate asked.

Buster smiled. "Trust me. I've been through a lot of trials."

Kate frowned. "So why do we care who the foreman is? Doesn't he have one vote like the rest of them?"

"Yes, but the foreman sets the tone, has a lot to do with how the tide washes back and forth through the jury."

"He'll be good?"

"I think so. There's just one person who I think could be a problem."

"Who's that?" Francis and Kate asked simultaneously.

"The first alternate, Mrs. Fitzgerald. I considered challenging her, but I thought it better to let it go."

Kate frowned. "What's wrong with her?"

"She's *really* conservative, probably the unforgiving type. She admitted to being a fundamentalist Christian, but it's tough to dismiss her for that. It's unlikely she'll get seated, but I worry about her."

Buster set his empty glass down on the floor. "The main problem we've got is we can't find Mrs. Shedrick. Roger, the private investigator I hired, has one more lead to check out—an old lady in some county nursing home—but it sounds doubtful." Buster looked at Kate. "We really need an objective witness who knows some damaging details about Leland's abuse."

While they were talking, Kate stared at the fire in the woodstove. "I've wracked my brain trying to think of others. String and I were loners; we spent most of our time avoiding Leland's rages. He would lose it if we even talked to neighbors or started

245

getting close to anyone. We basically moved from one cheap apartment to another."

Francis looked at Buster. "Can Stringer testify?"

Buster leaned forward on the couch. "I've thought long and hard about that and I don't think it's a good idea."

"But he could testify first-hand about what Leland did to him. Wouldn't it make the strongest impression on the jury?"

"It might. But he's angry and Chadbourne would hammer him about emptying the gun and that sort of thing. I'm worried she'd drive him to pop off at her; do himself more harm than good."

Kate looked at Buster. "So we don't have much of a defense, do we?"

Buster looked at her compassionately. "Mrs. Johnson, we'll keep looking for witnesses. And we'll find a way to mount a strong defense."

Buster straightened his tie then pushed himself up off the couch. "Time to get to the hotel. If I don't get some insulin into this old body, I'll be dead by morning. We've got a day off before the trial so we can get some rest and keep working on finding the elusive Mrs. Shedrick. I'm quite sure something will break our way."

After Buster left, Kate, dejected, went straight to bed. Francis went back to painting in the studio, eventually falling asleep on the cot. He was awakened the next morning by Kate standing in the doorway. "I'm going on a hike for the day. My head's a mess and I really need a break before the trial begins. I wouldn't be good around Stringer at the moment. I'll see him later."

Francis sat up on the edge of the cot. Kate had on a white turtleneck, a sweater, and a pair of jeans. Her hair, freshly brushed, fell over the collar of his field coat. "Do you need—"

"Francis," she said, holding her hand up. "Thanks, but I don't need anything. I have a map. I'm going to catch a noon meeting in Rockland. I'll be fine."

"Rockland's miles from here."

Kate crouched down next to him. "You are a dear man, but you can't take care of everything for me. If I got from LA to Winter's Cove on my own, I can make it to Rockland and back."

Kate kissed his forehead and walked to the door. "I love you, Francis," she said as she left.

Francis got up and walked out onto the frozen lawn, but she was already out of sight. He looked up into the sky, which was filled with fluffy snowflakes. He held out his hand and caught several large flakes that instantly melted in his palm. His feet freezing, he hurried back inside.

Francis spent most of the day at his easel, finishing two paintings by sunset. It had snowed off and on all day and the ground was covered with a good three inches. Hungry and tired, he made a bowl of corn chowder and pulled the rocker from the parlor to the front door where he could watch for Kate. He sat dipping pieces of Kasa's homemade bread into the thick chowder, waiting for Kate's return.

An hour passed and there was no sign of her. Francis repeatedly got up, checked the clock above the stove, and paced around in the hallway. By nine o'clock he could feel his heart pounding. Was she hurt? Should he call the police and report her missing? Fat chance they'd be of any help.

Around ten he walked upstairs to the bedroom. His hands felt unsteady as he struck a match and lowered it into the whaler's lamp. He stood in the spot his grandmother had stood so many nights, watching and waiting.

A short time later he saw Kate's figure immerge from the fog, slowly walking up the path from the cliff. He raced downstairs and out onto the lawn. He lifted her off the ground, turning around and around on the white grass. Her cheek was cold against his face, her hair windblown and knotted. She was so tired she felt limp in his arms.

Francis helped her inside and up the stairs. She lay down on the comforter covering the bed. He unzipped the field coat and slipped it over her shoulders then persuaded first one, then the other boot from her legs. He held her cold feet against his warm belly.

With the rest of her clothes still on, Kate crawled under the comforter. Francis leaned over and kissed her cheek.

"Stringer's okay, he's hanging in there," she said softly.

"Good."

Thinking of the miles she'd traveled, Francis shook his head. "You're something else."

He slid off the bed and looked through frosted windowpanes. Under the light of a partial moon, the pine tree's branches held the new snow with unusual grace. After a few minutes, Francis slid into bed next to Kate and gently curled around her.

CHAPTER 26

The first day of the trial, Tuesday, December tenth, dawned clear and cold. All over town, eaves lined with icicles soon began to drip in the warm sunlight. Trails of snow along the streets and sidewalks left by the town snowplows were starting to melt. Every business in Winter's Cove was decorated for the holidays and several coffee shops, including The Claw, sported signs enticing visitors to come in. Unfortunately most of the visitors were reporters and protestors in town for the trial.

The week and a half since Thanksgiving had been an emotional grind: pretrial hearings and attorney conferences. Stringer's ulcers appeared to be healing, but his appetite was poor and he continued to lose weight.

Kate had gotten home from the jail late the night before. Unable to sleep, she and Francis had spent the night cuddled on the couch by the woodstove, holding each other. At six in the morning Francis broke down and called Jacob in New York, who coincidentally said he had spoken to Buster the night before and that he felt Buster was ready for the trial. "Anyway you cut it, this is going to be a tough one," Jacob said. "Buster's the best, but I'll be there if you need me."

Buster wanted Kate and Francis at the courthouse at eight-thirty. While Francis got their things together, Kate paced, appearing more anxiety ridden than ever. Suddenly she ran from the house. Alarmed, Francis stepped to the window and saw her hunched over under the pine tree, retching. He stepped back from the window, wanting to run out and hold her, but knew she needed some space.

They held hands on the way to the courthouse. Main Street was blocked off with barricades, but deputies allowed Francis to park the Bronco next to the sheriff's department. Several TV news vans were set up in the parking lot and a small group of sign-carrying demonstrators were held back by a wood-slatted snow fence about twenty yards away.

A deputy hurried them inside where they found Buster and Stringer sitting in the defense room. Stringer sat at one end of the table in a navy blue suit. His hair had been trimmed short. Kate ran over and hugged him.

"Good morning," Buster said. He wore a well-cut, dark tweed suit. His hair was also freshly cut, his eyes much brighter than when he'd last come by the house.

"*You* look different," Francis said.

"Today's the day," Buster replied.

Francis shook Stringer's hand and patted him on the back. "How are you doing?"

"Okay, I guess. I'd rather be skateboarding."

Buster picked up a file. "Please sit down; we have just a few minutes. The judge ruled on a couple of matters this morning." Buster looked at Kate. "Even though it's your son on trial, you may have to testify as a material witness. If you do, he won't let them ask you things that could result in direct testimony against Stringer, but you'll have to answer questions about what you saw."

Buster looked at the file. "Now, the order of the proceedings will be this: an opening statement from the prosecution and then one from me. Ms. Chadbourne will then present her case. She potentially has five witnesses: Dr. Freid, the coroner, Dr. Krault, a criminal psychologist from Boston, Mrs. Mary Howard, one of Kate's neighbors, and you and Francis. If she ends up calling you, the jury will understand you both are hostile witnesses."

Kate turned to Stringer and slid her hand over his. Francis put his arm around Kate.

"Then it's our turn, and much of our case will come out when I cross-examine the two of you. In addition, I'm calling Delbert Ready, Dr. Conklin, and possibly Kasa. I'm not comfortable that Dr. Hardy who came up from Portland will help us, so we won't call him." Buster looked over his bifocals. "But if Santa is really good to us, we may yet get Mrs. Shedrick here."

"You found her?" Kate asked.

"I believe so. Roger found a lady with her name and description in that county nursing home. He said she's frail but still pretty with it. He thinks he can get her here in time."

"That's wonderful," Francis said. "So you think she'll be a good witness?"

"I don't know yet. Now one last thing."

Buster was interrupted by a sharp knock on the door. Sheriff McNeal's large head popped inside. "Judge is ready. Let's go."

"In a minute." Buster pushed his chair back and stood.

McNeal swung the door open wide and stepped into the room. "Now," he growled.

Buster snatched his glasses off his face and stepped directly in front of McNeal. "I said in a minute, when I'm finished speaking with my clients. Is that understood?"

The corner of McNeal's mouth curled, revealing a wad of chew. He glared at Buster. "You've got two minutes," he said and shut the door sharply behind him.

"As I was about to say," Buster continued, looking Francis and Kate in the eye, "I want you to remember it takes faith to get through a trial. This is a battle royal in every sense of the word. Though your faith may be sorely tested, you *must* trust me."

They all stood. Stringer turned and fell into his mother's arms. "I'm so scared, Mom. I can't stand it in that jail anymore."

Kate held him against her. She kissed his head and stroked his hair. "I love you, String. I'm here for you no matter—"

The door swung open. McNeal barged into the room with Charlie and another deputy right behind him. "We're going—now!"

Charlie and the other deputy each took one of Stringer's arms. Charlie did not look at any of them.

Buster nodded to Kate. "It's time."

Francis touched Stringer's shoulder. "It'll be better if you let the deputies do their work."

Still clinging to his mother, the deputies pulled Stringer away from her and led him out of the room. The door closed with a thud.

Francis started to hug Kate. Her jaw set, she pushed him away. She took in a long breath and looked at the floor. "If you guys want me to keep my shit together and not tear that fucking courtroom apart, don't crowd me. Don't pamper me. Don't treat me like a helpless woman. I'm not."

Kate wiped tears from her cheeks then, for a few moments, closed her eyes and meditated. When she was finished, she stepped into the hallway.

Buster slid his papers into his briefcase then looked at Francis. "That's one strong woman you've got there."

After Buster left, Francis stepped to the window and separated the dusty Venetian blinds with his fingers. The sky was clouding over from the north.

Back in the courtroom, while Lester went through the usual formalities, Francis found himself staring at the shiny gold eagle on top of the American flag at the side of the bench. He was aware of shadows from the large ceiling fans moving across the embossed tin ceiling. He didn't look at Stringer and he didn't look at Kate. He was lost in an unfamiliar courtroom in the middle of his hometown.

It wasn't until he felt a hand on his shoulder that Francis came fully into the moment. He turned and saw Kasa sitting straight-backed on the bench behind him, her countenance strong and determined, the way it was when Rachael was dying. Francis put his hand over hers as he noticed the sea of faces behind her. The clock on the balcony read twelve-ten.

Francis turned back to the front of the room. In her dark blue suit, Gwen Chadbourne stood straight as a sign post in front of the jury. The skin over her high cheek bones was tight and smooth. Her small hands were tensed as she completed her opening statement.

"I am confident the State will show beyond a reasonable doubt that Stringer Albert Johnson murdered his father in cold blood with five shots from a .22 caliber revolver he stole from his father and brought with him from California for the sole purpose of killing him. The State does not believe the defendant was insane at the time of the murder. He knew exactly what he was doing. He is a ruthless teenage killer from the streets of Los Angeles who needs to be put away so he can't endanger anyone else." She bowed slightly to the jury then turned back to the Judge. "Thank you, Your Honor." Without looking at the spectators, she returned to her seat, her high heels rapping on the hardwood floor.

Judge Thornton turned to Buster. "Mr. Hurd, are you prepared for your opening statement?"

Buster stood. "Yes, Your Honor." He walked over to the railing in front of the jury and took his bifocals off. "Ladies and gentlemen, I thank you for your time serving on this jury. Particularly with the holidays upon us, it is a considerable burden on you and your families."

The courtroom was still, Buster's deep voice respectful, almost soothing.

"While you are within this hallowed room, I ask that all of your attention be focused on the life and death matters before you." Buster turned and pointed directly at Stringer, who stared grimly at the jury. "This young boy has his whole life ahead of him, and now his life is literally in your hands. He is a remarkable boy who single-handedly, and at great risk to himself, saved the life of a local man he'd never met. A boy who is a talented painter with no prior criminal record of any kind."

Buster took a step back and turned toward Stringer. "Stringer Johnson is not a murderer. He had no intention of shooting his father that tragic day. When Leland Johnson brutally attacked Stringer, his mother, and Mr. Monroe, the defendant did everything humanly possible to stop him, including trying to beat him back with his broken arm which was in a cast." Buster turned back to the jury. "Stringer only resorted to deadly force when Leland Johnson, the man who had beaten and abused him his whole life, was in the act of killing his friend, Francis Monroe, and, most probably, his mother and himself as well."

Buster faced the jury squarely. "To save the life of these good people and his own, Stringer went and got a gun and, after repeatedly yelling at Leland to stop, pleading with him to drop the knife he held over Mr. Monroe's chest—" Buster raised his hands in the air, hands tightly grasping the imaginary knife, "Only *then* did Stringer—terrified, in desperation—reluctantly fire the gun that killed Leland Johnson."

Buster scanned the jurors' faces. "This is not a case of first degree murder or any kind of murder. Don't let the self-serving, politically motivated prosecutor lead you to believe otherwise. By listening carefully to the testimony, by looking into these witnesses' eyes, you will discover the truth. This boy murdered no one; in fact, he saved three innocent lives from the drunken rage of a madman named Leland Johnson."

Buster paused for a few moments. "I thank you," he said, bowing his head slightly as if doffing his hat to the jury. Squinting, Chadbourne watched him as he walked back to his seat.

The courtroom was silent. In less than five minutes Buster Hurd and Gwen Chadbourne had laid out their claims. Judge Thornton looked at Ms. Chadbourne. "We are ready for your first witness."

Chadbourne quickly rose. "Yes, Your Honor. The State calls Mary Howard."

Lester methodically rose from his small desk and limped up the aisle past the jury to a door in the back. He opened it and escorted a woman in her forties in a creased, gray dress down the aisle to the witness stand. Her hair appeared thin for her age and she looked uncomfortable as she stepped around Lester trying to get her hand on the Bible. The jury listened attentively as the lady stated her name and address and that she lived in an apartment above Kate.

Chadbourne stood in front of the witness. "After Kate and Stringer Johnson moved into your building, did you ever hear a fight downstairs in their apartment?"

"Yeah. Couple of times. Not at first. A month or so after they moved in."

"Did you ever see a man make visits to the apartment after dark?"

"Yep."

"Do you see that man here today?" Chadbourne turned away from the witness toward the spectators.

Mrs. Howard looked around the room then raised her hand and pointed at Francis. "That's him."

Chadbourne walked between her table and Buster's, pointing directly at Francis. He and Kate recoiled in their seats. "This man? Francis Monroe?"

"Yeah."

"Was Mrs. Johnson's son home when Mr. Monroe would come over?"

"I think so. Most of the time."

"How late at night did he stay?"

Buster raised his hand. "Objection, Your Honor. Relevance."

"Your Honor, I'm trying to establish a pattern of behavior—"

Buster stood. "May I remind Ms. Chadbourne, it is not Mrs. Johnson nor Mr. Monroe who is on trial."

Chadbourne turned to the judge. "Your Honor, I'm establishing a pattern of conduct that is relevant because it sets the stage for the brutal murder of Mrs. Johnson's husband in her apartment by her son."

The judge held up his hand. "Objection overruled. You may continue. But I ask both of you to not wander unnecessarily."

"Yes, Your Honor." Chadbourne ran her finger down a page of notes. "Mrs. Howard, did you ever notice any trouble, like people arguing or fighting, when Mr. Monroe was visiting?"

"One night before the shooting, I seen Mrs. Johnson go off with him. They come back a while later and he left her at the door and took off. Right after she went in I heard a wicked fight downstairs. Things crashin' around."

"Do you know who was fighting?"

"I s'pose it was Mrs. Johnson and her husband who musta come to get her and seen that Monroe fella with her."

Buster jotted a note on his yellow pad then looked over his glasses at Mrs. Howard.

"And did Mr. Monroe come back to the apartment?"

"Yup."

"When?"

"The next day, the morning of the killin', just before I heard them gunshots."

"Was there a fight that day?"

"Not really."

"Not like the fight the other time?"

"No. Nothin' loud."

Buster scribbled on his pad. His left knee began to jiggle.

"So would it be accurate to say that shortly after Mr. Monroe came over that next day, you heard gunshots?"

"Yeah."

"No real yelling or fighting. Just gunshots."

"That's right."

"Did you do anything at that point?"

"I was scared and called the police. I got a red 911 button right on my phone."

Chadbourne smiled at the witness. "Thank you, Mrs. Howard, that will be all." She fired a glance in Buster's direction as she returned to her seat.

The judge looked at Buster. "Your witness, Mr. Hurd."

Buster stepped over to the witness stand. "Mrs. Howard, I'm Buster Hurd, Stringer Johnson's attorney." Buster smiled at Mrs. Howard. She nodded and looked at the floor.

"Mrs. Howard, do you have a good memory?"

"Guess so."

"You don't remember much of any fight before you heard those gunshots in the apartment underneath you the day Mr. Johnson was killed?"

"That's right."

"Mrs. Howard, is it true you take care of your daughter's baby during the day while she's at work? I believe you said in your deposition that she works at the clothespin factory up near Skowhegan, is that right?"

"That's right. Tommy's my grandson. He's almost two." She smiled at the jury.

"Is he a pretty good sleeper?"

"Yup. Sleeps like a little bear."

Buster smiled. "I'll bet he does. And when does he take his naps, Mrs. Howard?"

"Oh, one in the forenoon, one late afternoon before my daughter picks him up."

"Was your grandson with you the day of the shooting?"

"Sure was."

"Where was he when you heard the gunshots?"

Mrs. Howard held her arms in front of her as if cradling a child. "Right in my arms. He was scared to death."

"Of what?"

"All the noise."

"The gunshots?"

"Well, yeah…"

"But hadn't you picked Tommy up from his crib *before* you heard the shots?"

"Yeah." Mrs. Howard glanced sideways at the jury.

"Why?"

"'Cause he woke up screamin'."

Francis looked at the jury. They appeared to be hanging on every word. Two older jurors leaned forward, their hands cupped behind their ears.

"So he woke up *before* the shots?"

"Yup."

Buster continued in a friendly voice. "So you went in, picked him out of the crib, and were comforting him before you heard the shots?" Buster mimicked her cradling motion with his arms.

"That's right."

Chadbourne raised her hand. "Objection, Your Honor."

"Overruled." Judge Thornton appeared as attentive as the jury.

Buster took a step closer to the witness box and stared straight at Mrs. Howard. "So what woke Tommy up?"

Mrs. Howard looked terrified. Her hands trembled in her lap. "The…the fightin', I guess."

"You mean fighting downstairs *before* you heard the gunshots? Fighting that was loud enough to wake your grandson, who you said sleeps like a little bear?"

Tears filled Mrs. Howard's eyes. Her head fell to her chest. Buster stood there for a few long moments watching her. "Thank you, Mrs. Howard," he said. "No further questions, Your Honor."

Several members of the jury shook their heads. Buster returned to his seat without looking at anyone. Breathing shallowly, Kate stared straight ahead. Francis couldn't stop looking at Buster. He was good.

Judge Thornton looked at the clock on the balcony. Outside the tall courtroom windows, the sky was darkening.

"Ms. Chadbourne, your next witness."

Chadbourne stood. "The State calls Dr. Lawrence Freid."

An older gentleman in a gray wool suit came through the door at the back of the room. Lester walked him to the witness box and swore him in. The man had a tightly trimmed beard and mustache. His left eyelid drooped slightly over his eye.

"Dr. Freid," Chadbourne began. "How long have you been a coroner in the state of Maine?"

"Thirty-seven years."

"Have you performed many autopsies on murder victims?"

"Several dozen I would guess." Dr. Freid spoke clearly, deliberately.

"Did you perform the autopsy on Leland Johnson in Winter's Cove on September 9, 1999?"

"Yes, I did."

"Could you describe your findings from that autopsy for the court?"

"Yes. Mr. Johnson suffered five gunshot wounds. May I use my slides?"

Chadbourne picked up a slide carousel from her table and handed it to Lester. "Your Honor, the State asks that these slides be entered into evidence."

Judge Thornton nodded in the affirmative. Lester limped to a small closet next to the judge's door, took out a stand with a slide projector, and rolled it to the front of the court room.

Dr. Freid stepped down from the witness stand and walked to the projector as the overhead lights dimmed. The projector whirred to life, a shard of bright light from the back of the machine shining across the faces of several jurors.

"This first slide shows the deceased in the condition he was in when he arrived at the morgue."

A six-by-eight foot image of Leland's body, his face and penis blocked out, flashed on the wall in front of the jury. Francis watched several jurors recoil from the sight.

Dr. Freid pointed a red laser at two holes in Leland's left chest. "These were the fatal shots. The upper bullet transected the patient's left pulmonary vein, causing him to exsanguinate—or bleed to death—into his thoracic cavity."

Gwen motioned toward the jury. "Could you explain to the court in layman's terms what that means?"

Buster rose. "Objection. I think we all get a pretty clear picture here."

Chadbourne glared at Buster. "The details are important, Your Honor, and the State would never be gratuitous about such a matter."

"You'd better not be," Thornton said sternly. "You may continue."

Dr. Freid clicked the remote. A close-up view of Leland's chest appeared on the wall. "Based on the track of the two bullets that entered the chest, the second, higher bullet tore a hole through one of the main blood vessels coming from the left lung that allows oxygenated blood to be pumped by the heart to the rest of the body. In such cases, the victim usually bleeds profusely into his chest and dies quickly."

Chadbourne put her hand to her chin. "That's what you believe happened to Mr. Johnson?"

In the dim light, Francis watched the jury's eyes.

"Yes."

"How do you know it was the later, second shot and not the first that killed him?"

"Because the other gunshot to the chest broke a rib and went through the lung, which had coagulated blood in it. After the fatal shot, there would have been nothing left to bleed so the blood formed into a clot."

Dr. Freid moved on to a slide showing the inside of Leland's chest cavity. There was a white plastic marker showing where the bullet tore open the pulmonary vein. The cut ends of his rib bones shone through the maroon muscles. Large clots floating in a sea of blood filled the dependent portion of the opened thoracic cage. It looked like the inside of a whale after it had been harpooned.

"And the other wounds, Doctor, did they have clotted blood in them?"

"Yes."

"Dr. Freid, can you, with reasonable medical certainty, tell us the order of the gunshots?"

Dr. Freid thought for a few moments. "Only that the fatal shot was the last shot."

"Is there anything else different about that wound compared to the others?"

"Yes."

"And what is that?"

Dr. Freid pointed to a dark ring of discolored skin surrounding the wound. "This is a powder burn from the blast of the gun. It indicates the firearm was very close to the victim at the time it was fired."

"Closer than with the other four shots?"

"Yes."

"How close do you think the end of the gun barrel was from Mr. Johnson's skin?"

"Objection," Buster said, standing. "This witness is a pathologist, not a firearms expert."

"Your Honor, the witness has many years of experience with this sort of thing. His opinion is valid and important."

"I'll allow it."

Chadbourne turned back to Dr. Freid. "How close, Doctor?"

"I would say a foot, eighteen inches at the most."

Chadbourne walked over, stared at the bloody slide on the wall, and shook her head. Then she turned toward the jury. "Thank you, Dr. Freid."

After a few moments the lights came back up. Juror number seven, Mrs. Endelman, was holding her hand over her mouth. She looked pale. The juror next to her put an arm around her as she appeared she would get sick.

Judge Thornton spoke to Lester: "Please take the juror to the rest room."

Lester helped Mrs. Endelman out of her seat and led her up the aisle. Several newsmen with cameras came out of their seats in the back. Murmurs filled the room. Many stared at Stringer, who held his head down.

Judge Thornton addressed the remaining jury members. "Court is in recess until nine tomorrow morning. Members of the jury, you are to speak to no one about this trial. You are not to read newspapers, watch news on television, or listen to it on the radio. Deputies will escort you on a bus to the hotel." He rapped his gavel on the bench, stood, and walked out through his oak door.

CHAPTER 27

A few spectators stayed in their seats, staring at the wall where the slides had been projected. Deputies handcuffed Stringer and locked his legs in chains. Her face gaunt, Kate made her way to the far aisle, held her hand out and touched Stringer's arm as he passed. His head was low, and the chains rattled on the floor as he passed.

Kate slumped onto a bench. Francis sat next to her.

Buster walked over, set his briefcase on the bench, and loosened his tie. "This is tough stuff. I knew Freid would do some damage. And sometimes it's not wise to push the jury too far. Juror seven, Mrs. Endelman, looked pretty bad."

Francis straightened. "That's not good. You thought she would be sympathetic."

Buster nodded as he rubbed the back of his neck. "Oh, I think she is."

"You'll cross-examine Dr. Freid tomorrow?"

"Yes."

"Can you undermine him like you did Mrs. Howard?"

"I'll be working on it tonight and hope to have something on him by morning." He picked up his briefcase. "I'm going to head out, get something to eat then get some rest. See you tomorrow morning." He started to walk away.

Kate lifted her head. "Mr. Hurd."

Buster looked back at her.

"Thank you. You're the only real hope we have."

Buster managed a bit of a smile. "You're welcome, and please call me Buster." Then he walked up the aisle and out of the courtroom.

On the way home, Kate leaned against the passenger's door. The CB radio squawked quietly under the dash: truckers heading south on I-95 hauling loads of fresh lobster packed in ice or tandem loads of fresh cut logs. Locals chitchatting about the traffic, the weather, and the trial. Kate turned off the radio and they rode home in silence.

After sleeping fitfully, Francis awoke the next morning at sunrise. He could hear Kate downstairs and smelled fresh coffee brewing.

"Good morning," Francis said as he walked into the kitchen. He poured himself a cup of coffee then walked to the door of the studio. Kate was sitting on his stool, holding a canvas. "This is my favorite," she said.

Francis looked over her shoulder. It was a painting of a giant lifting the roof off the jail. "It was the first thing Stringer painted after I brought the easel to the jail."

"Wow," Kate said, "it's amazing how much you've taught him."

"He's very talented and a quick study." Francis smiled. "I wish Andrew Wyeth could see this; he has a devilish side to him too."

Francis put his hand on Kate's shoulder. "I'm going down to say hi to Kasa, but I won't be long so we can leave for court by eight-thirty."

"Actually, I'm going in soon to try and see Stringer. If the grumps will let me in. I'll meet you there."

Francis cocked his head. "The grumps?"

Kate grinned. "That's what I'm calling the deputies from now on. All of them, including McNeal."

Francis smiled. "Does take some of the bite out of them, doesn't it?"

When the trial resumed that morning, Judge Thornton seemed agitated from the moment he appeared. He banged the gavel more sharply than before as he called the courtroom to order. "We will resume testimony with Dr. Freid. Do you have any further questions, Ms. Chadbourne?"

"No, Your Honor."

The judge looked at Buster, who wore the same suit as the day before but with a different tie. "Your witness, Mr. Hurd."

Francis glanced at the jury. Mrs. Endelman was back in her seat, appearing calm and composed.

"Thank you, Your Honor," Buster said, standing. He walked over to Dr. Freid, who sat statue-like in the witness box. "Doctor, yesterday you testified that you had worked on several dozen homicides—maybe forty or fifty. Is that correct?"

"Yes."

"How many of those were close-range gunshot cases?"

"Perhaps half."

"Interesting," Buster said, looking through his bifocals at his notes. "According to the county coroner's office records, since the day you started work there have been twenty-one shooting deaths. Thirteen were documented hunting accidents leaving only eight others, of which at least four were homicides by high-powered rifles from long distances."

Buster took his time reviewing his notes. "That would leave four cases that could possibly have been close-range gunshot deaths." Buster looked over the rim of his glasses at the witness. "So in reality, Doctor, assuming you've done every autopsy in the county for the last thirty-seven years, you haven't examined forty or fifty of these cases; you've done at most four."

Dr. Freid's drooping eyelid began to twitch as he appeared increasingly uncomfortable. He cleared his throat. "That doesn't sound right. I'm certain I've done more than that."

Buster stepped back to his table, picked up a manila folder then returned to the witness stand. "Would you like to examine your official records, Dr. Freid? I think you'll find you've performed only three such autopsies in thirty-seven years."

Adjusting himself in his seat, the witness started to mouth words then stopped.

"Doctor, would you consider someone an expert in something they had done three times in their entire career?"

The doctor looked at the floor and said something inaudible.

"I'm sorry, Doctor, I couldn't hear you."

Dr. Freid glared at Buster. "I said no."

Francis looked around the courtroom without moving his head. Attention was riveted on Dr. Freid. Buster had done it again.

"Doctor, I have one more question, rather a request of you." Buster tucked the coroner's office file under his arm and took a step toward the jury. "Yesterday I noticed you had blacked out the face of the deceased in every slide. Did Ms. Chadbourne ask you to do that?"

Chadbourne shot out of her chair. "Objection, Your Honor. This has no—"

Judge Thornton motioned for her to sit down. Obviously angry, she complied.

Dr. Freid hesitated, visibly squirming in his seat.

"Answer the question, Doctor," Judge Thornton directed.

"We discussed aspects of the case, of course. I don't remember if—"

Buster stepped closer to the witness box. "Your memory doesn't seem to be very good, does it, Doctor?"

Sweat beaded on his brow. "We decided the slides would be less offensive if the face was not shown." He looked over at Stringer. "It's more appropriate. This boy is only twelve."

Buster took off his glasses and turned toward the jury. "You mean to tell me, Doctor, the State is trying this twelve-year-old boy for first degree murder, but he can't see the face of the man he's accused of killing in cold blood?"

Buster's jaw tightened. He turned back to the witness stand. "Is the face of a man not a vital part of him? Does it not tell an important part of his story? Indeed, how are we to know these pictures are in fact of Leland Johnson at all?"

Francis glanced at the jury. They seemed puzzled by Buster's line of questioning.

"Doctor Freid, in your carousel, do you have any slides of the deceased that show his face?"

Chadbourne came out of her chair again. "Objection, Your Honor, Mr. Hurd has gone too far! He's needlessly badgering this witness who is a respected authority. This has no relevance to the case."

Judge Thornton looked over his glasses at Buster. "Mr. Hurd, I too am having a hard time following this line of questioning."

"Your Honor, if you would please indulge me a few moments further. Dr. Freid has already acknowledged lapses in his memory. I think it is only fair to my client that critical testimony be substantiated in every possible way. Particularly testimony as intentionally sensational as the slides Dr. Freid has shown."

Judge Thornton thought for a few moments while tapping his glasses on the bench. "You may proceed, but bring this line of questioning to a conclusion."

Her neck rigid, Chadbourne sat back down.

Buster looked at the judge. "Thank you, Your Honor." He turned back to the witness. "Would you like me to repeat the question, Doctor?"

Dr. Freid stared straight ahead. "The answer to your question—though I find it to be in very bad taste—is yes. I have a frontal overhead slide of the deceased that shows his face."

"Would you project it on the wall for us?"

Mrs. Endelman stiffened in her seat. Kate inched closer to Francis and took hold of his arm. Stringer looked down at the table.

Dr. Freid walked slowly to the slide projector and turned it on. The courtroom lights dimmed once again. He moved the carrousel to the particular slide and dropped it in front of the lamp.

He slowly turned the focus knob, bringing a grotesque image of Leland's face into view.

Across the courtroom people audibly gasped. Leland's thin lower lip was deformed by an irregular scar, partially hidden by a coarse, bristly beard. His forehead was set in a sinister frown, his eyes sunken deep in their orbits. His mouth seemed set in a snarl. It was the evil-looking face of the wild man who had driven Francis into the swamp that night. The face of a man who had tormented his wife and child for many years.

Mrs. Endelman shielded her eyes with her hand. Mr. Perry looked very upset.

"That's enough," Judge Thornton said. "Shut it off."

Lester turned off the projector, and the courtroom fell dark and silent.

"Thank you, Your Honor. No further questions." Buster quietly sat down.

As the lights came on, Judge Thornton looked over his glasses at the prosecutor. "Do you wish to re-direct?"

Chadbourne hesitated then stood. She frowned at Dr. Freid. "No, Your Honor," she said and sat back down.

The judge nodded to the witness. "You are excused."

The doctor stepped from the witness stand and walked, head down, up the aisle and out of the room.

Lester limped to the bench and spoke to the judge. They both looked at the jury box where Mr. Perry appeared terribly pale, his hand clutching his chest. Another juror knelt beside him. Lester made a quick phone call from his desk then leaned over Mr. Perry, loosened his collar, and held his head as he lay back on the floor.

Francis heard someone say, *heart attack*.

"We are in recess," Judge Thornton said, standing.

Shortly a siren was heard outside the courthouse. Two EMTs rolled a stretcher down the center aisle to the jury box, placed an oxygen mask over Mr. Perry's face, and started an IV.

Obviously frightened, Stringer turned and looked at Kate and Francis. Buster's expression was steely. Francis knew he was thinking about the conservative alternate juror. Francis glanced around the room, trying to read the tide that Buster had talked about, but everything just seemed chaotic. He could only imagine how hard it was for Stringer.

When court resumed, the judge announced Mr. Perry had been hospitalized with angina and the first alternate, Mrs. Fitzgerald, would take his place for the duration of the trial.

Buster didn't look up; he just made notes on his pad. Francis watched as Mrs. Fitzgerald sat down in seat number nine. He thought he detected a barely perceptible grin forming at the corner of her mouth.

Judge Thornton asked Chadbourne for her next witness. She rose and straightened her suit. "Your Honor, the State withdraws Kate Johnson from our witness list. Instead we call Mr. Francis Monroe."

Francis's heart began pounding so hard it frightened him. Heat rose up his neck to his face. He wasn't ready for this.

The judge turned to Buster. "Objections, Mr. Hurd?"

Buster looked over at Chadbourne, sized her up then looked back at the bench. "No, Your Honor."

Lester stood and motioned for Francis to come to the stand. Francis felt Kate's hand squeeze then release his arm. He stood slowly, as though finding his balance after sailing. He looked at Stringer then stepped into the aisle and walked to the witness stand. Lester swore him in, his left hand on a leather Bible, his right raised. It sounded like someone else was speaking his words. Francis stepped into the witness box and lifted his head to the sea of faces.

Chadbourne stood in front of her table and stared straight at Francis. "Mr. Monroe, how did you come to know the accused?"

Struggling to focus, Francis looked at Stringer. "One morning late last summer he came to my house while I was painting. He had just moved here from California." Francis paused to catch his wind. "He and his mother, Kate, had traveled across the continent to escape that monster, Leland Johnson."

Chadbourne stepped hard on the floor with her foot and looked at the judge. "Your Honor, would you please instruct the witness to answer only the question asked?"

Judge Thornton turned to Francis. "Please limit your answer to the specific question, without editorializing."

Francis nodded.

Chadbourne took in a slow breath as she looked at her legal pad. "Mr. Monroe, in the two months preceding the shooting of Leland Johnson, did you develop a romantic relationship with Mrs. Johnson?"

Francis looked straight at Chadbourne. "Yes."

"Did you visit her house late at night when Stringer was home?"

"Sometimes."

Chadbourne cleared her throat and stood at her full five feet six inches. "Did you have sexual relations with Mrs. Johnson?" Chadbourne made a point of emphasizing *Mrs.*

Buster's hand shot up. He started to rise, but Francis looked at Kate then answered Chadbourne in a softer voice. "Yes. After I fell in love with her."

Chadbourne's lip turned upward. "Did you know she was married, that she had abandoned her husband in California?"

Francis thought for a moment. "I knew she had escaped a madman who had beaten and abused her and Stringer for years."

Chadbourne pursed her lips. "Your Honor—"

"Mr. Monroe, I'm asking you again to answer only the question asked."

Francis looked down.

"Mr. Monroe. Were you aware you were sleeping with a married woman?"

Francis looked at Kate again. "I had been in mourning since my wife died last year. I wasn't looking to fall in love. It just happened—unexpectedly and in a wonderful way."

Judge Thornton frowned at Francis.

Chadbourne crossed her arms tightly against her chest. "Mr. Monroe, did you know you were having sex with a married woman?"

Francis looked at the jury. "Yes. In the end I was aware of that."

"Did Deputy Lord ever speak to you about the Johnsons's situation, that you should stay away from her?" She looked at her notes. "Did he warn you, and I quote, 'that this Kate lady is trouble?'"

Francis felt his heart sink. He didn't look up.

"Mr. Monroe, did he warn you that you were carrying on with a married woman, that you were committing adultery?"

Francis stared at the floor.

"Mr. Monroe, answer the question," Chadbourne snapped.

Francis slowly looked up. "Yes, something like that."

"But you ignored Deputy Lord's warnings?"

"There was a lot more to it."

Chadbourne became increasingly agitated. "Did you ignore his warnings?"

Francis waited until she was red in the face. "Yes," he said quietly.

Chadbourne took a few steps back and forth in front of the witness stand. "When were you aware Mr. Johnson had come to Maine to find his wife?"

"Stringer came to me the morning after he ambushed them in their apartment and asked me for help. After I saw him I realized it was Leland that had run me off the road earlier."

"Do you have proof Mr. Johnson ran you off the road?" Chadbourne took a step toward Francis. "And let me remind you, you are under sworn oath."

"I saw the driver's face; it was the same violent face we just saw in that slide."

Buster motioned for Francis to keep it cool.

"When you went to the apartment to allegedly help them, did Mr. Johnson express to you that he was upset because you were with his wife?"

Francis tried to contain himself. "You might say that. He started by punching out the window of the front door while I was on the porch."

"Did you then leave the apartment?"

"No. I couldn't leave Kate and Stringer there like that. They had bruises on their faces and the apartment was a wreck. Besides, Leland immediately attacked me."

Stringer and Kate sat motionless. Buster listened intently.

"Did Mrs. Johnson call the police and ask the authorities for help?"

"She couldn't. I told you he was attacking her. Besides, she'd called the police before and they'd never done anything. Leland always talked his way out of it."

"Are you aware of Mrs. Johnson calling the police since she came to Maine?"

"No."

"Mr. Monroe, it is well known that you are a famous artist and, we presume, a wealthy man. Isn't it true you thought you could do anything you wanted to with this new woman in this town and no one would stop you?" Chadbourne turned sharply in front of the jury box and stared at Francis. "You wanted to keep your affair with Mrs. Johnson going, even knowing her husband had come to town to bring her home to California. Isn't that right?"

Francis hesitated. Chadbourne's eyes were wide open and her neck was flushed. She marched over to the witness stand. "Isn't that the truth, Mr. Monroe?" she demanded.

Francis held on, glancing at Kate, then at the jury. For an instant he felt the trial's emotional ebb and flow, the tide Buster had talked about. He realized that letting Chadbourne rant at him worked in Stringer's favor. "I was trying to help a woman and her son, both of whom I care for deeply."

"Mr. Monroe, this jury isn't stupid. They know when a witness is being evasive, so let's cut to the chase. Did you not return to Mrs. Johnson's apartment the morning of the murder?"

Francis hesitated again while Chadbourne shifted back and forth on her high heels. "Yes, and I forbade Stringer to come with me. I feared for his safety."

"Then how did the defendant get to the apartment?"

"He found my bicycle and rode it into town."

"Did you witness Stringer Johnson fire a pistol at his father not once, but five times?"

"Stringer only got the gun out after fighting as hard as he could to stop his crazy father. By then, Kate and I had been savagely attacked by Leland—with a butcher knife, for God's sake."

Judge Thornton spoke again. "Mr. Monroe, I know this is difficult for you, but you must focus on answering the question Ms. Chadbourne is asking. I don't want to find you in contempt."

Chadbourne appeared to smirk at Francis. "Once again, Mr. Monroe, did you witness the defendant fire a pistol at his father not once, but five times?"

"I don't remember exactly how many shots there were."

"Where were you in relation to the victim when the shooting took place?"

"Leland was on top of me, holding a knife above my face."

"So you were very close to Mr. Johnson when he was shot?" Chadbourne stepped closer to Francis. "You must have had a very good view of him when the bullets entered his body."

Francis looked at Buster, who didn't move. "It all happened so fast."

"I'm asking you to think very carefully, Mr. Monroe." Chadbourne leaned in closer. Francis felt the hardwood spindles of the chair against his spine. The courtroom was silent.

"When the first shot hit Mr. Johnson, did he fall over dead?"

"No."

"The second?"

"I don't think so." Cold sweat formed on the back of Francis's neck.

"The third?"

Buster came up out of his chair. "Objection, Your Honor. She's badgering the witness. He's not qualified to judge when Mr. Johnson died."

Chadbourne glanced at the judge. "I'll rephrase, Your Honor."

Judge Thornton nodded and Buster sat down.

Chadbourne turned back to Francis. "Certainly after Mr. Johnson had three bullets in him, wouldn't you say he was incapacitated enough to not be able to kill you? That he could no longer be a mortal threat?"

"Objection, Your Honor. Mr. Monroe is not a doctor or a forensic specialist. This line of questioning is completely inappropriate."

Chadbourne spoke before the judge could. "I'll rephrase, Your Honor." She stared at Francis. "Did Mr. Johnson stop breathing, did he look like he was dead anytime before the fifth and final shot hit him?"

Most of the jurors were leaning forward, riveted.

"Mr. Monroe, you have testified Leland Johnson was directly on top of you when he was shot," Chadbourne said impatiently. "Was he still alive even after his son fired three bullets into him at point blank range? Do you want us to believe that is even possible?"

Francis's heart pounded uncomfortably. He felt sick, wondered if he was going to have a heart attack. His whole life seemed to narrow down to this tiny point in time. He slowly raised his gaze to Stringer, flashing back to the day they met, when Stringer thanked him for telling the truth. Stringer's heavy eyes looked back at him from the defense table.

Francis turned to Chadbourne and quietly cleared his throat. "I have no doubt Leland Johnson was still alive. His eyes were wide open and he was still clenching the knife over my head."

Visibly agitated, Chadbourne furiously thumbed through her notes. "Mr. Monroe, did Mr. Johnson fall over dead after the last shot was fired?"

Francis hesitated.

"Mr. Monroe?" Chadbourne pressed.

Francis looked at her. "Yes."

"So, in summary, the defendant killed his father right in front of you. Is that correct?"

Francis could still see Leland's nasty, scraggly face over him, then the blood drooling from his mouth after he fell to the floor. He looked up at Chadbourne. "In self-defense."

Chadbourne frowned. "How was it self-defense, Mr. Monroe? Did Leland Johnson ever turn the knife on Stringer or threaten him in any way?"

"He'd been beating them up—both Stringer and his mother."

"He was beating them up when he was shot?"

"No, he had been—"

Chadbourne squinted at Francis. "You seem confused with your facts, Mr. Monroe."

Buster raised his hand. "Objection, Your Honor."

"You may continue," the judge said to Chadbourne.

"The truth, Mr. Monroe, is that the defendant took advantage of a fight his mother's lover was having with his father to kill him in cold blood. Isn't that right?"

Francis felt his facade cracking, his strength draining out of him. Before he could answer her, Chadbourne turned and slowly panned across the faces of the jury. "No further questions, Your Honor."

After a few moments, Judge Thornton looked at Buster. "Your witness, Mr. Hurd."

Buster took his time pushing away from the table and standing. He took off his bifocals and looked at Francis, who had composed himself. "Mr. Monroe, at any time since you met Stringer Johnson, have you thought he *wanted* to kill his father?"

Francis shook his head. "No."

"Did Stringer ever talk to you about being scared of his father? Did he ever feel threatened by him?"

"Yes. He didn't like to talk about it, but he had been beaten and threatened by him many times. He and his mother had lived in fear for years."

Gwen Chadbourne dug her heals into the floor and rose. "Objection, Your Honor. The defendant has no direct knowledge of anything that happened back in California."

Judge Thornton thought for a moment. "Mr. Hurd, I'll allow you to go down this road a bit further, but don't go too far."

"Thank you, Your Honor." He turned back to Francis. "At the time of the shooting, did you think Leland Johnson was going to kill you?"

"Yes. I was terrified." Francis straightened in his seat. "If Stringer hadn't shot him, I'm sure he would have killed me. And Kate too." He looked over at Kate. "We wouldn't be sitting here today."

Buster stepped around the front of his table and spoke in a low, steady voice. "Do you believe Stringer, this twelve-year-old boy, did *everything* possible to stop Leland before he fired that gun?"

Francis looked at the jury and saw the pain on their faces. "Yes. Absolutely. He had no choice."

"Thank you, Mr. Monroe. No further questions, Your Honor."

Judge Thornton looked at Chadbourne. "Do you wish to cross?"

Her arms crossed, she shook her head.

The judge nodded to Francis. "You may step down. Court will recess for thirty minutes."

Francis sat there staring at Stringer.

"You may step down, Mr. Monroe."

CHAPTER 28

The metal prisoner's door in the back of the courtroom clanked open. McNeal and Charlie strode down the aisle, stopping beside Stringer. The sheriff slid a wad of chew from one cheek to the other. "Let's go," he said.

Charlie glanced at Kate and Francis then helped Stringer from his seat.

As McNeal led Stringer up the aisle, Kate slid across the bench, trying to get close to him. But McNeal hurried Stringer away, brushing against Kate as they passed.

"Pig—" she said, glaring at McNeal. She shook her head. "I need some air."

"Come," Francis said quietly. "Follow me."

He led her out of the courtroom into the vestibule. Camera flashes exploded around them. They put their hands up and hurried out the front door, running along the granite foundation to a small stand of pines behind the courthouse. Francis leaned against the trunk of a large tree.

"You did well in there," Kate said, catching her breath.

"I don't think so."

"That bitch pushed you hard, but she didn't get you to say what she wanted you to."

"I did my best to tell the truth and to protect Stringer."

Kate nodded. "I know." She stepped away from the tree into the sunlight, which illuminated her long, dark hair as it fell over her shoulders. "You know, Francis, when you were testifying, I had a moment of clarity, that telling the truth was the right thing to do, no matter what." Kate looked at him. "I had a similar moment crossing Canada on that train. We were coming out of the Rockies near Banff at dark, passing some little town, watching the lights come on in peoples' houses. It was really peaceful and I had a moment of hope. I just knew we would find this place. I didn't know its name or where it was, I just knew it was free of Leland and that we were headed here."

Kate laid the palms of her hands on his chest. "Even with Stringer in jail and on trial, I still feel a freedom we never had before. Strange, huh?"

"Not really. You've finally escaped your own imprisonment."

Someone approached from behind them. Francis looked over his shoulder. Buster pushed past a low-hanging branch and joined them. "Charlie thought you'd be out here." He unzipped his coat and leaned back against a pine, wiping his brow with a worn white handkerchief. "How are you guys holding up?"

"Okay," Kate said, crossing her arms.

Buster touched Francis's arm. "That was tough, but you did well in there." Buster took several deep, cleansing breaths as he looked out through the pines toward the harbor. After a few minutes he looked at Francis. "I suppose Thornton's relieved himself by now. We'd better get back. Don't want to be late for this next witness."

Buster had a bit of a twinkle in his eye. He turned and walked back through the opening in the trees.

"Ready?" Francis said to Kate.

"Not really." Kate took his hand and they walked back to the courthouse. A cold wind was blowing up from the harbor and only a lone picketer remained behind the snow fence. Francis squinted. In one hand she held a black shawl tightly around her neck. In the other a sign that read: "Every seven seconds. When will it STOP?"

Francis knew the battered women's struggle, the awful truth of its statistics. It frustrated him that so few people had a clue; it embarrassed him that until Kate came into his life he hadn't either. As they walked back to their seats, Stringer glanced over his shoulder at them. Charlie was posted by the steel door. He looked agitated, almost grief stricken.

Judge Thornton looked over his glasses at Chadbourne. "Is the prosecution ready to proceed?"

Chadbourne stood, her hair wound in a tight bun at the back of her head. "Yes, Your Honor. The State calls Dr. John Krault."

A distinguished but severe-looking man in his sixties walked down the aisle past the jury to the witness stand. Lester swore him in and he sat down. His tanned face was framed with a short gray beard that looked professionally trimmed. He wore a dark gray three-piece suit with a perfectly folded, monogrammed handkerchief crowning his breast pocket.

Chadbourne looked pleased with herself as she stepped in front of the jury box then turned to the witness. "Dr. Krault, you are a child forensic psychologist, is that correct?"

The witness leaned toward the microphone. "Yes." His voice was deep, his mannerisms smooth.

"Would you please tell the court a little about your professional training and qualifications?"

"Certainly. I attended Stanford University, majoring in psychology then received my doctorate from Harvard Medical School, where I also completed my Ph.D. in child psychology. I was in private practice in the Boston area for many years before I decided to write and lecture full time. I have published two books on the subject of violent children and often speak at scholarly seminars on the topic."

Buster kept his ear toward the witness, scribbling several lines of notes on his pad.

Chadbourne turned to the jury. "Doctor, would it be accurate to say you are one of the world's experts on such matters?"

Dr. Krault leaned toward the mike. "Yes, I believe it would."

"Are you familiar with the particulars of the case before this court involving the defendant, Stringer Johnson, and the murder of his father, Leland Johnson?"

279

"I am."

"Have you had time to review the police and medical reports regarding the murder?"

"I have."

"Have you had a chance to interview the defendant regarding this case?"

"Yes, as much as was possible."

"What do you mean?"

"I'm afraid the defendant wasn't terribly cooperative."

"How so?"

"On two occasions when I attempted to interview the defendant, he was very difficult to deal with. His demeanor was angry and defiant, contemptuous of the legal process and my role in it."

"Were you able to spend enough time with him to form an opinion?"

"Yes, I was."

"And have you dealt with cases such as this before?"

"Many times."

"So, Dr. Krault, do you think Stringer Johnson acted in self-defense when he shot and killed his father? Or is it your opinion that he acted with malice or premeditation?"

The doctor straightened in his seat and looked at the jury. "After careful consideration of the defendant's mental status and the circumstances and method of the killing, it is my opinion that the defendant was mentally competent at the time of the shooting; that he was prepared and waiting for an opportunity to kill his father, the man he and his mother hated. The man who had allegedly abused them."

Except for the rhythmic squeaking of the ceiling fan overhead, the courtroom was silent.

Kate's breathing became shallow. Francis knew it was taking every bit of control she had not to scream out or run up and strangle this cold-hearted man. Behind her sat Kasa who was frowning, her jaw set like angle iron.

Buster pushed his chair back. "Objection, Your Honor. This witness is rendering opinions beyond the field in which he is an expert. I move his testimony be disallowed."

Chadbourne looked at Buster in disbelief then turned sharply to the judge. "Your Honor, this is *exactly* the field in which Dr. Krault is *most* qualified to testify."

Buster glared at Chadbourne. "Ms. Chadbourne's brought in this slick hired gun to bolster a desperate attempt to distort a case of self-defense and parade it before the jury as first degree murder."

"That's a lie!" Chadbourne fired back at Buster.

Dr. Krault bristled, the corner of his thin mustache turning upward.

Judge Thornton cracked his gavel on the bench. "Approach—both of you," he barked.

Buster and Chadbourne walked to the bench, standing as far apart as possible. Thornton took off his bifocals. His forehead contorted in a deep frown. He spoke in a sharp, angry tone, first to Buster then to Chadbourne. When he finished his admonition, he glared at them both. "Step back," he said in an angry tone.

Chadbourne and Buster nodded then returned to their respective tables.

"The State may proceed," Thornton said sternly.

Chadbourne straightened her suit. "Dr. Krault, what evidence did you find to support your opinion?"

The doctor drew his thumb and forefinger tightly across his mustache. "Before the defendant and his mother left California, Stringer Johnson stole a concealable firearm from his father. He took ten rounds of ammunition with him and illegally transported it across Canada to Maine. He went to enormous effort to make sure he had a deadly weapon with him and he knew how to use it. And he made it clear he and his mother were certain his father would go to any lengths to try and find them. Furthermore, I found no evidence that the defendant was being threatened by anyone else. So why else would he want to have a gun with him?

Furthermore, the defendant appears to show little if any remorse for killing his own father."

Dr. Krault paused and took a sip of water from a glass on a stand next to him.

Francis could feel the shifting tide. The atmosphere was heavy, airless.

"Doctor, do you have other findings you feel are relevant?"

Dr. Krault turned toward the jury. "The defendant's profile is not that of a normal twelve-year-old, though it is not that of someone mentally ill either. *This* is the profile of a young socio-path, a street kid who wanted to kill his father. He made the necessary plans, stole the weapon, and fired it repeatedly until the gun was empty. He didn't want to just stop his father, he wanted him dead."

Murmurs spread through the room. The jury was obviously unsettled, several members moving in their seats as if trying to get comfortable. Even Mr. Mason, the bow-tied foreman, looked unnerved. Mrs. Fitzgerald stared at Dr. Krault, a knowing grin on her face. Chadbourne remained standing in front of the witness, savoring the moment.

Judge Thornton leaned forward, his arms on the bench. "Do you have any further questions for the witness?"

Chadbourne looked at him with an air of satisfaction. "No, Your Honor. That will be all." She turned to the witness. "Thank you, Doctor."

Buster was tense, his shoulders set. Francis slid his hand over Kate's, which was gripping the edge of the seat.

Judge Thornton looked at the clock on the front of the balcony, then at Buster. "Mr. Hurd, it's getting late. I'm sure the jury's tired. Let's wait to begin your cross-examination until morning."

Buster straightened his notes then rose from his seat. "If it would please the court, I'd like to ask the witness one brief line of questioning before we recess for the day."

The judge looked at Gwen, who said nothing. "Certainly, Mr. Hurd."

"Thank you."

Looking like a man about to go in for a kill, Buster stepped in front of Gwen's table and stood between her and the witness. "Dr. Krault, I know it's getting late, but I have one matter I'd like to ask you about before we go home, and that boy goes back to his cell for the night. Would you agree that your alma mater, Harvard University, is one of, if not *the*, best medical school in the country?"

"Yes. I'd agree with that statement."

"And does Harvard not have a superior academic reputation throughout the medical community?"

"Certainly." Dr. Krault suddenly appeared nervous, adjusting himself in the seat.

"You were on the faculty of Harvard Medical School for quite a number of years, is that correct?"

"Yes."

"Doctor, on September twenty-second of nineteen seventy-five, were you called before the Ethics Committee of Harvard Medical School and charged with falsifying psychological research data in order to support your post-doctoral thesis regarding violence and the teenage child? And did this investigation eventually lead to your resignation from the faculty?"

Kate and Stringer lifted their heads. The jury sat frozen. Dr. Krault's eyes opened wide with a look of terror. Blood drained visibly from his face. He looked to find Chadbourne but couldn't see around Buster.

Buster stepped closer, holding the railing of the witness stand with both hands. "Doctor, would you like me to repeat the question?"

Dr. Krault glared at Buster, fear and rage in his eyes. Perspiration broke across his forehead. Trembling, he turned to Judge Thornton. "Your Honor, that information is protected under confidential peer review statutes and is not to be made public."

Ignoring Krault's plea to the judge, Buster continued to speak in a calm voice. "Doctor, were you quietly forced to resign from the faculty because you lied about the findings of your research? Did they not consider you to be an embarrassment to the medical school?"

Dr. Krault glanced at the jury then back at Buster. He appeared disoriented. "Well, I don't know…I…"

Gwen shot out of her chair. "Your Honor, this is outrageous! I don't know where Mr. Hurd gets his information, but I know Dr. Krault is a respected expert. His record is impeccable."

Buster waited patiently. Francis prayed the judge would make Dr. Krault answer the question.

Thornton slowly turned to the witness.

Gwen crossed her arms, staring at the judge. "Your Honor—"

Judge Thornton spoke without looking at her. "Counsel, I have heard your objection. I will let the question stand."

Disgusted, Gwen sat down with a thud. Everyone else in the courtroom strained to hear the witness.

Dr. Krault looked down at the floor in front of the witness box where Buster stood. "Yes," he said in a barely audible voice.

Judge Thornton shook his head. "Repeat your answer, so the jury can hear you."

Dr. Krault raised his head and stared at the back of the room. "Yes," he repeated in a slightly louder voice. "What you say is true."

CHAPTER 29

Buster stopped by the bungalow after court recessed. He looked drained. Despite Francis's feeling he had delivered a major blow to Dr. Krault at the end of the day, Buster said he was uncomfortable with the tide. He couldn't undo what Stringer had done with those five gunshots. It was an enormous challenge to put a positive enough spin on the case to get a favorable verdict. Buster downed a shot glass of Jameson, rested for a while then left for his hotel.

After Buster was gone, Kate went for a walk and Francis sat down in his studio and thought of Wyeth. How he was physically challenged as a child; how he was able to develop under the enormous creative shadow of his famous father. How he painted to survive.

Francis worked on a painting for a couple of hours before the front door opened and Kate walked in. Without looking at Francis, she went to the kitchen where he heard her rattling dishes around in the sink. She opened and closed the refrigerator, and he started when she slammed a container down on the kitchen counter. He set his paintbrush on the edge of the easel and waited for her to say something, anything.

Finally Francis heard Kate hit something and then let out a deep, angry moan. "How can you sit in front of that fucking easel and paint?" she demanded, her voice coming through the house with startling clarity. Another bang and a glass shattered on the kitchen floor.

Francis winced.

Kate crossed the hallway to the studio door, her hair streaked about her face, her eyes red and swollen. She stomped her foot on the floor. "Goddamn it, look at me!"

Francis looked up at her swollen face. Then Kate lunged at him, pounding on his chest with her fists. "They can't do this to us!" she cried, weeping so hard her body shook.

Francis took her hands firmly in his and held them. She struggled a bit then her arms went limp and she fell into him. His chest smarting, he held her for a long time. Finally she straightened up and pushed tear-soaked hair away from her eyes. "I'm sorry."

"It's okay," he said quietly.

Kate walked back to the kitchen and began cleaning up the broken glass.

Francis stepped to the doorway. "Can I help you clean that up?"

"No, I need to do it. Go back and paint."

Francis hesitated. "Okay, but I'm here if you need me."

He walked back into the studio, picked up his brush, and continued to paint for another hour. A strange scene: a 1940s Ford woody, struck by a train at a desolate railroad crossing. An old couple beside the tracks, staring into the dark wreckage, wrapped around the iron cow catcher on the front of a black locomotive. A white sheet covered what was left of the front seat and at the bottom of the track embankment a young woman in a faded blue dress holds the limp body of a child.

Knowing where the inspiration for this painting came from, Francis strongly felt Andrew Wyeth's presence. On an October day in 1943, Andrew's father, the great illustrator N.C. Wyeth, stalled in his car on a railroad track near his home in Chadds Ford, Pennsylvania. Next to him sat his beloved grandson and namesake, Newell, just shy of the age of four. From her home on the hill above the tracks, Wyeth's sister, Caroline, heard the familiar whistle of the train then the terrible sound of a collision. When she and others reached the smoky wreckage, N.C. and little Newel were dead. Francis had read several times that Andrew had never fully recovered from the shock of losing his father and nephew in that horrific accident.

Around eleven o'clock, Francis heard Kate go out the door. Through the window he saw her shadow cross the yard, heading through the moonlit snow toward the cliff. He resisted the temptation to go after her. He knew she needed her space. Instead he sat back on his stool and stared at the steamy smoke rising from the wrecked Ford. He had never consciously acknowledged it before, but Francis had been disappointed that since his grandmother introduced him as a teenager to Andrew Wyeth, the man had never shown any interest in Francis's work. Now in his eighties, Wyeth still spent his summers just a few miles up the coast from Winter's Cove, but he had never once visited his gallery or come to a show.

What hurt the most was that Francis knew, at least in part, why Wyeth had never come. A long time ago Francis had stopped painting anything even remotely authentic. For twenty-five years, until he met Stringer and Kate, he had painted acrylic crap for tourists: beautiful cookie cutter lighthouses, delicate foamy spray rising off blue-green waves as they crashed against Maine's legendary rugged coastline.

Disgusted, Francis turned away from his easel, switched off the light, and looked out the window. Out on the lawn he noticed crescent moon shadows in Kate's footsteps in the snow. Lying down on the army cot, he fell asleep.

At two-thirty in the morning, Francis awoke to a noise. He sat up and heard Kate crying. He pulled on a pair of sweatpants and walked into the hallway. The woodstove had burned out and the house was uncomfortably chilly. He stepped into the kitchen doorway and saw Kate sitting cross-legged in the middle of the floor, a bottle of Canadian whiskey open in front of her. Her hair and clothes were a mess. Her hands fidgeted on her knees as she stared at the bottle, her eyes rimmed with red.

Francis slowly walked into the room, the slate floor icy under the soles of his feet. Though frightened by what he saw, Francis sat down in front of her, leaving a little space between them. He spoke in a calm voice. "What can I do to help you?"

Kate raised her head, looking at him with a shattered gaze. Tears streaked her cheeks. "Can you turn me into another person?"

He reached over and slid the whiskey bottle away from her. "I wouldn't want to if I could."

"I'm no good," Kate blurted out. "I've *never* been any good, except at being a goddamn drunk."

Francis touched her arm. "You know that's not true."

"No? I come from a crazy Indian mother who killed herself. I've been a pathetic addict who did damn near anything for drugs. I almost killed my baby in a dumpster—" She had trouble catching her breath. "Now he's going to die for shooting that asshole, who deserved to die. I should have killed Leland myself a long time ago."

Kate rolled over on her side on the floor, her body wracked with grief. Francis got a couple of flannel blankets from the pantry and covered her. Then he folded the other blanket and slid it between her head and the cold slate. He sat down again and gently stroked her hair, softly whispering to her. "You have more soul than anyone I've ever known."

After a few minutes Kate settled down. "Why do you care, Francis? We've ruined your nice life here. You should get away from me—just leave me alone."

"I can't." He looked deep into her emerald eyes. "Kate, I don't love easily or lightly. You have become an inextricable part of my heart."

"I'm a worthless drunk."

"You know that's not true. That's the terrified part of you that wants to give up, that lives in fear." Francis sat back against the cook stove. "Like it or not, we're each responsible for our behavior, our actions, and whether we stay sober or drink. And we all fall short and we're all fearful at times, something you've experienced more than most."

Francis reached out and lightly touched Kate's chest over her heart. "No matter what happens, finding peace is an inside job. We each have to learn how to find it, under any circumstances; otherwise we're lost to grief and fear."

Kate sat up and pulled the blanket around her shoulders. "It sounds like you've found the truth we all search for."

Francis thought for a moment. "With your help I'm finding *my* truth. And I believe you're finding yours." He looked at the clock. It was after three a.m. "Let's get some sleep. We've got a long day ahead of us."

He stood and offered his hand. Kate let him help her up off the floor. She curled her hair behind her ears. "I'm sorry I'm such a mess."

Francis kissed her on the forehead. "You're the most beautiful woman I've ever known."

Kate smiled shyly. "You're crazy."

"I believe we've already established that."

She stepped into the hallway. "I'm going to take a shower then I'll see you upstairs."

Francis walked to the staircase.

"Francis," Kate said, pausing at the bathroom door. "I didn't take a drink."

Francis nodded. "I know."

He walked upstairs and climbed into bed. The last thing he remembered was partially awakening to the scent of warm French oil as Kate slid under the covers next to him.

Before sunrise Francis awakened to someone calling his name. He squinted into the early morning light. Kate was asleep next to him, but someone was banging on the front door. "Now what?" he said to himself. He slid out of bed and stepped to the window where he saw Charlie Lord pacing back and forth on the front lawn in the snow.

"What's *he* doing here?"

Kate sat up in bed. "Who?"

"Charlie."

She swung off the bed and quickly pulled on a pair of sweat-pants. "I'll go down and talk with him."

Surprised, Francis turned from the window. The softer features of Kate's face were illuminated by the rose light of sunrise. "Why you?"

"You're angry with him and I know he's hurting."

"How do you know?"

"I've seen it in his face. And he's tried to help Stringer." She ran her hand over Francis's upper back. "Go back to bed and let me talk with him."

Francis heard the front door swing open as Kate greeted Charlie. Francis tiptoed to the top of the stairs, crouched down, and listened. He watched Kate and Charlie talking in the hallway through their vague reflections in the glass of one of Rachael's photographs along the staircase.

"I'm sorry to come out this early, but—"

Kate put her hand on Charlie's shoulder. "It's okay, Charlie. I understand."

"You do?"

Charlie's head dropped. He shifted his hands on his gun belt. "I feel confused and nervous as hell. Can't sleep." He took a step back. "But I shouldn't be talking to you. Mr. Monroe'll be furious."

"Charlie, Francis doesn't tell me what to do. Besides, my nerve endings are pretty damn raw. I feel what's going on."

Charlie's voice cracked. He sort of slumped into the chair by the phone. "I don't usually get emotional."

"Me neither," Kate said, sitting on the hall floor in front of him.

"I like your son a lot. Not at first, but the stuff I've heard at the trial—" He shook his head. "He's been through a lot. More than I coulda taken." Charlie pushed his sheriff's hat back on his head and took a deep breath. "Things in this town are just fucked up."

"What do you mean?" Kate asked.

Feeling a bit like a voyeur, Francis slid back from the stairs but continued to listen.

"I mean the goddamn sheriff is too powerful, runs too many things. He's got too many people scared. The boys and I are trying to treat Stringer right, but we can't do nothin' about the trial and how McNeal and Chadbourne twist things around."

Francis felt a strong wave of emotion rise inside. Not the anger he had felt so much lately but something different: a touch of gentleness, even compassion. To respect Kate and Charlie, he stepped back into the bedroom and stood silently by the window. He stared out at the cold sea beyond the bluff and found himself softly humming one of Kate's Lakota songs.

A short time later the front door opened. Charlie stepped backward into the snow as if leaving an embrace. Francis watched from the window as Charlie trudged through the snow to his cruiser.

After a few minutes, Kate came back upstairs. "Charlie's a bit of a wimp when it comes to the sheriff but he's still a decent man." Without saying another word, they got into bed and both fell asleep.

Around seven, Kate sat bolt upright in bed, her neck and forehead covered with sweat. She could barely catch her breath.

"What's the matter?" Francis asked.

She shook her head, pushing her hair back with her hands. "I was having a drunk dream—thought I was back in the old days."

"A what?"

"A drunk dream. I was at a bar in Venice Beach, drunk, coming on to some asshole, trying to score crack." She sat back against the headboard and pulled her knees up in front of her.

"Well you're sober here in Maine with me."

Kate looked at Francis. "These dreams are incredibly real. They scare the shit out of me. I haven't had one in a long time."

"What do they mean?"

"Some people say God sends you a drunk dream to keep you sober, scare you into going to more meetings, doing whatever it takes not to pick up that first drink."

"You're terrified you'll drink, aren't you?"

Kate nodded.

"How often are you getting to those meetings?"

Kate looked out the window. "Not enough. Especially since the trial started. I have to admit I'm feeling pretty crazy."

"Can I help?"

"No. I mean, you *are* helping me a lot, but you can't keep me sober." Kate pulled the comforter over her hips. "I went to great meetings three or four times a week in LA. It was comfortable. It's been hard going without them. The AA meetings here are okay, but there's only one meeting here I really like. It's me, though, not the meetings."

"Have you made any friends?"

"Not really. Most of the girls at The Claw drink a lot. Like Shelly. She was good to me, but I have to stay away from her. She drinks like a fish."

Kate looked at the clock on the bedside stand. "I gotta get going. I want to see String before court. Charlie said he'd get me in."

Francis put his hand on her forearm. "Will you get to a meeting soon?"

"I'll try, but Stringer comes first."

"Sounds like you need to put yourself first to stay sober. And you want to stay sober, don't you?"

"Yeah, I do."

After Kate left and he'd showered, Francis thumbed through his directory looking for the piece of paper Kasa had written the church phone number on the day Kate had called for help from Bucksport. He found it and dialed the number. A dozen rings. He was about to hang up when an elderly woman answered the phone. Her voice was soft and calm. In the background a child was crying.

Francis felt relief. "Hello, is this Madeleine?"

"No. This is Sister Magnus."

"Is Sister Madeleine there? May I speak to her?"

The woman paused. In the background, a woman comforted the crying baby.

"Ma'am? Can you hear me? It's very important I talk to Madeleine."

"I'm sorry," the woman said. "Sister Madeleine was taken back to the Lord by a stroke a week ago."

"I'm sorry. I had no idea."

"Can I be of assistance to you?"

"No. Thank you."

"God bless you, sir."

The line clicked. Francis sat listening to the dead sound in the receiver for a few moments then hung up. He put on his coat and was headed out the door when the phone rang. He answered it.

"Mr. Monroe? Pete Moses. Your Wagoneer's ready. Took a while, but we got her fixed up."

"Thanks, Pete. I'll pick it up later today."

Francis drove into town, purposely going by way of Cliff Street. The long wooden banking for the Festival chute had been erected and decorated with fur bows, large red bows, and tiny white lights. Three firemen were laying hose from a hydrant at the top of the steep street, preparing to flood the pavement down to the harbor.

Francis had always loved Festival. It was the one day of the year everyone, despite their differences, came together and got along. No hierarchy, no controversy. Even Sheriff McNeal acted like a human being for a day, even letting his few prisoners out of lockup to take a slide and watch the bonfire. He was also one of the "dignitaries" who handed out torches to the sliders at the top of the ice chute. Too bad it couldn't be someone else.

The fireman holding the nozzle raised a hand in the air. An-other fireman turned a crank on top of the hydrant and the hose quickly filled, snaking along the street. The nozzle man surged forward as the water reached him. He pushed a lever, releasing a powerful stream that shot fifty feet through the air. Steam rose as water spread over the frozen street.

One of the firemen, Jeb Fairbanks, glanced at Francis and waved. "Hey, Mr. Monroe. How's the chute look?"

Francis looked at the icy hill and smiled. "Never looked better, Jeb."

CHAPTER 30

When the trial resumed, the courtroom was uncomfortably cold. As Judge Thornton strode to his tall leather chair he didn't look to be in a terribly good mood. In the back corner of the room sat a dejected Dr. Krault.

The judge looked at the attorneys. "Counsel will approach."

Gwen and Buster walked to the bench. After a brief interchange, the judge motioned for them to step back and they returned to their seats.

"Mr. Hurd does not wish to further cross-examine the last witness. Dr. Krault, you are excused." Thornton looked at Chadbourne. "Does the State have further witnesses?"

Chadbourne glanced at Buster. "No, Your Honor. The prosecution rests."

Thornton turned to Buster. "The defense will now present its case."

Stringer looked at Kate and Francis. He appeared much older than when Francis had met him just months before. Francis slid his hand over Kate's, intertwining his fingers with hers. She was scheduled to be Buster's first witness. "You can do this," Francis whispered in her ear. Kate stared straight ahead.

Buster rose from his seat. "Your Honor, the defense wishes to call Francis Monroe back to the stand."

Surprised, Francis withdrew his arm. Buster turned and looked at him expectantly. Francis stepped into the aisle and walked to the witness stand. Judge Thornton reminded him that he was still under oath then Francis sat down. Under the windows, steam pipes creaked as the iron radiators hissed to life. Overhead, the slightly off-balanced ceiling fan continued turning.

Buster stood in front of Francis. "Mr. Monroe, I know being on the stand again is difficult, so I'll try to keep my questions as brief as possible. I'm sure you understand that you are a critical witness in this case. Perhaps no one better than you can help this jury get a realistic sense of what led to the death of Leland Johnson."

Buster unbuttoned his suit coat and slid one hand into his pants pocket. "From the time you met Stringer last summer until the present, have you ever seen him be mean or malicious? Lash out? Try to hurt anyone?"

Francis shook his head. "Never. He's a gentle kid."

"Have you spent much time with Stringer?"

"Yes. He came to my house after school many times to paint. He has a gift."

Chadbourne quietly tapped her fingers on the table.

"Have you ever seen Stringer go out of his way to help another person?"

"Yes. The day I watched him save Delbert Ready. Stringer could have easily drowned. I've never seen a human being put himself at such risk to save another—a man, in fact, Stringer had never met."

Buster turned away from Francis and stood before the jury. "So, Mr. Monroe, how do you explain the fact that this twelve-year-old boy, who is not mean or malicious, who's concerned enough for his fellow man to risk his own life to save a stranger's—how do you explain the fact he shot his father dead in front of you?"

Francis looked at Stringer then spoke slowly, deliberately. "This may sound strange, but in the moments before he fired that gun, I don't believe Stringer was feeling mean or malicious. I don't think he *wanted* to hurt or kill anyone." Francis turned to the jury. "Like Kate and I, Stringer was terrified."

Buster stepped closer to the witness stand. "Of what, Mr. Monroe?"

Chadbourne shot out of her chair. "Objection, Your Honor. This is pure speculation on the part of the witness."

Thornton spoke without looking at Chadbourne. "I'll allow it. You may continue, Mr. Hurd."

"Thank you, Your Honor," Buster said, politely. He turned back to Francis. "Mr. Monroe, what were you all so frightened of?"

Francis's chin began to quiver. Tears unexpectedly welled in his eyes. For a moment he saw Leland holding the knife over him, saw that crazed look on his face.

Francis struggled a bit but looked straight at Buster. "I..." His voice quavered. "I was scared to death. For the first time in my life, I thought I was going to die. I thought we were all going to die."

Francis paused, put his hand to his ribs. "Leland had stabbed me here, in the chest, and in the thigh. I was bleeding badly. He had kicked Kate in the head, driven her to the floor. He'd beaten Stringer up yet again. It was the worst moment of my life. The pain was awful. I could hardly breathe." Francis turned to Kate and Stringer. "I am so sorry I couldn't help you." Tears ran down Francis's cheeks. He turned back to Buster. "Leland was bringing the knife down at my throat when I heard the first shot."

"Did Leland stop attacking you then?"

Francis shook his head. "No. He reached up with his other hand and gripped the knife so hard his knuckles turned white."

Buster pressed on. "Couldn't you get up and throw him off of you?"

"No. He was strong; he had me pinned to the floor."

"Did you still think he would kill you? Did you still feel your life was in mortal danger?"

Chadbourne jumped up again. "Objection! Speculation."

Judge Thornton glanced at her. "Overruled."

"Mr. Monroe, you are a strong man yourself. After the shooting began, did you still think you were going to die?"

Francis sat straighter in his seat. "Yes. My lung had collapsed. I had no breath, no real strength left. I waited for that knife to cut through my throat—to end it all. Even with the gunshots, he kept trying to stab me."

"When did you know you weren't going to die?"

"Not until after the last shot. It was only then Leland's legs weakened. He finally dropped the knife and fell over. Then he stopped breathing."

Buster stayed close to Francis. "Mr. Monroe, this is very important. Do you think Leland Johnson would have continued to try and kill you if that fifth and final shot had not been fired?"

"Yes. He was crazy; hell bent on killing me." Francis shook his head and stared at the floor. "If Stringer hadn't kept shooting and finally stopped him, Leland would have killed all of us. He was a madman."

"Objection!" Chadbourne all but yelled at the judge.

Buster reached out and touched Francis's hand, which gripped the wooden railing. "Thank you, Mr. Monroe. No further questions." Then Buster walked back to his table.

For a few moments, Judge Thornton looked compassionately at Francis. Then he turned to Chadbourne. "Do you wish to redirect before we recess?"

"No, Your Honor," she replied coldly.

Judge Thornton tapped his gavel on the bench. "We'll resume with this witness in thirty minutes."

Chadbourne snatched up her briefcase and marched up the center aisle. Kate stepped around the front of the seats to Stringer, and Charlie allowed her to give him a hug. Buster stood watching them. With the jury still watching him, Francis stepped off the stand and walked straight up the center aisle into the vestibule.

As the doors opened, TV cameras with blinding lights confronted him. Reporters wanted to know how it felt to be on the stand and how he thought the trial was going. He put his hand up, frowning at the glare. He tried to step through the crush of reporters but couldn't. A woman stuck a foam-covered microphone in his face and he batted it away. Two more replaced it. He took a half-step back and gritted his teeth.

"You've been through some rough testimony, Mr. Monroe. Don't you have anything to say for yourself?"

Seething inside, Francis looked up at the cameras. "This isn't about me. It's about a great kid who's fighting for his life." Francis paused. "It's about truth."

He put his head down. The reporters and cameras fell away as he walked across the hallway and out the front door. He hurried along the granite foundation into the safety of the small pine grove. The sounds of the wind in the branches and the sweet aroma of pine pitch comforted him.

After a few minutes, Francis felt Kate's hand on his arm. He put his arm around her and she laid her head against his chest. In the distance, Francis saw steam rising from the area of Cliff Street where firemen had been flooding the chute. It was five days before Christmas and the usual warmth and good cheer of the season was absent. All was white and cold; a town frozen by the tragedy of the trial.

When the bell in the steeple of the Congregational Church rang eleven times, Francis and Kate realized they were late and rushed back to the courthouse. When they entered the courtroom, Buster fired a stern glance in their direction as Judge Thornton was already in his seat and the jury members were finding theirs. Francis left Kate and hurried down the aisle to the witness stand. He waited for Lester to motion him into his seat then sat down.

Judge Thornton turned to Francis. "Mr. Monroe, remember you are still under oath."

Francis nodded.

The judge looked at Chadbourne. "Your witness."

She stood and studied her yellow legal pad. She looked angry as she walked around the prosecution table, standing six feet from Francis. "Mr. Monroe, I'd like to clarify a couple of points." She put her index finger to her chin. "Before you were on the floor of the apartment with Mr. Johnson allegedly holding you down—"

"He *was* holding me down."

"Did you have life-threatening injuries?"

"I said that I had stab wounds to my shoulder, leg, and chest. I could hardly breathe. I had a pneumothorax."

Buster frowned and raised his pen. "Objection. Mr. Monroe is not a medical expert and he's already testified to this."

Chadbourne looked at the judge. "Your Honor, I'm asking for the patient's opinion."

"I'll allow it."

Chadbourne turned back to Francis. "Were they life-threatening wounds? Were you dying?"

Francis felt agitated. "He stabbed me with a large kitchen knife. It certainly felt life-threatening."

Chadbourne turned to her table and picked up a file. "According to the hospital record you had, and I quote: 'simple repair of two lacerations: one of the left shoulder and one of the right thigh. No evidence found of major vessel or nerve damage.'"

Chadbourne glanced up from the file. "You had a small tube inserted for a minor lung injury and were discharged in good condition two days later. At no time did you have unstable vital signs. Your condition was always listed as 'good,' and you were kept in a regular room, never in intensive care." She looked at Francis. "Does that sound correct, Mr. Monroe?"

"Yes, but that's not—"

"Mr. Monroe—" Chadbourne cut him off. "All of this testimony about mortal injuries and being scared to death was really just in your head, wasn't it?"

Francis felt like his blood was going to boil out of his veins. He looked at the jury. They looked unfriendly. He glanced over at Buster, who sat frowning, a pen firmly clenched in his hand.

"Answer the question, Mr. Monroe."

Francis brought Gwen Chadbourne's slender, business-suited person back into focus. "That's not how it happened."

"That's what the facts would support, Mr. Monroe. Juries come to verdicts based upon facts, not hysteria." Chadbourne snapped her head away from Francis. "No further questions, Your Honor."

Francis's face felt red hot.

Judge Thornton looked at Buster. Francis hoped he'd end it, not keep him on the stand.

"No further questions, Your Honor."

"You may step down, Mr. Monroe."

Francis took hold of the railing, feeling as if he'd gone nine rounds with Sugar Ray Leonard. And lost. He walked to the front row of benches and sat at the end.

Buster stood and motioned to the judge.

"Mr. Hurd."

"Your Honor, could we take a short recess?"

Judge Thornton nodded in the affirmative, rapped his gavel, and walked out.

Buster spoke to the deputies guarding Stringer, to Kate, and then walked across the front of the courtroom to Francis. "I'll meet you in the defense room." Francis didn't look up. Buster stepped closer, knocked Francis's knee with his own. "Now," he said sternly.

Francis followed Buster to the defense room where he shut the door with a reverberating thud. Stringer and Kate stood beside the table.

"Sit down," Buster said. He was breathing hard, his lips pursed.

The three of them did as Buster asked. Kate held one of Stringer's arms with her hands.

Buster frowned. "We have work to do. This prosecutor is even better than I thought she'd be. She's playing hard ball and playing it well." He took off his bifocals. "We have *got* to sway the sympathy of the jury in our direction, particularly now that Fitzgerald is sitting there. I fear that woman's veins—like Chadbourne's—are filled with antifreeze."

There was a sharp knock on the door and a deputy stuck his head into the room. "There's an old lady out here who says she needs to see Mrs. Johnson."

"Who is she?" Buster growled at the deputy.

"Kate, Francis…"

Francis perked up. "It's Kasa. Let her in."

Buster dropped a manila file on the table. "We don't have time, Francis." He waved the deputy away.

Kate stood. "I want Kasa here—with us."

Buster's face grew redder. He shook his head. "All right. Let her in. But hurry up."

The door opened wider. Kasa stepped into the room. Her cheeks red from the cold, she held a faded white handkerchief in her hand. Buster closed the door as Kasa lowered herself into the chair next to Kate.

Buster put his bifocals back on. "I'm putting Delbert Ready on the stand next. Delbert's been around the world a few times. He'll do well. And I've got a bit of good news. With any luck, Mrs. Shedrick will be here tomorrow."

Stringer looked up and smiled for the first time in days.

"She's weak, but Roger, the PI, is flying out here with her. He says she's a little out of it, but I think she'll help us."

Kate took Stringer's hand and squeezed it.

Buster looked at Kate. "Then I'm planning to call you. Somehow as a mother you have got to capture the hearts of this jury."

Kasa dropped her hand to the table. "You can't put that pressure on this girl. Don't you think she's suffered enough?" Kasa stood. "And now you're going to put her in front of those wolves so they can eat her alive?"

Francis reached out to her. "Easy, Kasa."

Buster straightened, took off his glasses again and looked at Kasa. "Mrs. Mokanovitch, you cannot barge in here like this and tell me—"

Kasa stepped within inches of Buster. "I can tell you this trial is a travesty! You're letting that skinny rail of a woman twist the truth anyway she likes. Mr. Hurd, you've got to get the truth told to that jury about how terrible it was for Kate and Stringer. How hard Kate struggled to escape that evil man."

In the silence, someone banged on the door. "Back inside in two minutes."

Buster looked at Kasa. "Mrs. Mokanovitch, I know how these people have suffered and I also know what I have to do to win this trial."

Kasa's brown eyes opened wide. She stared at Buster. "Do *you* know of suffering?"

Buster squinted at Kasa as his cheeks tightened.

"Put the boy on the stand," Kasa said. "Let *him* tell them the truth for himself."

Buster stepped closer to Kasa, so close she took a half-step back. "I do know what suffering is." He took a shallow breath, cocking his head toward her. "But for the good of *this* boy, the one we can save, I will not waste time and energy challenging you now."

Kate, Stringer, and Francis stared at Buster. Kasa didn't move.

Buster spoke through clenched teeth. "I will do everything in my power to save Stringer. I would bleed in front of this court if I thought it would help him. I have not practiced law for forty-two years to lose my head now. If you think the wolves will tear Kate apart, what do you think they would do to Stringer?"

Buster caught his breath. "Now, will you please leave me with my clients so we can prepare to go back in there?"

Dead silence took over the room. Large snowflakes fell slowly past the window. Kasa clutched her handkerchief and looked at the floor. She stepped around Buster, pausing beside Stringer and Kate. "God bless you," she whispered.

As Francis watched Kasa leave, he found himself both on the verge of tears and ready to fly into a rage. For everyone's sake, he had to keep himself under control. He turned to Buster, who was obviously distraught. "What do we do next?"

Buster straightened his tie. "I'm going to take a leak, collect myself, and put Mr. Ready on the stand and see if we can turn things around. As for you..." Buster looked at Kate and Francis. "Maybe you need a break. It's an awful pressure cooker in there."

Kate looked up, drying her eyes with her sleeve. "I'm not leaving."

"Neither am I," Francis said.

"All right. But if you stay, keep a lid on your emotions. The jury sees everything and I've got enough to worry about without you two falling apart. And you better keep that Mokanovitch woman under control."

Buster stepped to the door.

Stringer looked up at him. "Mr. Hurd..."

Buster turned back to Stringer. "Yes?"

"I'm sorry about your son. Kasa didn't know you're working twice as hard for me."

Buster's countenance softened. He took Stringer's chin in his hand. "Thank you for that, young man," he said, managing a bit of a smile.

CHAPTER 31

Delbert testified poignantly. There was no doubt in his mind he would have perished if not for Stringer's selfless, heroic act.

Because the jury looked tired, Buster kept his questioning brief and to the point. "Mr. Ready, would you consider yourself a good judge of character?"

"Yes.

"Why, sir?"

Delbert thought for a moment. "I was an editor at *Inside New York* magazine for twenty-six years, editor in chief for ten of those. I worked with hundreds of writers and had to cut through the BS of politicians and professors and the mercenary intentions of business tycoons. I had to become savvy about the workings and motives of human nature." Delbert turned to the jury. "I'm not an easy man to fool."

"What is your opinion of Stringer Johnson as a human being?"

Delbert looked at Stringer. "Even trying to put the fact that he saved my life aside, I'm impressed with him. He's honest and courageous and I suspect he has survived more hell in his short life than most of us sitting here many times his age."

"In your opinion, Mr. Ready, do you think Stringer Johnson would plot to kill anyone, let alone his own father?"

Chadbourne raised her hand. "Objection, Your Honor. The witness barely knows the defendant. How can he testify to such things?"

Buster fired a glance in Chadbourne's direction. "He knows him well enough to have an opinion."

Judge Thornton turned to Delbert. "You may answer, but remember you are under oath." Thornton turned to Chadbourne. "You will have your chance to cross."

Buster looked at Delbert. "Do you think he would plot to kill anyone?"

Delbert shook his head. "No, I do not."

"Do you think he could shoot a man if it meant protecting his own life or the lives of those he loves?"

Delbert thought for a moment. "I think he would have had to feel his or someone else's life was in imminent danger. Only then."

Buster turned toward the jury. "Mr. Ready, do you have any experience in domestic abuse cases?"

"Yes."

"Objection. Mr. Ready has not been entered as an expert witness."

Buster stepped in front of Judge Thornton. "Your Honor, I believe Mr. Ready has relevant testimony related to his experience that helped him form his opinions of Stringer."

Chadbourne ground the toe of her shoe into the floor. "Your Honor, I know you're trying to give each side ample leeway, but this is an improper line of questioning."

Judge Thornton motioned to the attorneys. "Counsel approach."

The judge spoke briefly then motioned for them to step back. "Mr. Hurd, you may continue if you quickly make the relevance of this line of questioning clear to the court."

"Thank you, Your Honor." Buster turned back to the witness stand. "Mr. Ready, tell us about the experiences you feel are relevant to this case, to having an opinion regarding Stringer Johnson."

Delbert looked at the jury. "When I was a reporter for the *Times*, I was assigned to the NYPD Domestic Violence Unit for two years. I followed them around, writing articles about the battered women and children that I saw and what had happened to their lives." Delbert paused. The jury was very attentive. Chadbourne sat bolt upright in her chair, ready to rise.

"Spousal abuse is an insidious crime. If the victims survive, their abusers gradually whittle away their hearts and minds, convincing them they are worthless trash and could never make it on their own.

"People I interviewed often asked: why don't these women just leave their abusers? From what I saw, it was terribly difficult for them to break free. Many truly believed they were worthless and most all of them felt imprisoned. Some couldn't leave because violence was the only kind of attention they had ever known from a man. And many would be in real danger if they left."

Chadbourne started to raise her hand then reconsidered.

Delbert leaned toward the jury. "Kate and Stringer somehow found the courage to leave. They got as far away from their abuser as they possibly could. They tried to leave no trace behind. I believe the only way that Leland Johnson found them was through TV reports of a freak accident that resulted in Stringer saving my life. Ironic, isn't it?"

Chadbourne stood. "Your Honor, this is total, unfounded speculation."

Judge Thornton held up his hand.

Delbert pressed on. "I don't believe Stringer wanted to shoot or kill his father. He was forced to do it — to defend himself, his mother, and his friend, Mr. Monroe."

"Your Honor!" Chadbourne said sharply.

"Sustained." Judge Thornton looked at Delbert. "Mr. Ready, that's enough."

Delbert nodded to the judge.

"Thank you, Mr. Ready, that will be all," Buster said then returned to his seat.

"Ms. Chadbourne, your witness."

Chadbourne's lips were drawn tight, her jaw set. She addressed Delbert from in front of the jury. "I have two questions for you, Mr. Ready. First, how much total time do you think you have spent with the defendant since you met him?"

"It's hard to say."

Chadbourne stepped closer. "Hard to say for a man of your intellectual abilities? Or do you not *want* to say?"

Buster raised his hand. "Objection. Badgering the witness."

"Overruled," Thornton said, without looking at Buster. "Answer the question, Mr. Ready."

"I'd say I've spent two or three hours with him."

The jury looked surprised. Several members frowned.

"And from these few hours you have derived your extensive opinion of him? The same quality of opinion you formed from twenty-six *years* as an editor?"

"I'm a good judge of character."

"You must be," Chadbourne retorted and turned toward the jury. "The truth is, Mr. Ready, you don't know much of anything about Stringer Johnson or the circumstances of his murdering his father. Isn't that right?"

Buster stood. "Your Honor, Ms. Chadbourne is—"

Thornton cut Buster off. "Sit down, Mr. Hurd. I will allow the prosecution the same latitude I allowed you."

Stringer's leg jiggled nervously up and down under the defense table.

Chadbourne continued. "Mr. Ready, do you have any firsthand information about the murder of Leland Johnson?"

Delbert stared straight ahead. "I do not."

"Thank you. Now, my second question. How much do you weigh?"

"Objection," Buster said. "This has no bearing on the case."

"Overruled."

Chadbourne stepped close to the railing in front of Delbert. "Please answer the question."

"I weigh about one hundred and seventy-five pounds."

"And would you say this twelve-year-old would have to be exceptionally strong—physically and mentally—to jump into the stormy Atlantic and pull your one hundred and seventy-five-pound injured body through the waves to shore?"

"I suppose, yes."

Chadbourne turned back to the jury. "Wouldn't you say that's a far cry from the picture you presented a few minutes ago? The poor little abused boy who had to run across the continent with his mother to escape his mean father?" She wheeled around and looked Delbert in the eye. "*After* he stole his father's gun with which he finally killed him." Chadbourne scanned the jury. All were sullen except Mrs. Fitzgerald.

Not waiting for an answer, she quickly walked past Delbert to her seat. "No further questions, Your Honor."

Francis slid his arm around Kate. He felt the bones of her shoulder through her sweater. She had lost so much weight.

The judge studied his notes then looked at the attorneys. "Christmas is fast approaching and I would hate to keep the jury sequestered over the holidays. However, this young man must get a fair trial, which means this court will afford him and his counsel the time he needs and deserves. I simply ask that we stay focused."

For the first time, Buster and Chadbourne actually looked at each other civilly and nodded.

"Court will be in recess until nine-thirty tomorrow morning."

As the courtroom emptied, Francis spoke to Stringer then left with Kate through the side door away from the crush of reporters waiting in the vestibule. As they hurried across the parking lot, they saw Sheriff McNeal standing guard on the courthouse steps.

Kate drove home in the Malibu. Francis drove to Gate's Garage to pick up the Jeep. They were closed for the night, but the red Wagoneer was sitting out front, keys under the mat. Francis walked around the Jeep, running his hand over the smooth sheet metal where the damage had been repaired. He climbed in, started the engine, and turned on the radio. A country song blared over the speakers. He turned the dial to his favorite station, and then drove home listening to James Taylor singing "Carolina In My Mind."

Francis had no more than stepped out of the Jeep when Buster roared up the driveway in his Buick. He pushed his large body up out of the car. "Good news, I hope."

"What?" Francis asked.

"Roger just flew in with Mrs. Shedrick. He's taken her to a bed and breakfast in town."

"That's great," Francis said.

"We'll see. She sounds a little crazy. He said she was quiet most of the trip then suddenly started shrieking when he was getting her off the plane. Got the flight attendants in a stir."

Francis frowned. "That doesn't sound good."

Buster pulled his coat together in front of him. "He thinks she's with it enough to testify and it sounds like she knows a lot about what happened out by that old trailer she used to live in. And she's all we've got."

"You know what's best."

Buster looked at him and shook his head. "Things aren't going well, Francis. I've *got* to put her on the stand." Buster lowered his voice. "This is costing you a bundle. I hope you..."

The door of the bungalow opened.

"I don't care about the money," Francis said quietly. "I'll paint more seascapes if I have to."

Kate walked out of the bungalow in a T-shirt, jeans, and a pair of Francis's winter boots. Her hair was wet. She hurried across the snow, her arms crossed to keep warm. Her steaming breath rose against the dark blue twilight sky. Her nipples pushed against her shirt in the cold air. "What's going on?"

"Mrs. Shedrick's here," Francis said.

"Thank God." Kate gave Buster a hug.

"Yes. A little out of it, but she's here," Francis said. He took his coat off and wrapped it around Kate. For a moment he felt guilty at how attracted he was to her; how much he wanted to make love to her. Then he felt an even more powerful wave of gratitude for having this amazing woman in his life. He smiled and stepped back.

Buster turned to Kate. "I'm taking a necessary gamble putting Mrs. Shedrick on the stand. If things go well with her, I may not need to call you. We'll play it by ear." Buster opened his car door. "I'm on my way to interview her now. I'll see you in the morning."

CHAPTER 32

After a quick breakfast the next morning, Kate and Francis drove to town in the Jeep. It was three below zero on the thermometer in front of the Casco Bank and sharp winds from the harbor had driven wave-like drifts of snow against the tires of cars parked along Main Street. It was too cold for protesters, and only one television van had arrived.

McNeal wouldn't allow a morning visit with Stringer, so Kate and Francis walked straight into the courtroom. They sat quietly holding hands, and though the cast iron radiators cracked and hissed at the sides of the room, there was a cold draft along the wooden floor. Soon the jury, bundled in sweaters and fleece pullovers, entered and settled into their seats.

Charlie and Ralph led Stringer to his seat. He looked over as he passed Kate and Francis.

Judge Thornton banged his gavel then motioned to Buster, who looked good in his dark blue, sharply cut suit. "The defense calls Carol Shedrick."

The heavy double doors at the back of the room swung open. Through them came a wheelchair carrying a small, hunched-over woman, a sparse shawl covering her bony shoulders, her thin black and gray hair revealing a balding scalp beneath. Her right arm was drawn up in a claw against her chest. Her gaze ran along the hardwood floor as she was wheeled down the center aisle. Lester had to swing his bad leg out to the side so he could bend down enough to slide the Bible under her contracted hand. He administered the oath then parked her wheelchair in front of the witness stand.

Buster left the yellow pad he was studying on his desk and stepped over to the wheelchair. "Mrs. Shedrick, we appreciate you coming all the way from California to testify."

Buster waited a moment. There was no reply. She continued to look at the floor. He leaned over and spoke louder. "Can you hear me, ma'am?"

Mrs. Shedrick pushed her chin up with her claw hand. "Yeah, I can hear you," she snapped at him. Her beady eyes were sunk deep in her wrinkled face. Her tongue darted in and out of her mouth as if she were a venomous snake. Several jury members appeared repulsed by her.

"Mrs. Shedrick, I'd like to ask you some questions regarding things you may have seen when you lived in a trailer near the Arroyo Grande Aqueduct in Los Angeles, California, in the summer of 1995."

Mrs. Shedrick said nothing, her jaw moving as though she was chewing her tongue.

Buster stepped to the railing and slid an eight-by-ten color photograph of Stringer into her lap. "Did you ever see this boy near your trailer?"

With her functional hand, Mrs. Shedrick took hold of a corner of the photograph and stopped chewing her tongue. "I don' know."

"Please, Mrs. Shedrick, it's important." Buster adjusted the photograph in her lap. She batted him away, tearing the edge of the paper.

Buster glanced over at Roger, the PI, who shrugged his shoulders.

"Maybe I seen him," she said, cocking her head at an odd angle to the photograph. "Not sure."

Stringer stared at Mrs. Shedrick. Francis squeezed Kate's hand so hard she had to pull it away.

Buster walked to his table and retrieved a second photograph from a folder. He stepped back to the railing and slid it into her lap. "Have you ever seen that boy with this man? Perhaps shooting rats in the canal?"

Chadbourne shot up. "Objection— leading the witness."

"I'll allow it."

Shedrick looked at the second photograph. Her eyes suddenly opened wide. She let out a muffled screech, like a young kestrel frightened in its nest. She awkwardly pushed the photograph off her lap onto the floor.

Buster picked up the photo and slid it onto the railing in front of her. "Do you recognize this man?"

She tried to push it away again with the elbow of her claw hand.

"Mrs. Shedrick, I know this is difficult, but it is very important you tell us what you know."

She glanced at Buster. With one corner of her mouth trembling, she let out another, though weakened, screech.

Buster leaned on the railing and compassionately touched her arm. "What do you want to say, Mrs. Shedrick?"

She leaned forward, jamming the photo under her claw on top of the railing. She pointed with a bony finger at the man beside the boy in the picture. "That man—" She took a shallow breath through clenched teeth then spoke haltingly. "Shot a hole through my trailer. Crazy son-of-a-bitch! Made that kid kill cats and rats and dogs in the ditch."

"Did you ever see this man abuse the boy?"

Mrs. Shedrick turned away, again knocking the photograph to the floor. She drew her deformed hand tight under her chin.

"Mrs. Shedrick, please tell us what you know about this man hurting this boy."

"Objection," Chadbourne called out.

"Overruled," Thornton said, staring at the witness, his glasses halfway down his nose.

Buster motioned toward Stringer. "Mrs. Shedrick, this boy's life is at stake."

The ceiling fan squeaked overhead. Buster held the photo of Leland and Stringer in front of Mrs. Shedrick. She shook her head as if trying to rid herself of an evil spirit. "No! Get away."

"Mrs. Shedrick, did this man hurt this boy?"

Her mouth gaped open. "Yeah. Terrible things." Her claw hand began shaking.

Buster leaned closer. "What things? What did he do?"

Mrs. Shedrick let out another screech.

"What things?" Buster encouraged.

Mrs. Shedrick looked at him, her eyes wild. "His privates." She hit the railing with her good hand.

"What did he do to the boy's privates?" Buster asked as calmly as he could.

Mrs. Shedrick grimaced at Buster. "Made him dance then shot his balls off. Blood run down the boy's legs. Said he'd kill me if I said any…" Tears streamed down Mrs. Shedrick's face. "I'd never dared come here if he was still alive."

Buster kept his composure, tenderly touching her arm again. "Thank you, Mrs. Shedrick. You're a courageous lady." He turned and walked to his seat. "No further questions, Your Honor."

After a few long moments, Judge Thornton turned to the prosecution. "Your witness."

Chadbourne cleared her throat and stood. Her otherwise perfect suit had developed a deep crease across her seat. She walked slowly in front of the bench, appearing to be giving the witness time to calm down.

"Mrs. Shedrick, I know you're tired and clearly not well, so I'll try to make my questions brief." Her voice was cool, manipulative.

Buster watched Chadbourne out of the corner of his eye. Francis slid Kate's arm beneath his own and held it tightly.

Chadbourne gestured across the courtroom. "Mrs. Shedrick, do you see the boy in Mr. Hurd's photographs here in the court-room today?"

The witness stared at the crowded courtroom. "Nope."

"Are you sure?" You could hear the pleasure in Gwen Chadbourne's voice.

"Don't see him," Mrs. Shedrick snarled.

"Your Honor, let the record reflect the witness could not identify the defendant." With a nasty look in her eye, Chadbourne turned back to Mrs. Shedrick and held the photograph in front of her. "You don't really know who this boy is, do you?"

Mrs. Shedrick looked away.

"Do you, Mrs. Shedrick? You can't even identify him when he's sitting right in front of you." Chadbourne's voice was sharp.

Buster's arm went up. "Objection, Your Honor. She's badgering the witness."

Chadbourne ignored him. "You don't really know anything about Stringer Johnson or any supposed abuse by his father, do you?"

Mrs. Shedrick raised her good hand as if protecting herself. "I told you what I saw."

Buster stood. "Your Honor, this is cruel; the witness obviously cannot see well."

Chadbourne's face lit up. She turned and faced the witness squarely. "Is that true, Mrs. Shedrick, that you don't see well?"

Mrs. Shedrick lowered her hand a bit. "That's right. Don't see good."

Chadbourne turned toward the jury. Blood appeared to drain from Buster's face.

"You never saw anything happen with this boy, did you?" She turned aggressively back to the witness. "You couldn't have seen any alleged abuse from your trailer, could you, Mrs. Shedrick?"

Mrs. Shedrick became very agitated. Her hand started to shake.

Chadbourne bore down. "You are under oath, Mrs. Shedrick. Now answer the question."

"I told what I seen."

Chadbourne continued pressuring her. "But you just said you don't see well, didn't you?"

Mrs. Shedrick cocked her head back and let out a weakened kestrel shriek.

Buster was out of his chair. "Your Honor, this is outrageous!"

Judge Thornton shook his head and frowned. "Ms. Chadbourne, I think the witness has done her best."

Mrs. Shedrick's eyes rolled back and her body began to seize. Her head fell into her lap, the bony knuckles of her claw rapping against her teeth.

"Call an ambulance," Thornton shouted to Lester. He banged his gavel on the bench then looked at Buster and Chadbourne. "In my chambers—now!"

Deputies, led by the sheriff, marched in. McNeal grabbed Stringer by the arm and yanked him out of his chair.

Kate looked as though she would scream at McNeal, but held herself back. Francis held Kate's arm and, in the commotion, glanced over at the jury. For a fleeting moment, he felt a glimmer of hope. Their faces said they were with Mrs. Shedrick, not with that bitch, Chadbourne.

As Kate and Francis made their way to the door, Buster motioned to them. "I'll meet you in the jail conference room in five minutes."

CHAPTER 33

Kate and Francis pushed through the reporters to the granite steps outside. Kate pulled Francis to the side. "What did that bastard do to Stringer?"

"I don't know." Francis glanced around then spoke in a hushed voice. "*You* don't know what Shedrick was talking about? What happened with his privates?"

"No. Only that Leland had embarrassed him that day at the aqueduct and then he took off up north. I didn't know he injured him. And Stringer never lets me see him naked. I just thought it was a guy-puberty thing."

Francis looked at his watch. "Come on, we've got to meet Buster." They crossed the parking lot to the jail. Charlie held the door open for them as they hurried up the steps. His face was drawn, his manner unnerved.

Inside, Buster stuck his head out of the interrogation room down the hall. "Kate, Francis, we must talk."

They hurried into the room and Buster closed the door. He immediately turned to Kate. "I am your son's attorney. I *have* to know everything that has happened to him that might be relevant to his case. Now what *exactly* was Mrs. Shedrick talking about regarding Stringer's privates?"

Kate turned toward the small window. Impatient, Buster motioned with his eyes for Francis to intervene. He stepped over to Kate, sat on the arm of a chair, and touched her shoulder. "I know this is terribly painful, but Buster has to know."

Tears squeezed from Kate's eyes. Every muscle appeared to tighten. "I know I sound like a terrible mother, but the truth is I don't know. The summer Stringer turned eight Leland suddenly took him up to the mountains with his drinking buddies. All I knew was that they had been out shooting rats in the canal and then they just took off. When they came back a couple weeks later he had some blood in his urine but he wouldn't talk to me about it. I took him to some doctor Leland knew, but String wouldn't let him examine him much." Kate crossed her arms and continued to face the window. "That was when I was so sick; strung out on cocaine, drinking all the time. The doctor was a weird guy who said there was nothing wrong with String. It was awful."

Kate turned toward Buster and Francis. "Leland was a bastard, but it's hard to believe even *that* animal would do something this fucked up."

Buster shook his head. "There are truly sick, wicked people in this world and I'm now certain Leland was one of them." He sat on the edge of the table. "Judge Thornton has recessed court for the day and ordered Stringer be examined by a physician this afternoon. They're contacting Dr. Conklin at the local hospital."

"Great," Francis said sarcastically.

Buster raised his eyebrows. "Is he not competent?"

"He's competent. It's just that he's under the sheriff's spell like the rest of them. Even though he did take good care of Stringer in the jail."

Buster looked at Francis then at Kate. "We could ask for an outside expert, but it will delay things, and my sense is Mrs. Shedrick's testimony can really help Stringer if a doctor—especially a local one—can promptly corroborate what she said.

"I feel the tide shifting," Buster added as he walked about the room. "Perhaps it's best if Dr. Conklin *is* under the influence of Sheriff McNeal. If Stringer has physical evidence of this hideous injury, either Conklin testifies to it or we get another physician to and Conklin looks terrible. It becomes obvious how McNeal has abused his power and that, in turn, could undermine the State's case."

Buster sat in a chair and drew Kate and Francis close to him. "You see, it's all up to the jury, and they are local people, affected by the same things that affect everyone else in this town. One way or another, more and more people are becoming affected by this very special kid. Delbert Ready, Francis, Charlie, and myself—we've all been changed by your son. You can see it in Charlie's face. Soon the county doctor may have to bring *his* own humanity and Hippocratic Oath to bear testifying for Stringer." Buster nodded his head. "Yup, the tide may be turning our way. Dr. Conklin's coming here around four o'clock. I'd like you both to be here in case Stringer gives him a hard time."

Kate nodded. "We'll be here."

"Good."

"But Stringer is very guarded. This is going to be very hard on him."

"I know," Buster said sympathetically. "We'll be as gentle as possible, but we have to remember that his life is at stake."

Buster looked them both in the eye. "Steady as she goes, my friends. Steady as she goes."

Kate and Francis drove back to the bungalow in silence. The snow clouds had moved farther west and the sky had cleared. Kate felt a little sick to her stomach, so she went out for a walk along the bluff. Francis tried to paint but couldn't concentrate. He mulled around the house for a while then pulled the painting of Rachael from beside his drawing table. He hadn't looked at it since he put it away after he met Stringer. He carried the painting outside to the bluff. Under the bright sun, the snow had melted away from the edge of the cliff, so he leaned the painting against a rock in front of him and sat down.

Francis stared at Rachael kneeling on the water-slicked rock. He gently touched the layers of paint that formed the breast she had lost. He looked into her eyes and, for the first time, admitted he had been afraid of her. Perhaps most afraid of being honest, of sharing his deepest fears and vulnerabilities with her. It had been so freeing painting from his heart these last few months with Stringer and Kate in his life. He wondered what it would have been like to have been authentic with Rachael. He had been hesitant to argue with her much, to step out of line lest the successful life and career she had built and managed for him would fall apart. And he always feared being abandoned—emotionally, physically—as he had been by his father.

Francis studied the curve of Rachael's hip, remembering the softness of her inner thigh. He turned and looked out over the whitecaps in the bay. Rachael was the only woman he had ever made love with, until Kate. Rachael was skilled and taught him how to be a good lover. He had followed her lead. But Kate was different. Sharing her love, her sensuality felt so natural, so unencumbered. He was so powerfully drawn to her. Sharing his body, his heart, and soul with her was the most wonderful thing he had ever done. So strong and disarming was her love, it had freed him. In so many ways, it was as if his life had started over.

After a while he walked back inside and put the painting away.

Kate and Francis arrived back at the jail at three-thirty. Charlie let them say hi to Stringer, who was in an especially bad mood. He did not want Dr. Conklin, or anyone for that matter, to examine him. Kate wanted to be alone with Stringer, so Francis walked back to the sheriff's office. He had a cup of coffee with Charlie, who had a hard time sitting still. Softened by Kate's fondness for Charlie, Francis found himself a bit worried about him.

"You okay?" Francis asked.

"Yeah, why?" Charlie paced under the gold sheriff's star on the wall.

"You seem awfully uptight."

"Been tough around here," he said, glancing toward Sheriff McNeal's office.

Francis knew he couldn't really talk.

Just then, Dr. Conklin arrived. He looked serious and carried a small black leather bag. Francis wanted to tell him to be good to Stringer, tell him how much hell he'd been through, but the doctor looked appropriately concerned as he headed for the cell block.

Stringer put up a bit of a fight. You could hear his and Kate's voices echoing in the brick hallway. "You must let him examine you," she said a few times, with increasing urgency and conviction.

Francis stepped into the shadows and listened. He heard Dr. Conklin ask Stringer to lie back on the cot and lower his pants. His heart pounding, Francis strained to hear. A zipper; the rustle of fabric. Kate quietly gasped.

"My God," Dr. Conklin said, half under his breath.

CHAPTER 34

Court did not convene until two p.m. the following day so the State could depose Dr. Conklin before he testified. When Kate and Francis entered the courthouse, there seemed to be a different feel in the air. In the lobby, one of Ginny's lobstermen patted Francis on the back and said quietly, "That sick bastard deserved to die."

Lester administered the oath to Dr. Conklin in front of a packed courtroom then Buster rose and walked to the witness stand. He looked relaxed, more confident than the day before. "Doctor, thank you for coming today. I appreciate the difficulty of testifying about one of your patients. Doctor, did you perform a physical examination on the defendant, Stringer Johnson, at the county jail yesterday?"

"Yes."

"What were the findings of your exam?"

Dr. Conklin adjusted his sport coat as he glanced at the jury. "I'll try to be as delicate as possible."

Buster stepped closer. "You can be delicate, Doctor, but you must tell us the important details of what you found."

Dr. Conklin's gaze went to the back of the room. Francis looked over his shoulder and saw Sheriff McNeal sitting in the last row near the metal prisoner door. He was staring straight at the witness.

"At the request of the court, I examined this young man at the jail. His chest and abdominal exam were normal except for what appeared to be three small round burn scars near his umbilicus."

"Did these appear to be old or new scars?"

"Old, from years ago."

"Did they resemble anything you've seen in the past?"

Dr. Conklin glanced at the back of the room again. "They could have resulted from a variety of things."

Buster stepped closer to the railing, blocking the doctor's view of McNeal. "In your experience, Doctor, do they resemble a particular type of burn?"

"Yes. Burns from cigarette butts."

"You said they were from years ago, so they would have been caused when he was a young boy?"

The doctor appeared more uncomfortable. "Probably."

Chadbourne came out of her chair. "Objection. Speculation."

"Your Honor, the doctor is expressing his medical opinion."

"I'll allow it. You may continue, Mr. Hurd."

Buster turned back to Dr. Conklin. "Did you find other abnormalities?"

"Yes." There was a long pause then he continued. "The boy is missing his left testicle."

A communal gasp spread across the courtroom.

Buster waited a few moments as the gravity of the doctor's testimony sunk in. "Did this look like a congenital defect?"

"No, absolutely not. He has an irregular scar on his left scrotum, where his testicle should be. He had an injury to that area."

Francis felt Kate losing strength next to him. He looked over at members of the jury who were intensely focused on Dr. Conklin.

"Did Stringer tell you what happened to his testicle?"

Dr. Conklin cleared his throat. "He was very hesitant to, but yes, he did."

Buster waited. Dr. Conklin looked at Stringer compassionately. "When he was eight, his father took him to an abandoned aqueduct in LA and made him dance on a picnic table in front of his drinking buddies." Dr. Conklin hesitated. "He said his father was drunk, shooting between his legs as he danced. Not surprisingly, he missed." Dr. Conklin looked at the floor in front of Buster. "His father shot off his testicle with a .22 pistol."

Murmurs spread across the crowd as many people shook their heads in disbelief. Several members of the jury put their hands to their mouths.

Buster stepped closer, leaned on the railing with both hands. "Who performed the surgery to repair his wound?"

With a haunted look in his eyes, Dr. Conklin looked at Buster. "Some hunting buddy of his father's. I'd say a butcher did it."

"Objection, Your Honor. Dr. Conklin has no idea what doctor the defendant might have seen years ago."

Ignoring Chadbourne's objection, Judge Thornton turned to the witness. "Doctor, please answer the questions without injecting your personal opinions."

"Yes, Your Honor," he said, settling himself. "After he was shot, Stringer bled badly. His father slowed the bleeding by duct taping a rag across his groin. They were drunk and didn't dare take him to a hospital so they drove him up to a hunting camp in the mountains where an old army medic buddy sewed him up with fishing line." Dr. Conklin looked over at the jury. "After that they continued drinking and making fun of him. Leland said he'd kill him if he told anyone what happened. And besides, Leland said if Stringer ever told anyone they'd know for sure he wasn't a real man."

"Why didn't Stringer ever tell anyone—at least his mother?"

Dr. Conklin shook his head. "Ashamed and scared, he's hidden it from his mother and everybody else for years."

Buster waited a few long moments after Dr. Conklin stopped speaking. "Doctor, have you seen many cases of child abuse?"

Dr. Conklin nodded his head. "Unfortunately, quite a few."

"Would you consider this a case of child abuse?"

Dr. Conklin looked at Buster incredulously. "Yes. Definitely. The worst I've ever seen."

"With reasonable medical certainty, do you believe these wounds could have been self-inflicted?"

"I do not. No way."

Buster glanced at Chadbourne, who appeared ready to rise again.

"Thank you, Doctor," Buster said. "That will be all."

Buster returned to his seat. The courtroom was deathly quiet. Lester leaned over and clicked on a switch on the wall. The ceiling fan over the jury box creaked to life.

Judge Thornton looked over his bifocals at the prosecutor. "Your witness."

Chadbourne stood. Appearing rather solemn, she addressed the witness from behind her table. "Dr. Conklin, what is your medical specialty?"

"Emergency medicine."

"Are you certified in pediatrics or urology?"

"No, but those areas are part of emergency medicine."

"But you're not considered an expert in those areas, are you, Doctor?"

"No."

Gwen stepped from behind the table. Her posture was rigid as she walked toward the stand. "Putting aside for the time being what the defendant may have told you, from your physical exam alone could you tell what had caused the defendant's condition?"

"I suppose not."

"Is it possible, Doctor, that lots of things could have caused it? A fall on something sharp? Getting caught climbing over a fence? That sort of thing."

"It's possible, but—"

"Many types of jagged cuts can heal in the way you describe, can they not?"

"Yes, but in this case, I—"

Chadbourne cut him off again. "So with no medical evidence—"

"Objection, Your Honor." Buster rose, setting his glasses on the table. "The State isn't even showing the courtesy of letting the witness finish his sentences."

Chadbourne stepped back from the witness stand and looked at the judge. "I'm sorry, Your Honor. I will let him finish." She turned back to Dr. Conklin and waited. He again glanced toward the back of the room where McNeal was seated.

Judge Thornton leaned forward. "Doctor, do you have something more to say in response to the previous questions?"

"No."

"You may proceed, Ms. Chadbourne."

"Doctor, with apparently no medical records and no objective findings to point to a specific cause, we really have only the defendant's story to suggest any abuse was involved. Is that correct?"

Dr. Conklin's eyes opened wider. "I believe him. He has psychological scars."

Gwen turned sharply. "And now you're a certified psychiatrist too, Doctor?"

Buster came out of his seat. "Your Honor, Dr. Conklin is a respected member of the medical community. He should not have to endure Ms. Chadbourne's callous behavior, her baseless demeaning of him."

Judge Thornton turned to the prosecutor. "You may continue, Ms. Chadbourne, but I ask you to limit your editorializing, which ill serves you and the State."

Chadbourne bristled then nodded politely and continued. "Dr. Conklin, have you seen this sort of wound on other young boys? Not necessarily on the scrotum, but anywhere on the body?"

"Yes."

"From what sort of injuries?"

"Getting caught on barb wire, farming injuries, that sort of thing."

She turned back to Dr. Conklin. "Did you think those injuries were from child abuse?"

Dr. Conklin frowned. "No."

Gwen stepped to the railing of the witness stand. "So, Doctor, is there *any* definite medical evidence that proves the defendant's injury was the result of abuse and not just some kind of kid injury?"

Dr. Conklin looked over at Stringer, a look of despair in his eyes.

Chadbourne leaned closer to the railing. "Doctor?"

Dr. Conklin hesitated.

Chadbourne took a couple of steps toward the jury. "Your silence answers the question." She turned and walked back to her seat. "No further questions, Your Honor."

Judge Thornton looked at the clock on the balcony then at Buster. "Do you wish to redirect, Mr. Hurd?"

Buster stood. "Just one question, Your Honor." He looked at Dr. Conklin. "Doctor, in your medical opinion and in your heart, do you have *any* question that Stringer Johnson lost his testicle by a violent act of his father?"

Dr. Conklin looked straight at Buster and shook his head. "No, Mr. Hurd, no question whatsoever."

CHAPTER 35

After court recessed for the day, Buster met briefly with Kate and Francis in the courthouse parking lot. The sun was quickly setting and a cold mist hung in the air. Kasa waited by her car a short distance away.

Buster loosened his tie. "We were just notified that unfortunately Mrs. Shedrick has died, poor thing." Buster shook his head. "It's time to call in the cavalry, so I just phoned Jacob. He's leaving New York and should be here late this evening."

In the golden light, Buster looked more worried than he had at any time since the beginning. Francis felt panic forming in his gut. Kate shook her head, working the crumbling pavement with her foot.

"Things are not going well," Buster said, his warm breath mixing with the cold air. "I've seldom seen a trial with such a strong, unpredictable rip tide." He faced Kate. "We have critical decisions to make. I think Chadbourne's going to offer us reduced charges—second degree murder or less. You're Stringer's legal guardian and you'll have to make the final decision whether we agree to let the jury consider them."

Kate's eyes lit up. "Second degree sounds better."

"A little, but don't get too excited. Stringer could still spend most of his life in jail. The other major issue is that time is running out. Who else should I put on the stand? You? Stringer?"

"I don't know. You're the attorney," Kate said, sounding annoyed.

Ignoring Kate, Francis looked at Buster. "How do you think Stringer would do?"

"I don't know. He's totally devastated by this injury being revealed; he's a teenager who's lost part of his sex organs. He dreads the thought of being on the stand, of having to be asked about it." Buster shook his head. "It's not clear how to proceed. I want Jacob's help on this. He'll offer an objective view."

Buster turned to Kate. "I'm cold, and if you'd be so kind, I need to speak with Francis for a few minutes alone."

Kate looked alarmed. "Okay," she said hesitantly. "I'll ride home with Kasa." She slowly turned away and walked over to Kasa's car.

Buster waited until Kate was out of earshot then turned to Francis. "When I defended Felix Giroux years ago in that logging murder, I had a clear vision going into the end of the trial that we would win. I could feel it. I have to be honest that I don't have that clarity now. This is the goddamndest case I've ever tried. The jury and everybody else are already worn out and they want this over before Christmas. If we're going to win, we have to make the right move, land the right punch—now."

Buster shook his head. "It's clear to me Stringer is not guilty of murder in any degree, but I'm worried because the circumstances are so complex, Chadbourne is so relentless, and the jury's understandably torn." Buster looked Francis in the eye. "I'm certainly not throwing in the towel, but you folks had better be prepared for anything."

Francis felt a well of emotion rise in the back of his throat.

"I know how much you love them," Buster said, patting Francis on the shoulder. "I'll bring Jacob out to the bungalow as soon as he arrives."

As Buster walked toward his Buick, Chadbourne came down the courthouse steps toward him. He stopped and they spoke briefly then walked to their cars and left.

As Francis opened the Jeep's door, he saw Charlie standing in the doorway of the sheriff's office. He looked like a terribly lonely man. Francis watched him for a few moments then climbed in and drove off. He drove down Main and turned onto Cliff Street. The firemen had gone home, but the ice chute they'd made glistened under the street lights. He got out and stood at the top of the chute. The cold wind blowing off the harbor felt good against his face, giving him a relief of sorts. He looked out beyond the frozen harbor where whitecaps dotted the horizon.

"You okay?"

Francis turned. A sheriff's cruiser had pulled up beside the Jeep. Charlie got out and walked over to Francis. "Pretty cold out here without a coat."

"I like it," Francis said, crossing his arms.

Charlie adjusted his gun belt on his hip and zipped up his coat. "I'm worried they're going to hang him." He stared out at the harbor, shifting his weight from one foot to another. "If you want, I'll let him out. Tonight."

Francis turned to Charlie. "What do you mean, let him out?"

"I go on duty at eleven. I mean, I'll spring him from jail, let him out the back door. They'll probably lock me up, but I don't care anymore." Charlie shoved his hands in his pockets. "I can't sleep. My stomach's a wreck. I think of..." Charlie paused, looking at the ground. "I think of Nate and how you helped him." Charlie took a few steps away. "Shit, Francis—"

Francis frowned. "I don't think that's it, Charlie. What you really want is for me to forgive you." He turned and looked Charlie in the eye. "Isn't it? You bastards allowed the county to charge this poor kid with murder when you knew Leland had beaten the shit out of him and Kate. You and Ralph went to the apartment. You *knew.*" Francis felt so angry he wanted to slug Charlie.

"We had nothing to do with charging him. That was Chadbourne's doing."

Francis glared at Charlie. "That's bullshit! You were all in on it. You, that asshole McNeal, the town council, and your secret meetings—all of you. Don't stand here and pretend you weren't. You could have stopped this goddamn freight train a long time ago, but you didn't. None of you like outsiders and you're all chicken shit afraid of the sheriff. It makes me sick."

Francis wiped cold sweat from his forehead. "Now, at the end of his trial, you want to let Stringer out of jail, to let him run off into the night? What, so you can shoot him down in cold blood trying to escape? Make a big name for yourself?"

As the words left his mouth, Francis saw Charlie's countenance fall, his shoulders drop. Hard tears formed in the corners of his eyes. "I would never..." Charlie said with half a voice. "I want to help—"

"It's kind of late, Charlie," Francis said, a bit more understanding in his voice. He walked over and climbed into the Jeep. "They'll never hang him. Never!" he yelled out the window as he drove off.

Francis didn't remember driving home. "Kate?" he called out as he walked into the cold house.

On the kitchen counter by the stove was the cap to the Jameson bottle. "Shit," Francis said. Not seeing her, he ran upstairs to the bedroom. On the hardwood floor in front of the windowsill was the whaler's lamp, smashed to pieces, its wire frame contorted.

Francis's heart sank. He knelt on the floor and lifted the remains of the lamp in his hands. Small pieces of ancient glass tinkled to the floor as he stood and set what was left of the lamp back in its place. He reached inside the metal frame and straightened the remnant of a candle. Stepping over the broken glass, he walked downstairs into the hallway. He turned on the light then saw Kate's legs on the floor in front of the woodstove. He rushed into the parlor where he found her half-wrapped in a blanket on the cold floor, the bottle of Jameson on its side against the wall. The floor was wet, the air heavy with the smell of whiskey.

Francis crouched on the floor and slid his arm under Kate's neck and shoulders. He lifted her against him. "Oh, Kate," he said, tears running down his cheeks into her hair. He rocked back and forth with her in his arms, crying harder than he had in many years. He cried for what a bastard his own father was; cried for Rachael, for Kate, and for Kasa. He cried for Stringer as Leland ground his childhood drawings into the floor with his boot. He cried for all the injustice, the hatred, and the cruelty.

Francis closed his eyes and fell back against the couch. As he caught his breath, he felt Kate lift her head. She slid her hands around his face. Her breath did not smell of whiskey.

"I'm sorry about the lamp. When I got home, I tried to light it, but I was shaking so badly."

Francis felt her shivering against him. She looked around the room. "I know it smells like a distillery in here. I *really* wanted to get drunk, but I ended up kicking the bottle across the floor. What a mess," she said. "Like me."

A huge wave of relief shot through Francis. He looked into her eyes. "I love you more than I have ever loved anyone." Kate leaned toward him and kissed his lips. Then they wrapped their arms around each other.

The phone rang, startling them both.

"It's probably Buster," Francis said. He got up and answered it. "Yes, we're here. Come right out."

"What is it?" Kate asked.

"Buster said Jacob's arrived from New York."

"Does this mean Buster thinks things are going badly?"

"To some degree, I guess. Things have been so tumultuous that he's just not sure. Mostly I think he wants Jacob's objectivity and moral support. They're on their way now."

Kate nodded. "I need to go outside and meditate for a few minutes then I'll clean up this mess."

"Take your time."

Kate pulled on his field coat and walked to the door.

"Kate," Francis said.

She looked back at him.

"We *will* get through this.

"I hope so," Kate said then turned and walked outside.

Francis cleaned up the broken glass then picked up the empty Jameson bottle. Buster wouldn't be happy. He walked upstairs and looked out the seaward window. Kate stood at the bluff. A large silvery moon was rising, illuminating tufts of whitecaps on the bay. He pushed the window open and listened. He heard Kate's song carried on the ocean wind. This time it was not a war song; it was more like a lullaby she was singing to herself.

Kate came back inside and brewed a pot of cinnamon spice tea. Buster's Buick came up the driveway just as Francis finished building a roaring fire in the parlor.

"Jacob," Francis said, opening the front door. Even in the dull light, Jacob's eyes were bright and penetrating, his face calm, self-assured. They embraced on the front step. "I am so glad to see you."

Jacob took Francis's arms in his strong hands and looked him over. "And I am glad to see you. I didn't expect it, but you look good, my friend."

Francis stepped aside, motioning for Jacob and Buster to enter. As they stepped into the bungalow, the warm scent of wood smoke and spice rushed past them into the cold night. Francis closed the door and took their coats.

Jacob turned and faced Kate, who was standing in the doorway to the kitchen. "You must be Kate." He walked over and offered his hand. "It's a pleasure to meet you. Buster has spoken very highly of you."

Kate looked embarrassed and gently withdrew. "Thank you for coming." She took a step back into the kitchen. "Would you like a cup of tea?"

"I'd love one. The aroma in here is wonderful."

"Come, sit by the fire," Francis said, motioning toward the parlor.

Jacob and Buster sat in the two easy chairs. Kate served everyone tea and squares of Kasa's shortbread then she and Francis sat on the couch.

Jacob sipped down half his cup and set it on the floor beside him. He looked at Kate. "Buster and I have discussed things by phone several times during the trial, and I hope you don't mind me speaking frankly." He paused for a few moments.

"I sense strong provincial politics running beneath the surface of things. This town is devastated that any of this happened here and they want it to never happen again. My read is people want to err toward public safety, to set a precedent to frighten other, trouble-making outsiders away. Fear is a very powerful force."

Jacob stared at the flames in the glass door of the stove. "On the other hand, these Maine folks have a long history of being fair minded; of having a sincere interest in the truth. I doubt that deep down they like men who abuse women and children much more than they like murderers."

Jacob loosened a finely woven scarf from around his neck. "The problem is the most undeniable truth in this case: Stringer's father is dead at the hand of his son. Five shots from his father's own gun—the gun that was cruelly used on him as a boy. Ironic, isn't it? Or..." Jacob said, lifting his eyebrows, "in the mind of the prosecution, is it a case of violent revenge? An eye-for-an-eye, so to speak?"

Jacob lifted the cup from the floor and drained the rest of his tea. He looked at his old law school friend. "Buster, I say to hell with years of appeals. You've got one real chance to win this. You *must* capture the jury's heart. I know you can mount one hell of a closing argument, but I'm not sure it'll be enough. So there are only two possible witnesses left: Stringer and you, Kate. You're both high risk. In a capital case, only rarely is the accused put on the stand, virtually never someone Stringer's age. Being his mother, you don't *have* to take the stand. You could be key, but it would put enormous pressure on you to try and save your son. It could backfire—and badly. On the other hand, if we think the trial is not going our way, what harm could it do?"

Francis watched Kate's face. She was in control of herself, but her pain was intense.

Buster leaned forward in his chair. "The other major issue is should we allow the court to instruct the jury to consider lesser offenses? Chadbourne caught me in the parking lot and asked us to consider them. She would rather be assured of a conviction on second degree, even voluntary manslaughter, than risk losing on first degree. She's mounted a good case, but I also sense she's worried."

Buster loosened his tie and leaned back. "I think she's willing to bargain. If Stringer pleads guilty to second, she'll ask for leniency, maybe fifteen to twenty."

Kate looked at Buster. "He'd be in jail till he's thirty-three?" She shook her head. "Forget it."

Jacob looked at Kate. "It would be better than life."

Kate crossed her arms and stared at the stove.

After a couple moments, Jacob turned to Francis. "Do you have any thoughts on this?"

Francis sat back on the couch. "It would be presumptuous of me to have a legal opinion. I have to trust your expertise." He didn't look at either Buster or Jacob.

There was silence.

Jacob continued to look at Francis. "We've known each other a long time, my friend. I feel you have something to say."

Francis looked up. "You know me well." He cleared his throat. "I may be way off base, but I don't think the jury will have the stomach to convict String on first degree but might find their way to conviction on a lesser charge. I feel unsettled, but I'd lean toward making them prove first degree."

Kate frowned, shifting to the opposite side of the couch. She stared at Francis. "And what if you're wrong? What if he ends up in jail for the rest of his life?"

"He asked my opinion, Kate. I've given it honestly."

Jacob glanced at Buster then sat back and clasped his hands together. "I think the best thing would be for Buster and me to confer alone. We must decide a course of action tonight."

"Okay," Francis said. "I could use a walk."

Kate stood. "Me too."

"Give us half an hour," Buster said.

Kate took Rachael's sheepskin from the closet. Francis grabbed the field coat and a pair of leather gloves and they walked out the door, heading across the snow in opposite directions: Kate toward the cliff, Francis toward Kasa's.

As he approached the bottom of the hill, a state plow truck scraped along the main road, sending sparks and a curl of dirty snow across the end of the driveway. The truck's brilliant amber strobe lights refracted in millions of ice particles suspended in the air and on the branches of the trees.

Francis stopped beside the fence surrounding Kasa's garden. A couple of pumpkin tops showed through the snow. The lights were off in her house so he assumed she had gone to bed. He turned and walked toward the main road.

"You can't sleep, either?"

He turned and saw Kasa sitting on her splitting block beside the summer kitchen. He walked over and leaned against a stack of firewood.

Kasa patted his leg with her hand. "How are you holding up, my friend?"

"We've been meeting with the lawyers. They have to decide if Stringer might plead to slightly lesser charges, but I have a bad feeling about it."

Kasa listened carefully until he was finished then looked up into the sky. "Do you know about the American explorer William Clark?"

"Of Lewis and Clark?"

"Yes. Legend has it that Clark was leading his men across the Rocky Mountains in the dead of winter. They were freezing, half-starved, and desperately discouraged. They had gone too far to turn back, yet they had treacherous mountain passes to conquer in order to make it to the other side. One morning after a heavy snowfall, Clark stood before his men and said: 'Faith dares the soul to go farther than it can see.' Three days later they made it safely to the west side of the Rockies."

Kasa turned toward Francis. "Stringer must be allowed to defend himself. Do not let them lower the charges. Make them prove their case or set him free. You must have faith in these Maine people to do the right thing. I do."

Francis saw the strength in her large eyes. "I will do my best," he said. He wished her a good night and walked back up the slippery hill to the bungalow.

Inside he saw Kate standing by the parlor talking with Buster and Jacob. She immediately walked over to Francis. Her countenance had softened and she looked scared. "They want Stringer to testify and they want to stay with first degree. Buster says because I'm his guardian, the final decision is up to me."

Francis looked into her eyes. "What do you feel in your gut?"

"Sick," she said. "I know what I feel as a mother, but I don't have a feel for things legally. Truthfully, I feel like I'm going to explode with anxiety and fear and at the same time I feel I need to trust them." Kate moved closer to Francis. "I have one favor to ask you."

"Name it."

"Buster said Stringer *really* doesn't want to get on the stand, but we have to see that he does. I think you're the best one to convince him. You have a special way with him; the same as with Charlie's son."

Francis took a step back.

"If you can't convince him, I'll let them put him on the stand anyway, but he may not cooperate, which could look really bad."

Francis thought for a few moments. "All right. I'll talk to him first thing in the morning."

Buster stepped into the hallway. "Tonight, Francis."

Francis looked at Buster then at Kate. "Okay. Tonight."

CHAPTER 36

Because of the heavy snow drifts, it was after midnight when Francis arrived at the jail. Charlie was on night duty and for the first time Francis felt like saying something to Charlie to relieve his angst. But he just couldn't find the words. So instead, Francis nodded cordially and walked straight to Stringer's cell. As he unlocked the door, Charlie spoke quietly to Francis. "He doesn't look good and he won't talk. I'm really worried about him."

Stringer stood at the far end of the metal bunk staring out the window. Francis stepped into the cell and sat on the edge of the cot. He spoke in a quiet, steady voice. "String, I need to talk to you about something that's very important. We want you to testify tomorrow. It's critical."

"No way," Stringer said, grabbing hold of the bars over the window.

"Why won't you help yourself? What are you afraid of?"

Stringer wheeled around. "I'm not afraid."

Francis stood. "I think you are. You're scared to tell the truth. I thought that's what you liked about me."

"It's not the same."

"Then tell me what you're thinking."

Stringer let go of the bars and leaned against the chalky bricks. "You didn't know my father. From when I was little, even before he shot me, he said I would never be a man." Stringer pushed off the wall and faced Francis. "Well, that bastard was wrong and now I'm going to be one. I'm not going to give up and collapse like a fucking wimp."

Francis was surprised at what he heard. "You think that not acknowledging your past—not fighting and letting these people put you away for the rest of your life—is being a man? You're smarter than that, Stringer."

Francis stepped toward him. "You think if you let down your guard and tell what Leland *really* did to you, he'll have beaten you?" Francis shook his head. "I think it's the other way around. You *can* get justice and relief from this hell you're in only by getting the whole truth out there."

Stringer didn't waver.

Unexpected anger rose in Francis. "You know, String, as awful as it was for you, you're not the only kid in the world who had to put up with an abusive father."

Stringer looked at him sarcastically. "What would *you* know about that? You and your money and your rich friends."

"You don't know as much about me as you think you do. You think money protects you from harm in this life? Well, think again." Francis stepped to the cell door and took hold of the bars. "My father did anything he could think of to stop me from painting. Every Friday night I lived in fear of his coming home from work in New York. He'd kick my easel across the floor, smash paints against the wall. He'd lock me out of the room in the attic where I painted and trash everything I hadn't hidden."

"Yeah, well did he ever beat you up? Kick the shit out of you?"

"As a matter of fact, he did." Francis pushed back his sandy hair, revealing an old scar on the crown of his head. Stringer looked away. "That's from a brass cane my father hit me with one night after too many cocktails. He chased me down the staircase from the attic beating me over the head. I was fourteen years old. Out in the middle of our street he kept yelling at me, said he wouldn't have a little faggot artist living in his house."

Francis let his hair fall over the scar then placed his hands on Stringer's shoulders. "The only way I survived was holding onto my truth with everything I had. One night, against my mother's pleadings, I finally told the police everything that bastard had done to me. I finally got out of that house and came here to live with my grandmother. And no matter what, I kept painting."

Holding Stringer's shoulders firmly, Francis stared into his eyes. "You *must* tell them what he did to you."

Stringer's eyes filled with tears. "I can't, Francis." He looked down at the dingy cement floor. "I think I'll fall apart if I do."

Tears streamed down Stringer's face as his shoulders gently shook. He turned away from Francis and collapsed on the cot. Francis sat beside him, curling an arm around his shoulder. Stringer cried into the rough woolen blanket.

Francis looked at the crumpled Wyeth print on the wall. He reached up and took it down so Stringer could look at it. "This painting is called 'Barracoon.' Do you know what that means?"

Stringer dried his eyes with his sleeve and looked at the painting. "No."

"Barracoons were small enclosures in which they kept slaves during Thomas Jefferson's time." They stared at the black woman's body. "Cooped up in that dark, claustrophobic space, I'm sure she had little idea how she could ever make it to freedom or even survive, for that matter. But she and thousands of others clung to a deep, enduring faith that got them through, and eventually they were set free."

Stringer looked into Francis's eyes. Francis knew he understood. Then Stringer laid his head back down and closed his eyes. Francis rubbed his back until he finally fell asleep.

CHAPTER 37

December twenty-second dawned sunny and cold. Despite the weather, a band of protesters had returned and the yellow sheriff's tape was back up along the snow fence. Several television vans were parked in the lot, satellite antennas telescoping skyward from their roofs. Everyone knew the end of the trial was near.

A deputy let Kate and Francis slip in the side door of the courthouse. The room was even more packed than usual. They walked down the aisle, slid across the bench to their seats behind Stringer, who sat attentively in a new suit between Buster and Jacob.

Judge Thornton put down the file he was reading and glanced at the clock. "Good morning. I'd like to mention that an additional defense attorney has joined us today, Mr. Jacob Bernstein from New York City."

Chadbourne looked at the defense table disapprovingly.

The judge looked at Buster. "Your next witness, Mr. Hurd."

Buster rose. "Thank you, Your Honor." Buster sounded unusually respectful as he stepped toward the jury. "The defense calls Stringer Johnson."

Several jury members looked surprised.

Charlie stood beside Stringer and motioned toward the witness stand. As Stringer passed him, Charlie mouthed the words, "Good luck."

Stringer appeared weak as he walked across the courtroom. He didn't look at Gwen Chadbourne or the jury or the many rows of people watching. He walked straight to Lester, put his left hand on the Bible, and slowly raised his right.

"Do you swear to tell the truth and nothing but the truth, so help you God?"

Stringer paused and glanced at Francis.

"Son?" Lester said quietly.

Stringer looked at him. "Yes."

"You may be seated."

Stringer stepped into the witness box. Though appearing thin and uncomfortable in his suit, he still looked like a handsome young man.

Buster spoke to Stringer in a calm voice. "After all you've been through, I'm sure you're worn to the bone, but only you can tell us the truth of what happened to you on September ninth in that apartment and how events in your life with your father led up to it." Buster gestured to the jury. "And the only thing that really matters to the members of this jury is the whole truth. There's too much at stake and we're all too tired for anything else."

Buster pulled his suit jacket back and slid a hand into his front pocket. "Stringer, when you got out of bed that morning, did you have any intention of killing your father?"

"No, sir." Stringer's voice sounded clear and mature.

"Had you been lying in wait for your father to come from California so you could kill him?"

"No, sir. I hoped he'd never find us up here in Maine."

"What did you think when he arrived in Winter's Cove?"

"I was mostly scared, afraid he'd start beating on us again."

"Did you have any good feelings?"

Stringer glanced at Kate, who looked down at the floor. "To be honest, part of me hoped he'd be different. I just wanted him to be nice to us. You know, be a normal dad. I always kept hoping for that."

"Was he different?"

Stringer shook his head. "Nope. It was worse than ever."

"How so?"

Stringer stared into space for a few moments.

"What did Leland do to you?" Buster continued.

Stringer did not respond.

Buster stepped closer. "Stringer, the jury needs you to tell them exactly what Leland did to you and your mom."

Stringer's shoulders fell.

Buster waited a few moments then put his hands on the wooden railing. "Stringer, you must tell us what happened. There is no other way for the jury to know."

Stringer raised his head and looked at Kate again. "Does Mom have to be here?"

Francis held his arm around Kate's shoulder.

Buster glanced at Kate and Francis. "If it would help you speak more freely, we could ask her to leave."

From the corner of his eye, Jacob watched the judge and the jury.

"I'm sorry, Mom," Stringer said.

Judge Thornton looked at Kate. "Mrs. Johnson, would you mind stepping outside?"

Without looking up, Kate curled in tighter to Francis.

The judge looked over his bifocals. "Ma'am, I think it might be best for your son."

Francis was sure she felt Stringer would be thrown to the lions without her there to protect him. But then Kate planted her feet under her and slowly rose. Francis stood, supported her with his arm, and helped her step to the center aisle. They started to walk toward the back.

"Not Francis!" Stringer called out.

Startled, Francis stopped and turned back. Kate slid out from under his arm and hurried out through the double doors.

Francis stood in the middle of the courtroom. It seemed like a thousand faces were staring at him. He returned to his seat and sat down. Attention turned back to the witness stand.

Buster looked at Stringer. "Now please tell us what Leland did to you and your mom."

Stringer stared at the floor again and said nothing.

Judge Thornton waited a few moments then leaned forward. "Young man, you are to answer Mr. Hurd's question."

Stringer remained silent.

Thornton stared at him. "Face Mr. Hurd and answer his questions."

Stringer turned to Buster who looked frustrated but kept his cool. He took off his glasses and stepped close to Stringer. "This is your life we're talking about here, son."

The jury began looking impatient. Jacob turned and looked at Francis. Francis stared at Stringer, hoping he would look up. Everyone waited.

Finally Stringer looked at Francis who nodded.

Stringer fidgeted with the microphone then began speaking. "For a long time Mom put up with my father beating her. The worst was late at night when he'd get drunk and lock her in their bedroom. I'd sit in my room listening to him slapping her and throwing her around. She'd scream in pain. If I tried to get into their bedroom, he'd come out and beat me up bad."

Stringer fell silent and looked at the floor. "Most kids couldn't wait for the weekend, but they were the worst for me. I still can't sleep much on Saturday nights."

"What happened on Saturdays?" Buster asked.

Pain crept across Stringer's face. "He snorted cocaine with his pals on Saturdays. He'd come home really crazy, usually with one of his buddies. Mom tried to leave with me lots of times, but Leland always found us. We didn't have a car and we were always broke. We didn't really have any friends or family to go to so we never got very far."

The jury paid close attention. Buster worked to keep Stringer focused. "What happened when Leland came home with his friends?"

Stringer's face turned beet red. "He and his buddies partied in our apartment. Some nights he—" Stringer's voice choked; he had a hard time catching his breath.

"Go on," Buster urged.

"He let them screw my mother." Stringer paused, his eyes brimming with tears. "One night she screamed so much I broke the door down with a dumbbell. This guy and Leland were abusing her. They had her tied to the bed. They poured beer on her, twisted her nipples, laughing while they raped her. She was screaming, trying to buck them off."

Judge Thornton sat back in his chair, grimacing. Buster looked shocked at what Stringer was saying.

"I tried to help her. Her face was bruised and her breasts were bleeding. When Mom saw me, she screamed for me to get out. I tried to pull them off of her, but Leland just kept slugging me. I think he knocked me out 'cause I woke up later outside on the living room floor."

Several jury members held their hands to their mouths. Even Mrs. Fitzgerald seemed appalled. Gwen Chadbourne didn't move.

"I wanted to help my mom, but I couldn't."

"I know you did," Buster said. He waited until Stringer got control of himself. "I know how hard this must be, but can you tell us what happened to you that day by the aqueduct, near Mrs. Shedrick's trailer?"

Stringer buried his face in his forearm and began to cry again.

Buster waited a few moments then stepped closer. "Please, Stringer. We need you to tell us everything."

Stringer caught his breath and looked at the judge. "Could I have a drink of water?"

"Right beside you there, son," Thornton replied in a sympathetic voice.

Stringer took a couple sips from the glass then cleared his throat. "My father took me to the aqueduct lots of times to shoot rats, stray cats, anything that moved. Sometimes he'd bring his drunk friends with him. The worst was the summer I turned nine. That was when Leland shot up Mrs. Shedrick's trailer. He was crazier than ever that day."

"Why did he shoot at her?"

"She saw something…"

"Saw what, Stringer?"

"I don't want to talk about it."

Buster stepped tight to the railing. "You *have* to talk about it."

Chadbourne stood. "Your Honor, this is not a psychotherapy session. He's badgering his own witness, for God's sake."

Buster turned to Judge Thornton. "I'm doing my job, Your Honor. What happened is terribly relevant to this trial. It's critical to this boy's defense. I need the boy to tell the jury what happened."

Chadbourne fired a glance at Buster. "Or do you want him to tell the jury what *you* want him to say? Push him till he makes up something good?"

Stringer banged his hand on the railing and snarled at Chadbourne. "I'm not making anything up!"

Judge Thornton rapped his gavel on the bench. "I'll not have outbursts in my courtroom."

Buster turned back to Stringer. "*Please*, Stringer."

Stringer awkwardly pulled off his suit coat. "He made me get up on a picnic table and take my pants off."

Francis stared at Stringer, encouraging him with his eyes.

Buster's voice was kind and calm. "Then what happened?"

"He made me spread my legs apart and then he…" Stringer stopped. He looked ill.

Buster put his hand on Stringer's arm to steady him. "It's okay. He can't hurt you anymore. Francis and I are right here with you."

Stringer took a deep breath. "He made me dance on the table. He and the other men were really drunk and yelling at me. They took turns firing shots between my legs with Leland's pistol."

Stringer's face contorted as he spoke. Several jury members gasped. Francis too suddenly felt ill.

"I was so scared, Mr. Hurd, I shit on the table. My father made me keep dancing and they kept shooting…" Stringer had a hard time catching his breath.

"And then what happened?"

"He kept screaming at me what a sissy I was. My feet were slipping in the shit on the table. He took the gun from one of the other men and came up close to me. The other guys tried to grab the gun from him, but he threw them off and shot at me."

Stringer bent forward, his hands covering his lap. "It was awful; it burned like a blow torch. There was blood all over my legs. That's when Mrs. Shedrick started yelling from the door of her trailer. I'm not sure exactly, but I think I fell off the table. I remember somebody loaded me into the back of a pickup. I was trying to hold my crotch together, but..." Stringer's head fell forward and he wept.

Buster kept his hand on Stringer's arm and waited.

"I only had one ball left," Stringer said between breaths.

"Your father shot off one of your testicles as Mrs. Shedrick testified?"

Stringer nodded then held his face in his hands and rocked back and forth.

Murmurs filled the courtroom.

Buster looked at Judge Thornton. "Your Honor, I have just a few more questions."

Frowning, Judge Thornton nodded.

Buster continued. "Stringer, did you have any idea that Leland would come to Maine?"

"No. We never wanted to see him again. I told you we thought it was far enough away."

"Then why did you take your father's pistol with you?"

"To protect us. I'd hardly ever been out of LA—never out in the sticks like this."

"Not to shoot your father..."

Stringer shook his head. "Of course not. But Mr. Hurd, I couldn't let him kill Francis and Mom."

"Do you know why there are no medical records about your scrotal injury?"

Stringer thought for a moment. "I guess 'cause my father took me out of town to some cabin. He had some old army vet sew me up. He didn't take me back to LA for a while. He let me call Mom a couple times but he was always right there holding the phone. She was pretty bad off that summer, but I know she was worried crazy about me. Leland said he'd kill me if I told anyone what happened. Mrs. Shedrick and his friends were the only ones who saw it. His friends would never tell 'cause they knew he'd kill them too."

Chadbourne raised her hand. "Objection, Your Honor. This is purely speculation by the defendant."

"I'll allow it," Judge Thornton said, without looking at her.

Buster nodded as Stringer spoke then turned to the jury. "I have just one last question for you." He turned back to Stringer. "If you could be anywhere in the world you wanted right now, where would it be?"

Stringer looked puzzled.

"Just tell us where you'd be, what you'd be doing if you were free."

Stringer cocked his head to the side and thought for a few moments. A bit of a smile came to his face. "I'd be skateboarding on the Venice Beach half pipe at sunset with my friends. Mom and Francis would be watching me do flips."

Buster listened, his hand under his chin.

"I wouldn't be scared anymore. It'd be awesome."

Buster smiled. "Thank you, Stringer. You're a remarkable young fellow." Buster looked at Judge Thornton. "No further questions, Your Honor."

CHAPTER 38

Francis looked around the courtroom. The jury, as well as many of the spectators, looked exhausted. He expected Judge Thornton to take a recess, but instead he asked Stringer if he was able to go on with the State's cross-examination. Stringer nodded.

Chadbourne rose, stepped around in front of her table, and leaned against it. "Stringer, when you were in California and Leland was mean to you, did you ever feel like you wanted to kill him?"

Stringer watched Chadbourne as if she were a rattlesnake coiling in front of him. He glanced at Francis. Francis knew Stringer was deciding whether or not to tell the truth. He also knew it was the only solid ground Stringer had left upon which to tread.

Stringer looked at Chadbourne. "Yeah. Couple times when he beat us up bad."

"Before you left LA, you broke into a locked box in your father's room and stole the pistol you used to shoot him. Is that right?"

"Yeah."

"And you knew how to shoot, right? Your father had taught you?"

"I already told you that."

"So your answer would be yes. Is that correct?"

"Yes."

"On the day of the shooting, how did Francis Monroe come to be in your mother's house?"

Stringer looked at Francis again. Buster straightened in his seat. "My father beat us up the night before. He'd gotten so drunk he was still asleep in the morning, so I got out of the apartment and ran to Francis's house. I told him Leland was crazy, that he'd been pounding on Mom and me."

"Why did you go to Francis?" Chadbourne bore down. "Was it because you knew he would help you kill your father?"

"No!" Stringer said sharply. "Because I trust him."

Chadbourne glanced across the jury. "So you went to your mother's lover, with whom she was committing the crime of adultery and—"

Buster came out of his chair. "Objection, Your Honor."

Judge Thornton looked at Chadbourne. "For everyone's sake, Ms. Chadbourne, please minimize the inflammatory rhetoric."

"I'll try, Your Honor." Chadbourne had a noticeable edge in her voice with the judge. "If you and your mother were really being abused by your father, why didn't you go to the police and ask them for help?"

"'Cause they never did anything. We'd had deputies come over before and he wouldn't let them in the door. They were just as scared of him as we were." Stringer shook his head. "It was the same in California. Nobody wants to deal with people like us."

"So instead of going to the proper authorities, you ran to Mr. Monroe and took him to your apartment to take care of your father?"

"I guess. But Francis wouldn't let me go with him. He made me stay at his house. But after he left I found his bike and rode into town."

"So really there were three of you against one of him."

"Yeah. But Mom couldn't fight him and I tried as hard as I could but with my broken arm I couldn't stop him. You don't know how crazy he'd get."

Chadbourne took a step toward Stringer. "Really?" she said slowly, sarcastically. "Let me get this straight. Aren't you the same 'kid' who dove into the stormy Atlantic and rescued Mr. Ready, pulling his water-logged body through the rocky waters of Wagner's Point to shore? Weren't you commended for your manly strength in saving his life?"

"Objection!" Buster said loudly. "This boy's strength is not at issue here."

"I'll allow it," Judge Thornton said without looking at Buster, who sat back down.

Chadbourne leaned in closer. Her voice was pressured, confrontational. "So I ask you, Stringer Johnson, why didn't you use your remarkable strength to subdue your father, especially in light of the fact that he weighed twenty pounds less than Delbert Ready? Why did you go for your father's gun and repeatedly shoot him at point blank range until the chamber was empty? Why did you drill five bullets into your own father's body if you didn't want to kill him?"

Buster stood. "Your Honor, this is outrageous. Ms. Chadbourne has gone beyond any bounds of decency."

Murmurs filled the courtroom. Many people were shaking their heads. Jacob looked over at the jury. Judge Thornton banged his gavel several times. Frowning, Lester rose from his desk.

"Quiet!" Judge Thornton said angrily. "I will not tolerate anymore outbursts." He held the gavel in his hand, pointing across the room with the handle. "If need be, I'll have the court officer clear every one of you from this courtroom."

He looked at Buster. "I will allow the prosecution the same latitude I gave you, Counsel. Now continue, Ms. Chadbourne."

"Thank you, Your Honor." She quickly turned back to Stringer. "I asked you why you shot five bull—"

"I heard you," Stringer snapped at her.

"Then answer me," she snapped back.

"'Cause Leland was crazy. Don't you get it? He was a madman; he was going to kill Francis and Mom and me."

"So why didn't you save Francis the same way you saved Mr. Ready in even more dangerous circumstances?"

"Nothing's more dangerous than being around Leland when he's drunk and crazy."

Chadbourne ignored him. "Was it because you'd been waiting to get your revenge for what your father had done to you with that same gun? Admit it, Stringer, you wanted him dead."

Stringer's face tightened. He squinted at Chadbourne. They were nearly nose to nose. The courtroom was hushed. Stringer took a breath through clenched teeth. He looked like he was about to spit at her. "Yes!" Stringer yelled in her face. "Sometimes I wanted him dead! Okay?" He rocked back in his seat.

Francis felt his heart thumping violently under his breast bone. Buster shot out of his chair. Jacob reached over, grasped Buster's leg, and held him. After a few tense moments, Buster sat back down.

"But I didn't *want* to shoot my father and I wouldn't have if he wasn't trying to kill us. I pleaded with him to put the knife down, but he wouldn't."

Anguish covered Stringer's face as he fought back tears. "If you want the truth..." he said, looking over at the jury. Buster, along with most of the courtroom, held their breath. "If you want the honest truth here..." His chin quivered and tears filled his eyes.

"The only way we could ever be okay, be safe, was if he was dead." Stringer started to cry. "He tortured us. He never stopped."

For a few uncomfortable moments, Chadbourne paced in front of the witness stand. She didn't seem to know what to do next. Then she planted her feet in front of Stringer and looked him in the eye. "One last question. Just so we're all clear on one point. Did you shoot and kill your father at point blank range with his own gun?"

Stringer got enough control of himself to answer. "Yes," he said, staring straight at her. "I had to."

CHAPTER 39

During the noon recess, Francis made his way to the far aisle and squeezed Stringer's arm before two deputies wearing black bulletproof vests escorted him from the room. Francis then went to the vestibule to find Kate. He could barely imagine how hard it was for her to leave her son alone in the courtroom. Not seeing her, he hurried outside where he was met with a gusty wind from the harbor that was blowing swirls of snow off the rooftops. He walked to the Jeep and found Kate tucked in a ball in the back seat. He chipped the ice and snow from the driver's door, climbed in, and started the engine.

He reached across the back of the seat and put his hand on Kate's leg. She was shivering. "You're freezing. We've got to get you warmed up."

Kate lifted her head. "Is String okay?"

Francis nodded. "Yes. He was a trooper. He told the jury the truth, and I think they appreciated that. The State has rested its case. Closing arguments are next."

"I hated to leave him."

"I know, but you did the right thing. It made it easier for Stringer to come clean. It was *really* hard, but I think he helped himself."

"Thank God," Kate said, straightening up in the seat.

Francis pushed the cuff of his coat back and checked his watch. "I'm going to take you some place warm."

He drove out of the parking lot, stopping in front of Zack's Coffee Shop. He ran in, picked up coffee and Danish then drove down Main Street to the gallery. He fumbled through the ashtray and pulled out a key.

"Stay here," he said, leaving the Jeep running. "I'll be back in a few minutes."

Kate nodded.

Francis took the bag from Zack's and climbed through the snow covering the gallery's steps and went in. A few minutes later he came back out and opened Kate's door. "Come on inside. We'll warm up."

Huddled under his arm, Kate walked through the snow into the gallery, which was cold and hollow sounding. Francis led her to a carved mahogany door in the back, which opened into a small, dark-paneled room with a thick Persian rug. Antique silk tapestries hung from ceiling to floor and a gas parlor stove blazed in front of a small sofa. Through frosted windows, the rock outcroppings of Wagner's Point could be vaguely seen in the distance.

Kate rubbed her hands together above the stove while Francis set the coffee and Danish on a glass-top table in front of the sofa. "Come, sit down," he said gently.

Kate sat beside Francis who tucked a soft cream and red plaid trapper blanket over her shoulders and around her legs. Then he handed her a cup of hot coffee, which she grasped with both hands.

"This tastes so good," she said. She stretched her neck in several directions then rested her head against the back of the sofa. "What is this place?"

"This was Rachael's room; where she'd come to get away from it all, especially in the summer when the gallery was very busy. Other times, she and Kasa and their friends would get together in here to discuss books they were reading or just to talk. And they enjoyed their fair share of wine and cheese in here too."

Kate took another sip of coffee. "Rachael sounds like an interesting woman."

Francis relaxed on the sofa next to Kate. "She was. And she was creative in her own, controlled sort of way. But she wasn't that nice to a lot of people. She had an upper class edge to her and always an agenda. And you know something?" Francis looked at Kate. "I didn't realize how much it turned me off until I met you."

Kate managed a subtle smile.

"After Rachael died I didn't think I would ever fall in love again. I didn't think it was possible." Francis shook his head. "You have so dramatically changed my life."

"Yeah," Kate said, sarcastically.

"I mean for the better." He touched her cheek. "I love you more than you can know."

Kate leaned against him.

After a while Francis stood and walked into the gallery. A collection of paintings leaned against the desk. "Where did these come from?"

Kate walked up behind him. "Kasa and I framed them. You agreed to have a show after the trial was over. Remember? In the parlor that night?"

Francis crouched down and looked through the collection of his new work. "The framing is excellent. How did you know how to do it?"

"Ginny helped us."

"Ginny Wentworth?"

"Yes. We've become friends."

"Really?" Francis said, surprised. "You get around more than I thought. Well, I doubt anyone's going to want to look at these, but if you agree to exhibit Stringer's work alongside mine, you can do a show."

Kate's eyes brightened. "You mean it?"

"Yes. He's done wonderful pieces, including several since he's been in jail." Francis glanced at his watch. "Speaking of which, we've got to hurry back. It's almost two o'clock."

When they pulled into the courthouse parking lot, Kate turned to Francis. "How do you feel it's going—really?"

He put the Jeep in park and looked at Kate. "I'm worried. Chadbourne is sharp, tough, and she keeps driving home those damn five shots. Buster has to give one hell of a closing argument."

Kate looked down.

Francis touched her leg. "We've got to go in. It's important that we're there."

As they walked inside, Charlie abruptly stepped away from Sheriff McNeal, crossed the vestibule, and took Francis by the arm. "Where is Mr. Hurd?"

"I'm right here," Buster said, walking out of the defense room.

Charlie turned to him. "I *have* to talk to you." Charlie's eyes were wide, his shirt collar loose about his sweaty neck.

"Buster looked Charlie in the eye. "About what?"

"I want to testify."

Suddenly McNeal charged across the vestibule, bumping into several people as he marched toward Charlie.

"For the defense?" Buster asked, frowning.

"Yes. I know things that could help Stringer."

"What the hell's going on here?" McNeal demanded. He grabbed Charlie's arm.

Charlie jerked his arm away and stared at Buster. "I *have* to testify."

McNeal stepped between them. "Are you stupid or just crazy? You're one of us."

Charlie's neck was engorged and red. "Not anymore. I quit." He reached up, tore his silver star from his chest, and jammed it into McNeal's hand.

McNeal winced as his hand began to bleed. Enraged, he growled at Charlie, "You goddamn traitor! You'll pay for this."

Charlie didn't move. He stared straight at McNeal. "No, you will, Sheriff."

Buster and the others in the vestibule stood in shocked silence.

McNeal glared at Charlie, Buster, and Francis. Then he turned away, motioned for Ralph to follow him, and stormed out the courthouse door.

CHAPTER 40

After the recess, Francis and Kate took their usual seats. With Charlie's surprise declaration, Francis felt some sense of relief. Buster watched intently as Judge Thornton walked to the bench. He looked tired and pensive. Chadbourne stood at her desk, her body stiff and a pen held so tightly in her hand she looked like she might stab someone.

Thornton took a drink of water and cleared his throat. "During the recess, defense council requested they be allowed to call an additional witness who has come forward. In light of the severity of this case and over the recorded objections of Ms. Chadbourne, I will allow it." He looked at Buster. "You may proceed, Mr. Hurd."

Buster whispered something to Jacob then stood and buttoned his wool suit jacket around his belly, which was smaller than when the trial had begun. "Thank you, Your Honor. The defense calls Mr. Charlie Lord."

Charlie entered from the back in a green chamois shirt and his uniform pants. Many townspeople looked confused and agitated. Charlie walked to the front and took the oath with his old friend, Lester, then sat down.

Buster stepped over to the witness stand. "Mr. Lord, you are testifying today at your own request. Is that correct?"

"Yes," Charlie said, watching as McNeal entered and sat in the back row. "I hope I'm doing the right thing."

Buster continued. "How long have you lived here, Mr. Lord?"

"All my life. I was born up in Rockland."

"And what have you done for work?"

"I worked lobster boats for a few years after high school then I went to the police academy and became a deputy sheriff. I've worked for the county under Sheriff McNeal for thirty-four years now."

Buster turned to the jury. "Are you still a deputy sheriff?"

Charlie looked down. "No. I quit. Just a little while ago."

"Did you like your job?"

"Loved it—at least most of it."

"Why did you quit a job you loved?"

"Objection," Gwen said. "Relevance."

"I'll allow it," Judge Thornton said without looking at her.

Buster repeated his question.

Charlie hesitated. "I couldn't do it anymore."

Buster stepped closer to the stand. "Couldn't do what?"

"Lie. Carry on the charade." Charlie frowned and looked at McNeal. "I couldn't work under the sheriff anymore."

"Why not?"

Charlie's jaw tightened. "'Cause he runs this place through fear and intimidation. Everybody feels threatened." He looked at Stringer and shook his head. "I've covered for him too many times. I can't do it this time."

Again, murmurs swept through the room. Buster waited then continued. "Mr. Lord, do you have information pertaining to Stringer Johnson or his mother, Kate, that is relevant to this murder trial?"

"Yes," Charlie said clearly into the mike.

"Did you ever see Leland Johnson abuse them?"

"Yeah, the night Leland beat them up in their apartment. I didn't see the actual beating, but I seen what he done to the boy and his mother. It was bad."

"But the official report from that night states you and another deputy went to the Johnson's apartment and found no evidence of significant injury to Stringer or Kate. The report is signed by

Sheriff McNeal himself. Are you saying you know something different?"

Charlie glanced at McNeal again. "Sheriff changed the report after Ralph and I wrote it. Said it'd be better if we didn't make a big deal out of it. He doesn't like people thinking there's trouble in town." Charlie shook his head. "Especially when he's up for reelection in the spring."

Chadbourne came out of her chair. "Objection, Your Honor!"

"Overruled."

Buster continued, "Are you saying Sheriff McNeal lied? Falsified official police records?"

Charlie's breathing quickened.

"Mr. Lord—"

"Yes. He's done it before."

McNeal shot out of his seat in the back of courtroom. "That's a goddamn lie!"

Judge Thornton cracked his gavel on the bench and glared at McNeal. "I'll have none of that, Sheriff."

"You ungrateful bastard!" McNeal yelled at Charlie.

"Remove him," Judge Thornton ordered.

"This is *my* courthouse—" McNeal shouted, his face a dark, purply red. He stepped into the center aisle, his right hand on his holster.

Lester limped up the center aisle to within a few feet of the sheriff. Judge Thornton rose from his chair and stared at McNeal. The courtroom was silent save for the irregular squeaking of the ceiling fan.

Charlie leaned on the railing of the witness stand with both hands, anguish overtaking his face.

Ralph was guarding the metal door at the far corner. He slid his right hand onto the grip of his gun and took a step in McNeal's direction.

Larry McNeal sucked hard on the wad of chew inside his lower lip, glancing back and forth across the room without moving his head. Slowly he stepped backwards until his left hand felt the large oak door. He pushed it open and backed out of the courtroom.

Ralph walked out after him. For a few moments, McNeal's yelling out in the vestibule carried into the courtroom then all was quiet again.

It took Judge Thornton a few moments to collect himself. He glanced at the door then looked at Buster. "Mr. Hurd, do you have any further questions for Deputy Lord?"

"Yes, Your Honor." He turned back to Charlie. "Mr. Lord, on the night of the fight with Leland Johnson, did you get a good look at Kate and Stringer? Up close, I mean. And if so, what did they look like?"

"I was on the porch, but I saw them pretty good through the open door. Their clothing was disheveled and torn. They both had bloody noses. Stringer's face was bruised pretty bad and he was holding his arm tight to his body—the one that had been in the cast."

Chadbourne rose again. "Objection, Your Honor. This witness is not a medical expert. He has no business testifying to this."

"Your Honor, I'm simply asking a veteran police officer for his observations relevant to this case."

"I'll allow it," Judge Thornton said, appearing impatient with Chadbourne's incessant objections. "Mr. Hurd, you may continue."

Buster turned back to Charlie. "Have you seen a lot of domestic abuse over the years?"

"Unfortunately, a fair amount."

"How did what you saw that night compare with other cases?"

"Pretty bad. He'd hurt them."

"Objection!" Chadbourne pushed her chair back and stepped toward the bench. "Your Honor, Mr. Hurd pulls this witness out of thin air—God knows how—and is now examining him as if he were an expert on medical injuries and domestic violence."

"Ms. Chadbourne—"

She dropped her legal pad on the table. "No, Your Honor, this is outrageous! You can't allow this."

Judge Thornton removed his bifocals and set them on the bench. "Ms. Chadbourne, this has been a difficult trial for everyone and I appreciate the stresses involved on all sides."

Chadbourne crossed her arms against her chest.

"In light of the considerable extenuating circumstances in this case, I have given both you and Mr. Hurd more than the usual leeway. However—" He leaned forward, looking directly at her. "*I* will decide what will and will not be allowed in this courtroom. Is that understood?"

Her lips pursed, Chadbourne arched her back. "Yes, Your Honor." She sat down and pulled her chair up tight to the table. "And I will certainly remember these proceedings when your judicial review comes up."

Thornton glared at her. "Are you threatening me, Ms. Chadbourne?"

Flushing red, her countenance softened a bit. "No, Your Honor, I was simply making a point."

"Mr. Lord," Buster continued. "If proper action had been taken that night instead of covering up what had happened, do you think the death of Leland Johnson might have been prevented?"

Charlie gave it a little thought. "Yes, I do."

"Objection. Speculation." Chadbourne looked infuriated but was trying to contain herself.

"They needed help," Charlie said directly into the mike.

"Mr. Hurd," Judge Thornton said, "you may not ask the witness to speculate in this manner."

Buster glanced at the jury, at Charlie, and then at the judge. "No further questions, Your Honor," he said, then walked back to his chair.

Judge Thornton frowned at Buster then turned and looked with some compassion at Charlie. "Deputy, are you ready to proceed?"

Charlie nodded. "Yes, Judge."

"Ms. Chadbourne, your witness."

Chadbourne stepped to the witness stand without looking at Judge Thornton. Charlie watched her carefully.

"Mr. Lord, you have been Sheriff McNeal's chief deputy for over fifteen years, is that correct?"

"Yes.

"And is this the first time you've ever claimed the sheriff has falsified records?"

"Yes."

Chadbourne turned toward the jury. "So if what you claim is true, you must have played a major part in covering up lies with the sheriff over the years." She turned back to Charlie. "Is that right, Mr. Lord?"

"Well, I—"

"Or are you lying now, Mr. Lord—to get at the sheriff or to help your friend, Mr. Monroe, and his girlfriend's kid?"

Buster raised his hand. "Objection. Argumentative."

"Overruled. Continue."

"Is it not true, Mr. Lord, that you are beholden to Francis Monroe for helping you with your difficult son who you and your wife couldn't handle? Did he not call you the day of Delbert Ready's wreck to help him by giving Kate Johnson a ride to the hospital? And was it not *you* who tried to cover up Mr. Monroe's involvement with that same married woman before the murder?"

"Yes, but no—" Charlie stumbled on his words.

People in the gallery looked back and forth at each other. The jury appeared concerned and confused.

"So you've lied one way or the other, Mr. Lord. Now you want us to believe your story about Sheriff McNeal, who has faithfully served this county for well over forty years?"

Charlie glanced around the room. "Other people know what the sheriff's like—how he scares people. Just ask them."

Chadbourne glared at him. "It's *you* who is under oath, Mr. Lord. You're the one who needs to answer the question."

Buster stood. "Your Honor—"

Judge Thornton looked at Charlie. "Please answer the question."

"*What* question?" Buster demanded. "All she's done is badger the witness. Is she the one testifying?"

Chadbourne stepped closer to Charlie. "The *question* is, Mr. Lord, are you trying to help Mr. Monroe because you are beholden to him?"

Charlie looked at the floor.

Chadbourne pressed on. "Years ago, weren't you and your wife under embarrassing pressure from county child services because you were not providing your handicapped son the education he needed? You went to Mr. Monroe for help. Wasn't he instrumental in keeping you out of trouble?"

"We did the best we could," Charlie said with anger and sadness. "Nate was difficult. Mr. Monroe helped, but—"

"And now you're trying to help him. Isn't that right, Mr. Lord? Well, it isn't going to work."

Charlie opened his mouth to speak, but Chadbourne turned away and walked back to her chair. "I'm finished," she said, thumping into her seat.

After a few moments, Judge Thornton turned to Buster. "Do you wish to redirect?"

Buster looked at Charlie for a few moments. Jacob didn't move. "No, Your Honor. Mr. Lord was quite clear about what really happened that night. The defense rests."

Judge Thornton adjourned for the day, and the courtroom quickly emptied.

CHAPTER 41

When court reconvened the following morning two State Police troopers stood guard at the back of the room and remained for the duration of the trial.

Judge Thornton looked up from the Bible on his desk and turned to the jury. "Ladies and gentlemen, you will now hear closing arguments. When the attorneys have concluded their remarks, I will give you instructions regarding your deliberations." Thornton turned to Gwen, who wore a navy blue suit, her sharp cheekbones highlighted with a touch of blush, her hair perfectly styled. "Ms. Chadbourne—"

"Ladies and gentlemen of the jury," she began, walking slowly toward them. "This murder trial is about to be put squarely in your hands. It is an awesome responsibility to judge another human being, and I thank you for the close attention you have paid these past two weeks. While it is never an easy task, I am confident you will do the right thing and convict."

Chadbourne's voice was softer, less confrontational than usual. "Since this trial began, I have been viciously criticized, truly vilified by the press. In fact, a Boston editorial called me a 'heartless, childless bitch.'" Protestors taunt me daily outside this courthouse. I have even had a threat made on my life."

She looked squarely at the jury. "I must tell you, it has not been easy prosecuting a twelve-year-old. However, when I accepted the position of county prosecutor, I swore an oath to uphold the laws of this state and to bring to justice those who broke them.

"There is a part of me that wishes the facts of this case were different; that this young man hadn't stolen his father's gun and fired five shots that killed him at point blank range. It is a terrible thing that a boy must admit—at his own murder trial—he had previously wanted to kill his father."

Chadbourne paused, putting a hand to her chin.

"The facts clearly show that despite whatever abuse there might have been in the past, the defendant is a young man of sound mind and strong body. During a fight between his father and his mother's lover, the defendant walked into his bedroom, came out with a deadly weapon, and repeatedly shot and killed his father."

Francis looked at the floor.

"The defendant had motive and took deliberate, premeditated actions to make sure he had a loaded gun at the ready. When the opportunity arose, he used it to kill his father. Not to stop his father; not to just protect himself or others. Stringer Johnson used that gun to *kill* his father dead."

Chadbourne leaned on the railing in front of the jurors. "This kid from the streets of LA committed cold-blooded, first degree murder and he is a danger to all of us—to this town and to society as a whole. You twelve citizens sitting here are the only real protection the good people of this community have. It is your responsibility, in fact your duty, to ensure he pays the price for his actions and never has a chance to kill again."

Chadbourne lingered for a few moments then bowed her head toward the jury. "I thank you for your attention and for your service to this court." She turned and walked back to her seat.

The courthouse was deathly quiet. Jacob leaned toward Buster and whispered something in his ear.

Judge Thornton turned to Buster. "Mr. Hurd—"

Francis could hardly breathe. Kate sat stone-faced beside him. Francis knew Chadbourne had had a powerful effect on the tide of the trial. The waters were dark, uncertain and turbulent.

Buster adjusted his glasses and rose. He straightened the front of his suit jacket, stepped around the table and walked over to the jury. "Mr. Foreman, members of the jury, I agree with Ms. Chadbourne that it is an awesome responsibility that rests upon your shoulders. However, as you deliberate and come to a verdict on this boy's fate you have a very important thing on your side and that is the truth. You have heard the unsettling, indescribably painful truth of what led Stringer Johnson to shoot his father, something he never intended or truly wanted to do."

Buster gestured toward Stringer. "This boy was forced by a madman to save his own life and the life of his mother and their friend. The same courageous instinct that led Stringer to risk his life to save Delbert Ready's—a complete stranger drowning in the stormy Atlantic—caused him to use the only force strong enough to stop his crazed father from killing three people. The same good person committed these seemingly different but actually quite similar acts."

Buster looked into the faces of the jurors. "Please remember for a moment Leland Johnson's face." He pointed to the wall where Dr. Freid had reluctantly projected Leland's horrifying image. "Think for a moment. If Leland Johnson had been on top of your loved one—your father, your brother, sister, son, or daughter—holding a twelve-inch steel blade over their throat, what would you have done? Leland Johnson, a monster who encouraged other drunken men to rape his wife while his child watched."

Buster swept his gaze across the jury. "If you had been in Stringer's position that day, how far would you have gone to save *your* loved ones? Would you have turned away and let this madman stab them to death only to then have him come after you?"

Buster stepped closer to the jury box. "Leland Johnson had already stabbed Mr. Monroe three times before he pinned him to the floor. Leland Johnson had punched and kicked and beaten Stringer and Kate before he climbed on top of Francis to finish him off."

Buster leaned on the wooden railing with both hands. "This was a man who shot off his nine-year-old son's testicle under ghastly circumstances and laughed about it with his drunken buddies. Stringer knew all too well how crazy his father was, and he had every reason to assume—to know—Leland was about to kill them all."

Buster shook his head. "A boy having to kill his father is a great tragedy under any circumstances. But Stringer had no reasonable alternative but to put himself in terrible peril—physically, emotionally, legally—by taking the life of one violent man to save the lives of three other human beings."

Buster straightened. "Ladies and gentlemen, I think in our hearts we all know there is no first degree murder here. In fact, there was no murder except in the mind of a cruel, power-hungry sheriff and a prosecutor anxious to make a name for herself and to please her conservative constituents who got her elected. This is really a case of a terribly abused twelve-year-old boy who faced a sudden, deadly situation and did the only thing he could do to defend himself, his mother, and their friend."

Buster paused and shook his head. "This is as clear a case of self-defense and defense of others as any I've ever seen. I can't imagine how, with clean conscience, you good people could convict this boy of the crime of which he is accused. I fear you would never sleep again."

Buster looked into their tired faces. Some looked back at him. Some had tears in their eyes. Several looked away or at the floor.

"Thank you," Buster said quietly. "I thank you for being such a good jury." Then he slowly walked back to his seat, sat down, and put his arm around Stringer.

Kate leaned forward over the railing behind Stringer's seat and touched his back. He didn't move.

Judge Thornton watched Buster and Stringer for a few moments then turned to the jury. He cleared his throat. "Members of the jury, I will now give you your instructions. You will be sequestered to deliberate the facts of this case until you reach a verdict or until you decide you are unable to do so, which would result in what we call a hung jury and a mistrial. Your solemn responsibility is to determine if the evidence supports—beyond a reasonable doubt—that Stringer Albert Johnson committed murder in the first degree in the shooting death of his father, Leland Johnson. In order to find the defendant guilty, you must believe there is credible evidence of premeditation, that he planned the murder before it actually occurred, and that it was not committed primarily in self-defense.

"If, on the other hand, you do not believe the defendant committed premeditated murder, you must find him not guilty. You are not to consider any other, lesser offenses."

Judge Thornton folded his hands in front of him. "You will now be excused to go to the jury room and begin your deliberations. You may speak freely among yourselves, but I caution you again on one vital point: your verdict *must* be based solely upon what you believe to be credible facts testified to at trial; not personal feelings, opinions, or prejudices. It cannot be based on any information you might have learned prior to or outside of this trial. If you wish to have any portion of the transcript read back to you, just bring that to your foreman's attention and it will be arranged. He will guide you in your deliberations."

Without further ado, Judge Thornton rapped the gavel on his bench. "Court is adjourned."

State troopers immediately escorted the jury from the room. Ralph walked down the aisle and handcuffed Stringer. Judge Thornton remained in his chair and watched the deputies walk Stringer up the far aisle. Before they opened the metal door, they hesitated for a few moments and kindly let Kate hold him. Then the door clicked open and they led Stringer away, leaving her standing alone.

CHAPTER 42

Kate and Francis arrived back at the bungalow about six o'clock. Unable to focus on anything for more than a few minutes, they both paced aimlessly. Francis was standing in the doorway of the studio when Kate came from the kitchen and stood behind him. "Would you do something for me?"

Francis turned to her. "Of course."

"I'm losing my mind here. I want a drink so bad I can taste it. I need to get to an AA meeting, but I think I'm too shaky to drive. There's a meeting at eight at the Congregational Church. Would you take me?"

"Yes, of course."

They rode to town in silence, pulling into the church parking lot at ten of eight. There were about a dozen cars parked along the snow banks, and three people stood outside the back door of the church smoking cigarettes.

"Thanks for bringing me," Kate said as they parked. "I've got to make it through all this sober, regardless of what happens to Stinger."

Francis looked at her. "You will."

Kate opened her door. "Do you want to come in with me?"

Francis looked surprised. "Go in to the meeting?"

"Yeah."

"Don't you have to be an alcoholic?"

"No. It's what's called an open meeting. You can come as my support person."

"All right. I'm feeling pretty crazy myself and you always seem calmer after you've been to one of these."

"Good," Kate said.

As they walked across the parking lot, the cold night air felt good. Overhead, the sky was clearing, revealing Orion's Belt between the clouds.

"What do I do in there?" Francis asked as they approached the back door to the church.

"Do what I do. Mostly listen. It's a speaker meeting. A recovering alcoholic will tell their story to the rest of us and then we'll discuss it. Let's go in; I don't like to be late."

Kate said hi to a young man who was standing by the door then led Francis down a set of steps into the basement where several rows of folding chairs were set up facing a simple wooden podium. On the front of it hung a hand carved sign: "You Are Not Alone." The room smelled of freshly perked coffee. Fifteen or so people chatted in small groups. On the wall was a poster that read: "There but for the grace of God, go I."

Kate got a cup of coffee, introduced Francis to two people she knew then they sat in the middle row of chairs. At eight o'clock, a broad-shouldered man in a NAPA Auto Parts cap tapped a wooden gavel on the podium and everyone stopped talking. The man's arms looked as big as Francis's legs though his voice was surprisingly gentle. "Welcome to the Thursday night Harbor Meeting of Alcoholics Anonymous. My name is Frank, and I'm an alcoholic."

Everyone said, "Hi, Frank."

"I've asked Mike to read the preamble."

A skinny, bespectacled man with a bowtie stood up and stepped to the podium. As he read from a weathered sheet of paper, Francis glanced around the room. He was surprised that everyone looked just like regular folks. They were not bottle-in-a-paper-bag drunks as he'd imagined.

Mike finished reading and Frank spoke again. "I've asked Ginny to read the Steps."

A woman walked down the aisle to the podium, put on her glasses, and picked up another sheet of paper. "I'm Ginny, and I'm an alcoholic."

Francis was shocked to see that it was Ginny Wentworth. He had no idea she was an alcoholic. She winked at Francis then read the "Twelve Suggested Steps of Recovery."

Francis had a hard time relaxing enough to focus, but he did hear two of the steps clearly. Step Two: Came to believe that a power greater than ourselves can restore us to sanity. Step Three: Make a decision to turn our will and our lives over to the care of God as we understand him.

Though Francis had never been interested in religion, at this juncture in his life, he liked what he heard. The words gave him an unexpected sense of relief. He turned to Kate who sat with her eyes closed, listening.

Frank introduced the featured speaker, a woman from Brunswick named Catherine. She began by thanking Frank and his group for asking her to speak. She said it was a pleasure to be there. Francis was amazed this woman had driven over an hour up the coast on icy winter roads to speak to a bunch of alcoholics in a church basement.

Catherine began by describing what an out-of-control drunk she was for over twenty years before she came to AA. She got sober at thirty-five and hadn't had a drink in eight years. She explained how she was about to be fired from her law firm when a friend got her into the "program," which she believed saved her life.

Francis listened intently.

"A year ago," she continued in a lowered voice, "my ten-year-old son, Joshua, was diagnosed with an aggressive form of leukemia, or cancer of his bone marrow. It has been a heart-wrenching year, to say the least."

Catherine paused for a moment. Kate took hold of Francis's hand.

"I never would have believed I could stay sober through something like this. As the cancer has progressed, Sam has lost much of his strength. He can no longer walk without a walker or with help. At times, the pain in his bones becomes unbearable and I give him morphine injections, but he doesn't like them because they make him so sleepy." She paused for a moment. "He's such a brave kid and doesn't want to miss any of the time we have left together."

Catherine wiped her eyes with her sleeve. "You know, people in this program have told me to be grateful for all I have, to thank God for this beautiful son I have to hold, even if there's only a short time left. Though it is the hardest thing I've ever done, I must tell you, it *is* such a gift to be able to be there for him. I'm not falling down drunk in some bar or alley, unsure of who's putting my son to bed. For whatever time Josh has left, I'm there for him, and we're loving each other the best we know how."

Catherine looked across the audience, her gaze coming to rest on Kate. "In order to stay sober and not die of this awful disease of alcoholism, I've had to surrender. I'm not exactly sure what or who God is, but I *am* sure there is a power out there somehow running the universe that is a lot more powerful than I am. It's the most I'm capable of understanding. And I think it's all I need to know."

Catherine smiled. "It's you folks in these rooms who have taught me how to live, to deal with life on life's terms. No matter how much pain my son and I are in, we will get through it together. And with your help, I'll stay sober. Thank you for listening."

After the woman fell silent, everyone, including Francis, enthusiastically applauded.

Frank stepped back to the podium. "Thank you, Catherine, for your wonderful message."

After a discussion session about the woman's talk, the meeting ended with everyone standing and joining hands in a circle. Those who wished to, recited the Serenity Prayer. When the meeting broke up, Kate walked over and spoke with Frank and Catherine. Francis stood in the back, watching. Everyone in the room seemed positive, energized by being with each other.

Francis said hi to Ginny, who seemed glad to see him. Then he walked over to Catherine and extended his hand. "I was very moved by your talk," he said, shaking her hand. "Thank you."

Kate joined him and they left the church, driving past the bright Christmas lights of downtown over to the ice chute at the top of Cliff Street. The firemen had laid down several inches of good solid ice that covered the street and the wooden side boards leading down to the harbor.

Halfway home, Kate took hold of Francis's arm. "What did you think of the meeting?"

"Listening to that woman was very powerful. I felt a little uncomfortable, but I'm glad I was there. It got me out of my own head for a little while."

"Yeah," Kate said. "There's an amazing power in a room of clean and sober people. I'll carry some of her strength with me these next few days. I know Stringer needs all I can muster."

Francis looked at her lovingly. "Your son has an incredibly strong mother. Beautiful too." Francis managed a smile. "Somehow, we're all going to make it through this together."

"I hope so," Kate said quietly.

Exhausted, they went to bed as soon as they got home.

December twenty-third dawned sunny and a bit warmer. Kate drove to the jail around seven. Beside her on the seat sat a small Christmas tree in a planter for Stringer. Ralph was on duty and he knew the sheriff and his brothers would be hung over from their annual Christmas party, so he let Kate in before visiting hours officially began. In fact, she and Francis spent much of the day in Stringer's cell, including sharing a pizza dinner with Cherry Garcia for dessert. Even Ralph had a piece with them through the bars. Though waiting while the jury deliberated was terribly difficult and draining, there was some sense of relief that the trial would soon be over.

As Kate and Francis prepared to leave, Ralph asked Francis if he could have a word with him. They stepped into the brick hallway outside Stringer's cell.

"Mr. Monroe, may I ask you something in confidence? You'll tell no one?"

"Yes. What is it, Ralph?"

"This place is already falling apart without Charlie. Even the sheriff realizes Charlie held everything together." Ralph glanced up and down the hallway. "Me and some of the boys have been talking. If we could get Charlie to run for sheriff in the spring, do you think he could beat McNeal?"

Francis raised his eyebrows then smiled. "That's a good idea. I'll bet he could beat that old bastard."

The phone rang out in the office.

"Thanks," Ralph said. "Not a word to anyone."

Francis nodded.

Early afternoon on Christmas Eve day, Buster called to say the jury had requested some of Stringer's and Mrs. Shedrick's testimony be read back to them. They also wanted to view one of Dr. Krault's autopsy slides.

Francis asked Buster about the tide. Buster said he didn't know, that like them, he was just holding on, trying not to drink too much Jameson.

Around mid-afternoon Kate brought the broken whaler's lamp downstairs and spread the many pieces of glass over a dark blue tablecloth on the kitchen table. That evening while they waited for the verdict, they fitted and glued the pieces of the ancient lamp back together. It was late in the evening when they glued the last piece, leaving out only one small triangle of glass that was shattered too badly to fix.

Then, just after midnight, the phone rang.

CHAPTER 43

It was Buster on the line. He said simply: "The jury's back with the verdict. I'll meet you at the courthouse."

Kate held tight to Francis's arm all the way to town. The moon passed behind scattered clouds over the frigid ocean. As they turned at the head of Main Street they were greeted by a huge white banner strung between light poles welcoming everyone to the eighty-first annual Winter's Cove Festival. Despite the hour, the parking lot was jammed and a gaggle of reporters waited on the courthouse steps.

Ralph and another deputy guarded the entrance to the lot. When they saw Francis's Jeep, they pulled a barricade out of the way and motioned for him to drive through.

Ralph escorted Kate and Francis in through the side entrance to the defense room door. Inside, Stringer paced back and forth in front of the window. Jacob and Buster stood by the table talking quietly.

Kate ran over to Stringer and took him in her arms. Buster waited a few moments then asked everyone to sit down. They all remained standing around the table.

"Well, this is it," Buster said, looking at Kate and Francis. "Before they read the verdict, I need to tell you something." Jacob remained silent, holding his hand to his chin.

"As you know, I asked Jacob to come up here to help. However, regarding the critical issues at stake the other night, I take full responsibility for what we did. Jacob thought we should go for lesser charges and not put Stringer on the stand. And while

I greatly respect his opinion, I believe we did the right thing. Though risky, I think it has increased Stringer's chance of acquittal." Buster shook his head. "I pray I'm right. Regardless, I needed to get that off my chest."

There was a sharp rap on the door then it swung open. Kate recoiled as Sheriff McNeal stepped into the room. "Jury's back. Let's go."

Ralph walked around the sheriff to Stringer. "It's time."

Kate hugged Stringer again then Ralph took hold of his arm. "I'm sorry, Mrs. Johnson," he said, leading Stringer out of the room.

Jacob walked out, followed by Buster. Francis stood with his hand on Kate's back. His legs felt unsteady as they stepped into the hallway. State troopers created a narrow corridor through the reporters as they walked into the courtroom, which was eerily quiet. People stared as Kate and Francis walked down the center aisle to their seats where they found Kasa waiting for them. She reached out and took hold of their hands. Francis felt the strength of her grip.

"God is merciful to those who believe," she said in a strong, hushed voice.

The jury filed in and sat staring straight ahead.

"All rise," Lester called out.

Judge Thornton entered, walked behind the bench, and sat in his chair. He did not look at anyone.

There was a long pause. Francis heard Kasa's shallow breathing next to him. Stringer pulled a crumpled piece of paper from his shirt pocket and carefully unfolded the print of Wyeth's "Barracoon" on the table in front of him. He sat silently, his palms on the soles of the imprisoned African woman.

Judge Thornton lifted his eyes to Stringer. "The defendant will rise." He turned to the jury. "Has the jury reached a verdict?"

Mr. Mason pushed himself out of his chair. "We have, Your Honor." The foreman looked tired and even older than his eighty years.

Lester limped forward, took a piece of paper from Mr. Mason, and carried it to the bench. His face steeled, Judge Thornton unfolded the paper and read it. Emotionless, he handed it back to Lester who returned it to Mr. Mason.

"Mr. Foreman, what say you?"

Mr. Mason looked confused.

Judge Thornton leaned forward. "Please read the verdict."

Mr. Mason carefully unfolded the paper. "Yes, Your Honor." His voice cracked. For a moment it looked as though he would lose his balance.

Kate's head fell forward. Kasa slid her large hand into Kate's lap. Francis couldn't breathe.

Mr. Mason steadied himself on the railing and raised his head to the courtroom. "The jury finds the defendant, Stringer Albert Johnson…" He paused, his hands trembling. "Finds the defendant, not guilty." Mr. Mason fumbled for a moment. "Did I say that right? *Not* guilty of murder in the first degree."

It wasn't until he said "not" for the second time that Francis really heard it. Kate slid off the bench onto her knees. Kasa leaned over her and they wept together.

Francis stood and steadied himself on the bench in front of him. Tears streamed down his cheeks.

Stringer shot an arm into the air. He hugged Buster, turned, and leapt over the railing into Francis's arms. Kate came up off the floor and wrapped her arms around her son. The three of them stood there hugging, holding each other for a long time.

When Francis stood back, he heard cheers coming from the back of the room. Judge Thornton must have adjourned the court, because he was gone and so was Gwen Chadbourne.

Jacob and Buster stood in the front of the courtroom; two old war horses smiling and shaking hands.

Holding his face in her hands, Kate just kept looking at Stringer. Finally Stringer said, "Let's get out of here," and they left the courtroom, carried on some kind of warm, powerful wave. Kate, Francis, Stringer, and Kasa drove home in the Jeep, past townspeople leaving the courthouse, many of whom waved or gave them a thumbs up. At the head of Main Street, Charlie stood beside his pickup. He nodded and waved as they passed.

When they got home, Stringer burst from the Jeep and ran like a cooped-up golden retriever through the snow. Kate made hot chocolate and they all ate warm cinnamon buns Kasa brought fresh from her oven.

Late afternoon, Buster and Jacob came out to the bungalow to say their good-byes. Francis brought out the Jameson, but Buster said he was too tired and had too long a drive back to Blue Hills to start drinking.

Buster sat for a few minutes in the parlor with Kate. Francis waited in the hallway. Buster took Kate's hand in his. "You will never know how grateful I am you let me defend your son—that you put such trust in me. This is the first time in the twenty-five years since my son died I have felt any peace at all."

With tears in her eyes, Kate thanked Buster and gave him a long hug.

Buster stood and turned to Francis. "Thank you, Francis. You are a remarkably good man. I've never met anyone quite like you."

Buster shook Francis's hand then stepped to the door where Stringer was waiting for him. He put his arms around Buster's large belly. "Thank you, Mr. Hurd. You are so cool."

Buster smiled. "You're welcome, my young friend." He ran his hand over Stringer's head. "Stringer, if my son had lived, I would have been very proud if he'd grown up to be half the young man you are. I will never forget you."

Then Buster turned to Jacob and they shook hands.

"You were brilliant," Jacob said. "And, as usual, your instincts were perfect." They both smiled. "We'll talk soon."

Buster opened the door, a gust of wind blowing a lick of snow into the hallway. He pulled his scarf around his neck and headed to his car.

Jacob put on his coat then turned to Francis. "I must be going too. My plane leaves in a couple of hours from Portland."

They shook hands then Jacob turned to Kate. "Best of luck to you and your son. You are an extraordinarily beautiful woman in many ways. Francis is very lucky, as are you."

Kate blushed and thanked him.

Jacob turned to Stringer and they said good-bye. At the door, Jacob spoke to Francis. "By the way, I came up here just to be of moral support. Buster did all the work." Jacob adjusted the collar of his coat. "At the beginning of all this I told you he was the smartest attorney I've ever known. I meant it." He opened the door and left.

Finally they were alone. Stringer and Kate ate a pint of ice cream together at the kitchen table. She kept reaching over and touching him, as if to make sure he was really there.

Francis planned to give Kate and Stringer the big bed upstairs, but Stringer wouldn't hear of it. He said he wanted to sleep on Francis's cot in the studio.

It was after three in the morning when Francis said good night to Stringer. He walked upstairs, pausing to look at the photographs on the wall. He wondered what Rachael would have thought about all that had gone on and, for a fleeting moment, thought she would have been proud of him.

By the time Kate came to bed, the sky had cleared and a bright moon was reflecting off the Atlantic. Francis lit the candle in the whaler's lamp, the dozens of pieces of cemented glass sending tiny prisms of light into the room. Kate climbed into bed and slid under Francis's warm arm. He stroked her hair as she quietly hummed one of her mother's Lakota peace songs.

As Kate drifted off to sleep, Francis heard Stringer climb the stairs and come into the bedroom. He sat on the side of the bed next to Kate. "Can I tell you something?" he said to both of them.

"Of course." Kate lifted her head from the pillow.

"I know how awful Leland was." Stringer paused and then continued. "But I never really wanted to kill him. If I hadn't thought he was going to kill you guys, I wouldn't have shot him. I hated him, but he was still my dad."

"Oh, String," Kate said, lifting her hand to his cheek. "I know," she said, hugging him.

Stringer kissed her, said good night to Francis, and walked back downstairs.

After Stringer left, Francis held Kate in his arms as she cried softly. They watched the candle flicker in the window as they fell asleep.

The next few days Francis and Stringer spent much of their time putting finishing touches on paintings for their art show. They also had some great snowball fights with Kate out in the yard.

Around nine in the morning on New Year's Eve day, Charlie suddenly drove up the driveway. Francis and Kate walked outside as Charlie got out and stood beside his rusty pickup. He mostly looked at the ground, seeming nervous and emotional.

As they approached, Charlie struggled to find his words. "I wanted to say that I'm glad everything worked out. And—" He paused, shifting his weight from one foot to the other, his face full of despair. "I'm sorry I didn't do a better job—that it went so far."

Kate stepped toward him. "Charlie, you did your best and in the end you took a huge risk. Your testimony made a big difference and we're grateful." Kate put her hand on his shoulder. "You've been working in a tough situation for a very long time."

Feeling a tremendous amount of emotions welling inside of him, Francis took a step toward Charlie. "I've always liked you, Charlie, and thought you were a good man." Francis shook his head. "We've all been through hell, and I've said some harsh things, but I want you to know I still think you're a good man."

Charlie's eyes opened wider; his expression lifted a bit.

Francis extended his hand and their palms met.

"Thank you, Francis," Charlie said, his voice quivering.

"Now, how about doing something to make things better around here?"

"Like what?" Charlie asked.

Francis continued to hold Charlie's hand in a firm handshake. "How about you run for sheriff?"

Charlie's eyes brightened. He straightened up and looked Francis in the eye. "You mean it? Are you serious?"

Francis smiled. "I'm not letting go until you shake on it."

"Okay," Charlie said. "I've never considered it, but I'll give it some thought."

"You'd be a great sheriff."

"Thanks, Mr. Monroe." Seeming embarrassed, Charlie walked back to his truck. "I'll see you at the ice slide tonight. Don't be late."

They waved as he drove off.

CHAPTER 44

Gradually winding down from the emotional roller coaster of the trial, neither Kate nor Francis felt much like being out in public. On New Year's Eve, however, Stringer insisted they all go in to town to join folks in celebrating at the annual Festival. Francis and Stringer finished a couple of paintings in the afternoon then around eight o'clock they drove to town where they found the whole downtown alive with hundreds of excited people. Festive lights and banners hung across Main Street and a bluegrass band with a whole family of fiddlers was playing on a platform near the courthouse. Children were making wildly decorated snowmen along the sidewalk while teenagers tortured them and others with firecrackers thrown every which way. The moon shone brightly and there was even a lighted Christmas tree on the deck of the harbormaster's shack.

At the top of Main Street, the three of them climbed up on a snow bank and dug out seats to watch the parade. At ten o'clock the Congregational Church bell rang and the town siren wailed from atop the firehouse. The annual parade began, led not by Sheriff McNeal as it had been for decades, but instead by Charlie and Ralph in a spotless sheriff's department cruiser.

"What's *he* doing leading the parade?" Stringer asked. "Where's the sheriff?"

Francis smiled and waved. "Maybe McNeal's finally got the message he's not welcome around here. I think there are big changes coming."

A Boy Scout float adorned with a ten-foot-high golden eagle came next, the top of which just made it under a banner. Mounted on its wings were rows of colorful Chinese fountains spraying brilliant sparks into the air.

A family dressed up as lobsters passed by on a farmer's hay wagon. They guarded a couple of kids locked in a makeshift lobster trap while a boom box played "Happy Days are Here Again."

Though most of the floats were pretty simple by California standards, Stringer and Kate seemed to get a kick of them. At one point someone threw a clump of firecrackers off the back of a logging truck into the snow beneath them. Stringer jumped off the pile and retrieved them. Only about half of them had gone off so he blew the snow off the rest and stuffed them in his pocket for later.

The parade ended around eleven and everyone migrated toward the top of Cliff Street. Near the ice chute stood Charlie's pickup, which was piled high with wooden torches that had small strips of burlap soaked in wax and kerosene wrapped around the ends.

Francis and Kate walked over and shook his hand.

"We're doing things a little differently this year," Charlie said. "We're going to have the kids give out the torches." Francis smiled and turned to Stringer. "Well, let's get to it."

"You bet." Stringer smiled and grabbed a bunch of torches.

When all of the torches had been handed out to the bravest of the crowd, everyone gathered around a wooden platform, and Mayor Horace Bagley stepped to the microphone. "It is my distinct honor to welcome you all to the eighty-first annual Winter's Cove Festival. In..." Horace struggled to look at his watch. "In just a few minutes we will ring in a brand New Year and here in Winter's Cove we have a wonderful tradition of lighting the way for the New Year by sliding down our world famous ice chute with these blazing torches. Each one of you will have a hand in lighting the great bonfire down there in the harbor. As always, the firemen have done a wonderful job of flooding the street, and I'd say the ice looks faster than ever."

The crowd erupted in applause then the mayor turned to Charlie and Ralph. "You boys ready?"

"Yes, sir," Charlie said.

"Okay," Horace called out, waving his arm through the air. "Let the slide begin!"

Charlie struck a match and lit a large torch on a long pole. He leaned down and lit Stringer's torch with his own. "You deserve to go first," he said. Stringer's torch burst into a bright yellow flame then he immediately began touching one torch after another, each person lighting someone else's until hundreds of people stood at the top of the chute, their cold faces illuminated by the warm light of the torches.

The ice was fast and most people screamed and yelled as they flew down the steep incline. Only a couple lost their torches, the flames skidding along the ice beside them.

After the majority of people had gone down, Stringer turned to his mother. "You ready?"

"Are you crazy? I'm already half-frozen. I'm not sliding down that thing."

"Come on," Francis said to Kate. "I've never missed a slide yet."

Kate frowned. "No way am I going down that!"

"'Course you are," a woman said behind her. They turned and saw Kasa, who was so bundled up she looked like an Eskimo. She put her arm around Kate. "I've never missed a slide either and I'm not starting now. Come on!"

Kate shook her head. "You New Englanders are crazy, but all right."

"Let's slide down together," Stringer said. Holding their torches high in the air, they all smiled at each other.

"Let's go!" Stringer yelled. They pushed themselves over the edge and started down the slide. The rush was so intense, even

Francis was taken off guard. Kate screamed most of the way down the chute until they came to rest near the crowd surrounding the bonfire. After they caught their breath, they looked at each other and started laughing.

Just then, the mayor bellowed over the microphone: "Three, two, one—Happy New Year!" A cannon on the hill above town fired a flaming ball that arced overhead, landing in the open water beyond the harbormaster's shack. Almost in unison, the crowd threw their torches onto the twenty-foot-high woodpile. Stuffed with newspaper and cardboard soaked in kerosene, the bonfire quickly roared up into the night. Cascades of fireworks exploded overhead as lines of people, arm-in-arm, swayed back and forth around the fire singing, *Auld Lang Syne.* There seemed to be a shared sense that a new day was dawning in Winter's Cove.

As the great fire gradually melted through the ice and sank into the harbor, the air turned much colder and most folks called it a night. On the way home, feeling full of new life and a bit nostalgic, Francis drove slowly by the gallery. "I was pretty hesitant at first," he said, "but now I'm glad you talked Stringer and me into having an art show. It should be interesting."

CHAPTER 45

The morning of the art show, Stringer could not contain his excitement. He woke Francis and Kate up early and by noon they joined Kasa and Ginny at the gallery, who helped them spruce the place up. They strung tiny white lights through fresh balsam boughs which they then used to frame the large windows at the front of the gallery. Francis and Stringer set up a display in the windows, showcasing their new paintings. By three o'clock, they had put out platters of fresh shrimp and cocktail sauce, crackers with mango chutney and cheddar cheese, plump grapes and baked brie wrapped in phyllo dough. A crystal punch bowl sat on an antique table in the middle of the gallery and a leather-bound guest book was open on the desk by the door.

By four-thirty, only a handful of people had showed up, mostly tourists from down country that were in town for Festival. They were looking for Francis Monroe's famous seascapes but there were none to be found. Feeling a bit embarrassed, Francis retired to the back room where he sat on the sofa next to the gas stove.

Around five thirty, Stringer burst through the doorway. "Francis! Get out here. It's incredible."

Francis realized he must have fallen asleep. Hearing a lot of activity out in the gallery, he walked into a surprisingly large crowd of people including several of Rachael's close friends whom he hadn't seen since her funeral. He was also happy to see several old artist friends including a fine watercolorist from Portland who had driven up for the show. "It's so good to have you back,

Francis," the man said. "Your new work is fabulous—so alive. I wish I knew what motivates you."

Francis grinned. "It's a long story."

After speaking with several other people, Francis stepped back and enjoyed watching Kate and Stringer, who seemed to be having a wonderful time. Many people stopped and studied Stringer's works. In fact, he sold three pieces before the crowd thinned out around seven-thirty. Charlie also stopped by and spent a long time looking at Francis's painting of people playing with a Frisbee in Central Park.

"This is great," Charlie said when Francis came over to him. "I didn't know you painted this sort of thing – you know, real life."

"Well, now I do." Francis was struck by Charlie's enthusiasm. "Would you like it?"

Charlie looked uncomfortable. "I could never afford one of these."

"It's yours," Francis said. He stepped to the canvas and wrote sold across the sticker. "I'd be very pleased for you to have it."

"Really?"

"Really. Happy New Year." Francis shook Charlie's hand. "You can pick it up tomorrow."

After Charlie left, Francis relaxed with Kate, Kasa and Ginny in the back room. Just before nine, a dark Suburban pulled up in front of the gallery. A woman got out, and helped an older man step down onto the sidewalk. For a few moments they just peered into the gallery, then the man opened the door and they came inside. His face barely visible behind the upturned collar of a heavy wool overcoat, the white-haired gentleman made his way from painting to painting, pausing the longest in front of Stringer's works.

Sitting in a chair in the corner, Stringer watched the man, who occasionally pointed to a canvas and spoke to his companion. When he was finished, he walked over to Stringer. Peering out from under heavy eyelids, his eyes were intense and thoughtful.

"These are good paintings, Son." He glanced over at Francis, who was in the back talking with Ginny. "You must have had a hell of a teacher."

Stringer smiled nervously. "I did. Francis Monroe."

The man looked Stringer straight in the eye. "Just keep working at it. Forget everything else. Paint."

Stringer couldn't take his eyes off him. "I will."

The man tightened the collar of his coat and walked to the door.

Suddenly, Stringer realized who this man might be. Thought he recognized his face. "Sir—"

The man stopped.

"Mr. Monroe had a great teacher, too."

The deep crevices of the man's face lifted into a subtle smile. After they left, Stringer closed the door behind them and, for a few moments, stood with his face against the glass.

Francis came over and put his arm on Stringer's shoulder. "Who was that last visitor? I don't think I know him." He wiped condensation from the window and looked down at the street.

"Oh, I think you do. He's a cool old man who admires your work."

Francis opened the door and walked out onto the snowy landing. He watched the man climb into the Suburban. As the headlights came on, he rolled down his window and looked up at Francis. Through the falling snow, Francis caught the unmistakable light in his eyes. Francis walked down the steps as if not on his own power. The man extended his arm through the window and shook Francis's hand firmly. "It took you a while but I knew you'd come around. I'm proud of you." He nodded then rolled up his window.

Francis stood at the edge of the sidewalk as they drove off, watching the tail lights disappear into the snowy night. Then he turned back to the gallery. In the window, Kate and Stringer stood waiting for him, the bright flame from the whaler's lamp dancing against the frosted glass.

AFTERWARD

There are life-saving things we can all do to help stop domestic violence. Good places to get information and to find ways to get involved are:

National Coalition Against Domestic Violence at www.ncadv.org.

Childhelp USA at www.childhelp.org or their national hotline 800-4-A-CHILD

Child Welfare League of America at www.cwla.org or 202-688-4200

Prevent Child Abuse America at www.preventchildabuse.org

Women Helping Battered Women at www.whbw.org

White Ribbon Campaign at www.whiteribbon.ca

These organizations offer a wealth of information on how to prevent abuse and to empower and assist its millions of victims. In addition, most large communities and all states, have programs you can easily access.

I would also like to recommend the following books: *The Illusion of Love*, by David P. Celani; *Getting Away With Murder*, by Raoul Felder & Barbara Victor; *It's OK to Tell*, by Lauren Book; *Trauma and Recovery*, by Judith Herman, MD; and *A Child Called "It"*, by Dave Pelzer. And, for simply being one of the most wonderful books I've ever read, *Bird by Bird*, by Anne Lamott.

To help those suffering from the disease of alcoholism, please contact the worldwide fellowship of Alcoholics Anonymous @ www.aa.org.

I hope you will learn more about these complex and devastating problems and consider lending a helping hand.

A portion of any profits from this book will be donated to worthy causes working to end spousal and child abuse.

Made in the USA
Middletown, DE
14 October 2015